Myths, Gods & Immortals
Morgana Le Fay
New & Ancient Arthurian Tales

This is a FLAME TREE Book

Publisher & Creative Director: Nick Wells
Editorial Director: Catherine Taylor
Senior Project Editor: Gillian Whitaker
Editorial Board: Gillian Whitaker, Catherine Taylor, Jocelyn Pontes,
Jemma North, Simran Aulakh and Beatrix Ambery

FLAME TREE PUBLISHING
6 Melbray Mews, Fulham,
London SW6 3NS, United Kingdom
www.flametreepublishing.com

First published 2025

Copyright in each story is held by the individual authors
Introduction and Volume copyright © 2025 Flame Tree Publishing Ltd

The Part Opener Quotations are from: J.J. Parry's translation of Geoffrey of Monmouth's *Vita Merlini* (University of Illinois, 1925); W.W. Comfort's translations of Chrétien de Troyes' work in *Four Arthurian Romances* (c. 1900); Mark Twain's *A Connecticut Yankee in King Arthur's Court* (Charles L. Webster & Company, 1889); *Sir Gawain and the Green Knight*, trans. William Allan Neilson (Houghton Mifflin, 1917).

25 27 29 30 28 26
1 3 5 7 9 10 8 6 4 2

ISBN: 978-1-83562-263-6

All rights reserved. No part of this publication may be reproduced, stored in a retrieval system, or transmitted in any form or by any means, electronic, mechanical, photocopying, recording or otherwise, without the prior written permission of the publisher.

Publisher's Note: The stories within this book are works of fiction. Names, characters, places, and incidents are products of the authors' imaginations. Locales and public names are sometimes used for atmospheric purposes. Any resemblance to actual people, living or dead, or to businesses, companies, events, institutions, or locales is completely coincidental.

Content Note: The stories in this book may contain descriptions of, or references to, difficult subjects such as violence, death and rape, but always contextualized within the setting of mythic narrative, archetype and metaphor. Similarly, language can sometimes be strong but is at the artistic discretion of the authors.

Cover art by Flame Tree Studio based on elements from Shutterstock.com: Kiselev Andrey Valerevich, Novikova-Asheulov Natalia, Jakub Krechowicz, and fotandy.

A copy of the CIP data for this book is available from the British Library.

Printed and bound in China

Contents

FOREWORD
Dr Marta Cobb 6

ANCIENT & MODERN: INTRODUCING MORGANA LE FAY
by Pamela Koehne-Drube 10
1. The Many Faces of Morgana le Fay 11
2. A Changing Britain 38
3. The Modern Morgana 67
4. The Once and Future Morgana 99

MODERN SHORT STORIES OF MORGANA LE FAY
His Head in Your Lap, Dear Brother
K. Blair 123
Morgana and the Morrigan
Chris A. Bolton 136
No Need for the Green Knight
Courtney Danielson 152
The Woman with the Bleeding Eye
Evan Davies 169
To Cut the Rot
Caroline Fleischauer 185

CONTENTS

Gelato
Micah Giddens 199

The Story that I Want
Lyndsay E. Gilbert 210

Under Avalon
Liam Hogan 224

An Offense of Memory
Larry Ivkovich 231

Mirror, Mirage
Alexis Kaegi 246

Destiny Forged
Damien Mckeating 262

To Catch a Name
Nico Martinez Nocito 275

The Many-Hued Land
John J. O'Hara 291

Hound, Hart, Crow, Queen
M.R. Robinson 306

Sea-born
C.J. Subko 322

She Made a Doll in Winter
Lana Voos 338

Every Son a Reaver
Holly Lyn Walrath 352

BIOGRAPHIES 361
MYTHS, GODS & IMMORTALS 367
FLAME TREE FICTION 368

Foreword
Dr Marta Cobb

or centuries, tales of Arthur and his knights have been retold, with each new telling shaping the narrative to suit the needs of the time. Through these stories, we explore what it means to be a hero, celebrate examples of valour and honour, and enshrine the values we hold most dear. Yet these are also stories of duplicity and violence where women, in spite of oaths of chivalry, are often the victims of the very men who have sworn to protect them. Arthur himself embodies these complexities: he is the product of an adulterous deception and the engendering of his son in an incestuous union leads to his death. Women in Arthurian legend also manifest these contradictions as sites of both desire and fear. The lady may be a prisoner in a tower, awaiting rescue or ravishment, but she may also be an enchantress ready to ensnare the unsuspecting. These tensions are central to the narrative and explain why these stories are still compelling.

Although an enduring character in the Arthurian canon, Morgana le Fay is also an enigma. One of Arthur's closest relatives (usually his half-sister, but sometimes his aunt), she is often relegated to the fringes of the Arthurian court, where she plots its downfall or at least tests the mettle of Arthur's knights.

A healer but also a sorceress, her actions contribute to Arthur's downfall, yet she is one of the women who escort him to Avalon, a place from which he may eventually return.

The first entry of Morgana into the Arthurian canon, Geoffrey of Monmouth's twelfth-century poem, the *Vita Merlini* (The Life of Merlin), focuses upon the more benevolent aspects of her character. In this text, she is not related to Arthur: Merlin describes her as one of nine sisters who rule the Fortunate Island. She is not only a skilled healer, but a powerful enchantress who can change her shape and fly. When Arthur is wounded in the battle of Camlann, he is brought to her realm in the hopes that she can heal him.

As time passes, Morgana's relationship to Arthur becomes closer, but her character darkens. In English narratives of the fourteenth and fifteenth centuries, such as *Sir Gawain and the Green Knight* or Thomas Malory's *Le Morte d'Arthur*, she is a more menacing figure, plotting against Arthur and his Round Table. In *Sir Gawain and the Green Knight*, she sends the Green Knight into Arthur's court in the hopes that the queen will be frightened to death. Yet, although she is revealed as the mastermind behind the events of the narrative, she only appears as a minor character, the older and uglier companion of the Green Knight's beautiful wife. Moreover, for all her supposed power, she does not speak a word. In *Le Morte d'Arthur*, she plots to overthrow Arthur by stealing his sword Excalibur. Although he manages to recover the sword, she then steals its magical scabbard, which has healing properties. Its loss contributes to Arthur's fatal wounding in his final battle.

The decline of Morgana's character occurs in tandem with the increasing association of magic with witchcraft in the later Middle Ages, which may help to explain why she becomes a more sinister figure. Yet Merlin, in spite of having demonic origins, is portrayed as Arthur's protector, while Morgana is condemned for seeking magical and political power for her own ends. Even in Malory, however, she is not simply a villain. After Arthur's final battle, she is one of the mysterious women who take him to Avalon for healing. Thus, her character is far more complex than it initially appears.

We expect women to have limited roles in medieval texts, that a woman who fails to comply with the patriarchal order will be punished. Yet, although Morgana refuses to defer to Arthur and his court, she too has her part; she exists to test their values, to see if they are the worthy knights and ladies that they proclaim themselves to be. Perhaps this role explains why she usually manages to escape Arthur's justice and retreat to fringes of the Arthurian world, later emerging again to offer another trial.

We might hope that more modern portrayals of Morgana would revel in and develop this complexity, but in film she is often removed from the story altogether, as she is in Antoine Fuqua's *King Arthur* (2004), or replaced by other sorceresses, as in Guy Ritchie's *King Arthur: Legend of the Sword* (2017). Where she does appear, as in Joe Cornish's *The Kid Who Would Be King* (2019), she is a two-dimensional and often monstrous villain bent on destroying Arthur, his followers, or his descendants. Television series, having the advantage of longer narrative arcs, often portray her as a more nuanced figure and offer deeper insight into her motivations. In

Merlin (BBC, 2008–12) or *Camelot* (Starz, 2011), she features as the main antagonist but also as a character who, to some extent, deserves the viewer's sympathy. Yet, despite compelling portrayals of the sorceress, both shows ultimately portray Morgana (or Morgan) as lesser than her masculine counterparts and condemn her for seeking power on her own terms.

Perhaps the problem is that medieval romances, as well as more modern retellings in film and television, tend to centre upon the world of Arthur and his court, offering them to audiences as aspirational figures. A character's moral worth is determined by their willingness to align themselves with these values. A woman who challenges this moral order inevitably becomes the antagonist. Yet this alone should not make Morgana evil, nor, in the twenty-first century, should a woman be condemned for seeking power in her own right.

Modern literary portrayals have the power to challenge these assumptions. In fiction, we can see events from Morgana's perspective, often offering a critique of the patriarchal values of Arthur and his court. In these reimaginings, Morgana's refusal to defer and her search for knowledge and power become heroic. She is not necessarily virtuous or an unmitigated force for good, but these portrayals open up the complexity of the Arthurian narrative and allow us to explore other options and retellings. New stories, such as the tales in this volume, have the power to reshape how we perceive the Arthurian world, moving Morgana from the periphery into the centre.

Marta Cobb

Ancient & Modern: Introducing Morgana le Fay

by Pamela Koehne-Drube

1.
The Many Faces of Morgana le Fay

She who is first among them is more skilled in the healing art, and also surpasses her sisters in beauty. Morgen is her name, and she has learned what useful properties all the herbs contain, so that she can cure the body ills. She knows, too, the art by which to change her shape, and to fly through the air, like Daedalus, on strange wings.
– From Geoffrey of Monmouth's *Vita Merlini* (c. 1150)

A PERSONAL QUEST

It was on a winter's evening when I, a bookish nine-year-old, hunkered under the blankets in my Australian home with a flashlight to read an omnibus edition of Susan Cooper's *The Dark Is Rising Sequence* (1965–77) – the book that would change my life.

While Morgana le Fay does not appear in that book, its influence started me on a desperate search to get my hands on any fiction or non-fiction book on the Arthurian legends that I could. I even announced to my parents that I would find the Holy Grail. The second I read about Morgana, however, I was completely hooked. She stood out because she was never the same in any two iterations. In some, she was kind; in others, fiendishly clever and manipulative. She could be whatever a writer needed her to be.

All through school I kept gravitating toward stories that included Arthurian myth. But always in the back of my mind was that promise I made to my parents that day: that I would find the Holy Grail. So when I went to university, I became a historian. I even used the Grail as the inspiration for my thesis, looking at the trajectory of storytelling from myth to popular culture. Morgana led me into my career and inspired my writing. She even enticed me halfway across the world to make my home in Wales, the heartland of Arthurian legend.

As an adult, I now know more about mythology and the ideas that stories represent. I know that I'll never find the one true Holy Grail – but I would argue that I have found something just as essential instead. I've discovered how we share fundamental ideas of our society through the stories we tell.

In Morgana we can clearly see the burden that society has placed on her as a character. Through all her literary interpolations she has undergone the most change – precisely because she represents the things that are most essential or frightening to those who tell her story. In some senses, we could call her a literary Holy Grail.

The way in which we use myths and legends is timeless. We reshape them to our needs, and they change and grow like living things. They represent our past, present and our hopes for the future. Also, I would argue, few characters from myth and legend represent this in quite so stark a way as Morgana le Fay. She has been used, abused, elevated and ignored, making it almost impossible to tie her down to a single fundamental representation. She is of the world, but also exists outside of it.

Morgana le Fay is all of us. Her appeal is undeniable, both as a modern-day feminist icon, speaking truth to power, and as something ancient and magical, beyond the realm of our understanding. How could I not be fascinated by her? Her complex legacy spans history, mythology and fiction; no singular truth can define her. Perhaps you will find your own truth in the embrace of Morgana le Fay.

ORIGINS

Celtic Beginnings

Morgana le Fay's origins can be found in early Celtic mythology and folklore. But in order to understand truly how this came to be, we must first understand some aspects of Celtic history.

There is no singular Celtic nation, nor one Celtic language. Instead the Celts consisted of several unique ethnic groups that covered much of Western and Central Europe. Rather than using a single language, they shared an Indo-European language group of which there were two branches: Brittonic and Goidelic. Many Celtic languages are now extinct, but some remain and are still in use today. Irish, Manx and Scottish Gaelic are still spoken from the Goidelic language family in Ireland, the Isle of Man and Scotland. Welsh, Cornish and Breton are still spoken from the Brittonic family in Wales, Cornwall and Brittany (France).

The Celtic nations had strong oral traditions. They shared their tales through spoken word and song, weaving narratives through the senses rather than on the page. For this reason, much of what we know about them is second hand, seen through the testimony of those with a written tradition, such as Greek and Roman chroniclers. These chroniclers approached their re-tellings with a strong emphasis on showing their own superiority. Meanwhile the early chroniclers of the Welsh and Irish tales sought to preserve the remaining oral traditions, with their own views on how they wanted to present their legacy.

We can also gain insights from the archaeological remains of Celtic societies and culture. Such places and objects offer us something concrete to investigate, although it is still up to researchers to interpret what they find – often within the confines of knowledge acquired from an already biased written record. Consequently, much of what is written about Celtic history is filled with the prejudices of those who wrote it down, so we must view it through that lens, meaning that a lot of what we think we know of Celtic history is guesswork as much as fact.

The Triple-Goddess

The result of survivorship bias in Celtic mythology is that the true origin of Morgana le Fay is difficult to pinpoint. Some scholars have suggested the Irish goddess, the Morrígan (roughly translated as 'Great Queen' or 'Phantom Queen'), as a possible inspiration for her character.

The triple-goddess archetype is a recurring theme in many Celtic traditions. The various roles that Morgana le Fay has played throughout Arthurian legend, from youthful enchantress to wise healer, echo this tripartite nature. This archetype – maiden, mother, crone – is a fundamental part of the Morrígan.

A goddess of battle and war, she is a guardian of her people and their sovereignty as well as a manifestation of the earth. She is a prophet, protector and portent of downfall who appears to warriors, foretells their fates and influences the outcome of battles. This connection to fate and prophecy is mirrored in later depictions of Morgana le Fay.

The Morrígan is often described as a group of three sisters, known as 'the three Morrígna'. In mythology they are named Badb, Macha and the Morrígan, although some sources claim these are three different names for the same goddess. She is also known to be a jealous shapeshifter, and linked to the banshee in later folklore.

In her early appearances in Welsh legend, Morgana is often portrayed as a young and beautiful enchantress, aligning her with the maiden phase of the triple-goddess. In this aspect she represents the potential for both creation and destruction, using her powers either to aid or to hinder Arthur and his knights.

As her character develops, Morgana's role changes to one of nurturing, and she assumes the aspect of the mother, particularly in her relationship with the character of Mordred. Fiercely protective of those she loves, she has at various points used political influence, magic and violence to deliver that protection.

As a wise woman and healer, Morgana represents the crone archetype, as when she tends to a wounded Arthur after his final battle and carries him to Avalon. In this aspect she has a deep connection to the mysteries of life and death, acting as a guide between the two realms.

The 'Ulster Cycle'

The Morrígan's first narrative appearance was in the *Ulster Cycle*, a collection of tales from Irish mythology that were preserved in manuscript form between the twelfth and fifteenth centuries. In the *Ulster Cycle* the Morrígan has an undefined relationship with the hero Cú Chulainn. He insults her and she prophesizes his downfall.

The *Ulster Cycle* is a collection of medieval Irish legends and sagas about the Ulaid – a dynastic group of people who lived in what is now eastern Ulster and northern Leinster. The stories, set in the distant past, feature the mythical king Conchobar mac Nessa and his court, the hero Cú Chulainn and their conflicts with the Connachta and queen Medb. The stories are written in prose narrative and include epic battles, brave and cunning warriors and conflict between clans, as well as love and elopements.

In the text, the Morrígan appears as one of the daughters of Ernmas. She is a member of the mythical Tuatha Dé Danann, a supernatural race of kings, queens, bards and heroes who reside in the Otherworld. In the first tale in which the Morrígan appears, *The Cattle Raid of Regamain*, the hero, Cú Chulainn, encounters her as she drives a heifer from his land. He doesn't recognize her and immediately insults her. Before he can attack, she transforms into a black bird and alights on a nearby tree, revealing her identity. Cú Chulainn acknowledges that had he known who she was, he would not have behaved so rudely, but tells her that she can't harm him. In response, the Morrígan foretells his death in a forthcoming battle.

In *The Cattle Raid of Cooley,* Queen Medb of Connacht invades Ulster to steal the bull, Donn Cuailnge. The Morrígan, in the form of a crow, warns the bull to flee. Cú Chulainn defends Ulster in single combat and is approached by the Morrígan, disguised as a young woman. She offers Cú Chulainn her love and aid, but he rejects her. She then interferes in his next fight, attacking him in the forms of an eel, a wolf and a heifer (reiterating the importance of threes in Celtic mythology). Cú Chulainn wounds her in each form, ultimately emerging victorious. Later the Morrígan appears as an old woman with the same wounds, and she manipulates Cú Chulainn by offering him three drinks of milk. He blesses her after each drink, unwittingly healing her.

Many tales of Cú Chulainn's death have been told. However, in the most common version, the Morrígan portends his death as he rides to meet his enemies. She appears as a hag, washing his bloody armour in a ford. After being mortally wounded, Cú Chulainn binds himself to a standing stone with his own entrails so that he can die on his feet. Cu Chulainn meets his end when the Morrigan takes the form of a raven and lands on his shoulder. This signals to his enemies that he is dead and they behead him, sending him to the afterlife.

In the tales, the Morrígan is both Cú Chulainn's protector and enemy – mirroring Morgana's roles as Arthur's enemy and healer. Both possess magical powers, including the gift of prophecy and, as revealed in some Arthurian tales, the ability to shapeshift. They also exist outside of the mortal plain. As a member of the Tuatha Dé Danann, the Morrígan exists in the mythological Otherworld, while Morgana is tied closely to the mythical Isle of Avalon.

Connection to the Otherwold

Much has been written about Morgana's connection with the Morrígan and the triple-goddess archetype. However, it's important to note that, despite a clear similarity in their names and some aspects of their stories, there is very little evidence that the Morrígan served as direct inspiration. Many of Morgana le Fay's other characteristics appear in no depictions of the Morrígan, so much wider Celtic influences are probably at play. Most importantly, Morgana's first literary appearance is in *Vita Merlini* by Geoffrey of Monmouth (*c.* 1095–1155), which derives from the Welsh tradition. *Mor* in the Britonnic branch of Celtic languages means 'sea'; it does not share the same root as the Irish Morrígan (although this does not completely discount a shared mythological influence).

Modron, the Welsh mother goddess based on the Celtic goddess Matrona, is the most likely influence on Morgana le Fay. She has the most direct connection to Arthurian legend, appearing first in print in the poem *Pa Gur yv y Porthaur*, from the thirteenth-century manuscript *The Black Book of Carmarthen*, collected from centuries of Welsh oral tradition. *Par Gur* takes the form of a dialogue between King Arthur and Glewlwyd Gafaellfawr, the gatekeeper of his court. In the conversation Arthur boasts of his exploits and those of his companions; one 'Mabon am Mydron', the son of Modron, is listed as one of King Arthur's warriors. In the Welsh Triads, a collection of Welsh folklore, mythology and tradition, Morgana's father is listed as Afallach, a figure connected to the Isle of Avalon.

ANCIENT & MODERN: INTRODUCING MORGANA LE FAY

The mystical Isle of Avalon is an otherworldly realm shrouded in mist and magic. Like the Otherworld of Celtic mythology, it serves as a bridge between the mortal world and the realm of the gods and the dead – a place in which boundaries between worlds are thin.

There are other, less direct influences on Morgana le Fay's character. In many of her appearances, her role as a healer is an important face she wears. This aspect carries influences from the Irish goddess Brigid, who was a healer, protector and sage with the gift of prophecy. Brigid was also associated with water, especially at the point where three streams join together (another example of the triple-goddess archetype), drawing parallels with Morgana's representation in some tales as the Lady of the Lake.

Morgana's association with Avalon places her firmly within a Celtic tradition of liminal figures who move between the mortal world and the Otherworld. The Otherworld, in Celtic belief, is a place of transformation and regeneration, while Avalon too is a place of healing and renewal. After his last battle Morgana takes Arthur to Avalon to tend to his wounds, fostering the hope that he will one day return. Her connection to Avalon enables her to mediate between the mortal and the divine, emphasizing her connection to these ancient Celtic myths.

A Celtic Legacy

Rather than being a direct legacy, Celtic folklore, especially that of Ireland and Wales, serves as a cultural backdrop to Morgana's character. In these Celtic stories we can see hints of the woman Morgana le Fay would become: a prophet of death, a powerful sorceress of ambiguous morality and a character deeply linked with magic and the Otherworld.

These mythological roots are further bolstered by the name by which she is most commonly known: Morgana le Fay (Morgana of the Fairies). In more modern Celtic traditions, the supernatural folk of mythology are often referred to as the Fair Folk, Faery or the fae. Although this is an addition to the mythology, dating from the beginning of the nineteenth-century Celtic Revival, it still connects Morgana to the Otherworld and is a clear influence on her character.

While there may never be a clear Celtic root from which Morgana's character 'grew', the influence of the mythology of both Ireland and Wales is undeniable. Arthurian legends have evolved over time, influenced by changing cultural and religious contexts, and Morgana's character has changed along with them. However, her roots in Celtic mythology continue to inform her characterization and role in the narrative, even as the stories themselves have shifted.

Morgana le Fay stands as a fascinating figure who bridges the gap between ancient Celtic mythology and medieval Arthurian legends. Her character, with its roots in goddess figures, healing traditions and concepts of the Otherworld, provides a unique window into the ways in which pre-Christian beliefs and traditions were incorporated into – and transformed by – later medieval literature.

MEDIEVAL GENESIS

Geoffrey of Monmouth's 'Vita Merlini'

Morgana le Fay appears in her first iteration as 'Morgen' in Geoffrey of Monmouth's *Vita Merlini (The Life of Merlin)*. Written around 1150, the work focuses on Merlin's life after the decline of the Arthurian court, particularly in the aftermath of the Battle of Camlann. *Vita Merlini* tells the story of Merlin's retreat into the Caledonian Forest after a descent into madness caused by the battle's traumatic events. There he lives as a wild man, embracing nature and sharing prophecy, and the story focuses on the attempts of other characters, including his sister Ganieda and his former student Taliesin, to bring him back to civilization. It is Taliesin who, using his knowledge of music and poetry, eventually succeeds in calming Merlin's troubled mind.

The poem is rooted in early Middle Welsh Celtic legends. It is clearly influenced by the traditions of the bard Myrddin Wyllt, who features in the *Black Book of Carmarthen* but was also a staple figure in pre-twelfth-century Welsh poems. *Vita Merlini* also draws heavily upon tales of Lailoken, the wild man, prophet and madman said to have lived in the Caledonian Forest in the late sixth century. It also features an early depiction of King Arthur's final journey to the place that, in later re-tellings, became the Isle of Avalon.

Geoffrey's Morgana is a healer and a shapeshifter. She is benevolent and wise, teaching her sisters the art of healing and astrology. Her home is described as the 'Island of Apples' or 'The Fortunate Isle', where the land is fertile. In his poem Monmouth describes it as a land that 'produces all manner of plants spontaneously. It needs no farmers to plough the fields. There is no cultivation of the land at all beyond that which is Nature's work'.

When a knight brings Arthur to Morgana's 'Fortunate Isle' after being wounded in the battle of Camlan, there is no question of her trustworthiness and integrity. She is capable and beyond reproach in her desire to heal the fallen king, with no sign of the mistrust that future writers would show.

Chrétien de Troyes' Arthurian Romances

Chrétien de Troyes (c. 1160–1191) presents a similarly positive view of Morgana in his poem *Erec and Enide* (c. 1150), the first in his five-poem cycle that makes up his Arthurian Romances. The love story of a young knight, Erec, who is accompanying Guinevere, it describes how he is ordered to chase down another knight who mistreats her. On his journey Erec falls in love with a beautiful woman named Enide, whom he eventually marries. Their adventures are full of chivalric romance motifs and hardships, and the pair encounter many of the characters who are influential in later Arthurian re-tellings.

It is in Chrétien de Troyes' Arthurian Romances that Morgana is first named as Morgan and appears as Arthur's sister. He highlights her almost unlimited healing powers, emphasizing the care and skill with which she heals Erec after he is wounded on his adventures. Morgana is a benign figure and talented healer through most of the poems, and it is in Chrétien's work that the first subtle hints at a connection between her and Guinevere are revealed. Her healing is trusted not just to Arthur himself, but is also extended to his knights. It can even cure insanity, as mentioned in *Yvain* (c. 1170), the final poem of the Arthurian Romances.

In *Yvain*, the titular protagonist seeks vengeance for the defeat of his cousin by a mysterious knight named Esclados. After defeating him, Yvain falls in love with Laudine, Esclados's widow. The two marry, but shortly after their wedding his friend Gawain convinces him to leave Laudine and join him on a knightly quest. Laudine agrees, but insists that Yvain return within a year. He promises, but becomes so engrossed in his quest that he breaks his vow. Yvain is then, in turn, rejected by Laudine.

Laudine's rejection pushes the distraught Yvain into madness. However, he is eventually cured by Morgana and sets out to redeem himself and win back his wife's love. On his journey, he rescues a lion from a dragon, and the animal joins him as a companion. Together they defeat a giant, three knights and two demons, as well as preventing an unjust execution. Lunete, the woman thus rescued, helps Yvain reconcile with Laudine, who welcomes him back.

In both Monmouth's *Vita Merlini* and Chrétien's Arthurian Romances, Morgana is a minor figure. She appears in only a few lines and yet, within those brief moments, she shines as a beacon of goodness and benevolence. We also see the genesis of elements that will become such fundamental parts of her character: her ability to heal, her relationship with Arthur and her connection to the mystical Isle of Avalon. These early works of medieval European literature laid the groundwork for her evolution through the Arthurian canon. While later writers would expand on – and often darken – her role, Monmouth and Chrétien's Morgana stands as a testament to her origins as a powerful and beneficent figure.

The Vulgate Cycle

In the thirteenth-century French *Vulgate Cycle* (c. 1215–35), Morgana emerges as a more antagonistic figure, often at odds with King Arthur and his knights. The *Cycle* is a series of French prose narratives written by an unknown author or authors, and it significantly shaped Arthurian legend. It consists of five interconnected works that recount the rise and fall of King Arthur's court. They focus upon the quest for the Holy Grail and the tragic love story between Lancelot and Queen Guinevere.

In the *Vulgate Cycle*, Morgana loses some of her Celtic roots. Still closely associated with magic, she no longer holds a deep connection to the Otherworld. Furthermore, instead of wielding a benevolent, healing power, Morgana's magic has become more malicious. She is firmly human and lives in a castle rather than an otherworldy plain. Her magic is used for vanity and to bring harm to others.

The other striking change to Morgana's characterization in the *Cycle* is that she becomes a much more active agent. In the works of Chrétien and Monmouth, she was alluded to as a distant, ephemeral, yet benevolent figure, but in the narratives of the *Vulgate Cycle* she is integral to events. This shift in Morgana's character may reflect a change in attitudes towards magic and powerful women in medieval society, as well as the influence of Christian themes on the Arthurian legends.

These more negative aspects of Morgana (or Morgaine, as she is known in the story) appear primarily in *Vulgate Estoire de Merlin* (*Story of Merlin*) or *Prose Merlin*. It recounts the life and prophecies of Merlin, including the birth of King Arthur, his upbringing and the events leading to his claim to the throne after drawing the sword from the stone. The stories also introduce significant characters who play vital roles in Arthurian legend, such as Lancelot, Guinevere and Morgana herself.

In the story, she appears as King Arthur's sister and Merlin's student. Morgana is described as young and merry yet with a sombre face; clever and comely, with a good singing voice. However, the text also describes her as lustful and lewd, especially in relation to Guimoar, the nephew of Queen Guinevere. This moment serves to cement Morgana's more negative aspects, pitting her in a cycle of revenge against the queen. Her actions become vengeful, capable certainly of anger and hate, but also of deep, all-consuming love.

In the *Prose Lancelot*, which recounts the adventures and quests of Lancelot and other Knights of the Round Table, Morgana is described as beautiful. However, her beauty diminishes as the story progresses. She flirts with Lancelot and attempts to thwart the love affair between him and Guinevere in revenge for the queen's attempts to come between herself and Guiomar. Arthur is the tragic king, Lancelot and Guinevere the ideal of courtly love and Morgana the evil temptress. The more her dark nature reveals itself, the more her physical beauty diminishes.

The Post-Vulgate Cycle

The *Post-Vulgate Cycle* (c. 1230–5) expands significantly on Morgana's characterization. Anonymously written, and pieced together from various fragments, it is widely considered a reconstruction of the *Vulgate Cycle*, with some parts left out and others added. The work also incorporates elements of *Prose Tristan* – an adaptation of the story of Tristan and Iseult, and the first to tie it to Arthurian legend.

Tristan is a young knight who arrives at the court of his uncle Mark, King of Cornwall. Wounded in a battle defending his country against the Irish warrior Morholt, he is healed by Iseult, Morholt's niece, but is obliged to flee to save his life. He returns to Iseult in disguise to bring her to Cornwall as a potential bride for his uncle. The couple accidentally drink a love potion, however, leading to a tragic affair that results in Tristan's banishment. Meanwhile he has many adventures and eventually becomes a Knight of the Round Table, reuniting with Iseult. When Mark discovers their rekindled affair, he stabs Tristan with a lance given to him by Morgana. In his dying moments Tristan embraces Iseult, crushing her heart, so the lovers perish together.

In many circles *Prose Tristan* is considered a direct sequel to (or at least an elaboration of) the *Vulgate Cycle*. In the poem Morgana seeks to enact her revenge on Tristan for the death of her lover, Huneson. And yet, while her actions inflict and have the intent to do harm, they are driven by love rather than simply a desire for violence.

While Morgana has magic at her disposal, however, many of the manipulations she uses are distinctly human. She causes pain where necessary and employs physical substances to mould men to her will. Although elements of her character as a healer remain, *Prose Tristan* sees those powers twisted and warped. Morgana uses her ability to heal to manipulate others into doing what she needs them to, rather than through a natural desire to help.

The *Suite du Merlin* of the *Post-Vulgate Cycle* develops Morgana's character even more, even though it follows the same general premise as *Prose Merlin*. In previous representations Morgana's enmity was reserved primarily for Guinevere, but in this poem, for the first time, her destructive nature is expanded to include Arthur himself. As in the *Prose Merlin*, she becomes violent when her love affair with Guiomar is discovered. Her desperate attempt to gain revenge on both Guinevere and Arthur leaves a trail of collateral damage in her wake, yet it also reconnects her back to her magical roots.

In this story Morgana created Excalibur's magical scabbard on the Isle of Avalon, so she knows its power. She steals it and is pursued, turning herself into stone to escape. Once again Morgana is connected to the Otherworld in the form of Avalon; her shapeshifting powers are restored, she lures characters to enchanted locations and she creates magical artefacts. *Suite du Merlin* also restores her powers of prophecy, and she foretells the deaths of both Arthur and Gawain.

Gawain and the Green Knight

The fourteenth-century English chivalric romance *Gawain and the Green Knight* shares many aspects of the tales that preceded it. Drawing more extensively upon the Welsh and Irish roots of Arthurian legends (especially the Irish *Ulster Cycle* and the Welsh *Mabinogion*), Morgana's character seems less overtly malicious than in the French chivalric traditions of the *Vulgate Cycle*.

Appearing as Morgan le Fay in the text, this Morgana is not so focused on the destruction of her half-brother Arthur and his court; she rather seeks to shame and test them. The Green Knight is enchanted in order to frighten Guinevere to death, once again casting the queen as the main focus of Morgana's ire, rather than to harm Arthur or his court.

The story begins on New Year's Eve, with the arrival at King Arthur's court of a mysterious Green Knight. He proposes a 'game': anyone may strike him with his axe, but must agree to accept a blow in return when a year and a day have passed. Sir Gawain accepts the challenge and beheads the Green Knight – who calmly picks up his severed head and reminds Gawain of their future meeting at the Green Chapel. As the deadline approaches, Gawain sets out to fulfil his side of the bargain. He encounters a lord who invites him to stay at his castle. His host proposes a daily exchange of winnings, while his wife tests Gawain's virtue with advances. These Gawain resists, but he does secretly accept a magical protective sash which he conceals from his host. At the Green Chapel the Green Knight reveals himself to be the lord in disguise, lightly wounding Gawain for his fault in concealing the sash. The knight forgives him, explaining that the quest was a test orchestrated by the sorceress Morgan le Fay. Gawain returns to Camelot in shame, believing that he has failed. However, his fellow knights honour his humility by adopting the green sash as a symbol of integrity.

When Gawain meets Morgana, he is introduced to an older woman who commands the respect of those in the castle. She sits at the high table and appears stately. Despite this, however, the unknown poet of *Gawain and the Green Knight* highlights her darker character in the way he describes her: black brows, black eyes and an almost nun-like garb. This gives the sense that there is more to Morgana than first appearances would suggest.

Despite having no overt role in the story of *Gawain and the Green Knight*, Morgana is the lynchpin that holds the story together. She is the conspirator behind the sequence of events; the one who brings each element of her plan into being. Her magic exists not only to disguise, but also to heal. When the enchanted Green Knight is beheaded by Gawain, he is magically restored and healed by Morgana's magic to reveal the plot to the reader.

From her origins, and through the medieval period, Morgana le Fay had already undergone a remarkable transformation in the Arthurian canon. From her origins as a skilled healer and shapeshifter in Geoffrey of Monmouth's *Vita Merlini* and the Arthurian Romances of Chrétien de Troyes to her more antagonistic role in the French *Vulgate Cycle* and *Post-Vulgate Cycle*, she has remained a captivating and enigmatic figure.

As the Arthurian canon evolved, so did Morgana's character, reflecting the changing attitudes towards magic, women and power in medieval society. While early depictions of Morgana emphasized her benevolence and healing abilities, later works explored her darker aspects. Through these she was cast as a vengeful and manipulative figure, often at odds with King Arthur and his court.

Despite these variations, certain elements of Morgana's character have cemented themselves as being essential to how she is viewed. For example, her deep connection to magic, her complex relationships with Arthur and Guinevere and her association with the mystical Isle of Avalon have endured throughout the centuries and across multiple re-tellings. She thus emerges as a woman of many faces, with a character that can be used and adapted across time.

THE DEATH OF ARTHUR

Thomas Malory's 'Le Morte d'Arthur'

What we know of Morgana le Fay's character is firmly cemented in the late fifteenth century by Sir Thomas Malory's *Le Morte d'Arthur* (c. 1469–70). This century compiled much of what had gone into previous Arthurian tales, culminating in what is probably the best-known work of Arthurian literature to date – and the most influential.

Le Morte d'Arthur recounts the rise and fall of King Arthur and his knights of the Round Table. It begins with Arthur's miraculous birth and chronicles his rise to the throne after pulling Excalibur from the stone. As Arthur establishes his kingdom of Camelot he faces several challenges, including wars, before the Round Table can be founded and peace secured. His court becomes a symbol of chivalry and valour, highlighted by the eventual quest to pursue the Holy Grail (in which many knights fail and Sir Galahad achieves the ultimate spiritual victory). *Le Morte d'Arthur* also includes several tragic love stories, for example that of Sir Tristram and Isolde and the doomed romance between Lancelot and Guinevere, which are used to foreshadow the eventual decline of Arthur's court. The collapse of the Round Table eventually occurs through betrayal and civil war, driven by the treachery of Arthur's son Mordred and the repercussions of Lancelot and Guinevere's affair. Arthur's tragic death marks the end of his reign, but the work's ambiguous conclusion leaves hope for his return.

In *Le Morte d'Arthur* Morgana is immediately recognizable as the character developed in the French tradition of the *Vulgate Cycle*, resulting in a fascinatingly inconsistent characterization. She appears in one tale as an evil enchantress and in another as a benevolent healer.

In Malory's tale Morgana (named as Morgan le Fay) is Arthur's half-sister, daughter of the Duke of Tintagel and Igraine, Arthur's mother. After her own father's death she was placed in a nunnery at the request of Uther Pendragon (Arthur's father). Here she became skilled in black magic, later marrying King Uriens and bearing a son, Uwaine.

For reasons that are not clear, Morgana is jealous of Arthur's strength and glory. She betrays him by stealing Excalibur's scabbard and giving it to her lover, Accolon, hoping to have him kill Arthur and become king himself. However, Nimue, the benevolent Lady of the Lake, thwarts her plans and saves Arthur. Morgana's lover Accolon then confesses her treachery before dying. Morgana herself also attempts to kill her husband, but is stopped by Uwaine.

After learning of Accolon's death, Morgana flees Camelot, stealing Excalibur's scabbard and throwing it into the lake to prevent Arthur from using its power. Although Arthur pursues her, she escapes by transforming herself and her followers into stone. Morgana continues to oppose Arthur and Guinevere, going so far as to send a cursed mantle as a false gesture of reconciliation.

She also targets the Knights of the Round Table and even abducts Lancelot, holding him captive in her castle.

When the affair between Lancelot and Guinevere is finally revealed, Arthur sentences Guinevere to be burned. In mounting a rescue mission, several of the Knights of the Round Table are killed, and Arthur and Lancelot enter a lengthy war. During this conflict Mordred, Arthur's bastard son by his half-sister Morgauwse, is able to seize the throne. In the final battle Arthur is wounded and brought to Avalon by both the Lady of the Lake and Morgana.

A Magical Rivalry

While Malory's emphasis in his work is on the chivalric heroism of its male protagonists, the women in the story act as incentives, through either positive or negative means. Malory's female characters serve to motivate his male ones, some through goodness and beauty, others by wielding incredibly powerful magic. They are larger than life, powerful symbols of either virtue or evil. In *Le Morte d'Arthur*, for the first time, Malory creates an opposite of Morgana le Fay in the form of the Lady of the Lake. In early Celtic legends Morgana and the Lady had sometimes been the same person. Yet in his tale Malory pits the two women against each other, drawing a direct contrast between their motivation and magical skills. This opposition creates a binary that makes Morgana appear far more evil compared with the unquestionable goodness of the Lady of the Lake.

Such a contrast can exist because Malory gives Morgana much more character in his work than she has had before. Previous texts often referred to Morgana in passing, or as acting behind the scenes. Malory not only gives her a far more prominent role, but also makes a great effort to create consistency in her character. An active presence in the story, she is able to rival her male counterparts in both strength and skill. As a woman, she exists at the margins of courtly society – yet she becomes a very real threat and danger to it.

On the surface, Malory seems to paint Morgana le Fay as a quintessential villain. As King Arthur's half-sister, she commits the ultimate betrayal by attempting to usurp his kingdom, using black magic to do so. Worst of all, she defies the very idea of chivalric love so essential to the Arthurian tales. She takes a lover, tries to kill her husband, is excluded from Camelot and thrives outside the court. In many ways Morgana embodies the worst fears about powerful women in the medieval imagination: that their independence and abilities will lead them to sin and destructive behaviour. Such malice is in direct contrast to the benevolent magic of the Lady of the Lake, who uses her powers to empower the narrative's heroic men. However, at Arthur's end, it is the two women together who carry him to Avalon.

Guinevere and Lancelot

Much of Morgana's story is related directly to her hatred of Guinevere. Her rivalry with Arthur is never deeply explored in the *Morte d'Arthur*, but her troubled history with Guinevere would have been long-established by the existing Arthurian canon. Given how much influence the *Vulgate Cycle* had on Malory's epic, we can assume that their enmity derives from the rift Guinevere created between Morgana and Guiomar off the page.

According to Stephen Knight, in his 2009 book *Merlin: Knowledge and Power Through the Ages*, Malory would have been acting on the authorial assumption that readers were already well-versed in his source material. For this reason Malory was able to omit motivation, name characters without introduction and avoid backstories completely, secure in the knowledge that his readers already possessed the necessary information.

What is most interesting is that Guinevere's motivations for seeking to come between Guiomar and Morgana are never explored, not even in the *Vulgate Cycle*. Since Morgana is sister to the king, and there is never any explicit shame attached to her character at the time, it is odd that Guinevere would have opposed the match so vehemently. It is possible that there were social taboos at play which contemporary readers of the tale would have recognized, perhaps surrounding bloodlines and family ties; these may be further evidenced by Morgana's marriage to Uriel and her infidelity with Accolon in *Le Morte d'Arthur*. Regardless of motivation, a lifetime of hatred for the queen is the result of the *Vulgate Cycle*. It marks Morgana's character for the rest of Arthurian legend, which directly informs her portrayal by Malory.

Morgana's capture of Lancelot is directly related to her hatred of Guinevere. It is she who uncovers the affair with Sir Lancelot, whereupon he becomes the focus of her anger, as she knows she can hurt the queen through her love for him. She captures Lancelot and attempts to seduce him into confessing his love to her. While this is a fundamental part of many of the previous tales, Malory makes this explicit. Morgana knows that Lancelot loves Guinevere, and thus forces him to choose to become her own lover or remain her prisoner. In doing so Morgana is aware that either his betrayal or his death will profoundly hurt Guinevere.

More Than a Villain

It is overly simplistic to label Morgana as purely a villain from a modern standpoint. She questions the legitimacy of her brother's court, true, but she also ends the tale as a wise healer, carrying Arthur to Avalon where she can tend to him. While she betrays Arthur through much of the story, her compassion and familial loyalty win out in the end.

The ambiguity of Morgana's character is also hinted at in other elements of Malory's story. Lancelot is not the only knight whom Morgana captures, and it is through these encounters that her less overtly villainous traits shine through. While an initial reading would cast her purely as the evil villain, she actually has very clear and targeted motivations, rather than simply indulging in wanton destruction.

In *The Book of Sir Tristram of Lyonesse*, Tristram is captured after an ambush and held captive in Morgana's castle. While he was specifically targeted, she promises to release him if he answers her honestly with his name. He does so, and she keeps her word. Morgana thus shows herself as true to her promises, even if she does manipulate the situation to her advantage.

While she acts with honesty in releasing Tristram, before he departs she gives him a shield decorated with the image of three figures: a king, a queen and a knight standing above them, one foot on the head of each. The king and queen clearly represent Arthur and Guinevere, while the knight is Sir Lancelot. Morgana's intent is to have Tristram use this shield in an upcoming tournament and, therefore, reveal the affair between Guinevere and Lancelot to the court in a public way.

In the same tale, Morgana shows care for a woman whose brother has been wounded in battle. While not directly named, the woman shares with Lancelot the fact that a sorceress from the nearby castle has told her how her brother's wound may be healed. The assumption is therefore that this unnamed sorceress is Morgana, as Tristram has just come from her castle. The woman sends Lancelot on a quest into the Chapel Perilous, where he will find a sword that, when touched to the wounds of the woman's fallen brother, will immediately heal him. Here Morgana's magic is used for no other purpose other than to heal, although her power is still used to test the mettle of one of Arthur's knights.

Ultimately, despite the conflicts and betrayals between Morgana and Arthur that occur throughout *Le Morte d'Arthur*, her final act, carrying her brother to Avalon, demonstrates a redemption. When it matters most, Morgana chooses to prioritize her role as Arthur's sister over their previous animosity.

The Demonization of Powerful Women

Morgana's portrayal in *Le Morte d'Arthur* reflects medieval anxieties about women in power and has had a significant impact on interpretations of her character. As opposed to the benevolent magic of the Lady of the Lake, Morgana uses her power to challenge the patriarchal structures of King Arthur's court rather than to sustain them.

For its medieval audience, Morgana's kick against the chivalrous patriarchy of Camelot would have made her an embodiment of evil. She personified the decadence of society, the result of a tradition fed with misogynistic views on empowered women and the progressive prosecution of pagan magic (along with beliefs that tied it to witchcraft) as a danger to the established social structure.

Moreover, Morgana's association with the negative elements of pagan magic further vilified her in the eyes of a medieval Christian audience. The practice of magic, especially by women, was increasingly linked to witchcraft; it was thus viewed as a direct threat to the authority of the Church. By portraying Morgana as a powerful sorceress who uses her power to manipulate and challenge the status quo, Malory taps into these fears. In so doing he reinforces the idea that women who step outside their prescribed roles pose a threat to the social order.

Malory's *Le Morte d'Arthur* is the culmination of a long series of re-interpretations of Celtic tales in a Christianized world. These tales sought to re-imagine folk tales in a way that would suit their world-view, giving moral lessons to their readers through the way in which individual characters were represented. They were influential stories in a changing world, told by those in a position to control the narrative.

2.
A Changing Britain

The King draws a deep sigh at the sight of them, and has a plaster brought which Morgan, his sister, had made. This plaster, which Morgan had given to Arthur, was of such sovereign virtue that no wound, whether on nerve or joint, provided it were treated with the plaster once a day, could fail to be completely cured and healed within a week.
– From Chrétien de Troyes' *Erec and Enide* (c. 1170)

CHIVALRY AND CHRISTIANITY

What is Chivalry?

Chivalry plays an important part in the genesis of Arthurian legend as we know it. Chrétien de Troyes, Sir Thomas Malory and even the unknown authors of the *Vulgate Cycle* all work together to create an idea of the chivalric ideal.

Chivalry originated as a code of conduct for knights in medieval Europe, blending martial, social and religious ideals. It evolved from early warrior traditions into a more formalized system during the twelfth century, closely associated with the rise of feudalism and the knightly class. The term 'chivalry' itself comes from the

Old French word *chevalier*, roughly translated as 'horse soldiery', reflecting its roots in the military service of mounted warriors.

As knights became more central to early medieval warfare between the eighth and eleventh centuries, the concept of chivalry began to evolve. It became more than simply military service and loyalty to a liege lord, with greater emphasis being placed on moral or ethical guidelines. As Christian ideals became more intertwined with knighthood, the idea of knights as defenders of the weak, protectors of the faith and champions of justice started to form.

These ideals were popularized in medieval literature, particularly the literary cycles known as *The Matter of France*, *The Matter of Britain* and *The Matter of Rome*, which detailed the exploits of Charlemagne, King Arthur and interpretations of Greek and Roman mythology and history respectively. *The Matter of Britain* in particular was largely informed by Geoffrey of Monmouth's *Historia Regum Britanniae* (1130). The work popularized the legend of King Arthur and his knights of the Round Table and was a precursor to his *Vita Merlini*.

By the fourteenth century chivalry had become more formalized. Knights were often inducted into chivalric orders such as the Order of the Garter (founded by Edward III in 1348). These orders, which aimed to promote the highest ideals of knighthood, were often tied to monarchies and political power.

In this period knighthood became more ceremonial and rituals such as dubbing (the act of knighting) were standardized. Tournaments and jousts became popular ways for knights to demonstrate their prowess and honour, further romanticizing the knightly image.

Paganism vs Christianity

Christianity played a significant role in shaping the ideal of chivalry. It ties closely to the Crusades that occurred between 1096 and 1291, in which those called to take up arms and fight in the Holy Land saw themselves as fighting to protect Christianity.

Knights were expected to uphold Christian values, fight for the faith or another noble cause and protect the helpless, including women, children and the poor. This blending of religious and martial duties was codified in various chivalric orders, such as the Knights Templar and Knights Hospitaller – both founded to protect pilgrims and to fight in the Crusades.

At the same time pagan traditions, including the belief in magic and supernatural powers, were increasingly viewed as a threat to Christian doctrine – and yet, to maintain the primacy of their religion, certain concessions had to be made. Chivalric tales that utilized pagan belief systems were used to portray the primacy of Christian beliefs in overcoming their pagan roots. Morgana's character serves to illustrate that. Her magical abilities became more and more tied to pagan traditions, and thus a symbol of the dangers they represented.

The conflict between Morgana and the Christian heroes of Arthurian legend provide a metaphor for the struggle between paganism and Christianity. Benevolent forms of magic, such as those displayed by the Lady of the Lake, or even Morgana's own healing abilities, are portrayed positively when they uphold Christian values and support the status quo. When they step beyond this, however, and represent anything that runs counter to the values of Christian chivalry, magic becomes a symbol of evil that must be vanquished.

An important point to note is that the medieval Arthurian romances are fundamentally Christian texts. The Knights of the Round Table act to glorify God; significant references are made to Christian feast days and holidays throughout the tales. By the medieval period Arthurian legend had been well and truly Christianized, with only literary allusions to their Celtic roots.

Courtly Love

Chivalry evolved further during the twelfth century with the rise of the concept of courtly love, which idealized knights' romantic devotion to noble ladies. This literary and social tradition was popularized by troubadours and poets; it introduced a more humanist rather than Christian theme to the Arthurian tales, as it elevated the role of women to more than just side characters mentioned in passing. Although courtly love was a fiction created for the entertainment of the nobility, it spread quickly across Europe, attracting a large audience who sought to emulate its ideals.

In his twelfth-century treatise commonly titled *De amore* (or *About Love*), Andreas Capellanus codifies courtly love as having four fundamental rules. The first states that 'marriage is no real excuse for not loving' and the second that 'he who is not jealous cannot love'. The third rule declares that 'no one can be bound by a double love' while the fourth urges secrecy: 'when made public love rarely endures'.

We can see these rules play out perfectly in Arthurian legend. Guinevere's marriage to Arthur is no boundary to her love of Lancelot, which is considered pure and perfect. The pair often show jealousy, despite having no true love other than one another. Morgana plays a vital role in this element. In Malory's *Le Morte d'Arthur* she tries to seduce Lancelot away from Guinevere, but is unsuccessful; he would rather die than betray his love for the queen. Morgana also plays a fundamental role in proving Capellanus's fourth rule of courtly love. Her primary motivation is apparently to publicize the love affair between Guinevere and Lancelot – not just to Arthur, but to the entire court.

While certain elements of courtly love can be seen to run counter to Christian ideals of chivalry, some scholars have suggested that it sprang from the Church's efforts to refine the feudal codes of the late eleventh century. Arranged marriages were common, leaving people to create alternative channels to express romantic love – channels that would work within the customs of their time, not outside of them.

We can see this view of courtly love play out clearly in both the marriages of Guinevere and Morgana. Guinevere represents the ideal. Her marriage to Arthur was not a match of great love, so they do not share a truly romantic bond. She and Lancelot look outside their marriages to create a love that is both pure and idealized as the epitome of romance. Morgana, interestingly, has a similar marriage with Uriens. Yet, rather than seeking her own romantic ideal, she focuses instead upon destroying Guinevere. She also manipulates her romantic partners and tries to murder her husband.

The Christian Patriarchy

Regardless of the idealized romance of courtly love that held women as ennoblers of their male partners, medieval society was deeply patriarchal. Men held roles of power and authority, especially within the Christian framework, and many stories were rewritten in order to represent this new world order more clearly.

In Celtic mythology, magic often lay with women. They might be powerful sorceresses, using their magic for reasons that were often morally ambiguous, yet they were never portrayed as purely evil. Such women often used their powers to heal or uplift heroes. However, by the late medieval period magic and sorcery had already started to become associated with witchcraft and the devil. By the time the Arthurian romances were written and compiled, the Inquisition, which would brand any unsanctioned non-Christian worldviews as heretical, was only a few decades away, so the benevolent power of magic was shifting.

Modern audiences will immediately recognize Merlin as being connected to magic. He takes on the magic role previously reserved for women and is treated kindly in Arthurian tales. The protector of both Arthur and Camelot, he contrasts with Morgana's portrayal as the woman who wishes to bring them down. Merlin has agency as a character, whereas both the magical women of Arthurian legend, Nimue (The Lady of the Lake) and Morgana le Fay, act only in the service of, or to counter, the acts of men.

What makes Morgana such a fascinating character in Arthurian legend, especially in Malory's portrayal of her in *Le Morte d'Arthur*, is that she does not fit the prescribed definition of femininity that we see in so many other texts of the day – and even in the other female characters of Malory's tale. Morgana's greatest threat to Arthur and Camelot is that she never fully embodies the masculine or the feminine roles of magic and power. She exists outside of that binary.

Like her half-sister Morgauwse, Guinevere and her mother Igraine, Morgana is of noble birth. Like those women, she has the privileges afforded by birthright. However, she transcends that birthright, wielding more power than the other women in the story purely by transcending her socially dictated patriarchal role. She betrays her marriage, but moves beyond the dictates of courtly love; she embraces her feminine (and, dare I say, pagan) power and makes a place for herself outside Arthur's court. She represents a woman unbound by patriarchy – and thus she must be evil.

The Quest for the Holy Grail

When discussing the nature of chivalry and Christianity in Arthurian legend, the most fundamental aspect to draw on is, of course, the quest for the Holy Grail. The Grail plays a pivotal role in the tales of King Arthur and his knights and has had almost as many versions as Morgana herself. It has been represented as a goblet, platter or even a mystical stone imbued with extraordinary healing abilities, able to bestow eternal youth or provide boundless sustenance.

The Grail first appears in Chrétien de Troyes' unfinished *Perceval, the Story of the Grail* (c. 1190), becoming a staple of Arthurian legend from that point. While it was always a magical vessel, it was Robert de Boron, in his work *Joseph d'Arimimathie* (1190), who first drew a parallel between the Grail and the cup used to collect the blood of Christ at the crucifixion.

ANCIENT & MODERN: INTRODUCING MORGANA LE FAY

In Malory's *Le Morte d'Arthur* and the earlier *Vulgate Cycle*, the quest for the grail is a holy mission representing chivalric ideals. The knights who embark on the quest must be not only skilled warriors, but also display incredible humility, piety and self-sacrifice. The Grail quest is an act of pilgrimage, in which the knights embark on a journey of spiritual purification and enlightenment. Along the way they face trials and temptations that test their faith and commitment to the Christian chivalric code.

Morgana's role in these quests is as a temptress to the knights who embark on this journey. It is through her manipulations that those unworthy of finding the Grail are revealed. Even the most celebrated knights, such as Lancelot, are ultimately found wanting due to their moral failings and their inability fully to reconcile their earthly desires with their spiritual aspirations. While Arthur sends his knights off to seek spiritual enlightenment, Morgana reveals the cracks in the perfect image of Arthur's Camelot.

It is ultimately Galahad, the son of Lancelot, who emerges as the epitome of the Christian chivalric ideal. Born from Lancelot's illicit union with Elaine, Galahad is conceived because of deception and magic, with Morgana le Fay as the catalyst. Jealous of Elaine's beauty, she ensnares her in a boiling bath from which she is rescued by Lancelot. Elaine falls in love with him and uses magic to seduce him, tricking Lancelot with one of Guinevere's rings into believing that she is the queen. When he discovers her deception, Lancelot threatens to kill her. Elaine reveals that their coupling has left her pregnant, so he lets her live, and she gives birth to Galahad.

Galahad is destined to be the purest and most perfect of knights, untainted by the sins of his father. His success in the Grail quest, where he ultimately achieves the Grail and ascends to heaven, represents the triumph of Christian virtue over the worldly temptations and moral compromises of the chivalric code.

THE ISLE OF AVALON

King Arthur's Britain

Arthurian legend has always been deeply connected to the Anglo-Celtic Isles and has become a fundamental founding myth of modern Britain. These stories link Arthur to a common poetic idea of Britain as a paradise and paragon of Christian goodness, with a past upheld by its Celtic roots but unspoiled by them.

Following the Norman Conquest in 1066, Celtic legend was reimagined and repurposed to tell different stories depending on the teller. Many Celtic strongholds, particularly Wales, managed to resist Norman incursion; their retellings were thus designed to highlight their triumph over outside forces. Arthur became the conquering hero who would speak to that triumph and the inherent rightness of their victory.

Geoffrey of Monmouth was instrumental in bringing Arthurian legend into the zeitgeist and is considered one of Britain's founding historiographers (the study of written histories). A Catholic cleric from Monmouth, in Wales, he established the Arthurian canon as we know it today. We have already discussed his *Vita Merlini*, but it was his earlier work, *Historia Regum Britanniae* (or *The History of the Kings of Britain*, c. 1136), that first introduced Arthur and his knights into the mainstream.

Monmouth represented his *Historia* as a work of fact, claiming it was based on a lost Celtic manuscript given to him by Walter of Oxford. While scholars now agree that Walter probably did provide Monmouth with some Welsh texts that formed a basis for his tales, they also agree that the claim of a lost manuscript is largely fabricated. By representing his book as a history, however, the damage was done. Early scholars had accepted Monmouth's *Historia* at face value, so it entered popular history as a work of fact rather than fiction.

In *Historia Regum Britanniae* Monmouth recounts Arthur's whole life story, from his birth at Tintagel through to his betrayal and death. It introduced many of the fundamental elements of Arthurian legend, including Guinevere, Merlin and even his magical sword, Excalibur (known as Caliburn in the text). The work was hugely influential and perceived as a founding truth of British identity until its re-evaluation by modern historians.

The Genesis of Avalon

Monmouth's *Historia Regum Britanniae* didn't simply introduce the characters of Arthurian legend to a wider audience; it was the first work really to cement Avalon as a physical place. He connected it immediately with Morgana le Fay, casting her as the island's ruler. While Avalon still maintained its mystical ideal, it had less of the sense of the Otherworld, separated from the mortal plain, than in older Celtic works.

In the *Historia* Monmouth refers to Avalon as the *Insula Avallonis*, meaning the 'Isle of Avallon' in Latin. In his later work,

Vita Merlini, he names it *Insula Pomorum*, or the 'Isle of Fruit Trees'. The name Avalon actually comes from the Britonnic languages for the word apple. The Welsh word for apple is *afal*, and *aball* or *avallen* means either 'apple tree' or 'fruit tree' in Old Welsh, Cornish and Breton.

Avalon as we know it did not really appear in early Welsh or Breton tales. In his *Historia* Monmouth drew inspiration from the Irish Otherworld, but represented the isle as something far more tangible, directly connected with Morgana le Fay. British chroniclers such as Monmouth used Avalon as a political tool, legitimizing the rule of English monarchs by presenting them as Arthur's successors and using superstition and religious rights to dismiss political dissent.

Presented to the public as a place of healing and abundance, where Arthur remains until his triumphant return to rule England, Avalon cast his rule as good and pure. It connected to Celtic traditions while creating something new – revealing that the otherworldly Avalon and its denizens had legitimized a Christian king as the rightful ruler of Britain. Fittingly, Morgana, as the representation of pagan magic, often ends her story by bearing Arthur to Avalon or healing him there.

In the end, the woman who fought against Arthur and his rule accepts Arthur's legitimacy; she takes him to her magical isle, cementing him as the rightful king. Writers adopted and adapted her character to suit their own political and literary agendas, changing Morgana from Arthur's foe to his healer in Avalon in order to discredit narratives of Arthur's return as a political threat.

Real or Otherworldy?

While modern-day scholars agree that Monmouth's *Historia* is largely a work of fiction, there have still been many attempts to draw parallels between the locations of Arthurian legend and real-world places. In some cases this is simple, especially when we look at the pre-*Historia* sources such as the *Vulgate Cycle*.

Monmouth names Caerleon, in Monmouthshire, Wales, as the location of Camelot and the Round Table. I lived in Caerleon when I first moved to Wales. It was once a Roman fortress town and there are excavated Roman ruins to be seen throughout the village, including a Roman amphitheatre. Many locals believe that the pre-excavated amphitheatre is where this myth originated, as it left a large, round depression in the ground. Surrounded by the ruins of a Roman fortresses, it is easy to see how it could have been perceived as the place of a large round table, set within a sprawling castle-city in a country so deeply connected to the legend.

Carmarthen is another Welsh location strongly associated with Arthurian legend. It is named *Caerfyrddin* in Welsh, which translates as 'Merlin's Fort', while the *Black Book of Carmarthen* describes it as Merlin's birthplace. Many other tales also mention Arthur specifically travelling to, or through, Carmarthen.

The real place with the strongest modern ties to Arthurian legend, however, is Glastonbury Tor in the southwest of England. Now a grassy hill with a ruined church tower at its summit, it would at the time of the legends have been an isle surrounded by marsh. According to Gerald of Wales, a chronicler of the twelfth century, it was an island surrounded by a vast lake called *Ynys Afallach*, the Island of Apples.

In 1191 the monks of Glastonbury Abbey excavated to find the bones of two people who they claimed were Arthur and Guinevere. They are said to have found an unmarked tomb and a lead cross that not only named both Arthur and Guinevere, but also referred to Glastonbury as the Isle of Avalon. After the dissolution of the monasteries the tomb was lost, and historians today question its authenticity. The story stuck, however, and has become a very real part of British folklore and identity.

With the Celtic Revival of the nineteenth century, the Tor once again became connected to the Otherworld. It was believed to represent an entrance to Avalon, the land of the fairies and the world of the dead, reconnecting Avalon back to Morgana le Fay. The Tor is the gateway to her realm.

Also connecting Morgana to the Tor is the nearby Chalice Well (or Red Well) that sits on a nearby hill. The water from the well has a reddish hue due to the iron oxide, making it a popular place of connection to the Goddess movement. Wells feature heavily in Welsh and Irish mythology, often providing links between different worlds. Due in part to the reddish colour of its waters and in part to the Tor's association with Avalon, the Chalice Well was also co-opted by Christian mythology as the resting place of the Holy Grail. As we have observed, in many Christian and pre-Christian versions of the legend it was Morgana who carried a wounded Arthur to Avalon, over which she ruled. She is the goddess who presides over Arthur's final resting place.

Fata Morgana

Given her villainy through so many of the Arthurian tales, it is surprising that Morgana le Fay's connection to Avalon has so strongly endured. The motif of Arthur resting in Morgana's care has become such a crucial element of the legend that it is hard to reconcile the two conflicting images of her villainy and benevolence. She is at once humanly fallible, using her sorcery to manipulate and do harm, while at the same time ending the tale as the goddess figure who bears Arthur to Avalon. This duality has led to an interesting real-world phenomenon bearing her name: Fata Morgana.

Fata Morgana is an Italian name derived from *la Fata Morgana*, or Morgan the Fairy. A phenomenon that causes a mirage, often seen in the Italian Strait of Messina, it has been described as fairy castles or false land appearing in the sky or on the horizon, once thought to be conjured by magic. The name has led some scholars to connect the island of Sicily with Avalon in some reports, due to how often the mirage occurs there.

A Fata Morgana mirage occurs when the curvature of light is distorted between two layers of air that are of different density. Because the atmospheric conditions that cause this can change quickly, the mirage can appear differently in just a few seconds, often causing it to flicker and shimmer. It can often look like land shimmering on the horizon, or even make objects appear to float in the air.

In the case of a Fata Morgana, it is both an atmospheric manipulation of our reality and a phenomenon that appears otherworldly and magical. I can't think of a more perfect phenomenon to carry Morgana's name.

Avalon and the Lady of the Lake

A large amount of the ambiguity surrounding Morgana's characters is the distinction between the Lady of the Lake and the Lady of Avalon. This is often far from clear; in some instances, Morgana is both, but in others they are different people. It is always Morgana who has strong ties to Avalon, yet the Lady of the Lake is never explicitly linked.

In Monmouth's *Vita Merlini* Morgana and the Lady of the Lake are separate people (Nyneve is the Lady in Monmouth's retellings). However, Morgana is explicitly named as the Lady of the Lake in earlier versions of the tale. This ambiguity extends to the possibility of multiple Ladies of the Lake – but it is often unclear whether they are distinct figures or varying interpretations of a single archetype.

There is some consensus among scholars that all versions of the Lady of the Lake, even those when Morgana is present in the text, derive from Morgana le Fay's early characterization. Her portrayal as a magical woman associated with lakes and water is consistent with the Lady of the Lake's characteristics. Even when she appears as a villain, therefore, her original spirit lives on through the continued re-tellings.

Despite their often contrasting portrayals, both Morgana and the various Ladies of the Lake are associated with similar motifs. These include giving magical gifts to knights, engaging in tests and challenges, and possessing the ability to shapeshift, often into birds. This blurring of boundaries contributes to the difficulty in definitively separating the characters. It is almost as if Morgana's original character of ambiguous morality was split into two, creating a direct dichotomy of good and evil. The only remnant of this original characterization emerges in her ultimate act of carrying Arthur to Avalon.

Despite the Lady of the Lake's clear association with water, it is only Morgana who has the unquestionable connection to Avalon. There may be multiple Ladies of the Lake, but there is only one Lady of Avalon – and she is Morgana le Fay.

MAGIC IN THE MEDIEVAL WORLD

The Role of Magic

Magic played a significant role in medieval society, impacting daily life and influencing religious thought. It was deeply intertwined with medieval life, despite official condemnation by the Church. People from all levels of society, from peasants to the aristocratic elite, engaged with magic in some form. They might use charms for protection, seek healing through rituals, recount tales of folklore and magic, or simply fear the power of witches.

In the early medieval period especially, the stance of the Church on magic was often contradictory. While the official opinion perceived magic to be demonic and heretical, many Christian practices resembled magic to ordinary people. The demarcation between religion, magic and superstition was thus blurred.

Christianity had to navigate the cross-section between ingrained cultural mythology and the religion's ability to control the narrative of salvation. The Arthurian legends sit exactly at the crossroads.

The concept of natural magic emerged as distinct from demonic magic. Natural magic came from the bounty of God, the other from the devil. Natural magic was more likely to be seen as an acceptable form of magic potential. However, this was not a blanket acceptance; some authorities denied the existence of natural magic altogether. However, because of the way in which magic was entwined with the folklore and culture of the Anglo-Celtic Isles, it became more or less accepted by most Church leaders for much of the early medieval period.

Although the Church actively sought to define and control magical practices, these remained deeply embedded in popular culture, continuing to challenge the boundaries of acceptable belief. The character of Morgana le Fay perfectly encapsulates this duality in belief. In medieval texts she displays both the negative aspects of magic and the good elements of natural magic – especially regarding her connection to the Isle of Avalon.

The Magic of Morgana le Fay

In many versions of her story through medieval sources, Morgana le Fay is described as possessing vast magical knowledge and power. She uses spells and rituals to manipulate and control through self-serving acts to meet her own goals. Despite this, however, her motivations remain complex.

She sometimes aids and sometimes hinders Arthur and his knights, clearly mirroring the ambiguity that medieval writers faced when categorizing magic. While they could easily condemn harmful magic as something inherently evil, healing magic or love magic were more blurred. While Morgana's magic is undeniably potent, it resists easy classification.

A crucial concern for medieval writers was the potential of magic to challenge religious, social and patriarchal hierarchies.

Magic thus represented a dangerous force operating outside the established structures of power, rather like Morgana herself. She uses her magic to disrupt the moral order of Arthur's court and to threaten his rule.

An intriguing example of Morgana's ambiguous magic occurs in *Sir Gawain and the Green Knight*. Gawain enters the tale as a representative of the chivalric ideal, a knight devoted to upholding Arthur's honour and engaging in noble acts. Morgana le Fay orchestrates the challenge to test Gawain's courage, honesty and loyalty, which ultimately leads him to confront his failure and shame.

The story itself has a far more nuanced and restrained approach to magic, obscuring its more magical elements. While certain features of Morgana's magic are clearly supernatural, it is this ambiguity that fills the reader with suspicion. The more magical elements function as trials of faith. In these Morgana's magic is not only a threat to social order, but also a dangerous temptation away from God's grace.

Interestingly, while Morgana is ultimately revealed as the orchestrator of the challenge, she remains a shadowy figure whose motivations are never fully explained. The poem resists easy answers, leaving readers to ponder the nature of magic and its potential for both harm and, perhaps, unexpected grace. Morgana is left as neither a hero nor truly a villain.

The Ambiguity of Magic

Morgana le Fay is a figure of uneasy power throughout the medieval Arthurian romances. Complex and contradictory, she rarely assumes the same character across any two tales. Although we may like to consider her a villain, her magical knowledge and power are never aligned with either good or evil; many of her powers are in fact shared with characters who are considered good. That leaves the nature of the character herself as the arbiter of that ambiguity, rather than the magic she wields.

Morgana's position as a figure who operates outside the accepted structures of power is what makes her magic ambiguous. She challenges both social norms and the divine order through her command of magic. Her motivations frequently involve manipulating the Knights of the Round Table, sowing discord within Arthur's court and even posing a threat to the king's rule. Her ability to command powerful magic positions her as a figure capable of disrupting the established order – precisely because she operates beyond it. If we look at other magical women in the legends, such as the Lady of the Lake, their magic differs only in its use. One seeks to uplift, the other to subvert.

As discussed, the medieval world-view struggled to reconcile the potential of magic and its deep links to folklore and the imagination with its capacity for harm and its connection to forces opposed to God. Morgana's character embodies this tension. Her magical abilities are captivating, yet her connection to the supernatural, her ambiguous morality and her willingness to challenge authority have marked her as a figure of suspicion and fear.

A Threat to Established Order

In her various interpretations Morgana has represented the fundamental ways in which magic was seen as a threat to order in the medieval world.

ANCIENT & MODERN: INTRODUCING MORGANA LE FAY

Magic was repeatedly associated with the demonic and the heretical. This was not as prevalent in the early medieval period, but by the time of the most popular Arthurian works such as the *Vulgate Cycle* and *Le Morte d'Arthur*, scholars and writers were beginning to explore this unease. In pre-Christian texts, we see magic as morally ambiguous, but in Morgana le Fay a more sinister representation emerges. Although not yet purely demonic, we see the first hints at the ease with which benign magic could mask something far more sinister. Morgana's magic is heretical not because of what it is, but because of how she uses it.

Another concern for the medieval writer would be the ways in which magic challenged established social and patriarchal hierarchies. Male magic practitioners such as Merlin were described in positive terms because they operated within the status quo. Female magic practitioners, however, were empowered beyond their marginalized status as women, giving them the potential to challenge medieval society's rules and norms directly. Those who operated within the structure maintained their status of 'good', but Morgana le Fay maintained a generally negative characterization until the moment she upheld the status quo by leading Arthur to Avalon.

Magic was also seen as a vehicle for personal gain and social disruption. The medieval world was fragile, increasingly defined by suspicion and fear – emotions often enhanced by the idea that magic was inherently rooted in deception and manipulation. While I would argue that Morgana's magic is rarely used for personal gain, she was certainly characterized as a disruptor, with much of her magic used for manipulation toward that end. Morgana's use of magic eroded trust in it, creating a fascinating bedrock from which further distrust could flourish in the later medieval period.

From Medieval to Modern

The longevity of Morgana le Fay and her role in Arthurian legends speaks to the power that medieval magic still has on storytelling and myth-making. This influence can be seen everywhere, from literature to modern systems of belief.

Natural magics, such as those practised by Morgana, are widely viewed as precursors to modern science. Consequently, modern fictional magic systems often incorporate elements of alchemy, astrology and herbalism. These are all elements that Morgana le Fay has embodied, making them constant elements of her character that have endured through countless retellings. From her earliest appearances she has used poultices and potions to heal, employed magical concoctions and enchanted objects and even studied the constellations with her sisters on the Isle of Avalon.

Medieval magic was a system of belief within its context, with its own logic and coherence. Such a system has carried over to inform a lot of modern storytelling. The ambiguity in how magic is presented within Morgana's character has almost directly led to the way in which modern interpretations of magic are written. They are intertwined with the beliefs, values and social structures of their fictional world. The magic itself is neither good nor evil; morality is applied simply in the way that it is used.

Morgana's character has always explored themes of power, responsibility and the consequences of wielding magic – traits that have endured across multiple representations over many centuries.

Her character also serves as a focal point for anxieties about female power and the unknown. While we see its beginnings in early medieval representations of Morgana, this element is expanded in more modern interpretations. This reveals an interesting continuation of these anxieties, which have been reimagined and explored through various lenses, including the Celtic Revival of the nineteenth century and more modern feminist perspectives.

MEDIEVAL WOMEN

A Complex Position

Just like Morgana herself, the role of women in medieval British society was varied and complex. Despite being limited in how they could operate inside more formal power structures, they were active participants in many spheres of life.

As is the case for many people throughout history, a woman's role depended on where she stood in the social hierarchy. Noblewomen could exert far more influence than women of lesser privilege. They had a level of agency and active engagement in religious and political discourse that allowed them more of a voice. Morgana le Fay, as Arthur's sister, daughter of a duke and wife to a king, as well as the Lady of Avalon in her own right, is a perfect illustration of this. Her social standing allowed her the agency her character displays, giving her an active role in the story that might otherwise have been denied her.

Women also played a vital role in healthcare. Midwifery is a common practice in which women are documented as being prominent. However, traditional remedies were also often important and necessary in their roles as caregivers to their families. With more regulation from the fifteenth century onward, women's activity became more restricted in this sphere. Traditional healing knowledge, often passed down orally through generations, made women vulnerable to being targets of witch hunts, giving rise to a medical field far more dominated by men. At the time, Morgana's role in legend was being solidified by writers such as Chrétien de Troyes and Geoffrey of Monmouth. However, women were still active participants as community healers, which we see clearly in Morgana's character.

While women did play an active role in medieval British society, their activities were restricted. This was particularly the case in urban areas, with public spaces associated with male dominance, such as taverns, discouraging women's presence through notions of 'respectability'. Dress codes were also used as means of control, facilitating a clear distinction between 'respectable' and 'disreputable' women. Morgana is interesting as she holds a space outside of these restrictions. Exiled from Camelot, she thrives on the outskirts of normal urban and social boundaries, creating a life of power for herself in which she is the architect of her own destiny.

The Medieval Household

Women were essential to the household in medieval British life and, due to restrictions within patriarchal social structures, it would have been their primary sphere of influence. Women's contributions were vital to the family's economic wellbeing – especially in rural settings where they would have actively participated in agricultural tasks, working alongside their husbands and other family members. However, there would have been a greater division in more urban settings, with men's work being outside the home and women's work centred within it.

Women would have been expected to manage household affairs and to oversee servants within their domestic sphere. There was a strong emphasis on a wife's obedience to the man of the household, as well as on her piety. The Virgin Mary was seen as the ultimate role model for all wives and mothers. Her chastity, obedience and patient suffering were virtues to which all women should aspire, and the respectable literature, theatre and music of the time were often written with a subtle undercurrent of guidance on proper female conduct.

Through marriage, a woman's legal and economic rights came under her husband's authority, limiting her ability to act independently in legal and financial matters. Despite this, women still found ways to exercise agency within these constraints. In the early medieval period, healthcare and childcare allowed women to exercise a degree of authority. Choosing a religious life also gave them access to education and influence, without the need for husbands or children.

Morgana le Fay once again exists outside these constraints. Various texts describe her as having different levels of privilege – whether with her father as ruler of Avalon, in a nunnery receiving an education, as Arthur's sister in Camelot or married to a king. She transgresses many of the expectations of women in the domestic sphere by attempting to kill her husband, plotting to overthrow her brother and thriving as the head of her own household.

Education and Literacy

It is important to remember that medieval Arthurian tales would have been written primarily for a male audience. There is a scarcity of sources that refer specifically to women's literacy, but it is true that noblewomen were more likely to have an education than those from a more common background.

However, there is also evidence that a wider variety of women would have been able to read a limited number of religious texts. They may also have had works read aloud to them, enabling them to participate in a literate culture even if they were not fully literate themselves. In her 1946 book, *Woman as Force in History*, the historian Mary Ritter Beard draws a parallel between the rise in female literacy and the profusion of romantic adventure stories – a genre in which the chivalric tales of Arthur and his Knights most certainly feature.

The source of most education for women was in religious institutions. Convents especially played a pivotal role in educating women, offering them a structured environment for learning and intellectual development. There they were given the opportunity not only to receive religious instruction, but also to read Latin, scripture and other religious texts, and to learn practical skills such as embroidery, spinning, weaving and music. Some convents even went beyond this by offering instruction in Greek, medicine and classical literature, enabling nuns to contribute to society in periods of conflict and instability.

Noble families would often send young girls to receive instruction in convents at an early age. Morgana le Fay herself was educated in a nunnery, alongside her sisters in some of the early

ANCIENT & MODERN: INTRODUCING MORGANA LE FAY

Arthurian tales. There she learned both astrology and sorcery, which in the early tales was when her character was the most sympathetic. These early representations of Morgana seem to align with a noblewoman educated in the ways of religious life. In those early tales she is a strong, capable, respected healer. Only when she moves away from those religious beginnings and moves into the domestic sphere does her character become demonized.

An educated woman who has given herself to the Church poses no threat. However, a strong, independent woman who works outside of those patriarchal structures most certainly does.

A Complex Relationship with Christianity

Morgana le Fay's magical abilities and evolving portrayal through the medieval period reflected broader anxieties about female power within a Christian context. In Monmouth's *Vita Merlini* Morgana is strongly associated with healing, a quality often associated with divine grace or saintly intercession. This connection is further emphasized by her association with Avalon, a place linked to healing and otherworldly bounty.

As Morgana's character developed in the later romances, her healing abilities became increasingly overshadowed by her association with darker forms of magic. In many of the sources these are described as 'black magic' or 'necromancy'. Such a shift reflects a broader trend in medieval literature, which began to portray women with knowledge or abilities that exceeded social expectations as dangerous.

With Morgana operating outside of the bounds of traditional female roles, medieval writers sought to highlight the 'unnatural' nature of female power. Her ability to shapeshift and control powerful magic, as well as her desire to undermine Arthur's Camelot and operate outside the confines of her marriage, challenged conventional ideas of femininity in a world that emphasized obedience and piety.

Morgana le Fay was a figure whose actions served to disrupt the established order. She actively challenged the values held by the male heroes of the medieval Arthurian legends, all of which were written to uphold Christian ideals. Arthur was a symbol of Christian kingship, and by being at odds with him Morgana undermined prevailing Christian morals.

This forms a powerful contrast with the representation of the Lady of the Lake. Another powerful woman who wielded magic, she represented a more acceptable version of female power within Christian society. While Morgana is led by her emotions, and is often perceived as destructive and self-serving as a result, the Lady of the Lake uses her powers to support Arthur and uphold the status quo.

Women's Roles in the Chivalric Ideal

The Arthurian tales are deeply rooted in the chivalric ideal. In understanding them, and the characters that they portray, it is important to consider the role of women – not just within early medieval society, but also within the literature of the day.

Women in chivalric tales were often passive figures who acted as catalysts for the male heroes. The chivalric code was primarily concerned with male conduct, with women simply providing a reason for their actions. Recurring motifs included damsels in distress, their plight serving as the impetus for the knight's heroic actions, or beautiful women forming the objects of romantic pursuit, in which they were idealized love interests. Their love was the reward that a knight could receive for his prowess in tournaments or on the successful completion of a quest. The courtly love story of Lancelot and Guinevere perfectly illustrates this ideal.

In contrast to that, women could also play the role of disruptors to the established chivalric order. Like Morgana le Fay they could wield power, most often supernatural or magical in nature, to challenge patriarchal structures. Women could manipulate expectations to achieve their own ends, often using the perception of weakness by the male knight to influence their decisions or to gain an advantage.

The nature of chivalry as an ideal underwent profound change during the medieval period, so the representation of women within that framework was also dynamic. As the ideals of courtly love became more commonplace, a knight's treatment of women, particularly with respect to courtesy and honour, became important markers of a man's worth. The women in these stories could actively try to uplift and inspire the heroes, or to manipulate them away from their ideals. Morgana le Fay often employed those very ideals to corrupt the knights, or to expose their own follies and hypocrisies.

Morgana's character would have been challenging to readers of the Arthurian romances, as she directly confronts and breaks down the limitations traditionally placed on women. Her role in society, combined with her magical powers and willingness to use these for her own ends, would have cemented her character as a disrupting force. Both Arthur, the chivalric ideal of kingship, and Lancelot, the chivalric ideal of courtly love, fall foul of her manipulations, serving to refute the traditional belief that women should be passive recipients of chivalric protection.

Instead of playing a socially expected role, Morgana actively shapes the events of the stories in which she appears. It is this characterization that became the most common view of Morgana, recurring in various re-tellings across the centuries.

3.
The Modern Morgana

I knew Mrs. le Fay by reputation, and was not expecting anything pleasant. She was held in awe by the whole realm, for she had made everybody believe she was a great sorceress. All her ways were wicked, all her instincts devilish. She was loaded to the eyelids with cold malice. All her history was black with crime; and among her crimes murder was common. I was most curious to see her; as curious as I could have been to see Satan. To my surprise she was beautiful; black thoughts had failed to make her expression repulsive, age had failed to wrinkle her satin skin or mar its bloomy freshness.
– From Mark Twain's *A Connecticut Yankee in King Arthur's Court* (1889)

THE CELTIC REVIVAL

A New Celtic Identity

n the late eighteenth and early nineteenth centuries there was a huge resurgence of interest in Celtic culture and history. Celtic Studies was a growing field and many significant texts were translated, making them accessible to a much wider audience.

During this period artists and writers were inspired by Gaelic and Welsh-language literature, portraying an often romanticized view of the past. In many ways this growth of interest was a reaction to the modernization brought by the Industrial Revolution. It promoted an intriguing, though generally historically inaccurate, view of the Celtic world, driven by a fascination with traditional, medieval, imaginative and supernatural themes.

Lady Charlotte Guest's translation of the Welsh *Mabinogion* (1838–49) was a seminal text that brought interest in Arthurian legend to ordinary people. Her translation made the stories accessible to those not previously familiar with the Welsh language and culture, arousing a Europe-wide interest in the tales. Guest also connected the tales to other medieval romances and even made the stories a popular source for children's literature of the day. This in turn led to further re-tellings of Arthurian legends, updated for a new audience.

The Celtic Revival impacted all aspects of the arts. It brought in new folklore re-tellings, gave rise to new literary voices and influenced artists and craftspeople, who began to incorporate more Celtic designs and motifs into their work. However, it was not without criticism. The romanticized view of the Celtic past perpetuated simplistic stereotypes about Celtic cultures, obscuring any real investigation of their nuance and complexity. Some scholars considered its focus on elaborate rituals and ceremonies of questionable authenticity to be a distraction from the cultural realities of the remaining Celtic nations.

Despite such scruples, the Celtic Revival profoundly impacted how people viewed and engaged with Celtic culture – not only in the nineteenth and twentieth centuries, but well into the modern day. The movement left a lasting legacy on literature, art and the national identities of the Celtic nations that still reverberates today.

Reimagining Arthurian Legend

Re-tellings of Arthurian legends in the Victorian era blended Celtic traditions with elements of fantasy. They combined mythology, romance and adventure, and spoke to those looking for a connection to a romanticized Celtic past.

In Arthurian re-tellings of the Celtic revival, we see a shift from the historicity of the medieval period to a more literary representation. Rather than trying to represent its characters as real people, in the manner of medieval chroniclers, writers of the Celtic Revival chose to use the characters to explore literary themes such as chivalry, heroism and romance.

However, one thing that remained was the tie the tales had with national identity. Much as the medieval chroniclers used Arthur as a representation of the divine right of kings, in the Victorian era Arthur became a symbol of a bygone era, as well as an emblem of a glorious past and potential future for Celtic identity. Arthur's court at Camelot, in which its knights were bound by a code of chivalry, became an idealized model of virtue and righteous conduct.

Meanwhile, fascination with the visual and tangible aspects of the Arthurian legends grew. This led to a surge in artistic depictions of characters from the tales, notably Morgana, Guinevere, Arthur and the Knights of the Round Table. These depictions often drew inspiration from medieval art styles. They emphasized the beauty and grandeur of the Arthurian world, even influencing fashion. Elements of medieval imagery and Celtic design appeared in textile design and fabrics, creating a rich Arthurian aesthetic.

Arthurian legends were popular because they were seen to embody the ethical and moral principles important to Victorian society. A reimagined chivalric code, emphasizing honour, duty and selflessness for readers of all ages, was especially appealing for a culture undergoing rapid social and industrial change. The legends provided a template for idealized behaviour, while simultaneously warning against conduct that transgressed Victorian ideals. Arthur and his Knights embodied the chivalric ideal, whereas Guinevere and Morgana le Fay were often re-imagined as examples of morally impure women.

Morgana's Absence

What is notable about the Celtic Revival in the case of Morgana le Fay is her relative absence. Many Arthurian tales of the Victorian age removed her from the narrative, focusing instead on more 'traditional' Celtic tales or the more romantic and chivalric stories of Arthur and his Knights.

In her translation of the *Mabinogion*, Lady Charlotte Guest collected tales that originally inspired, and would later be incorporated into, the Arthurian canon. While it doesn't follow the same narrative arc as later Arthurian romances, the *Mabinogion* does feature characters and motifs that later became intertwined with them. Morgana's role in the legends was a gradual evolution. Not always a central character in earlier works, she was often overlooked in the re-tellings of the Celtic Revival.

ANCIENT & MODERN: INTRODUCING MORGANA LE FAY

Victorian writers and artists, centring on the romance aspects of Arthurian legend, chose rather to concentrate on the women of Arthurian legends such as Guinevere and Elaine of Ascolat (the Lady of Shalott). In so doing they highlighted the women's femininity and the tragedy surrounding their romantic entanglements with Lancelot. They were the focus of much of the art of the Pre-Raphaelites, who brought the intense colours and complex compositions of Quattrocento Italian art back into popular favour.

Artistic and literary representations of Arthurian women often grappled with ideas about morality and female agency. Guinevere, for example, is frequently depicted as a tragic figure caught between love and duty, reflecting Victorian anxieties about female sexuality and societal expectations. Elaine, on the other hand, is a tragic figure who falls in love with Lancelot from afar and is doomed to die before she can ever reach him.

William Morris's *The Defence of Guenevere* (1858) is another work where Morgana is notably absent. The poem reimagines Arthurian legend from the perspective of Guinevere herself. It takes the form of a dramatic monologue in which Queen Guinevere defends herself against accusations of adultery with Sir Lancelot, taking place during her trial, as she recalls key moments of her life. *The Defence* tackles themes of love, guilt, betrayal and the subjectivity of judgement; its ending is deliberately ambiguous as to her ultimate fate.

Idylls of the King (1859–85), a 12-part epic poem by Alfred Lord Tennyson, is essentially a re-telling of Malory's *Le Morte d'Arthur*. Once again, Morgana is never mentioned by name. However, in the penultimate poem, titled *The Passing of Arthur*, three un-named queens lay him in a barge and carry him to Avalon. Morgana thus features in the story as a benevolent, otherworldly queen in spirit, even if never explicitly mentioned in the text.

Given how instrumental Morgana le Fay is in Arthurian legend, her absence in a lot of Victorian literature dealing with Arthurian themes is surprising. With a strong emphasis on character-driven stories and the aesthetics of romance and chivalry, Morgana was often overlooked as a character in these stories. Yet elements of her character are imbued into the other women of the reimagined works. As more nuance and duality emerge in those other characters, Morgana's legacy remained in stasis – cocooned and ready to re-emerge gloriously in later re-tellings.

A Connecticut Yankee

One of Morgana le Fay's most prominent appearances in the Victorian era does not come directly from the Celtic Revival in Britain. Instead, it comes from halfway across the world in Mark Twain's satirical fantasy novel *A Connecticut Yankee in King Arthur's Court* (1889).

The novel begins with a framing narrative in which an unnamed narrator encounters a man claiming to be Hank Morgan, a nineteenth-century Yankee who travelled back in time to sixth-century Britain to document his experience. The narrator reads Morgan's manuscript, which tells the story of his adventures in King Arthur's court.

Hank Morgan, finding himself in Arthurian England, uses his knowledge of modern technology and science to gain power and influence. He amasses a following, establishes industries and schools, and attempts to modernize the kingdom. Throughout his adventures Morgan encounters three significant figures who challenge his beliefs and methods: Sandy, a superstitious and romantic woman who becomes his wife; King Arthur, the embodiment of feudal authority; and Clarence, his devoted page and scribe.

Despite his technological advancements and attempts at social reform, Morgan's efforts ultimately end in disaster. He triggers a catastrophic battle that decimates the kingdom and leaves him isolated and disillusioned. The novel concludes with Morgan's death. The framing narrator returns after reading the manuscript to find Morgan delirious. He listens to his ravings until he draws his last breath, leaving the reader to ponder the meaning of Morgan's experiences and the limitations of progress.

Many Victorian Arthurian legends served as comments upon a lost world. Twain turned this perspective on its head, showing that this lost world could have been modernity itself. He critiqued romantic ideals and literary conventions, quoting heavily from Malory's original *Le Morte d'Arthur*. He explored the nature of progress and technology and the rights of monarchy, while also satirizing social injustice and political corruption – as well as the very nature of history and how it is viewed.

Morgana's role in Twain's story is unashamedly negative. She embodies the oppressive aspects of 'tradition' as a counter to Hank Morgan's attempts at reform. When Morgan meets her in her castle she wields authority and power, inflicting punishment at will. Her own family fears her, and her dungeons are full of people imprisoned for minor offences or slights on her character.

Morgana satirizes the unquestioning belief in magic and the supernatural that Twain saw as characteristic of the Middle Ages; she is thus someone who must be overcome to establish a more just and rational society. This is evident in Morgan's attempt to challenge her authority by liberating prisoners and disrupting her control over the kingdom.

Mark Twain uses Morgana le Fay in the opposite way to the medieval writers from whom he drew so heavily. For him she is a figure of the old world order, a character who must be overcome if progress is to be made. Rather than disrupting the status quo and operating outside of it, in Twain's work Morgana is a villain, representing the superstition and extrajudicial power that forms a barrier to modernity.

Pre-Raphaelite Art

While Morgana's appearance in literary works through the Celtic Revival is sparse, she fares slightly better in the art of the Victorian period. While much pre-Raphaelite art drew from popular literary traditions of the day, Morgana's depictions came from medieval sources rather than Victorian ones.

The Pre-Raphaelites were a community of English artists, poets and critics. Dating from the mid-nineteenth century, they aimed to reform art by kicking against the classical and academic standards dominant at the time. They saw the Mannerist influence of the High Renaissance, especially that of the painter Raphael, as being too elegant and idealized, and believed this had led to a loss of truth in art (hence the name Pre-Raphaelite).

The Pre-Raphaelites sought rather to draw inspiration from

earlier art styles, particularly those of the medieval and early Renaissance periods. They saw these styles as more genuine and 'true'. Their art was incredibly detailed, using vibrant colours and incorporating naturalistic elements. Pre-Raphaelite artists often depicted religious, literary and medieval themes, and included elements with symbolic meaning.

Guinevere, Arthur, Lancelot, Camelot and the Lady of Shalott were popular subjects in the Pre-Raphaelite movement. However, Morgana le Fay also received some striking visual depictions that would inspire her representations in film, television and literature from the twentieth century onward.

The British painter Frederick Sandys created the most famous image of Morgana from the Victorian period. *Morgan le Fay* was painted in 1864 with Keomi Gray, Sandys' mistress, as her model. She wears a green robe and is draped with golden fabric, stitched with Celtic iconography. Behind her is a loom on which she has woven an enchanted robe that will consume her brother Arthur in fire. Her hair is loose and her face contorted; the leopard skin draped over her shoulder suggests an almost bestial sexuality.

Similarly, John Roddam Spencer Stanhope's *Morgan Le Fay* (c. 1880) depicts a red-haired beauty draped in red satin. She is surrounded by orange lilies, representing both passionate desire and hatred, and a darker cloth snakes around her, reminiscent of Eve and the serpent. The Pre-Raphaelites were fascinated by the idea of the fallen woman, painting her as both alluring and tragic. As a powerful female figure often associated with forbidden love and transgression, Morgana represented the complex, often contradictory Victorian attitudes toward sexuality and agency.

Through her artistic depictions in Pre-Raphaelite art, Morgana entered the modern era as more than simply a sorceress or a villain. She entered it as a woman and an object of desire.

A MODERN FANTASY

A New Genre

The Celtic Revival was influential, not just at the time, but also through the modern fantasy genre which it inspired. Arthurian legends in particular had a huge influence on high fantasy. The genre harks back to a world defined by order and meaning, an incredibly strong attitude in the Victorian era.

Several influences from the Arthurian canon can be seen through fantasy fiction. Character archetypes such as noble knights, wise wizards and fearsome dragons originate in medieval literature, appearing regularly in the folklore, romance and epic poetry of the time. Themes of chivalry, heroism and the conflict between good and evil are also common. Much of high fantasy revolves around re-establishing order in a world beset by chaos. The power and role of individuals in a world governed by supernatural forces is also something tackled in modern fantasy. Characters must learn to embrace their destinies, often undertaking trials and quests to prove their worthiness.

We don't have to look far to see a shared aesthetic between Arthurian literature and modern high fantasy. Medieval-style settings are common, but used to explore modern anxieties. Using the hierarchical structure of a universe in which magic and the supernatural exist as reality allows for explicit exploration and representation of contemporary issues. In the medieval period this was often around the divine right to rule or the ideal of courtly love, but modern fantasy writers have used it to explore political ideologies and the changing role of women in society.

Such changes are not without criticism, however. Using medieval aestheticism in fantasy literature has led to a romanticized and homogenized view of the past. While the fantasy genre has never claimed to be historical, it has still led to a specific way in which modern readers have internalized the medieval past. It filters the medieval period and Arthurian legends through the lens of the romanticism of the Celtic Revival, already a romanticization of a distant Celtic past. As such, Arthurian characters such as Morgana le Fay became increasingly divorced from their origins.

Morgana evolved from Celtic goddess to otherworldly enchantress to evil sorceress within written memory. Now, with the rise of fantasy fiction, she can be re-written and reimagined over and over again to suit the narrative of her authors.

The Once and Future King

T.H. White's *The Once and Future King* (1958) is perhaps the most seminal work of modern Arthurian literature. Loosely based on Malory's *Le Morte d'Arthur*, it creates a more cohesive narrative, especially beloved among children. The work is split into four books, each having had various adaptations over time.

In book one, *The Sword in the Stone*, a young Arthur (known as Wart) meets the magician, Merlyn. He becomes his tutor and teaches Wart valuable lessons by turning him into various animals. When King Uther Pendragon dies, Wart unknowingly pulls a magical sword from a stone, proving his right to the throne of England. In book two, *The Queen of Air and Darkness*, Arthur faces rebellion, particularly from King Lot of Orkney. Arthur forms the Knights of the Round Table to bring justice, but an incestuous union with his half-sister Morgause sows the seeds of his downfall.

Book three, *The Ill-Made Knight*, follows the turbulent love affair between Lancelot and Queen Guenever. He goes on quests to escape his feelings, but is eventually drawn back into an affair with the queen, complicating his loyalty to Arthur. In book four, *The Candle in the Wind*, Mordred, Arthur's illegitimate son with Morgause, seeks revenge; he exposes the affair of Lancelot and Guenever, leading to civil war. Arthur tries to restore order, but Mordred seizes the throne. On the eve of battle, Arthur reflects on his life, accepting that while he may die, his legacy will endure.

Morgana le Fay, despite a relatively minor appearance in *The Once and Future King*, plays an important role. She is the embodiment of female power and a figure who disrupts the stability of White's patriarchal world. In *The Sword in the Stone* Morgana attempts to entice the young Arthur with magical food; in *The Ill-Made Knight* she imprisons Elaine in a boiling cauldron. Morgana's magic is a disruptive force, providing the axis on which much of the narrative will rotate.

In the original 1938 edition of *The Sword in the Stone*, Morgana is represented as a young, beautiful, seductive figure named Mim. However, in later editions White rewrote her as an older, far less attractive woman. This change in appearance suggests White's own anxieties about female sexuality. A complicated relationship with his mother and early twentieth-century ideas of rigid masculinity meant that White struggled to create realistic female characters. He diminished their roles in his work, yet granted them power and influence beyond what is warranted by those roles.

The women in *The Once and Future King* are often either underdeveloped, demonized or placed in a position subservient to their male counterparts. As such, Morgana's role in his book changed from a seductress to a demonized enchantress through rewrites of her character – a symbol of shifting ideas of womanhood and power.

The Mists of Avalon

In *The Mists of Avalon* (1983), Marion Zimmer Bradley created the most iconic modern image of Morgana le Fay. Bradley's representation of Morgana (named Morgaine in the narrative) centred her not only as the protagonist, but also as a woman misrepresented and misunderstood through history. In doing so, she singlehandedly changed how the women of Arthurian legend were imagined and represented.

The story is narrated by Morgaine, a priestess of Avalon and King Arthur's half-sister. It tells the story of Arthur's rise and fall from the perspective of women in the Arthurian legends. Morgaine's mother, Igraine, marries Uther Pendragon, the high king, after her first husband dies. Uther, using magic, tricks Igraine into conceiving Arthur, and Morgaine is taken by her aunt Viviane to Avalon, where she is trained to be a priestess of the Mother Goddess. As part of a fertility rite, Morgaine unknowingly conceives a child with Arthur, her half-brother. After Uther's death Arthur claims the throne with the help of magical artefacts from Avalon, but a growing divide between paganism and Christianity causes tension.

Morgaine leaves Avalon and gives birth to her son, Mordred. Meanwhile, Arthur marries Gwenhwyfar, who struggles with guilt over her love for Lancelet and her inability to conceive an heir. As Gwenhwyfar's Christian zeal grows, she influences Arthur to replace his pagan banner with a Christian one, further straining the relationship between Avalon and Camelot.

Years later, Morgaine plots with her lover Accolon to reclaim the kingdom for Avalon, but Arthur defeats them. Mordred grows up and eventually challenges Arthur for the throne. A final battle between Arthur and Mordred leads to Mordred's death and Arthur being mortally wounded. Morgaine takes the dying Arthur to Avalon, where she remains to tell the story as Avalon retreats into the mists.

Bradley not only reimagines Morgana as a powerful woman, but also explores the very essence of the medieval reimagining of Celtic tales by highlighting their Christianization. The transition is not straightforward, but is the consequence of political machinations and the inherent conflict between patriarchal and matriarchal societies in which Morgana exists.

In traditional Arthurian tales Morgana is portrayed as an antagonist. However, in *The Mists of Avalon*, she is a complex character, caught between two clashing worlds. Torn by her loyalty to Avalon and her love for Arthur, she explores the possibilities of co-existence between two seemingly opposing world-views: an intersection that Morgana represents. She is deeply connected to the old ways, but also central to the changing world of the narrative. She is a complex and intriguing bridge between the old and the new.

In Bradley's work, Morgana directly challenges the patriarchal structures threatening her world. She is powerful, has agency and is driven by her beliefs, even if some of her actions are morally ambiguous. In this way, she is tied back to her Celtic origins. Morgana's actions are her own; they do not fall into the camp of good or evil. She is a woman in a complicated situation, doing the best she can for the people she loves.

In contrast to other versions of Morgana, Bradley represents her as a nuanced and sympathetic character driven by conflicting loyalties. Returning to Avalon as paganism fades from Britain's shores, she illustrates the marginalization of the old ways and the women who represent them. She stands as a testament to social change and a warning of what can so easily be lost.

The Pendragon Cycle

Stephen R. Lawhead wrote *The Pendragon Cycle* in 1987, hot on the heels of Bradley's *The Mists of Avalon*. His representation of Arthurian legend is grounded in the older tales, drawing inspiration from the *Mabinogion*, Monmouth's *Historia Regnum Britaniae* and the writings of the bardic poets of the early Middle Ages such as Taliesin, Gildas and Nenius.

Fascinatingly, Lawhead blends the story of King Arthur with the legend of Atlantis, giving a nod to the early chroniclers of the Celtic tales, while setting his story in the aftermath of the Roman legions' withdrawal from Britain between 383 and 410 CE. Morgana le Fay (named Morgian in the text) is a central antagonist. While his books do have strong female characters, they contain none of the feminism so apparent in *The Mists of Avalon*.

The first book, *Taliesin* (1987), is about the relationship between the Atlantean princess Charis and the British bard Taliesin. They become Merlin's parents while battling the influence of Charis's half-sister, Morgian. *Merlin* (1988), the second book, follows Merlin (Myrddin Emrys) through his rise to kingship, his descent into madness and his role as a witness to Arthur's birth. The third book, *Arthur* (1989), tells of Arthur's rise and fall through the perspectives of Merlin's servant Pelleas, Arthur's friend Bedwyr and Aneurin, a bard-in-training.

The series was originally released as a trilogy but, due to plot holes in the original sequence, Lawhead released additional books to provide more plot details. In *Pendragon* (1994), Lawhead details the legendary hunt for Twrch Trwyth, the Black Boar, which is reimagined as the invasion of Britain by a Vandal king. And *Grail* (1997) follows Gwalchavad (the series' version of Galahad) on his quest to recover the Holy Grail, stolen from Arthur's court by Morgian.

Lawhead's world is a very Christianized one. Morgana is one of the series' antagonists, representing the fading pagan forces that oppose the rise of Christianity. Rather than being associated with Avalon, she and Charis are descended from Avallach, the war-obsessed king of Atlantis. Morgana also directly challenges Arthur's attempt to establish a Christian nation, the Kingdom of Summer.

Morgana once again becomes the evil sorceress. Her use of magic runs counter to the Christian themes of the novels – in which magic, in general, is once again divided along the lines of good or evil. Morgana's magic is evil, whereas Merlin's is a Christian miracle; he is protected by his faith. Unlike Bradley's more sympathetic view of paganism, in which Christianity is a force for change that is not always good, Lawhead firmly supports the triumph of Christianity over paganism. In his work, Christianity is represented as a force that brings order and justice to a Britain steeped in pagan traditions. Morgana is the ultimate embodiment of the negative aspects of pagan ways.

FILM, TELEVISION AND COMIC BOOKS

A Modern Supervillain

In 1955 Stan Lee gave comic readers their first introduction to Morgan Le Fay in an Atlas Comics series called *Black Knight*. After the series ended, she was reintroduced in the *Spider-Woman* series under the Marvel Comics umbrella in May 1978. Only a few years before, DC Comics had also introduced their own version of Morgana le Fay (named Morgaine le Fey) in *The Demon* (1972).

DC's Morgaine le Fey draws extensively from Malory's *Le Morte d'Arthur*. However, the influences of Stephen Lawhead and Marion Zimmer Bradley are also evident as her character developed in later works, for example *Madame Xanadu* (2008–10). She is represented as a gifted sorceress skilled in the art of black magic, the sister of Nimue and Vivienne and the Lady of the Lake – all of whom are survivors of the fall of Atlantis. True to the vision of good vs evil, Nimue is represented as a bearer of magic that is kind and good; Morgaine uses her powers more callously.

The earlier DC comics showed Morgana using her sexuality and violence as her defining characteristics. With the release of *Camelot 3000* (1982–5), however, she becomes far more monstrous. Driven by her hatred of Arthur, she becomes a spider-like creature as a punishment for her ambition and rebellion against male authority.

By the release of *Madame Xanadu*, Morgana is less physically monstrous; instead she proves her villainy through action. Throughout the series she is often contrasted with Nimue, who adapts and thrives by supporting the male heroes. Morgana's pursuit of power and autonomy are viewed as divergent, once again revealing the dichotomy that female characters are only 'good' when they conform to traditional gender roles.

While still a villain in her Marvel Comics representation, Morgana fares somewhat better. She has been described as one of Marvel's most powerful villains, especially in the *Doctor Strange* canon. Her character begins as a cult leader from the early sixth century in Camelot who attempts to summon a dark god. When she is unable to control it, the god is sealed away and her apprentice wrests the power of the cult away from Morgana. Doctor Doom, a villain from the future, seeks out her help to free his mother's soul from Hell, agreeing in return to help her lead an army of undead warriors against her half-brother King Arthur. Iron Man thwarts Morgana's plans, however, leading to further adventures of time travel and battles with supervillains.

Rather than take inspiration from early tales, Morgana's Marvel Comics representation is based almost entirely on fantasy. She conspires, schemes and performs villainous deeds, but is also a capable and interesting foil to the broader, time-spanning canon of

Marvel's superheroes. More than simply a villain, Morgana is clever, capable and incredibly powerful. She may be a villain, but she deserves respect. She is a woman with choice, power and agency.

Excalibur

Once again loosely inspired by Thomas Malory's *Le Morte d'Arthur*, the Oscar-nominated *Excalibur* (1981) set the aesthetic tone for Arthurian re-tellings. Originally intended as an adaptation of Tolkien's *The Lord of the Rings* (1954–5), the film incorporates many of the high fantasy elements that have become so fundamental to the legends' visual representation, such as full suits of armour and longswords, even though they may be historically anachronistic. Morgana is played by a young Helen Mirren, whose dark sorceress energy oozes sensually off the screen.

Directed by John Boorman, *Excalibur* tells Arthur's story with the sword as its focus. Uther Pendragon, driven by lust for Igrayne, has Merlin magically disguise him as her husband so he can bed her. Arthur is born of this union, but is spirited away by Merlin. Uther drives Excalibur into a stone, declaring that only his son can wield it.

A now adult Arthur pulls Excalibur from the stone unawares and is declared the rightful king. Arthur establishes Camelot and marries Guinevere, bringing his Kingdom into an age of stability. However, all the while, Arthur's half-sister Morgana plots to destroy him. When Lancelot and Guinevere fall in love, manipulated by Morgana, Camelot is again thrown into chaos. She seduces Arthur, bearing his son Mordred. A despondent Arthur drives Excalibur into the ground and the kingdom falls into ruin.

Arthur's knights embark on a quest for the Holy Grail to restore both the king and the land. Perceval finds the Grail and Arthur reclaims Excalibur. He forgives Guinevere, only to confront an adult Mordred, now heading an army. With Lancelot's help Mordred is defeated, but not before Arthur is mortally wounded. Excalibur is returned to the Lady of the Lake and Arthur is taken to Avalon.

Boorman's film explores themes of humanity's relationship with nature, the conflict between paganism and Christianity and the power of myth. His is a world where magic and reality are intertwined and human passions have the power to shape destiny. Morgana is the dark heart at its centre, a character as complex as the world she inhabits. She desires power and struggles against the patriarchy.

Excalibur delves into Morgana's relationship with Merlin, giving her actions a context. She sees his magic as a way to gain power in a world where she has little. Merlin shares with her the knowledge that their world is changing from a pagan world of magic to a Christian world, in which magical powers will fade. Morgana's actions are thus driven, at least in part, by the need to hold on to a world in which she can still exercise that power.

While her actions are those of an antagonist, Morgana is subtle. She is sensuous and she schemes – but her actions have a reason. She bears Mordred to produce a patriarchal figure that she can, in some ways, control, and she bewitches Arthur's knights on their quests for the same reason. Yet it is all for nothing. Merlin forces Morgana to speak an incantation that depletes her magic, and when her own son sees her aged and true self, he murders her in disgust. Try as she might to make her way in a world controlled by men, she is ultimately erased – and with her goes the force that kicked back against the patriarchal Christendom represented by Arthur and his knights.

Merlin

In 1998 Hallmark Entertainment released *Merlin*, a two-part miniseries that loosely adapted Arthurian legend into a new story. Despite relying less on historical tales, it attempted a far more historically accurate depiction of post-Roman Britain. However, that is where its historicity ends. It is fundamentally a tale of magic, enchantment and the fae, with Queen Mab, the fairy queen, playing a pivotal role as antagonist.

In a war-torn Britain, Mab, the fairy queen, creates Merlin, a powerful wizard, to restore faith in the Old Ways. Religious change in Britain threatens the existence of the pagan deities. Raised by Ambrosia after his mother died in childbirth, he grows up free of magic and falls in love with the lady Nimue. When Merlin displays his magical ability he is claimed by Mab, but when she lets Ambrosia die Merlin vows to defeat her. Years later Merlin aids Uther Pendragon in his rise to power, but is betrayed. Uther's obsession with Igraine, fuelled by Mab, leads to Arthur's birth, and Merlin vows to raise the child as a good man to defeat Mab.

Arthur eventually becomes king by drawing Excalibur from the stone, thus uniting Britain. However, Mab continues her schemes, corrupting Arthur's half-sister Morgan le Fay. She seduces Arthur and bears a son, Mordred, destined to be Arthur's downfall. Meanwhile, Merlin brings Lancelot to Camelot, but Lancelot's affair with Guinevere leads to tragedy. Mordred, raised by Mab, rebels against Arthur, leading to the Battle of Camlann in which both Arthur and Mordred perish. Merlin, having failed to save Camelot, confronts Mab, realizing that her power will fade as people forget her. In the end Mab disappears into nothingness as she is abandoned. Merlin reunites with Nimue, his lost love, and the pair live out their lives together, free from Mab's influence.

Merlin takes a fascinating approach to the Arthurian canon. While the conflict between paganism and Christianity remains central to the story's settings, neither is approached as being inherently better than the other. They are just different ways of experiencing the world, the underlying message being that sometimes we must simply embrace change.

Morgana (as Morgan le Fay, played by Helena Bonham-Carter) is both a victim and an antagonist in the story. She is manipulated by Mab, rather than being the primary manipulator, and is also deeply hurt by Merlin's actions. When she witnesses an enchanted Uther violate her mother, the trauma stays with her and colours her character from childhood onward.

Mab plays the role traditionally reserved for Morgana: a villainess driven by a desperation to retain power. Morgana, on the other hand, is driven by a desire for acceptance. In a world that prioritizes traditional beauty, Morgana's lack of it leaves her an outcast. Mab and Frick, her sidekick, allow Morgana to feel visible. They shower her with colour and magic, promising her an existence free from rejection.

When *Merlin*'s Morgana seeks the crown, it's because everyone around her does the same. All the strong men in the narrative vie for the same prize – why shouldn't she seek it for herself?

Morgana's story highlights the world's hypocrisy. When the men of the narrative seek power and are corrupted by it, it's simply a case of 'boys will be boys'. But when Morgana does the same, she highlights the folly of male pride.

Morgana's intention is to avoid weakness. Having felt weakness and cruelty at the hands of men she trusted, she desires never to feel that again. The only way to be strong in her world is to have power, and she cannot hold this without magic and manipulation. She turns to Mab because Mab offers her the power that Merlin's world will deny her. In her final moments, Morgana wants nothing more than to be seen as inherently worthy.

Merlin (Again)

The BBC's 2008 television series *Merlin* gives the Arthurian tale a much more youthful glamour. It speaks to younger audiences and focuses on friendship and magic. Morgana is revealed as the primary antagonist as the series progresses.

The series takes place in a version of Camelot in which magic is outlawed by King Uther, who has imprisoned a dragon in the caverns beneath the Kingdom. The dragon tasks Merlin with protecting Uther's son Arthur, as he is destined to be a great king.

Arthur and Merlin, of similar ages, do not initially get along. But after Merlin saves Arthur's life and becomes his manservant, the two embark on many adventures that bring them closer, with Merlin always obliged to hide his magic. Over time, the two young men come to respect and trust each other, ultimately joining forces to protect Camelot from the machinations of Uther's ward Morgana (played by Katie McGrath) as she turns toward evil.

The series has a very high fantasy feel. Rather than taking its aesthetic cues from the post-Roman period as did 1998's *Merlin*, this series uses a more late medieval 'sword and sorcery' fantasy aesthetic. Similar to that introduced in *Excalibur*, it features full suits of armour and great swords aplenty. It celebrates sorcery, magical creatures and political intrigue, with many of the roles and characters changed and reinterpreted for a modern audience.

Morgana's character, while a force of evil in the series, is complex; how she is represented evolves significantly over the course of each season. She appears initially as a kind and compassionate character with the potential to be a force for good in the Kingdom of Camelot. She also pushes back against Uther's injustices and his persecution of magic. But this complicated relationship with her father and magic eventually leaves her vulnerable to the influence of her half-sister Morgause, who gradually turns her to the dark.

When Morgana discovers her own latent magical abilities and suffers rejection from Uther, whom she views as a father figure, we can explore her conflicting emotions. As she grapples with the changes in her circumstances, her initial desire for a just kingdom is corrupted into something dark. Morgana's feelings of betrayal and a thirst for power ultimately win out, drawing a parallel between her and Uther. While she may position herself in opposition to Uther, her arc ultimately mirrors his, emphasizing the corruption of power – thus making her villain arc all the more tragic.

The role of magic in *Merlin* is also mirrored by the character journeys of Merlin and Morgana. Merlin embraces his magic, even if he must do so in secret. Morgana, on the other hand, discovers her magic at a time when it isolates her. She approaches it first with fear, then eventually with a twisted sense of empowerment, which leads her to delve into the darker aspects of magic and sorcery. This is displayed visually, with Merlin appearing in colourful clothing and using light and morally ambiguous magic. Morgana, on the other hand, is shown in dark clothing, wreathed in shadows.

Much of this speaks, once again, to Morgana as a representative of the dangers of women who challenge the patriarchal order. The nature of magic is that it can be dangerous. The female characters of *Merlin* appear to be particularly vulnerable to such corruption, especially when we view Morgana's character development over the series. Her initial strength and outspoken nature establish her goodness – yet without power she cannot bring about change. Magic grants her that power, but with that power comes corruption. Morgana is ultimately punished for embracing her ambition, reinforcing traditional patriarchal views that equate female ambition with corruption.

While *Merlin* offers a far more nuanced depiction of Morgana as a character with her own inner life and motivations, the result is a fallback to traditional Arthurian themes. She ultimately represents the danger of unchecked female ambition and desires for power.

A FEMINIST PERSPECTIVE

Magic and Power

Morgana's characterization in Arthurian legend, even in modern tales, is a matter of much complex debate. While her role in the stories has become more fleshed-out and nuanced, she is often still portrayed in a way that reinforces traditional views by punishing female power. She is a fascinating example of how long-standing the patriarchy can be.

Originally a figure of female power and magic, Morgana has been demonized for seeking power that challenges male authority. Even in more modern re-tellings where she possesses agency and strength, such striving for her own autonomy is depicted as 'unnatural'. In this way, anxieties surrounding female empowerment have changed very little since the early medieval period.

In a patriarchal world, Morgana's magic is her source of strength. Without it, she is just another woman in a world controlled by men. Magic gives her power and agency. It is a tool that she can use to subvert both the constraints of patriarchal structures and the expectations placed on her by society.

Marion Zimmer Bradley's *The Mists of Avalon* is the most explicit example of this in action. Morgana's magical training gives her access to knowledge often denied to women. She learns how to heal, which herbs to use and what powerful spells to cast. Her ability to control the elements and predict the future gives her a platform from which she can challenge the authority of the men in her life, and even influence the fate of Camelot itself.

The duality of female magic, especially in more modern portrayals of the Arthurian legend, shows that we are not so far removed from the fears of the past. Magic can be a source of empowerment, but it is also a cause of suspicion and fear, leading to the demonization and punishment of those who wield it. Morgana's tale often ends in tragedy – usually with the death of her son Mordred. However, she also represents hope and the desire for a better existence. In many of the tales in which she appears, Morgana is the one who carries Arthur to Avalon, showing that peace can be found for a woman outside of the confines of the Camelot patriarchy.

Reclaiming the Narrative

The women of Arthurian legends are often voiceless archetypes. In response, contemporary authors have done a great deal to reclaim the narrative by focusing on the perspectives, agency and motivations of the female characters. Over the years Morgana has evolved from being a character with only a few lines from which to determine her character to a woman with clear goals, motivations and internal conflicts.

Recent Arthurian fiction has shifted towards presenting Morgana with greater depth and complexity, avoiding the 'evil enchantress' trope so common in earlier fiction. *The Mists of Avalon* is the best-known example of this, but other novels such as Fay Sampson's *Daughter of Tintagel* (1889–92) series and Nancy Springer's *I Am Morgan le Fay* (2001) also aim to explore the legends through Morgana's perspective, and her role in the events of the legends.

In works that centre on Morgana as a protagonist, she is often depicted as powerful and assertive, challenging her traditional role in the story. Her magic is embraced as a sign of her strength and independence, while her non-conformity is celebrated as a form of rebellion against patriarchal constraints. Her sexuality and ambition are not depicted as purely negative, while her skills as a warrior and strategist – even in less overtly feminist portrayals, such as that in the BBC's *Merlin* – reveal her to be a competent woman with agency in traditionally male-dominated endeavours.

That said, even in more sympathetic and outwardly feminist perspectives, her ambitions and pursuit of power often end with tragedy or are met with suspicion. While some would argue that this ultimately reinforces the idea that female ambitions must be contained, I'm inclined to disagree. The very fact that actions and choices have consequences is what makes us human. To deny Morgana a realistic arc for a purely positive portrayal would simply create another woman on a pedestal. The reality is that through most of the Arthurian literary canon, Morgana has been primarily a villain. Investing that villainy with meaning and realistic consequences means that Morgana grows into an adult woman with agency and control of her story.

We cannot underestimate the importance of authorship and editorial decisions in how we perceive Morgana's character. Medieval texts downplayed her agency to fit the norms of their day. Contemporary authors may do the same, but in reverse. Every legend's characters represent archetypes that can be shaped and moulded to reflect the anxieties of the author, and Morgana is no exception to that. She is given agency, so her choices have consequences. Her decisions matter, even if they don't conform to our ideas of 'goodness'. In contemporary depictions, she is an active agent in her own story, for good or bad.

The Complexity of Identity (or Why Beauty Matters)

Women's beauty has long been used as a tool of oppression. How a woman looks on the outside has often represented how she is on the inside – and yet Morgana has always had a complex relationship with outward vs inner beauty.

Morgana's physical beauty has often been not only a source of strength, but also a means of control. At the same time, it is a tool used to undermine her agency by reducing her to an object (or not) of male desire. When portrayed as beautiful, she uses this to manipulate men to achieve her goals. We see such behaviour in representations such as the film *Excalibur* or in Hallmark Entertainment's *Merlin*. When she is not traditionally beautiful, however, the subtext is that her outer shell represents her inner evil. We see this in the character of Mim in T.H. White's *The Once and Future King* and its 1963 Disney adaptation, *The Sword in the Stone*.

In the original medieval Arthurian texts, physical attractiveness was often entwined with perceptions of moral goodness and Christian worthiness. It is also worth noting that Morgana was usually not described in detail in those early stories; when she was, it was often not as the great beauty that she would later be known as. Morgana's beauty is actually a more contemporary addition to the legend – one that subverts the idea of beauty being tied to morality even as it ties her to the idea that a woman's value is inherently connected to her outward appearance.

For this reason, Morgana's appearance has become a central part of her identity in many of the more modern Arthurian tales. It is fundamental to her character in Hallmark's *Merlin*, for example. In the mini-series Morgana is shown with a facial difference. While the characters in the story never react to it, it does mean they overlook her. Mab can manipulate her because of this facial difference; when she is made 'beautiful' to the standards of her day, it gives her power. However, she is at her most villainous when she wears her glamour of beauty. Morgana reveals her vulnerability when she seeks validation from her lover Frick, in her final moments as the enchantment fades. Here the inference is almost that her perceived beauty was a corrupting force, but one that she knows is only temporary.

It's also worth noting that none of these stories exist without context. Each sits within the social framework in which they were made. In the case of modern film and television adaptations in particular, there is less of an authorial choice in how Morgana is portrayed and more a necessity of casting choices expected to reflect contemporary beauty standards. We can see this in the original book of *The Mists of Avalon* and its 2001 television adaptation. In the book Morgaine is described by the Christian characters of the novel as 'small and ugly' because of her fae looks. She laments this, because she wishes that Lancelot could view her as beautiful. However, in the mini-series she is played by Julianna Margulies – a gorgeous woman who plays Morgana as dark and mysterious.

Ultimately, there is no single representation of Morgana, nor of how she looks. While some re-tellings aim to challenge traditional associations of beauty with female worth and power, others play into the idea, exploiting it to represent ongoing cultural anxieties around female agency and empowerment. Beautiful or not, Morgana is certainly powerful.

Why Agency Matters

A lot of modern discourse surrounding Morgana le Fay is about reclaiming her as a powerful female figure. Whether in early Arthurian depictions or more contemporary ones, Morgana has almost always had agency and authority over her own life. While her motivations were not always driven by goodness, they were hers, and hers alone.

If we dive into what makes Morgana such a compelling figure in the Arthurian legends, much is due to what she can achieve from outside the established system. A cunning strategist, she exerts control where she can and manipulates others to achieve her goals. Whether by arranging political matches or using her sexuality as a tool, she is a woman who can make independent choices to influence and exert power in a patriarchal system.

Her magic is a strong force. Often depicted as forbidden or dangerous, it is also a source of agency. Having that power gives Morgana autonomy. In *The Mists of Avalon*, for instance, her training gives her access to knowledge and abilities typically denied to women – an idea that goes all the way back to *Le Morte d'Arthur* and her childhood in a nunnery. Her mastery of magic gives Morgana independence and control, to the point where she can challenge the authority of male characters such as Merlin and Arthur.

This agency also allows Morgana to reject traditional feminine roles and embrace more masculine-coded pursuits. In Hallmark's *Merlin*, she seeks but one thing: the crown. She wants it and believes she deserves it; every action is in pursuit of that goal. It is a goal shared in some way by almost all the male protagonists, but she is never championed in that pursuit in the way that Merlin champions Arthur. However, this subversion of female stereotypes can also be physical. In DC's *Madame Xanadu*, Morgana has a far more masculine-coded physical representation. She dresses as an Amazon warrior, challenging traditional ideas of femininity and asserting her dominance through her dress and physical strength.

Ultimately, Morgana's autonomy matters because it can so easily be undermined. In Morgana's varied representations through literature there is a recurring pattern, in which her pursuit of power and her independent ambition are ultimately punished and undermined by reinforcing patriarchal norms. While female strength and leadership exist, they often end in punishment, death, isolation or madness. When she is a one-dimensional villain, it reinforces patriarchal stereotypes of powerful women. Yet when she has agency and the power to make decisions, Morgana moves beyond being a one-dimensional villain to become a woman who chooses, and whose choices have consequences.

Giving Morgana a character, a backstory and motivations means that she becomes far more than an archetype. She becomes a real person with dreams, hopes, ambitions and tragedies. She doesn't have to be palatable or sympathetic – but she can be *real*.

4.
The Once and Future Morgana

> *She has acquired deep learning, hard-won skill,*
> *many of the masteries of Merlin; —*
> *for she has at times dealt in rare magic*
> *with that renowned clerk, who knows*
> *all your knights at home.*
>
> *Morgan the Goddess*
> *is therefore her name;*
> *no person is so haughty*
> *but she can tame him.*
>
> – From *Sir Gawain and the Green Knight* (translated by William Allan Neilson, 1917)

SHE'S A WITCH!

A Witch or a Wizard?

While Morgana is rarely called a witch in Arthurian legends (she is usually referred to as a sorceress), she does display elements associated with the archetype of the witch. This is especially true when we compare her to the wizard Merlin.

While essentially the two terms, witch and wizard, refer to people who practise magic, their connotations are often very different. Wizards, who are usually masculine, chase intellectual pursuits and seek knowledge to enhance and control their power. Witches, on the other hand, are usually feminine and possess more carnal or manipulative powers.

Witches, and by extension Morgana, thus reflect a range of social anxieties about different types of magic and those who wield it. A wizard's magic is earned, learned and deserved, whereas a witch's access to knowledge often derives from outside sources. Someone must give them an unnatural access to power from beyond the established systems of control.

Witches are often portrayed as inherently evil, while the motivations of wizards are often more ambiguous. Merlin is generally considered a hero in Arthurian legends, whereas Morgana's role is traditionally that of a villain. She is a force of destruction, regardless of her motivations. Merlin's role is to uphold the stability of Camelot, guiding Arthur with wisdom; Morgana's role is to tear it down, acting against Arthur's best interests.

Essentially Morgana's status as a witch sets her up in contrast to the positive magic exhibited by Merlin. She represents that archetype by running counter to the needs and desires of the men of Arthurian legend, drawing power from outside the status quo to achieve those ends. In these tales the wizard is the hero and the witch is the villain, drawing a clear distinction between male and female power.

Fear of the Devil

Morgana le Fay's magic is steeped in that of the early pagan traditions from which the Arthurian legends originated. With the Christianization of Europe and an increasing fear of magic, Morgana represents the cross-section between paganism and Christianity. She is a woman who possesses pagan power and her actions run counter to the godly miracles worked to assist Camelot and its king. She is not of Camelot, and so her magic represents 'the other', working against the Christian mainstream.

As Christianity spread, beliefs and practices from a pre-Christian time were regarded as heretical or demonic. Women traditionally seen as healers or wise women, such as Morgana, were rebranded as witches and cast in a more negative light. Healing with herbs and pagan beliefs became linked with the devil, leading to a suspicion of anything possibly associated with witchcraft. Magic and powers from beyond the established order of the Christian Church were vilified and labelled, creating the archetype of the witch.

Morgana le Fay is at the centre of this change; her character exemplifies the association between paganism and witchcraft. In the early Arthurian tales, before she became a villain, Morgana was a sorceress with knowledge of healing and the gift of magic. She served as a remnant of pre-Christian belief in the oral traditions of Welsh and Irish folk legend. However, as the Arthurian legends developed under the influence of Christianity, medieval writers changed this portrayal, shifting her character towards that of a malevolent witch who uses her power for evil. Such transformation mirrored a broader cultural trend towards demonizing pagan practices and associating them with witchcraft.

Sir Thomas Malory's *Le Morte d'Arthur* perfectly represents this shift. Not only does his work reveal a cultural move toward the primacy of patriarchy and suppression of female power, but his association of Morgana's name with 'the fae' clearly marks her as an outsider, reinforcing the idea that her powers come from an evil source. Her power is 'othered' through her name in a way that other magics in the legends are not, aligning her magic with a Christian world-view that demonizes pagan beliefs, often associated with feminine power.

However, it is not only medieval sources that grapple with this fear of the devil. Even in modern re-tellings, the conflict between paganism and Christianity is a central aspect of Morgana le Fay's character. In *The Mists of Avalon*, for example, Marion Zimmer Bradley attempts to reclaim Morgana's connection to pre-Christian traditions by exploring the conflict between the pagan past and the Christian future. Such a dichotomy is also central to the story of Hallmark's *Merlin*, where the characters must navigate a world caught between two changing and conflicting world-views.

This ongoing tension, even in modern adaptations, feeds into Morgana's role as the archetype of the witch. It illustrates our evolving cultural understanding of paganism, witchcraft and female power, as well as the enduring influence of traditional narratives and stereotypes. Morgana embodies these complexities as a character who often bridges the divide yet falls prey to established fears of a pagan association with the devil in a Christian world.

The Temptress in the Dark

A long-standing association with witchcraft is the ability of a witch to tempt men from the path of righteousness. It has long been associated as an expression of female sexuality, which Morgana embodies throughout Arthurian legends.

The archetype of the witch developed in a context of misogynistic beliefs and anxieties around female sexuality. The *Malleus Maleficarum* (1487), written by the German Catholic clergyman Heinrich Kramer (c. 1430–1505), was a guide to the heresy of sorcery and its prosecution. This work, which became foundational in the history of witch hunts, effectively demonized female sexuality, linking it to weakness, deceit and the propensity for evil. It claimed that women were more susceptive to the devil's influence because of their insatiable lust, and consequently more prone to witchcraft.

The character of Morgana feeds into these fears of female sexuality in the Arthurian legends. In the tales, she uses her body to challenge patriarchal structures and societal expectations placed on women, rejecting traditional female roles, such as those of wife and mother, that would give her a benevolent but limited power to embrace magic and an almost unrestrained sexuality instead. In many early tales Morgana does actually kill her husband and take several lovers. She uses her seductive allure to lead men to their ruin and to make them act on her behalf, even if to do so goes against their best interests. Her sexuality is a powerful, uncontrolled force that can undermine male authority – a fear often associated with women accused of witchcraft. Their sexual deviance is perceived as a threat to the community, and so demands punishment.

Love magic is also a fundamental association with Morgana's character. In various re-tellings Morgana uses her powers to influence romantic relationships, sexual desire and even fertility. She has, in multiple stories, been the agent of Elaine's love for

Lancelot and her eventual demise, tried to seduce Lancelot herself using illusion, employed potions and manipulations to tempt men into her bed and manipulated her appearance to tempt Arthur into an incestuous coupling. She uses magic to exert agency over the men in her life, a trait closely associated with the archetype of the witch.

Although Morgana's magic gives her power, it can't be divorced from the idea that accusations of witchcraft were used as a means of social control, a punishment for those who transgressed societal norms. Authorities could target women who displayed independence and challenged male authority by targeting their sexuality and its association with witchcraft. The often tragic end that Morgana's character meets with feeds into such a premise. She exploits her sexuality to challenge male authority figures and to manipulate events in the kingdom of Camelot. Her transgressions go well beyond patriarchal boundaries – and so she must be punished.

Black Witch or White Witch

Morgana may be powerful, but she is far from the only witch in the Arthurian canon. While she is the most recognizable of the sorceresses, other female characters share her magical abilities. So why has Morgana become the wicked witch of Camelot, while other women escape the same villainization?

The idea of good or bad forms of magic is itself an ambiguous one. However, characters such as the Lady of the Lake and Nimue are often considered practitioners of beneficial magic. This ambiguity is especially obvious when we consider that Nimue and

ANCIENT & MODERN: INTRODUCING MORGANA LE FAY

the Lady of the Lake are often combined into a single character; Morgana has even played the role of the Lady herself.

Whether as separate beings or a single entity, Nimue and the Lady of the Lake are often shown in benevolent terms. They uphold justice and the patriarchal status quo, protecting Arthur and his court from magical threats. In many stories, the Lady creates Excalibur to aid Arthur in his time of need. Even when Nimue (in her role as the Lady) imprisons Merlin in *Le Morte d'Arthur*, it is shown as necessary to safeguard the kingdom, aligning her firmly with the side of the good. Nimue is a white witch who uses her power to support the existing order and protect Camelot.

The archetype of the white witch is someone who uses their magic only for good purposes, never for evil. In the world of Arthurian legend, characters such as Nimue and the Lady of the Lake maintain that ideal. In contrast, Morgana often represents the opposite of that ideal, being cast as the black witch.

Rather than upholding Christian ideals and patriarchal values, Morgana kicks against them. Her magic is often selfish; if not, it is at least self-serving. In Geoffrey of Monmouth's *Vita Merlini* we see a less binary version of Morgana and her magic. His stories echoed a pre-Christian ideal surrounding magic and wise women, with Morgana cast as a healer. However, following the Christianization of Europe and the rising fear of magic, demons and female empowerment, we see Morgana's magic turn darker; its interpretations are less ambiguous. The good witches of the tales conform to the patriarchy and align with the dominant religious ideology; the evil witch, in the form of Morgana, acts directly against it.

Even modern interpretations of Morgana's status as a witch fall into these binaries of good or bad. In the BBC's television series *Merlin*, screened in 2008, Morgana turns to dark magic, her appearance changing in response to her choices regarding magic. In John Boorman's film *Excalibur*, made in 1981, we see her associated with black magic through dark clothes and make-up. In *Merlin*, the Hallmark mini-series of 1998, Morgana is free from magic herself, yet she still aligns herself with Mab and *her* magic to achieve her own ends. She may not use such dark power herself, but she is prepared to benefit from it. Mab and the Lady of the Lake, both played by Miranda Richardson, reveal the binary of dark vs light. Mab wears black or shades of night purple, complemented by vampish make-up and claw-like nails. The Lady of the Lake wears a glowing white gown, her hair framing her head like a floating halo of white light.

In the battle between light and dark, Morgana, more often than not, represents the dark. Such conflicts derive from an age-old trope in which the archetype of the witch has become commonplace: day and night, good versus evil. These are themes central to the Arthurian canon. Ambiguous as she may sometimes appear, Morgana is a character most often aligned with the narratives' darker aspects.

THE FAE

The Realm of the Fae

Morgana le Fay's name ties her closely to the realm of the fae and the Celtic mythology from which it derived. Her character has always had a multifaceted relationship with the Otherworld and the fae realm, explored in different ways throughout her various representations.

The Otherworld of Celtic mythology was always a place in which magic was a reality; supernatural beings and creatures roamed freely there. The passage of time was also different from in the mortal realm, enabling humans to step outside their existence and experience something divine or perilous. Since the early tales, Morgana has had a deep connection with this otherworld and the fae, as is evidenced by her name – especially when Avalon comes to represent this facet of her character.

The fae realm was a place of duality. In some ways full of beauty and enchantment, it contrasted profoundly with the world of mortals. Morgana's Avalon existed as an idyllic paradise, away from the struggles and feuds of Arthur's court life and Camelot. Morgana straddled both worlds. However, the home of the fae was also a place of danger and deception. Beautiful and inviting it might be, yet this world was often governed by rules and customs alien to the mortals who strayed there. The fae, although lovely and magical, could also be unpredictable, capable of both great kindness and terrible cruelty.

The realm of the fae was not simply a place of fantasy; it was also a literary realm in which storytellers could explore moral and spiritual themes. Morgana fits firmly into this tradition. The challenges and trials faced by those who entered the home of the fae, or who came into contact with its denizens, provided opportunities for growth and self-discovery. While Morgana's character was often cast in the role of the villain, she served a crucial narrative purpose – to uphold and challenge the protagonists' beliefs.

Morgana is a being as strange and ambiguous as the fae realm itself, making her name all the more fitting. In a single character she encompasses all the complexities of the fae. She is beautiful, dangerous, magical and manipulative. Yet she also challenges and captivates, making her such a fascinatingly versatile character for all manner of stories.

The Otherworld of the Celts

The Celtic Otherworld encompassed several realms or concepts. Mythologies from all over the world have similar mystical spaces associated with magic and the supernatural, often used to represent the gateway between life and death.

The concept of the Otherworld pre-dates Christianity, which is why Avalon became such a fundamental part of Arthurian mythology. Morgana draws from ancient traditions and knowledge often seen as a threat to established order, especially as the stories became more Christianized. Her magic is frequently tied to paganism or 'the old ways', connecting her to these ancient forces.

However, the connection of the Celtic Otherworld to healing and resurrection made it possible to Christianize the concept of Avalon itself. A mystical place, invested with ancient traditions, it can also be linked to the Christian idea of heaven. After all his worldly trials, Avalon is where Arthur finds his final resting place, and eventual peace. Morgana's association with Avalon is the one aspect of her character that has never quite been overcome, no matter how villainous writers have made her. This connection to Avalon makes her a liminal figure, spanning the ambiguous morality of the Celtic Otherworld and the rigid moral structures of a post-Christian world.

Increasingly across various stories, Morgana represents the rebellion of a Celtic past against the rise of Christianity. Her rebellion is no longer a personal vendetta against Arthur and his court. It is driven instead by a desire to preserve ancient traditions and beliefs threatened by change. In some ways her motivations are rooted in a desire to defend a marginalized way of life that will be lost without intervention.

Morgana's connection to the Otherworld creates a rich and varied character. Her connection to magic gives her remarkable powers, which she can use for either good or evil. Intriguingly, her connection to a mythological past that has been restructured and propagandized in both positive and negative ways means that she can serve as either villain or a hero, depending on the storyteller's desire.

Interpreting the Text

While Morgana le Fay shares many similarities with the fae folk and the Otherworld of legend, she is never expressly connected to them in the text despite her name. Much of her character is defined by clues from the context of Celtic oral traditions.

Morgana le Fay translates to Morgana of the Fairies, which connects her to the Fair Folk or fae; so does her connection to magic. However, her characterization often goes further than these. Readers of the Arthurian legends would have been able to recognize tropes and themes in Morgana's character drawn from other powerful women of Celtic mythology.

In her early life, Morgana was described as a student of magic, astronomy and the healing arts. Figures such as Brigid, the triple-goddess, and Airmid, the Irish goddess of healing, were associated with healing wells, springs and herbal magic. Morgana has maintained a modern connection to these ancient tales through the Chalice Well at Glastonbury Tor.

Much of what modern researchers have uncovered about the Celtic nations, in so far as we can interpret them, also suggests a profound connection to astronomical events. Solar events such as the summer solstice are often considered fundamental to Celtic life. Monuments such as Stonehenge have long been considered a focal point for celebrating these events, integrating directly into mythology and rituals. Through her connection to the Otherworld and education in astronomy, Morgana is bound up with this Celtic past.

The triple-goddess archetype is a connection to a Celtic past that has already been discussed. However, this archetype has a further connection to the importance of numbers three and nine that occurs in much of Celtic mythology. Birth, death, rebirth – maiden, mother, crone. Groupings of three occur throughout the myths. In *Vita Merlini* Morgana is first introduced as the most beautiful and powerful of nine enchantresses who possess the powers of transformation, healing and prophecy. The number nine is a ninefold representation of these groupings of three (a triple representation of a tripartite aspect), which directly connects Morgana to the Celtic pantheon.

Shapeshifting is also a fundamental part of the Celtic canon. The Morrígan of Irish mythology, considered to be an inspiration behind Morgana's character, was known for her shapeshifting abilities; she appeared in various animal forms, particularly as a crow, to influence events and deliver prophecies. While Morgana lost much of her shapeshifting powers as the legends evolved, they were a fundamental part of her early characterization and still exist, at least in part, in later characterizations. She uses illusion and glamour to change her appearance.

However, perhaps the most significant connection for Morgana le Fay as a character to her Celtic roots is in her very nature. Her motivations are often morally ambiguous, despite being cast as a villain; like the fae creatures of Celtic tradition, her motivations have an ambivalent duality. She heals and prophecies, but she also manipulates and enchants. She puts the other characters through trials and challenges, but ultimately ferries Arthur from life into death. Morgana is thus poised between the mortal and immortal realms, shepherding the characters from life into legend.

The Fae of Legend

Morgana's developing character highlights the changing perception of fae and Celtic beliefs throughout time. Faery themes are used in the Arthurian canon to speak to a perceived Celtic past that readers of the original chivalric tales would have recognized.

Morgana is often portrayed as the master of trickery and deception, manipulating those around her with cunning intelligence. Faery tropes frequently speak to the mischievous nature of the fae and their ability to blur the lines between what is real and what is illusion. Morgana uses trickery and illusion to disguise herself and others, sowing chaos in Arthur's court and testing the loyalty of his knights.

This illusion also extends to the faery tradition of bestowing gifts, often accompanied by unseen conditions that mortals are manipulated into upholding. Many faery stories warn of accepting presents or food from the faery realm. Morgana exists within this tradition. She offers magical items or assistance to the Knights of the Round Table, but these gifts often come with a hidden price or unforeseen consequences. Like a faery bargain, such gifts have unpredictable outcomes; invisible dangers and implications that come with accepting her aid.

Beauty and seduction are also common tools of the fae. Faery women lured unsuspecting mortals to their realm or to their deaths, even as Morgana often uses her own beauty, or the illusion of it, to manipulate men into doing her bidding. Modern re-tellings represent her as a vampish beauty, exploiting her sexuality to influence Camelot's fate.

While her sexuality has often created a villainous persona in a Christianized world, this may have been more morally ambiguous in the pre-Christian era. A morally ambiguous nature, or shifting allegiances, are common themes in faery lore. The actions of the fae defy easy categorization because they work outside the boundaries of human morality. Much of this comes from their association with nature, often considered ethically neutral – an association that Morgana shares.

As the Lady of Avalon, an abundantly beautiful island, Morgana's connection to the natural world is clear. Her healing power is derived from her knowledge of herbs and her magic manifests itself in control over nature. Her Celtic connections to the Welsh goddess Modron, Brigid and the Morrígan tie Morgana to ancient Celtic beliefs that revered female deities connected to nature, fertility and the fae's dominion over the forces of nature.

While many interpretations of the Arthurian canon attempted to demonize this aspect of Morgana's character, modern interpretations have tried to show her fae connections in a more positive light. In Marion Zimmer Bradley's *The Mists of Avalon*, Morgana is a priestess deeply connected to the cycles of nature. This role emphasizes the strength and wisdom of the natural world, in turn aligning Morgana with a feminist reinterpretation of the power of the ancient deities of the fae folk of Celtic lore.

RECLAIMING THE GODDESS

Witch or Goddess?

While we have spoken about the nature of the witch and goddess in the Arthurian legends, it's important to note how both elements of Morgana's character have been reconstructed for the modern day. The maleficence of witchcraft in the late medieval era has seen a gradual shift to another form of magic; more morally neutral, it promotes personal agency above all else. In medieval tales the fae-like nature of the Celtic goddesses was readjusted for a medieval world-view, losing the goddess aspect so fundamental to Celtic legend.

In the modern day, feminist witches challenge the traditional 'witch/goddess' dichotomy which presents characters such as

Morgana le Fay as polarized representations of female power. They remove the distinction between them, claiming both as sources of empowerment. Whether a witch or a goddess, both are magical representations of female agency and the divine feminine.

The conscious act of claiming these labels by the modern neopagan and Goddess movements allows writers to redefine these ideas on their own terms, stripping them of previously negative connotations. By renegotiating the meaning of these words to a modern audience, we can invest characters such as Morgana le Fay with new meanings, creating a more inclusive understanding of feminine power.

Morgana is at the forefront of those conversations. She has a history as a goddess, a pagan priestess and a witch with demonic powers, but she has always retained a connection to the divine. She is a character who perfectly encapsulates society's changing views of women, and who has been at the forefront of centuries of representations that highlight those shifts.

Neopaganism and the Goddess Movement

The Goddess movement emerged in the United States during the 1970s as a reclamation of pre-Christian, Goddess-worshipping cultures. It sought to reinterpret ancient religious traditions while emphasizing the value of a woman's spiritual journey, reacting against the rigid patriarchal doctrines often found in mainstream religions.

The Goddess movement comes under the broader umbrella of neopaganism. The term encompasses several modern religious movements that share an influence with the beliefs of pre-modern civilizations. It is an incredibly diverse movement with no pre-defined beliefs, practices, texts or structures. Some neopagan movements attempt to revive ancient religions; others blend elements of select philosophies to create something entirely new. Some have strong religious tenets, while others are more humanistic, naturalistic or secular, seeing their spirituality as more of a personal practice rather than a strict dogma.

Within this scope, the Goddess movement is one of the neopagan groups that draws influence from traditions and mythologies worldwide, strongly emphasizing personal experience and individual interpretation. Deeply rooted in feminism, its adherents view the Goddess as a symbol of female strength, creativity and the interconnectedness of life. They seek to reclaim elements of womanhood that have historically been demonized or suppressed, especially around sexuality, fertility and a connection to nature.

Modern interpretations of Morgana le Fay take inspiration from the Goddess movement in how she is portrayed. The binary of good vs evil is no longer at the forefront of her characterization. Instead, her womanhood, agency and choice are more widely explored, as is her connection to a pre-modern world-view.

Given Morgana's strong association with Avalon, there is one place deeply connected to the Goddess movement where she is at the forefront: Chalice Well at Glastonbury Tor. It is also known as the Blood Well or Red Well due to its reddish colour, a result of iron deposits in the water.

While Chalice Well is a place that welcomes visitors of all faiths and spiritual beliefs, it has become especially important to the

Goddess movement. The colour of the waters has been likened to the red of menstrual blood, or to the blood spilled in childbirth. The well connects practitioners to the divine feminine and, as the Lady of Avalon, the spirit of Morgana feels significant to the location. The Winter and Summer Solstices are often celebrated at the well. Such events reconnect visitors with nature and bring a much-needed peace and tranquillity to the story of a woman who has endured so many changes at the hands of her writers.

A Return to Celtic Roots

While the Goddess movement may seem quite ephemeral in how it relates to modern interpretations of Morgana le Fay, her most iconic characterization stemmed directly from it. *The Mists of Avalon* is perhaps the best-known modern interpretation of Morgana, an interpretation born almost directly from Bradley's involvement with the Goddess movement.

In the 1960s Marion Zimmer Bradley co-founded the Aquarian Order of the Restoration, a group dedicated to reviving Goddess worship. Members of the group were influenced by the teachings of Dion Fortune, an occultist and ceremonial magician active in the early twentieth century. Bradley was also a founding member of The Society for Creative Anachronism (SCA), a living history group that aimed to study and re-create pre-seventeenth-century medieval European cultures and their histories.

The Mists of Avalon is a powerful example of how Bradley incorporated Goddess spirituality into her work. Its eventual success contributed hugely to the broader popularity of the Goddess movement that occurred after its publication. She reframed Arthurian legend from a female perspective, giving Morgana a voice as a complex woman devoted to Goddess worship rather than a one-dimensional evil sorceress. The novel, and indeed Morgana herself, resonated with women who were seeking alternative spiritual paths and challenged traditional patriarchal representations of female characters in literature.

In Bradley's work, Morgana's character aligns with the goals of the Goddess movement, seeking to reclaim and celebrate female divinity. She trains on Avalon, where the Goddess is revered, and learns magic there, coming to understand the Goddess and her cycles profoundly and to connect deeply to the natural world. Through Morgana's character, Bradley explored the conflict between the perceived ancient worship of the feminine divine against the encroaching power of patriarchal Christianity.

Through her portrayal of Morgana, Bradley made the concept of the Goddess accessible to a wider audience by packaging it in a captivating narrative. She showcased the full spectrum of feminine power through its light and dark aspects, from creation to destruction. Morgana is both a witch and a goddess; she is neither inherently evil nor good. This is the version of Morgana le Fay that has captured the attention of modern audiences, and the one that I believe will continue to influence future interpretations of her character.

What Comes Next?

The fascination of modern media with the Arthurian legends in general and Morgana le Fay in particular seems to be as strong as ever; we are sure to see many more reinterpretations in the future.

So what might these look like? Can we really predict how Morgana might change?

With the emergence of the Goddess movement, and a focus upon the more feminist aspects of neopaganism, writers are reclaiming Morgana as an embodiment of female power and resistance to patriarchal oppression. Such a trend will probably continue as writers and artists explore traditionally vilified female characters, perceiving them as potential symbols of female strength, spirituality and autonomy.

Future explorations will likely move beyond Morgana's villainous image and present her as flawed and sympathetic – especially with the current interest in morally grey villains in much of popular fantasy. Morgana's character has always been full of ambiguity, so she is perfectly placed to explore the nuance of the grey zones between being a hero and a villain. She has a range of capabilities and possible motivations that defy easy categorization, enabling her easily to play the role of healing or destruction, protection or challenge.

Looking at Morgana's past portrayals, we can see how she has reflected the social anxieties and cultural changes surrounding her writers. It isn't too much of a stretch to believe that she will continue to play that role in future interpretations. From grappling with a Celtic past to representing a threat to patriarchal Christendom, as well as portrayals in current media that explore themes of female leadership, power and ambition, we can expect to see her character evolve further to explore the issues of the day.

Possible future interpretations could lead to discussions around issues of environmentalism and our relationship to the natural world, an issue that becomes ever more pressing and potentially politically divisive. With her strong connection to Avalon and her role as a healer and guardian of the natural world, Morgana is primed for use by writers to present their viewpoints and explore these issues through her archetypal qualities. As a powerful sorceress, a villain, a wise woman and a social disruptor, Morgana can assume many roles that will resonate with modern audiences, no matter the context.

In whatever way she is reimagined, whether through art, the written word, across genres or settings, or in new and innovative contexts, she will retain her essence as a fascinating, multifaceted figure of female power. Morgana le Fay is a woman shaped by the creative choices of writers, artists and the cultural landscape through which her character is shaped. Complex and intriguing, she provides us with an enduring legacy of female power, identity and the impact of myth and legend.

AN ENDURING LEGACY

Morgana le Fay is a character who has undergone much evolution, yet kept many of her character's essential traits across many reinterpretations over literally hundreds of years. She has moved from a figure associated with healing and wisdom to a vibrant symbol of female power, whether this occurs through casting her as a villain or as an anti-hero. She has reflected both the values and anxieties of those who portrayed her and their societies, significantly shaping modern beliefs about female spirituality and divinity. It is precisely this complexity that ensures her lasting appeal.

Morgana is now more than simply a character; she has become an archetype in her own right. Her image as a powerful sorceress and a figure who defies societal expectations continues to resonate with audiences, inspiring re-tellings to this day. The common thread that binds her across seemingly contradictory interpretations is her unwavering strength and her ability to challenge the status quo.

No matter her role in the stories, Morgana consistently demonstrates intelligence, cunning and determination to forge her own path. It is this unwavering commitment to her own agency that has given her such lasting appeal. She remains relevant and intriguing because her multifaceted nature reflects the human experience.

Everyone grapples with conflicting motivations, emotions and desires. All of us are capable of great good or great evil – we carry the potential for each within us. Morgana embodies both the light and the dark, good and evil. This makes her someone we can all relate to, despite her connection to the supernatural and the mists of mythology. Her ambiguity invites readers and audiences to interpret her actions on their own merit, leading to a range of artistic interpretations through varying media: fiction, graphic novels, art, television and film. No matter what the creative vision may be, Morgana's character can be adapted to suit and speak to audiences on a fundamentally human level.

To modern audiences, Morgana le Fay has been a powerful symbol of female agency, fighting against the patriarchal status quo. She resonates with contemporary audiences, especially women, who face similar struggles in their own lives. Her magic, knowledge, intelligence and cunning give her power, challenging the idea that women are inherently weaker or less capable than men. Her complex relationship with other characters in the Arthurian canon, especially with Arthur and his Knights, also highlights the dynamics of power, loyalty and betrayal – common themes in modern fantasy that continue to be relevant in contemporary storytelling.

When I look at my own fascination with Morgana, and why I was so drawn to her as a character, it is fundamentally because she is complex. She is at once the evil queen of fairy tales and the independent heroine that I love in modern fantasy. She is timeless and defies any kind of neat categorization. She breaks every limit placed upon her, shifting and bending to reflect not only the intent of the author, but also the interpretation of the reader.

Ultimately Morgana le Fay is a woman who challenges our assumptions and invites us to question the world around us. Through her many faces, she reflects the rich diversity of what it is to be human and reminds us that in a world of myths and legends, there are essential truths to be found, if only we know where to look.

Modern Short Stories of Morgana le Fay

His Head in Your Lap, Dear Brother

K. Blair

Your brother is dying and they will say it is your fault.

* * *

From a young age, you like to make your brother laugh. To amuse your older sisters is an achievement, a hard-won treasure, but compared to joyful giggles, suppressed behind fingers, there is no contest. Your little brother has the warmth of late summer in his laugh. It gives you that first citrus burst of golden quince on your tongue to hear it echo off the castle walls.

You are fond of tricks and japes, coins pulled from behind ears, a sewing needle left upright on a chair, incense powder cast through a candle flame to give the illusion of breathing fire. You spend an afternoon, knee deep in murky pond water, patiently waiting to catch the perfect toad to hide in his riding boots. You will hide close by his chambers, all to hear your brother's startled pig squeal of shock more clearly.

The King, the man your sisters speak of with thinly veiled disdain, thunders that your behaviour is not ladylike. Deceit is an unbecoming look upon a young maiden's face.

Your tongue wishes to lash this man with his own hypocrisy. Your head knows better than to bait this particular bear.

You promise not to play any more tricks on your dear brother.

This is your first lie.

* * *

You are sent away to a convent for your schooling. Your brother worries you will forget him, that your head will grow so full of knowledge there will be no space for the memory of him.

You ruffle his dark hair, tell him that nothing you learn could replace him.

He smiles, gap-toothed, and does not notice your other hand dropping a spider down the back of his tunic.

* * *

The other girls at the convent are God-fearing. You suppose you would find God fearsome too, if he were ever interesting enough to hold your attention. Your studies are what capture your focus, the simple elegance of geometry and arithmetic, the rigorous discipline of rhetoric and logic. At first you struggle with the coordination required for the hurdy-gurdy, but your determination ensures that you soon master this as well.

It is here, within these hallowed walls, that your magic reveals itself to you, that glimmer gold unfurling beneath your skin. A secret kept close to your chest, you practise in the lofty heights of trees in the convent garden, tracking the movements of the heavens and crafting illusions in the palm of your hand.

Though there are girls you enjoy the company of, there are others who find you unpalatable. You do not hold their opinions in high esteem, though a few turn your head with their beauty. Still, their behaviour towards you is unsettling.

They flick ink across your parchment, trip you upon entering the chapel, exclude you from their circle and try to encourage others to do the same. At night you bewitch their beds to rattle and rock as if the frames are troublesome geldings trying to unseat their riders. When you see them walking from the dormitory, you conjure ravens to swoop down upon their heads, chasing them all the way to the cloisters. You pour salt in their cider and hide nettles in their chemises.

They lessen their unpleasant attentions on you, but their distaste remains apparent. You consider yourself the victor of these little games, your ire sated but their slights not forgotten.

* * *

Your brother's wounds are fatal. This is something that cannot be denied. You wish there was a way to unweave this tapestry before it is finished, but that is beyond your capabilities, learned though you are. You push the hair slick with sweat back from his forehead, hoping that it soothes him.

* * *

It is the spring of your fourteenth year when Merlin comes to you, eyes like the first sign on the horizon of some terrible storm. Dressed in a cloak spun from strands of twilight, he regards you in the tree with wry amusement as if you are a dog that has learned how to walk on its hind legs and perform a rondle.

You swing your legs back and forth, considering the wizard before you. You have seen only the blurred shadow of him in the castle walls, have heard the whispers of the servants who have witnessed his presence in the company of the King. When you enquired further, Morgause told you that he was a great sorcerer and to not ask any more questions. Some things are better left unsaid.

"There is much to show you," Merlin says, "if you are willing to learn."

You tilt your head, imagining the very tips of Merlin's beard setting alight. A spark. The edges of his moustache flash orange. A small singe, a brief burning. You laugh, deliberately raucous, though you know it only happened because Merlin allowed it.

"Teach me then, great sorcerer," you say, "if you are up to the job."

* * *

You return to fair Camelot an accomplished mage. There is no beast you cannot shift your form to take, no minor wound you cannot stitch together. You have studied the shape of things, the edges where the world comes together and can mimic its splendour.

Much has changed in your absence. Your nephews, who were mere toddling babes when you left, have the beginnings of beards on their chins and swords in their hands. Their voices crack with the weight of their newfound piety.

The King, frail in his old age, is not long for this world. Still, he voices demands you have no interest in. The sacrament of marriage, the noble cause of motherhood. Paths you do not find unpleasant on their own, but you rankle at the lack of choice in the matter.

The suitors offered reminds you of unripe medlars. You think perhaps that a little bletting would not go amiss.

Your little brother is not so little anymore. A foot taller than you, he is beginning to fit himself into the shape of kinghood. He speaks with authority, holds himself straight-backed.

When you hide behind the hunting tapestry in his chambers, face shape shifted into that of a slavering wolf, he jumps a foot in the air and screams like a startled goat. You snap your jaws at him, lolling out your big pink tongue while he rants and raves about your conduct, the reprimand undercut by the boyish laughter he is suppressing.

You are pleased to find there is still youthful joy beneath the mask. That he speaks shyly of Gwenhwyfar, his soon-to-be bride, the faintest of blushes in his cheeks, another glimpse of the softness beneath the polished armour.

There is still that slant of light in his laugh. There is still citrus on your tongue.

* * *

The King is dead. Long live the King.

* * *

Gwenhwyfar. Heaven-struck stained-glass woman. Wedding veil woven from starlight, she is revealed to you at the altar and your throat forgets how to construct meaning. Your mouth, heavy with desire, fails to recite hymns and prayers. There is only her face, the cloying of incense, the finality of vows.

It is difficult for you to make merry, set upon as you are by unexpected feeling. You sip wine, wave away offers to dance, sneak glances along the high table to Gwenhwyfar – bright, beautiful Gwenhwyfar – averting your eyes before the look is returned. You do not know what you would do if the look was returned.

Merlin, posture loosened by mead, clatters into the chair beside you, a gleam in his eye that betrays his roguish nature.

"There is rancour among those who would seek the throne for themselves about the best way to challenge Arthur's legitimacy," Merlin tells you conspiratorially, "but there is a plan."

"A plan?"

Merlin winks, bawdy as an alehouse. "It involves Uther's sword and a churchyard stone."

It is not often that the tapestry threads are so apparent, nor does Merlin ever admit he is the one with the needle.

You wonder what this means for the happy couple, for your brother freshly crowned. You wonder what it means for you, what stitches are keeping you in place and whether Merlin would ever reveal to you how to unthread yourself.

* * *

Arthur pulls the sword from the stone and you know in the marrow of your bones that nothing will be the same again.

* * *

You are known by many titles. Empress of the wilderness. Queen of the damsels. Lady of the isles and governor of the waves of the great sea. As your brother bleeds, his head in your lap, the only title you'd answer to now is sister.

* * *

You do not mean for it to happen. Trickster though you are, you would never seek to interfere with your brother's happiness.

And yet, as winter eats its fill of autumn, you find yourself in the firelight company of Gwenhwyfar, fashioning illusory delights for her amusement. Beasts of legend, Fae creatures found only in the space between dreaming and waking. You conjure what you can of dragons, of unicorns, of the white hart that eludes your brother.

You do not mean to, but the fire casts long shadows to hide desire in. To steal a kiss is a small sin in the grand scheme of things, but steal it you do.

Gwenhwyfar gasps your name, and it sounds like the falling of a great oak, the toppling of a mountain, the crumbling of a cliff into the sea. It is the power of destruction and your undoing.

* * *

Before you vanish into the wild woods, you make a copy of the sword from the stone, just to see if you are able.

You have a sense of the threads that guide your hand to do this, but you chose to ignore them.

* * *

You wander, seeking to learn from others like you. Sorcerers who praise the spirits of river and forest, those who reject the notion of one God for the worship of many. You have found it is more flesh and blood than you can stand, the King's circular table blessed for Christian saints. You are adrift, but not undetermined.

You sail for Avalon, known refuge of those who honour the old ways, and spend many moons under their tutelage. You find you prefer this to castle life, this community that seeks to embolden and empower you. For the first time, your magic is judged on its own merits, and not as a reflection of Merlin's teachings.

The distance provides clarity. Even when you learn of Lancelot, the most pious of the King's knights, and how he has turned the Queen's head, there are those you now know who distract you from this path of melancholy.

Sebile is witty. She draws you out of the mirrored chambers of your mind, reminds you that your body is here, that you reside in this earthly realm.

HIS HEAD IN YOUR LAP, DEAR BROTHER

Sebile is the one to tell you that the Lady of the Lake has gifted the King an enchanted sword. Excalibur, deep magic that will protect and keep him.

"I say we exclude her," Sebile says, as you braid her auburn locks, "for throwing her lot in with the world of men."

You laugh and kiss Sebile's shoulder. "Let my brother have his magic sword. We need not concern ourselves with their affairs."

* * *

Merlin comes to you in the spring once more. You allow him entry, serve him ale, wish he would not smoke such a foul-smelling pipe. He has come to you before, following a spat with the Lady of the Lake, the details of which he kept deliberately vague. He lounged around spouting prophecy and cluttering up the place. You are not eager for a repeat performance.

"Arthur must be tested," Merlin says, blowing smoke rings across the table.

A refrain you have heard before. A sword can be taken to a whetstone only so many times before it must make its first cut. Your brother has long since been sharpened.

"And if I refuse?"

Merlin regards you, sombre as standing stones, immovable as the coming dawn.

"Morgayne, empress of the wilderness, it is already written."

* * *

First you send a mantle that will render any who wears it to cinders. Red as common barberries, soft as lambs' wool, your servant carries the mantle as though it were a holy relic.

Sebile reports that were it not for the Lady of the Lake, the King would have donned the cloak without hesitation. Instead, your servant bears the brunt of the flames, reduced to ash in the great hall before the entire court.

Second you send a magical drinking horn from which no unfaithful lady can drink without spilling. A mere jape, it is intended to embarrass and stain. You did not expect the revelation of Isolde's infidelity, though you cannot say you are surprised. Your brother's Knights are horrific in their beauty. Like wounded birds, they draw people in with their noble suffering, only to blind them with hidden talons, the slick sheen of their devotion. To be enraptured, to want a taste was understandable.

You had seen it yourself, when arguing with Sebile about Lancelot. Sebile takes great pleasure in testing Lancelot's purity, so ardent is her desire to see him spoiled.

"He shines so brightly," Sebile tells you, as together you weave the enchantment that will keep Elaine of Corbenic within the confines of the boiling bath, "so desperately in love with the King and Queen is he. To bring about his ruin would be a great prize indeed."

"And when he kills you for that service," you snap, hands caught in the complex curves of this magic.

"He would never harm a woman," Sebile replies, obvious in her self-satisfaction. "He considers it discourteous."

This is true, though you wish it were different. To fight, to have the opportunity to shift shape into something magnificent, something beastly, long in tooth and claw, would release the tension you carry in your chest. But the King's most beloved knight has learned the tells of your changing.

You wonder if your brother confided in him where to look.

Third, at Christmas time, overcome by festive spirit, you ask a favour of the only Knight you've ever been able to tolerate. A worshipper of the old ways, green as the ivy, spry as the willow, the Green Knight agrees to the game you lay out for him.

Your nephew Gawain, eager to prove himself a man in the eyes of his King, responds with the impatience expected of his youth.

You wonder if the Queen gasped as the head hit the floor. Wonder if it sickened her as it rolled across the stone, laurels of blood spilling out towards the thrones, or perhaps, wonder if it delighted her to see such a display of brutality.

Wonder if she knows who sent such a strange gift.

* * *

From a young age, you liked to make your brother laugh. Now at the end of things, you struggle to think of wittiness. You have missed the sound of his laughter, the warmth of his teasing. His laboured breathing is loud in your ears, at odds with the soothing sound of the water lapping the side of the boat as you sail for Avalon.

* * *

Though you have remained hidden from your brother for many years, he finds you, almost by accident. He stumbles across your threshold, waylaid by the forest itself. A mighty King, tricked by oak and birch.

You regard each other from a distance, both wary as if the other is a deer in a meadow that might spook at the slightest noise. Perhaps this is merely an illusion, a clever piece of magic made from longing.

"Morgayne," your brother whispers, voice deep and cracked as if it has been long neglected. "Come home."

"Dear brother," you reply, your own throat aching as if you have swallowed splinters, "I cannot."

* * *

This is the consequence of your last joke.

You take Excalibur while the King slumbers and craft a clever likeness. He will know, the pommel so moulded to his palm. It is an extension of him, another limb. But within the scabbard, it is well disguised, a lamb in the wolf's den.

The Knights pursue you on horseback, a fearsome charge through woods and pasture. You elude them, slip ahead like the white hart of bewitching ruin.

You fling the sword, that foredoomed sword, into the lake from whence it came, trusting Sebile to keep its lady preoccupied. On the shore, autumn's wind caressing your skin, you turn to stone, a sculpture to mischief. Though they wail and rage, their weapons cannot make purchase.

HIS HEAD IN YOUR LAP, DEAR BROTHER

The sword is lost.

And so, your brother can be wounded.

You do not see it happen, this battle in that so called merry month of May. An ill-fated affair, an ill-conceived child. The blade strikes true, a wound so great it cannot be sewn shut. Merlin is long gone, meandered into the mists of his own myth. There is none, save you, to wipe the sweat from your brother's brow, to make him comfortable in the belly of your boat. His head in your lap, your dear brother.

For a moment, you thought you saw Gwenhwyfar on the shoreline, hair whipping in the wind, loyal Lancelot at her side. The only souls in the world whose agony echoes yours.

You look away.

There is only the water. There is only the mist. The quiet of siblings, alone with one another in the twilight.

The glint of a coin pulled from an ear, the wet wry chuckle that ensues. There is quince on your tongue once more.

* * *

You leave your brother's helmet in the cave for those that would seek to find the body. Let your brother rest in secret, far from the prying eyes of wayward pilgrims. If they seek a shrine, let them build it themselves as distraction. They need not know the truth, let the tapestry be enough for them.

This is your true last jape.

Morgana and the Morrigan
Chris A. Bolton

The Morrigan awakens in darkness, disoriented. How long has it been since she ventured from her slumber? The world has changed. Her name no longer spoken. Her image no longer worshiped. Her power no longer admired – or feared.

She feels something coming to her land from across the sea. A mere human, yet dangerously powerful. Her caution grows as it approaches shore. What does it want? Shall she embrace it – or destroy it?

From deep within the ancient shadows that entomb her, she waits… and observes.

* * *

When the curtain of fog finally draws back, Morgana le Fay sees shore for the first time in a week. The so-called Emerald Isle looks little different from the banks of the land she has fled *(been forced to flee)* – perhaps a brighter green, but not remarkably more verdant. Then again, no place is as lush and vibrant as her memories of Avalon. Her chest prickles at the thought that she'll never set eyes upon it again.

Her escorts hop into the shallow water and drag the small boat ashore. Their decorum is admirable but misplaced; the moment Morgana steps off the boat, her foot sinks into mud that splatters the front of her dress. Scanning the hills and glens to all sides, she realizes nothing will stay clean for long in this still-wild and primitive land.

"I'll scout ahead, my queen," says the fox, already bounding toward a thicket of brambles and ash trees, "and locate a suitable dwelling to occupy."

Morgana nods, and his bushy tail vanishes under thorny blackberry vines. The only dwelling she expects him to find is a cave or mud hut. There will be nothing that resembles the comfort of her castle in Camelot.

"Wretched land of bog-dwellers," she grunts, noticing the mist slither to shore like it's hunting them. "We'll be lucky if pagan savages don't flay us alive before nightfall."

"Oh, please don't say such things, Milady," the hedgehog says, his quills shivering with fright. "Surely you'll feel better with food in your belly."

The badger points to a large brown hare nosing through a clover patch, a short hop from the safety of the brambles. "There's a fine meal," he says in his forever-growling voice. "Shall I kill it for you, Mistress?"

"The last time you caught dinner, your claws made such a horrid mess, there was scarcely enough to nibble on." She glances at the hedgehog, who is bigger than the hare – but not much. "I'll do it."

Morgana aims one hand at the hare and murmurs a brief incantation. The hare's ears perk straight up, and it hesitates long enough for Morgana to wonder if she used the correct spell. A heartbeat later, the hare springs across the field straight at her. It runs toward the knife in her other hand and, with a mighty leap, skewers itself on the blade.

She breathes a sigh of relief – a small one, so the others don't notice. Her magic is weaker here, but still effective.

"Magnificently done, Milady," the hedgehog says, holding his paw out. "Shall we clean and gut it for you?"

She hands the impaled animal to the hedgehog, who steps gingerly past the badger. Their natural animosity has been tempered by Morgana's enchantment, but some instincts are too innate to curb entirely.

He carries the hare a short distance and extracts the blade. Then he makes a small incision near the tail and starts to tug the skin away.

The hare springs upright, its eyes huge and red. Its mouth draws back to reveal long incisors that gnash ferociously. It snaps at the hedgehog, narrowly missing his throat. He scurries backwards, whimpering.

The badger runs up and swipes his massive claws, but the hare dodges with unnatural speed. Even with blood spurting from its chest and nethers, it pounces on the badger's back and rips hunks of fur from his neck.

Morgana seizes the pointy ears and hoists the hare upright. Summoning her pastoral upbringing, she plunges her hand into the rear incision and grips the edge of the creature's fur. With a mighty yank, she tugs the hare's skin. The creature flails, spattering blood across Morgana's face and chest, but she continues to pry the skin over its body in one, unbroken piece, all the way past its ears.

What should be exposed muscle and tendons is instead a green-skinned creature with small horns, yellow eyes, and wings like a giant dragonfly. From the stories of her youth, Morgana came prepared to encounter these creatures. Still gripping its horns, she unsheathes an iron knife at her belt and presses it flat against the creature's belly. The frantic beast wails as its flesh sizzles.

"You're one of the Fae," Morgana says. "And far more gruesome than has been suggested by fairy tales."

"Please don't hurt me," the creature whimpers, "I'm only a brownie! I gots no magic pixie dust, I just makes mischief—"

"Still your tongue or I'll skewer it to your jaw," Morgana says, waving the knife blade. The brownie falls silent, though its body never stops squirming. "Lead me to your queen and I'll set you free."

The brownie clamps a hand over its mouth and nods eagerly. Its other arm straightens, a long finger pointing toward the brambles.

As Morgana and her entourage approach, thorny vines and leaves tremble. The fox emerges from the thicket, his fur covered in burs and twigs.

"I've found a place, my queen," he says. "Follow me and stay low."

Morgana removes an iron chain from a pouch on her belt and binds the brownie's foot. It whines and fidgets as if being coiled in metal spikes. Then she sinks to a crawl – cursing the soggy ground and the dark stains spreading across her dress – and drags the chained brownie behind her.

The fox maneuvers deftly on four legs, frequently stopping until Morgana catches up. When at last they reach a clearing, she beholds a castle ruin whose standing stone walls are choked with moss and ivy.

Pulling herself to her feet, Morgana ignores the helping paws offered by the hedgehog and badger. The bottom half of her dress is heavy with muck, and she wishes yet again she'd had time to grab leather clothing before she fled.

"I sniff a presence in these walls that's stronger than any I've felt since Merlin," the fox says. "Maybe more."

Morgana feels a curl at the corner of her mouth and purses her lips to hide it. If the others knew of her plans, she might have to face the presence alone.

A portcullis blocks the only entrance on this side. Behind it is a wooden door that looks far too thick for them to chop through.

"How do we get in?" she asks.

Still covering its mouth, the brownie jabs its finger toward the north side of the castle. Morgana walks around but sees no entrance – only solid stone, ancient but sturdy, glimpsed between clumps of ivy. The brownie's wings carry it to a cluster of vines that seems dense and impenetrable. It pulls at the vines, and – at Morgana's gesture – the fox, hedgehog, and badger hurry to its side to help. The badger sweeps most of the vegetation aside with a slash of his claws, revealing a jagged hole swirling with dust motes.

"Straight through there," the brownie says, "and you shall meet my queen. But, seein' as you been so kind to me, I feel duty-bound to warn you—"

Morgana silences the brownie with a swipe of the iron blade across its throat. The ugly thing drops to the ground, choking and gasping as life drains from it.

"I pledged to set you free," Morgana says, wiping its green blood on ivy leaves, "and so I have. Back to the underworld from whence you crawled."

"You are wonderfully terribly murderously kind," the hedgehog whimpers.

Morgana sheathes her knife and ducks under the crumbling stone. The fox slinks ahead of her and sniffs his way through a narrow tunnel. After several minutes of feeling along dank walls and stumbling over uneven ground, Morgana enters the remains of what must have been the great hall. Half the ceiling has collapsed, revealing large swaths of gray sky.

"This might not be entirely unbearable," Morgana says, sweeping her gaze around.

"W-what mightn't?" asks the hedgehog.

"Exile. The castle needs repair, but it seems salvageable with hard work." A look passes between the fox, hedgehog, and badger; she chooses to ignore it. "When I was raised in Avalon, I wasn't afraid of hardship and struggle. But after finding my half-brother – foolishly misreading his guilt for generosity and his scheming deception as loving embrace – I've grown soft. Even spoiled, one might say."

She steals another glance at her escorts. Their faces, wisely, reveal no emotion. "I have the power to command the animals, yet I let Arthur's drooling knights chase me away from what should be my birthright. And for what?"

"For having compassion, my queen," the fox says. "For telling bitter truths to a world that feeds ravenously on lies."

Morgana feels a tremble at her chin – a welling in her throat, with a salty sting at her eyes – and she forces all of it back with a mighty breath. No tears. Not now. "Compared to that kingdom of decadence and rot, this place shall be a respite."

A high-pitched scream fills the hall, scathing their ears. It rattles in Morgana's skull like church bells clanging an inch above her head. She flinches as if slapped and can't get her hands over her ears fast enough.

An apparition of a hooded maiden shimmers into view, just below what remains of the ceiling. Her eyes are red and shining, her face twisted with rage, her robe flowing behind her until it vanishes into the walls.

A banshee.

As a child, Morgana was warned that their ghostly wails can warp minds, driving stout men to suicide for the relief of silence. She's suspicious of this spirit – but if she's wrong, the punishment will be horrifying.

As the animals writhe in agony on the floor, Morgana withdraws a trembling hand from one ear – flinching at the pain, like a blade is twisting into her head – and lifts a chain from beneath her collar. She closes her hand around a silver medallion etched with a Vesica Piscis. In the center ellipse is a crystal not of this world – said to have been plucked from the eye of a demon – its red the color of fresh blood. She takes a quick breath to steady her nerves, then utters an incantation. The crystal glows brighter, until her fist seems to be engulfed in hellfire.

The banshee's scream crescendos to a level that would shatter glass if any were left in the windows. Then it ceases abruptly, leaving behind a deafening silence as the ghostly maiden dissolves like morning mist.

"H-how did you do that, Milady?" the hedgehog asks.

"It wasn't a real banshee," Morgana says, "or I'd have gone mad when I took my hand away. It was only a conjuration."

"Right clever girl, you are," a voice as dry as autumn leaves cackles in the darkness. "But cleverness won't save you. Leave this castle or be forever entombed within it."

"So, you are here," Morgana says. "A pleasure to meet you, Morrigan."

"*Who?*" the badger snarls, flexing his claws as he joins the fox and hedgehog in a protective circle around Morgana.

"The goddess who protects this realm from invaders. I learned of you in Avalon, where your power is greatly admired. But time trudges forward and glory fades. Christianity has forced you from the memories of all but the most devout Druids."

"I'm pleased you know of me, lass." The voice seems to slither around Morgana and her consorts. "Then you must also know it's unwise to suffer my wrath. Leave now or I'll hang your heads over my battlements."

"Not until I've taken what I came here to acquire. I am Lady Morgana le Fay, mistress of all animals, half-sister of King Arthur, and witch of Avalon."

Morgana touches the medallion around her neck, a farewell gift from her sisters. The air around her feels charged, as in a lightning storm; it crackles with the Morrigan's power. Although she is a long way from Britain, the source of her power, the medallion gives Morgana strength enough to outmatch a typical foe.

The Morrigan, however, is anything but typical.

A glow emanates from the far corner of the hall, where shapes that Morgana had overlooked as detritus begin to move. They rise, revealing pale white skulls with hollowed-out eye sockets. They wear suits of dusty armor festooned with cobwebs. Morgana recognizes old coats of arms from small fiefdoms that resisted Arthur's soldiers, the crests dying off with the families that had worn them.

"Your people have not fared well in my realm," the Morrigan hisses. "Now you shall follow them into the Otherworld."

The skeletal knights stand at attention in a single line. They raise swords, axes, and shields, few of which appear to have suffered the decomposition that afflicted their flesh and organs. Their implacable grins chill Morgana's blood.

"Destroy them," Morgana commands.

Swallowing whatever fear they might feel, her trio of warriors steel themselves for battle. Compared to the wolves and bears she could summon in Camelot, they're a scrappy fighting force, small in stature and horribly outnumbered – but they are loyal, steadfast, and fierce without equal.

As the fox, badger, and hedgehog charge into battle, Morgana rubs the ellipse crystal and murmurs a spell under her breath. But it does nothing to slow the skeletons' advance. Not for the first time, she curses her limited training.

The fox darts between the knights' legs, tripping several of them and drawing the attention of others. They swing and stab at the red blur swirling around their boots, but he's much too swift and agile to catch.

While the knights are distracted, the badger leaps into their midst and claws at their skulls, necks, and arms. Bones and armored pieces clatter across the stone floor. With no heads to guide them nor arms to wield weapons, the hobbled warriors stumble about until they crash into a wall or each other.

The smallest of the escorts and least equipped for combat, the hedgehog bounds headlong into the fray. He unsheathes his sword and swipes at skinless knees and ankles. But it's barely a dagger to them and does little more than chip bone, not even scratching armor. One warrior catches him from behind with a kick that launches the ball of fur over the heads of other skeletons. He lands hard and staggers to his feet as the knight advances swiftly on him.

The badger plows toward the hedgehog, knocking a pair of skeletons aside, then leaps up under the breast plate of the advancing knight. He thrashes its ribcage in a growling frenzy that flings bones and plate metal in all directions.

"Surrender," the Morrigan whispers at Morgana's ear, "and I'll give you a quick death. Or be flayed alive and hung from my tower as a warning to future invaders."

"I don't know if you've been counting," Morgana replies, "but you seem to have run out of dead things to fight for you."

Morgana smiles as the fox and badger reduce the last knight to a pile of bones. "The plague of Christianity has infected your followers. Even the Druids and witches who remember you are tortured until their tongues will no longer form your name. Your time is at an end, Morrigan. Your power fades like starlight crushed by the sun. It's of no use to you, so give it to me. I would return to Britain and wipe King Arthur's reign from the world. I'm the only thing that can stop him from crossing the sea and stomping your island beneath his boots."

Morgana waits for a response but receives only silence. "If you refuse, I shall return to my ships, waiting just beyond the fog, and rain soldiers down on your shores. Enslave your people and make Ireland the hub of my empire."

The Morrigan's chortle rattles bones scattered across the floor. "I smell your feeble lies, Morgana le Fay. There's no fleet of ships, only your rickety boat that barely made it across the Celtic Sea."

The shivering bones rise off the ground and pile upon one another. Linking together, they form a skeletal mass that towers over Morgana, nearly scraping the ceiling. A dozen skulls assemble into a giant face that opens its maw to expose hundreds of gnashing teeth. Six arms unfurl from each side, clacking long fingers made from thigh bones.

The Morrigan's voice emanates from the writhing bone-mass: "And if it's my power you seek, it'll never be gifted. You'll have to take it – if you can."

Growling, the fox lunges. Snarling, the badger charges. Barking, the hedgehog races.

The first blow drops from above – a boulder-sized fist smashes the badger with a thud that shakes the castle walls. The hedgehog is fortunate to be swatted aside with a backhand, sending him tumbling toward the hole from which they entered. He rights himself and looks over in time to see the fox's tail stabbed by a 'claw' – a rust-tinted spear pierces the stone floor and pins the creature in place. The hedgehog flees through the opening before he sees what falling axeblades do to his comrade.

The melee is over before it's hardly begun. Stunned, Morgana gawps at her fallen escorts. *Mere servants, nothing more*, a voice inside her insists. The icy fist gripping her heart counters that they *were* more – they were her faithful companions, the only beings in the world she could trust any longer. But now isn't the time to mourn.

Morgana stands alone in the shadow of the lumbering beast. It draws toward her on clattering legs, lifting itself higher until its ring of skulls peaks above the collapsed ceiling. Dozens of green eyes flare at her.

She barely turns to run before the first hand smacks her side. Morgana bounces off a pillar and slides into a pile of armor. The ache in her ribs makes every inward breath agony, but Morgana forces pain from her mind to focus on survival. She snatches a sword from the wreckage and spins, raising it above her shoulder to strike.

But the Morrigan anticipates her move, and counters with two arms swinging together from opposite sides. The bone-hands clap against Morgana, knocking the air from her lungs and sending the sword whirling from her grasp.

Morgana collapses, fighting for air. She caresses her medallion but hasn't enough breath or time for a healing incantation. She coughs up blood and slumps over the floor, wielding what remains of her strength to choke back a sob.

"You're right," she gasps with agonizing effort. "I have no army. No power. I'm a lowly witch who dreamt she could be queen. And believed her half-brother's promises of family and fidelity. Abandoned my sisters in Avalon to become part of his court. I was a fool, Morrigan, and I deserved to be cast out."

The skeletal mass stomps the ground by her head. Morgana doesn't look up at it, only stares at the blood pooling beneath her, pelted by her tears. She tenses her body, bracing for the crushing impact.

She waits, holding her breath.

After a long silence, the Morrigan's voice booms: "Why were you banished?"

"I found his beloved wife, Guinevere, in the arms of his most faithful knight. Tried to warn Arthur. Feared they'd betray him. Steal the crown of Camelot for Lancelot's head." Despite her pain, a bitter laugh shakes her shoulders. "And what was my reward for exposing this torrid affair?"

"Blame." The Morrigan's voice is softer now, almost mournful. "Accused of plotting against your queen. Besmirching the honor of Arthur's knights."

"Worse. He charged me with masterminding the affair. As if I'd pervert the magic of Avalon to lure Guinevere into Lancelot's bed. Even now, I've no doubt the penitent lovers resume their carnal liaisons, but with greater care and secrecy, while I am banished to this accursed land."

The bone-mass sways unsteadily. Morgana curls her whole body and squeezes her eyes shut, expecting it to topple forward and pulverize her.

Instead, the bones tumble backwards, crashing and breaking against the floor. She opens her eyes and sees the silhouette of a naked woman, glowing luminous green.

"I recognize your pain," the Morrigan says. "I, too, know the sting of betrayal. Dagda, father of the gods, promised to appoint me the ruler of the Otherworld on the feast of Samhain. Instead, he gave the throne to the Welsh king, Arawn. And when I dared express my wrath, Dagda drove me from my cave in Cruachan. Separated me from my followers and forced me to hide like an animal."

A grim smile plays at Morgana's lips. "Why do we trust the men who would hurt us most? We sharpen the sword that carves out our own hearts."

The Morrigan stretches toward Morgana. She flinches, expecting to be struck for suggesting anyone could harm the Morrigan. Instead, the spectral hand reaches past Morgana's throat and caresses her medallion. "I recognize the symbol of Avalon," she says. "Though it's a distant land, I'm aware of its power. But Avalon's magic is healing. Mine is darkness. You command the animals, Lady Morgana. I command death itself."

The crystal glows again – not red this time, but emerald. Pain leaves Morgana's wounds and strength fills her muscles. She rises on sturdy legs and breathes deeply.

"You're no longer a lady of the court," the Morrigan says, "and this gown doesn't suit a warrior."

Chainmail and plate armor float toward Morgana, even as her filthy, sopping dress falls away in tatters. She holds out her arms and lets the armor fold over her.

"Aye, this'll do until you find a smith to forge a suit that befits a witch queen," the Morrigan says. "Go, take your revenge. Turn the imagined glories of men into the triumph of the women who suffered for it."

As the Morrigan moves away, the medallion continues to gleam with her energy. But the Morrigan herself has a dimmer glow, as though she's fading.

"What will become of you?" Morgana says, tucking a spiked helmet under her arm.

"I'll rest for a bit. Let the old beliefs wriggle up through the crust of Christianity like a lily sprouting from a charred battlefield. One day, my believers will return, and I'll rise with them."

Morgana opens her mouth to express gratitude, but the words don't form. She bows deeply to the Morrigan, then leaves the castle through the hole.

Outside, the hedgehog sits on a log, wringing his paws. His eyes widen with shock at the sight of Morgana. "Milady, you… you're alive."

"Come," she tells him. "We've an arduous journey ahead of us."

"Would you have me at your side, even after I fled so cowardly?"

"If you'd stayed to fight, you'd have died like the others." She raises a hand and, with a mere thought, causes the briars to curl away from her, leaving an opening to walk through. No more crawling on her knees. "I hope we find able-bodied animals in this thicket, or it'll be an excruciating voyage to Britain."

"How will you face King Arthur and his army?"

"I'll raise the revenants of soldiers slain by Arthur's own hand," Morgana says, "and lead them against him. As he lies bloody and broken, it will be my exquisite pleasure to rip Excalibur from his grasp."

Morgana pauses to cast a glance at an upper window of the castle, filled with a faint green silhouette. "And when a queen sits on the throne of Camelot, surrounded by her witches, then the world will look very different, indeed."

No Need for the Green Knight
Courtney Danielson

Sometimes, on the darkest nights, Morgane could see colors swirl in the night sky. Tonight was no exception. She touched the crescent tattoo on her brow that marked her a Priestess of Avalon, and the lights seemed to jump with excitement. She laid on her back on the cool grass of Avalon, enjoying the rare spectacle. The half-crescent tattoo on her forehead burned, like the gods were communicating with her. It often did on these lonely nights after her training was completed and she had been declared a fully actualized priestess of Avalon – though she never heard of anyone else having the same experience.

She had only told anyone about the lights once, when a priestess of Avalon had asked her if she ever saw anything odd. Morgane had answered her, and their small dining hall filled with a familiar tension. Her stepfather, Uther Pendragon, spit on the ground before declaring that it was "because she has that fae blood in her. Look at her skin!" He hadn't been named king yet, but that didn't stop him from acting like a tyrant.

So, Morgane kept her mouth shut, even as they dragged her to Avalon. Arthur screamed in their mother's arms, confused and probably about to be sent off himself, but Morgane kept her back straight and her head forward. Their cousin Gwaine had been visiting that season. He watched her go too. She dared one glance back at him, his complexion the same soft brown as hers, and nodded. She held the memory in her head through the last four years of training. When she lost herself to the work, there was Gwaine, in her mind, sending her his quiet strength through their 'fae blood'.

The colors begin to fade, rousing Morgane from her reverie. The mist surrounding the little island rose, blocking out the stars and their troupe of dancing colors.

"Morgane... Aggh." A familiar voice called through the distance. "Morgane, please."

"Gwaine?" She sat up, searching through the night.

"Please, help." His voice penetrated the mists, a feat only accomplished by the high priestesses and the gods. "Come to the house of Morgause, before it's too late."

"Are you hurt?" She shut her eyes against the mists, settling herself into a loose meditation. She pushed her consciousness into the thickening fog. "Gwaine, what's happened? We're preparing for Beltane. Avalon won't let me go."

"You must."

The world collapsed on itself, and the colors began their frolic anew. Morgane saw them for a second before everything went black.

* * *

Morgane awoke to the sun streaming through the window of her dormitory. Three sets of eyes peered out at her. She groaned.

"You need to tell us what happened," Blanchefleur crossed her arms, her glare pinning Morgane in place.

"Uh, I'm not sure. I think I need to go to Orkney." Morgane rubbed her temples.

"That's not good enough, especially with Beltane this moon." Blanchfleur screeched. "Answers. Now."

"Oh, I'm sorry, I didn't realize this was an abbey," Morgane spat. The girl had been annoying before, but since she got her crescent mark, Blanchefleur had become insufferable.

Blanchefleur raised her hand in response. High Priestess Sunniva put a tanned, wrinkled hand over Blanchefleur's.

"She's right; that's not how we operate here, even if her delivery was less than to be desired." Sunniva threw a disappointed glance at Morgane before turning back to Blanchefleur. "Maybe, it's best if you sit this one out."

"But the goddess..."

"The goddess has other plans, it would seem." Aelfwynn, who had remained silent until now, lifted Morgane's hands to show to the priestesses. An elaborate stain sprawled across her hand and tapered at her wrist. It formed the braces of a delicate branch of applewood. Tiny buds littered the limb.

There was a collective gasp from everyone, including Morgane. There was no disputing

"It can't be...it's not fair." Blanchefleur slammed the door behind her. Morgane smirked; it seemed Nimue had chosen her.

"What did you see, child?" The high priestess sat on the edge of Morgane's bed.

"I didn't see anything," Morgane confessed. "But I heard my cousin, Gwaine." The memory flooded back to her. "He's in trouble. I have to go." She tossed the blankets off her.

"Shhh shh, easy, child." Sunniva laid a gentle hand on her shoulder. "It's likely he is unharmed. Visions in Avalon don't always align with our notion of time."

"Still, I need to journey to the house of my Aunt Morgause."

The priestesses exchanged pointed glances with one another.

"If you go now," Aelfwynn said, "you'll miss your initiation rights and Beltane. You were chosen to be this sun cycle's Mother Goddess. It is a great honor, one that may give another daughter to our dying coven."

"I know."

Gwaine's voice ricocheted in her mind. *You must.*

"I'll pass this honor to another. I *have* to go."

"Perhaps we let the Lady of the Lake decide," Sunniva said. "She gave you her applewood, after all. If the boat moves you across the lake we will grant you this sabbatical."

"Thank you, High Priestess." Relief flushed through Morgane's body. "I'll start to pack."

* * *

The three priestesses watched her depart on the long wooden boat. The usual oarsman stood on the shores with the three priestesses. None of them seemed happy, like fate had foiled some secret plan hatched not by the goddess, but by them alone. Guilt threatened to turn Morgane's eyes back to Avalon; the sensation tampered when the memory of Gwaine's pained groan ricocheted back to her.

The mists enveloped her as the boat steered out of view from the island. She breathed in the thick air like it was an old friend and relaxed against the wooden vessel. She couldn't quite believe the turn of events – though, if she was being honest with herself, she was relieved to be free of Beltane. The spring ceremonies celebrated the warming air with a mixture of fire, hunting, and sex. Some part of Morgane always knew she'd be picked to play the Mother Goddess – picked to lose her virginity in the hunt. While she had never admitted, she always dreaded the spring, wondering if this change of the seasons would be 'the one'.

"I've seen that story." A wispy voice broke out from the mist. "The one where you stay."

Morgane leapt to attention. "Who's there?" She picked up her staff.

"Down here, silly," the voice echoed from the edge of the boat. A girl materialized out of the water. Waves turned into soft chestnut curls, and the foam transformed into an immaculate white dress.

"Goddess," Morgane breathed and scrambled to pull the girl onto the vessel. The indigo ink in her applewood tattoo shimmered when she touched the girl. The surprise of it almost made her let go, but she gritted her teeth and yanked The Lady of the Lake onto the ship.

"I prefer enchantress extraordinaire, personally, but you can call me Nimue. I see you got my message." She gestured to Morgane's hand tattoo. "I can remove it if you like. I just had to let *them* let you go. You were in for a really shitty month otherwise."

"You speak…differently from what I expected."

"Yeah, well, see, the thing about being an ancient goddess is that time doesn't actually exist like you think it does. Sometimes the diction, connotation…the syntax, if you will, well, it gets jumbled in my head, so you're gonna have to cut me some slack on the whole talking thing."

"I suppose," Morgane said. "What did you mean, I was 'in for a shitty month'?"

"Ahh, how many weeks until Beltane?"

"Three…"

"Perfect, Beltane. Beltane was about to be a real bummer for you. Those priestesses think they're clever. I just couldn't watch that storyline unfold again, you know?"

"No."

"Okay, let's reset, because we are getting nowhere. Man, Zeus may have been right on the whole importance of being vague and mysterious thing." Nimue waved her hand in the air like she was erasing an invisible tally.

"Zeus?" Morgane asked.

"Ahh, you might know him as Jupiter. Anyway, it's not important. Here's what you need to know. If you had stayed in Avalon, your life was going to be completely run for you. Like you might have *thought* you had a say, but you didn't. Now you do. And don't worry, Arthur's still King, especially after Uther, ya know." The goddess made a slashing motion across her neck with her finger.

"Arthur's the king?"

"Yeah, but this isn't his story." The goddess clasped Morgane's hands. "It's your story now. Be wild, selfish, be anything you want, but be you." The mist thinned around them. "Shit, that's my cue. Please, sweet girl, go on this journey, heal Gwaine, and when it's time to make a big decision, don't think about anything but your own happiness." Nimue turned from Morgane and dispelled with the thinning fog.

"Wait! Gwaine! Is he hurt?" Morgane called out as the last of the mist evaporated. Her only answer was the crash of the waves against the wood of the little boat. A small traveling party waited for her to dock. With a deep breath, Morgane stepped foot onto the shores of Somerset for the first time in four years.

* * *

Morgane stopped at court first – though Arthur was not at Camelot. Igraine, their mother, sent her to Orkney with a horse, a guard and not much else. Morgane scribbled a quick note to her aunt and uncle letting them know she'd be arriving after a week's worth of travel.

Gwaine and a small party of servants waited for her at the border of his parents' province. He was a man now, with his sword at his hip and a respectable amount of light leather armor. She waved to him as they approached the shore. Unexpected joy warmed her body against the cool air. His face broke out into a breathtaking smile when he recognized her. Her heart squeezed. She slipped off her horse and ran toward him, bunching the loose priestess robes in her hands. She launched herself at Gwaine, who caught her mid-air and spun her around. She ignored the hard grooves of his muscles pushing against her soft body.

"I've missed you." He held her close for a beat longer than he should have, but no one around them seemed to notice.

"I've missed you, too." She beamed up at him. His tanned face had grown handsome, and his hazel eyes were sharp and clear. The memory of his agonized scream shattered their reunion. "Wait, are you hurt?" She gripped his arm and examined the man before her.

"Why would I be hurt?" He tilted her face so that she met his eyes again. "My favorite person just returned home. Come, Mother is waiting for us. Maybe you can talk some sense into her."

"What's wrong with Morgause?" Morgane asked and accepted her small bag of belongings from a sailor.

"She wants me to marry a princess, but I've decided not to." He took her sack and slipped it into his saddle bag before mounting his horse. "Unfortunately, my decision defies her and the king. I'm hoping you're the distraction they need to forget about all this nonsense."

"Oh." She pushed a traitorous thought away. "Arthur's here?" She grabbed his hand and mounted the horse.

"Wow, I'm impressed, priestess." Gwaine winked at her. "News travels to Avalon fast."

"A...friend told me."

"Ah, well, unfortunately no. Arthur was called away for some Beltane celebration. He had to act as a Hunter God, so that the people of the old ways still recognized him as king... or something like that. I'm not really sure. Neither Christianity nor the Goddess seem like they're worth the time nor power we attribute to them."

A pit formed in Morgane's stomach. *Those priestesses think they're clever.* Nimue's words echoed back to her, a spiritual slap in the face.

"Morgane? Hey." Gwaine touched her face, pulling her back to reality.

"Sorry, what were you saying?" She smiled, shoving down her realization.

"I said there is a local coven that heard you were on your way. They want to host Beltane for you. Probably won't be as big as Avalon's but it's close, I think… Are you sure you're okay?"

"Of course, I'd love to meet them!" she said, and after a tick added, "I'm just happy to be away from Avalon."

* * *

Morgause embraced her in the cold way her aunt interacted with everyone. They sat at the long table, waiting for Lot and the boys to make their way to the dining hall. The servants arranged the table under their mistress's keen eye. A silent moment later the oak doors swung open and Lot and his sons walked through. They joined the women at the table, Gwaine sliding into the seat next to Morgane.

"So what brings you to Orkney?" Lot asked in between large bites of turkey.

"Well, to be truthful, Uncle, the high priestess deemed it necessary for me to see how the followers of the old ways celebrate outside of Avalon." Morgane smiled through the lie. "Naturally, I thought of you, Uncle Lot. You and Aunt Morgause have done such a good job protecting those who cling to the Mother Goddess."

Lot seemed pleased with her answer and continued his meal. Morgane always found him rather simple. Any word of praise, even self-attributed, appeased the knave that still lingered in the King of Orkney's heart. Morgause, ever shrewd, narrowed her eyes at Morgane's response.

"Gwaine, you should introduce Morgane to your betrothed. She's a lovely girl, doesn't even care that Gwaine favors our fae ancestry. A princess in the French court, which is a fair compromise, I suppose," Morgause said.

"Compromise?" Morgane asked.

"Mother," Gwaine said, with unusual steel in his voice.

"Fine, I'll stop, but if Arthur is anything like Uther, this won't just disappear." Morgause took a slip of her wine.

"Arthur is *not* Uther and I have until after the equinox to send my answer. Which you know, Mother, will be 'no'." Gwaine gripped his fork.

"Foolish boy," Morgause laughed. "Arthur is king now, and the knights set an example for the court. You'll marry one way or another."

Gwaine slammed his silverware into the table. He kicked back his chair and stalked out of the dining hall.

Morgause turned to Morgane. "Maybe you can talk to him. He rejects the advice of the bishops, but perhaps a priestess…or better yet a beloved cousin can get through to him."

Morgane swallowed the lump of food in her throat. "I'll see what I can do." She set her utensils down and gently pulled away from the table to follow Gwaine's path. She exited the castle to find Gwaine's discarded armor at the door. She caught a glimpse of him as he marched toward the estate stables.

"Gwaine!" She scooped up her heavy dress to follow him.

"Go away, Morgane."

"Your mother is right. You'd be a fool not to make this match." Morgane stomped after him into the barn. "You still have fae blood, even if Arthur doesn't see it like Uther did. It's a generous match. What are you holding out for?" The words burned her tongue.

Gwaine's spine stiffened for a moment before he jammed a pitchfork into a large stack of hay. He lifted a large chunk into a barrel.

"She sounds like a good girl. A princess even." Morgane's tone softened. "What more could you ask for?" She touched his arm to slow his work.

"She's not you." He stabbed the pile again.

"What?" Her heart squeezed with tentative, forbidden hope.

"You heard me." He hefted another forkfull of hay.

"Gwaine."

"We were betrothed once, you know. When we were children." He slammed the pitchfork into the haystack. "It's so foolish, but I actually remember being relieved that I'd get to spend my life with my best friend. Even as a *kid*, I knew, I *saw* how rare that was."

"Gwaine, I'm a—"

"A priestess, I know," he interrupted her. "I've thought about you every day since that damned place took you away. Every. Day. And, now, what? You're back, but you're not back for me, at least not for long. God, I know how selfish I sound. But what am I supposed to do? Am I just supposed to marry a stranger? Because Arthur says so."

"He's the king now," Morgane said.

"I want the life I was promised." He spun to face her, closing the distance between them. "It's been *four years*, Morgane, four years. Yet, you walk through my mother's door, and it all snaps back into place, like you never left. Tell me, please." Anguish coated his features. "Tell me this is all in my head, that I've just made a grand idiot of myself. Stomp out this fire in my soul before it consumes me, I beg of you."

She looked into his hazel eyes. "I can't tell you that."

It was all he needed. His lips crashed into hers, slamming her into the barn wall. Her legs found their way around his waist, despite the numerous skirts between them. Gwaine's fire spread to her, transferred by the ravenous, consuming kiss. She barely registered her back hitting the barn wall. His hips pinned her there, freeing his hands to roam across her body. A warmth curled in her lower belly; the sensation of it was new and raw. A moan escaped her lips as he cupped her breast. He sealed the sound off with another hungry kiss, quieting her so they wouldn't get caught.

Gwaine held her tighter to him, like someone or something might take her away at any moment, painfully aware that this blissful moment was temporary. He broke the kiss to press his forehead against hers.

"I can't have you, but I *can* only have you," he pleaded. His eyes begged her to understand.

She did understand, but didn't say anything in response. A stray curl fell into his eyes; she pushed it back into place, behind his ear.

"Avalon stole my bride, and I refuse to take another." He eased away from her, making sure she recovered her footing before stepping away.

She watched him leave the barn, unsure of what to do next. Gwaine grumbled something just out of earshot before a little dark-haired head peeked into the barn.

"Hello, Mistress." Mordred, Morgause's youngest, beamed at her. "Liltha's here if you want to talk with her about Beltane."

She smiled at the boy who had replaced the newborn she left all those years ago. She followed him out of the barn and across the estate. A group of women sat under some trees. They all wore the soft blue robes of a priestess. Relief washed over Morgane as she and Mordred approached the group. This she could handle. Mordred ran, embracing the oldest women in their party while Morgane hiked her skirts to catch up.

"Liltha, this is my cousin Morgane. She has fae blood like you."

The old lady smiled in response. "Hello Morgane, sit, join us. We're honored to have a priestess of Avalon in our midst. You'll have to forgive our Mordred. He'll be a strong defender of the goddess one day, but, alas, today he is still only four."

The boy curled into the older woman's side and the other priestess smiled up at her.

"I'm happy to be here. Avalon is beautiful, but so isolated. I hear you're working on a Beltane celebration. I'd love to hear your plans."

"Yes," a younger woman said, clasping her hands together. "My husband is an animal during Beltane. We never miss it."

"And all you kids have birthdays in the same month," another chimed.

"Oh hush, your Tessa is just as bad! She'd go toe to toe with any man and come out on top."

"Wait. You have partners. Are you not priestesses?" A swirl of mixed emotions sank into Morgane's heart.

Liltha placed a tan hand over Morgane's. "While we respect the authority and traditions of Avalon, it's difficult to uphold the same traditions. Cerao is without a partner, because they serve as a wand-wife for one of Lot's lords, and the situation suits their preferences. The rest of us, however, take up partners if we want to. We've found a way to serve the Mother Goddess, and live the life we want to live. I think the goddess is happy with our compromise.

"I meant no disrespect," Morgaine corrected. "I've just never seen anything like this before. Morgause is among your ranks?"

"We have offered the queen a place, but she refuses. Her heart belongs to the Isle, I fear. Though she has our unwavering loyalty as she's protected our little coven all these years."

"She's different than I remember her," Morgane said. "Softer, almost like the Orkney waves have smoothed out her edges."

"Oh, she has edges a-plenty." The speaker nodded her head. "Just wait until you see her at the festival."

"Yes, Beltane! Tell me what you've got so far," Morgane said.

The ladies began to chatter.

* * *

The fires of Beltane roared in the center of a clearing that Morgane and Mordred had found at the edge of the castle grounds. Lot was skeptical at first, but the two of them wore him down until he agreed to host the rites. Morgause said nothing during their attempts, but Morgane could sense she was pleased with the outcome.

"It's beautiful." Liltha hobbled next to Morgane to watch the fires blaze. "We're glad for your help – though I'm sure Avalon puts on a better show."

"I'm glad to have been here for it. I've seen the Isle's work for countless holidays. But this? This is magical." She smiled down at the old woman.

"Now, I don't mean to pry, but why did you travel all the way to Orkney?" Litha asked.

"Nimue told me to. Well, she tricked me a bit. I thought Gwaine was hurt, so I rushed to be of aid," Morgane said, glancing at the somber knight barely sipping his ale. Their eyes met for a second before he set his drink down and began to walk over.

"Lord Gwaine has a deep wound in his heart. It's similar to yours, I think," Liltha said. "Perhaps, your work is not yet done." She patted Morgane's shoulder while she merged into the crowd.

"Hey—"

"I'm sorry—"

Their words collided, fighting to fill the space.

"I'm sorry about the barn," Gwaine said. "I know you're a priestess. I had no right to insinuate that you should give that up for me." He bowed his head.

"Are you going to marry the princess?" Morgane lifted his chin so that their eyes met.

"No," he said firmly. "I sent Arthur my response today. Maybe I'll marry later, but I don't have the stomach for it right now."

A bloom of blood rushed to Morgane's cheeks. Her relief blanked her emotions, surprising her by its strength. She intertwined her fingers into Gwaine's.

"I'll always be a servant of the Mother Goddess. She is my reason for living. That includes rituals, studying, prayer…a lot of prayer, and I even have a knack for shapeshifting and chaos magic when I put my mind to it. That *is* my life, and I'm never giving it up." She scanned his eyes, making sure her words settled around him.

"I understand that, I kno—"

She silenced him with a finger on his lips. "None of what I listed was Avalon."

He stared at her, confused. She shifted him to look at a young priestess, whose name she learned was Orva, jump over the center fire, grasping her husband's hand.

"What if there was a way we could have both worlds? Would that be enough for you?" she asked, avoiding his eyes.

"Enough?" He spun her to face him. "Morgane, that would be everything. *You are everything.*" He cupped her cheek. The pad of his thumb brushed the moon tattoo that denoted her status as a priestess of Avalon. "Would that be enough for you? Leaving the Isle?"

She smiled up at him. "I left Avalon to save you, as silly as it sounds. I'd leave it again in a heartbeat."

"Save me?"

She waved the question away. "A goddess lied to me to get me to leave, but I'm glad she did." Morgane turned to look at the celebration. "I'd never have found my home otherwise." She squeezed his hand.

"I don't think she lied to you," he whispered, pulling her closer to him, peppering each word between kisses down her neck. "You did rescue me. I can only hope to even the score." He tilted her head so he could find her lips in the firelight.

The kiss was soft and gentle but no less hungry than the one they shared in the barn. She reached up to grab his loose curls, sinking into the embrace. A wayward peek in between the breaths of their feverish kiss revealed the colors of the night sky taking up their dance once more. The gods were happy, she was happy, and the path laid out before her held a rare shimmer of hope.

For the first time, Morgane discovered what a happy ending felt like.

The Woman with the Bleeding Eye

Evan Davies

"One must beseech the Tuatha de Dannan in their own tongue," Anwen said, tracing her fingers over the crinkled parchment. "This is where the mundane notion of spell casting comes from. Commonfolk hear the ancient dialect and assume the words themselves have power... Morgana, are you listening to me?"

Morgana was not listening to her.

She sat in the far corner of the cottage, watching a moonlit stream glimmer through the darkness. In her lap, a tabby cat purred gently in its sleep, the only affection that particular cat showed anyone. It was mangy, ill-tempered, and missing most of an ear. Morgana called him Princess.

Anwen sighed and moved to close the window.

"What's a Fomorian?"

The woman froze with the shutters drawn but not latched. Even at so young an age, Morgana recognized the tension in her shoulders. She turned slowly. "Where did you hear that word?"

Morgana's eyes flicked to the leather tomes stacked above the mantlepiece, supposedly where a girl of thirteen could not reach them.

Anwen followed her pupil's gaze, perhaps noting the subtle differences in how she had arranged the volumes and where a select number of them now lay. She pursed her lips and thought about getting angry. When she was older, Morgana would realize that, in these moments, Anwen was wondering whether a punishment would do any good. "Fine," she said, with a sharp sigh. "Come here."

Princess hissed as Morgana set him down.

"I'm going to tell you this exactly once," she said, closing the book of elder script and steepling her fingers, "and only because you'd figure it out on your own if I didn't, and that would be worse... The Fomorians were the enemies of the first people."

"But I thought the Tuatha de Dannan couldn't be killed."

"They can't," Anwen said, slipping into the sing-song rhythm of her daily instruction, "nor could the Fomorians. Their battle lasted more years than history remembers. Champions rose and fell, and in falling, were not killed but crippled, rendered down to a lesser state of being."

Morgana's brow furrowed. "They left the world, you mean? Went beyond the pale like Lugh and the Dagda?"

"No. The Dannan were creatures of the air, their souls alighted from the world, but the Fomorians were... *are*... of the earth. They lie beneath the mountains and the seas, not quite living, but a long way from dead."

"Do they bargain with us, like the Dannan?"

Anwen's lip twitched, and she pulled back slightly. "Some try, but they are wicked creatures, Morgana. Though their words may be coated in honey, the taste in their mouths is for blood."

"I don't understand."

Anwen ran a hand down her face and grimaced. She did not want to continue, but to stop now would be worse than saying nothing to begin with. "You of course understand that the Dannan, being beyond this world, yearn for its peculiarities."

Morgana nodded.

"That is why you might offer them a piece of wormwood, or eye of newt, in exchange for some minor spell craft. The greater the spell, the larger the offering. Even with benevolent spirits, it can get out of hand. A chunk of birchbark might buy you a candle flame from Brigid, whose domain is the hearth, but ask for a bonfire, and you could wipe out a forest."

"Only if you were careless in your wording."

"Or open-ended, that is true, but what if the being in question was not concerned with trees?"

A cold hand crept its way down Morgana's spine, a chill both nerve-wracking and alluring. "What do the Fomorians demand?"

Anwen's gaze drifted to the fire crackling softly within the chimney. Morgana supposed she was thinking about her pupil's entwining ceremony, the first strands in a thread of worry that would span the next five years. "They are scarce heard from these days, but the most fearsome of them, the first to rise and the last to fall, was Balor of the Bleeding Eye. I will not speak his name again. When he reaches out to our kind... it is always for flesh and bone."

"Flesh and bone," Morgana whispered.

"To rebuild his mangled body," Anwen spoke softly, her expression slipping into the long ago and far away, "and he does not sell his power cheaply."

"But he is powerful?"

There was a thin scratch as Anwen dug her nails into the table. "You are not the first of our kind to think thusly," she said, with a look Morgana would remember, for it was the first time her teacher's anger had nothing to do with instruction. "There were once far more of us than there are now."

* * *

Five years later, Morgana thought back on that conversation as she stared into the depths of a witchwood fire. Amidst the shadows of the deep forest, a dozen pairs of eyes shone bright as stars, the faces that held them obscured by heavy cowls.

"What do you see?" Anwen asked, her voice an anxious whisper. Morgana was taking longer than she ought have.

She licked her lips and said, "A stone well beneath a broad tree."

Anwen's sigh of relief was well hidden. "Dian Cecht. This is good, I think. We've gone a long time without a skilled healer in the order."

Morgana said nothing, for what she had truly seen within the flames was a single, bleeding eye.

* * *

Morgana wrinkled her nose as the summer sun bore down on her, just warm enough for a sheen of sweat to prickle her forehead. She drew a pair of dandelions from her pocket and whispered something in the old tongue. The flowers vanished from her grasp, and a cool breeze came snickering across the hillside. She let out a contented yawn and shifted her hips to take better advantage of the soft grass.

She was in the clutches of a late afternoon doze when the cottage door creaked open. The sound of approaching footsteps roused her just slightly, the tip of a boot in her ribs decidedly more so. Morgana yelped and sat upright. The wind stopped sifting through the grasses.

"I did not teach you those words so you could barter for idle comforts," Anwen said, folding her arms.

Morgana rubbed her side and peered up at the woman. The sunlight brought out the gray around her temples. "I've done my rounds," she muttered, without much conviction.

"And done them *shoddily*," Anwen said, looking down the slope to the river. "I've just had word the Farrel boy's tooth is still bothering him."

"Mouths are hard," Morgana said, feeling a familiar pit widen within her stomach. It only widened these days, never shrunk. "It's hard to get Dian Cecht to understand what I'm asking for."

"It shouldn't be."

The discomfort in Morgana's stomach turned sharp. She looked at her mentor, seeking what, she did not know. She found a blank expression and an empty stare and not a shred of feeling in either of them.

"Go fetch us some water." Anwen managed to speak without breaking the silence. "We'll go through your lessons again."

Morgana didn't dare let her disappointment show. There would be no more use in that than in telling Anwen the truth. She trudged up the slope for the bucket and trudged back down to the stream.

She was sweating by the time she reached the bottom. She dared not do anything about that either.

She'd already stooped down toward the water, when she recognized the coppery tinge to the air. There was a faint splash as she dropped the bucket into the current. "Anwen!" she cried, sloshing hurriedly through the shallows. "There's a man in the river!"

* * *

It took both of them to drag him from the reeds. His mud-streaked armor clattered softly as they lay him down. Morgana knelt and undid the straps of his helmet. The face beneath was young and fair, with eyes that stared vacantly into the open sky. She felt for a pulse, held her breath until she found one. "He's alive."

Standing above her, Anwen grunted. "A wonder he didn't drown."

The copper smell was more pungent now. It didn't take her long to find its source. Gelatinous blood seeped from the edges of his breastplate. "We need to get him inside."

When Anwen did not reply, Morgana turned to look at her. The woman was staring upstream, where the river's course ambled out of sight. "Perhaps we should not interfere."

"I can help him."

"Can you?"

The two words struck Morgana more viciously than a boot to the ribs ever could. She clamped her jaw shut and glowered. "Don't tell me you're afraid of a wounded man."

THE WOMAN WITH THE BLEEDING EYE

Anwen, gaze still fixed upon the river bend, shook her head. "It's not so much the man as what comes after him."

A few heartbeats later, the little stream went from clear blue to crimson.

* * *

Morgana wiped a trickle of drool from her patient's mouth and grimaced. She'd always thought people looked foolish when they were sick, probably another reason she wasn't cut out to be a healer. The man lay, slack-jawed and snoring, upon a straw mattress at the back of their cottage. His sword and armor were piled up in the corner. Morgana had cleaned and dressed his wound, a long, thin slit running from his abdomen to his bellybutton.

She slumped back into her chair with a huff, glanced at the potted sapling at the foot of his bed. The little tree's leaves were already starting to shrivel. It was a reliable method. Dian Cecht siphoned the vitality from the plant, and in return, eased the wounds of the patient. The best healers could cut recovery time in half by such means. The most Morgana had ever managed was to ward off gangrene.

Anwen had made a snide comment about that before leaving for the village. There, she would procure supplies for a planned journey upriver, seeking news of the battle in which this man had played a part. The cottage felt empty without her, and the unconscious soldier was making for poor company.

A high-pitched squeak pierced the silence, and she turned to find Princess clutching a mouse between his jaws. "Oh, for the love of... drop it," she said, reaching for a broom. Princess abandoned his prize and attacked the bristles like the old adversaries they were.

When the mouse failed to make its escape, Morgana scooped it into one of Anwen's glass jars. It scrabbled futilely at the walls for a moment, before lying down and accepting its fate. Placing the jar upon the table, Morgana got a better look at the puncture marks in its stomach. Poor thing wouldn't outlive the hour.

She looked from the mouse to the injured soldier to the wilting tree doing scarce little to aid him and felt a familiar chill tickle her nerves. She drew an uneasy breath. Could she...

Morgana's brow furrowed before the thought was even finished, and she cleared her mind in the way she had been taught. "Balor," she said, in the old tongue. "I offer you flesh and bone from a wounded animal, in exchange for the health of this man."

The mouse let out a screech and curled in upon itself. Blood began leaking from every orifice in its body, splattering the walls of the jar as it writhed. Morgana stood up so sharply, her chair clattered to the floor. She stumbled back, covering her ears against the crunching of bone, closing her eyes to the desperate, dying spasms. When it finally stopped, there was nothing in the jar but blood and mangled fur.

Morgana ran to the wash basin and vomited.

It was a great effort to approach the bedside once more. She felt cold and cruel, and worst of all, a disappointment.

She nearly choked when she saw the man's wound, or rather, the lack of it. Dried blood still clung to his bandages, but the gash itself had vanished. A jagged scar, already faded, was the only indication he had been injured at all. Not even in the stories of the elder days had one of the fae folk healed such a grave wound so quickly. Morgana felt an unfamiliar lightness, as if the eternal pit in her stomach were finally drawing shut. Her eyes stung when she imagined what Anwen would say.

"MRRRAAAWRRR."

Her relieved breath shuddered and died.

* * *

"He was an old cat, Morgana. He lived a good life."

Morgana sat on the steps, legs huddled tightly against her chest.

Old wood creaked as Anwen took a seat beside her, preparations for the journey momentarily forgotten. Morgana didn't look at her, couldn't. "I know I've been, or rather I haven't been…" Anwen sighed and looked to the horizon. "It's easy to forget how much pressure we put on you."

Morgana blinked tears from her eyes and said nothing.

"I've been a wretched mentor."

That brought Morgana's gaze snapping upward.

Anwen showed her a sad smile. "I feared for your place in the order, and that fear, having nowhere to go, became…" She closed her eyes and shook her head. "I was never disappointed in you. I never could be."

There was no blinking away the tears that came then. Fearing the truth might be read from those tears, Morgana threw her arms around Anwen and buried her face in the woman's cloak.

"Oh, my poor girl," she said, putting a hand on the back of Morgana's head. "Your greatest breakthrough with Dian Cecht, and I wasn't even here to see it."

Morgana shut her eyes tighter and sobbed.

"I know it's not fair." Anwen pulled away and lowered her hand to Morgana's cheek. "But I need you to look after the place while I'm gone. If that boy comes around, send him on his way. We've done as much for him as decency demands, and if he was on the losing side of that battle…" Her gaze drifted to the ambling waters of the creek, no longer crimson, but not quite clear. "Can you be strong for a few more days?"

She swallowed a lump and nodded.

"Thank you," Anwen said, rising with a shudder and a groan. "No lessons when I get back. We can sit in the grass and enjoy the sun and swap stories about all the times I nearly chased out that wretched cat."

Morgana let out a strangled laugh despite it all. "Anwen," she said, as the woman set foot into her stirrup. The words fled when her mentor glanced back at her. There was a fondness in those wrinkled eyes that she dared not poison with the truth. "Ride safe."

* * *

The knock came just after midnight. It was soft enough that one wouldn't have thought it belonged to three armed men, but there they stood. "We're looking for someone," said the largest and baldest and meanest of them.

THE WOMAN WITH THE BLEEDING EYE

Morgana closed the door behind her. "That's no business of mine."

The man glanced at the shuttered windows, torchlight deepening the scars of his face. "Folks in town say you took a fella into this house… fella wearing armor."

"And if I did?"

"Why don't we just go and see him?" He moved for the door.

Morgana stuck a boot into his path. "No one's setting foot in this house while I'm alive." She'd heard Anwen say that to a pack of brigands, some years ago. It sounded weaker, coming from her.

The bald man raised an eyebrow. "Think you could stop us?"

"You're deserters," Morgana said, licking her lips. "Raise a hand against one of the folk, you won't make it ten leagues before someone gives you up."

The two goons glanced nervously at the trees, but the man himself did not falter. "Times are changing," he said, though he did step back off the porch. "The fae folk ain't as beloved as they used to be. King Arthur says you practice dark magic. Last I heard, he was offering a reward for your heads."

"Who the hell is King Arthur?"

"Fella set on ruling all Briton."

Morgana shrugged, a performative gesture if ever there was one. "Seems far-fetched."

"Not to the man inside your cottage."

Every muscle in Morgana's body tightened. Her neck tingled, as if there were hostile eyes behind her as well as before.

The scarred man must have seen something in her reaction because he nodded gravely and said, "Not too late to let us in."

She almost did. The only thing that stopped her was the thought of another shameful secret, buried away where Anwen couldn't find it.

* * *

The air inside the cottage was cold. The deserters' torches had left the night darker than they found it. Slits of moonlight revealed glimpses of the injured soldier, glinted softly off his discarded armor. Morgana crept toward the bedside, every footstep a cacophony of creaking floorboards. She looked down upon his expressionless features, listened to the dull rhythm of his breathing.

Her chest tightening around every movement, she bent down and lifted his sword from the heaped-up belongings. Her hands shook as she drew it a quarter inch from the scabbard. Coagulated blood clung to its edges. She glanced once more at the wounded man.

She found a bloodshot eye staring back at her.

Morgana gasped and reeled away from the bedside. The corner of a table dug into her ribs. Her heart shuddered as a second pair of footsteps met the floor. She pulled the bloody sword free of its sheath and pressed her back to the wall, panting heavily.

The cottage was silent, save its usual nighttime groaning, or perhaps that was something else entirely.

She remembered the birchbark in her pocket and whispered an exchange. A candle on the kitchen table flickered to life.

The soldier froze halfway across the room. He straightened out of his hunched posture and stared. The candle cast darkness

THE WOMAN WITH THE BLEEDING EYE

across everything save his eyes, those darted from Morgana to the blade to the door. The ceiling shuddered beneath a night wind as he weighed his options.

Morgana prayed he would make his choice quickly. The thrumming tension was already fading from her body, the sword beginning to weigh heavily upon her arms. She drew a breath and lifted the weapon as high as she could without trembling.

The man cast a wide glance around the room, took in the glass beakers and the black cauldron, the bottled components and the ancient tomes. There was no hiding what kind of place this was. There had never been any need to.

He took a hard step forward.

When Morgana didn't flinch, he flung the door open and disappeared.

* * *

As soon as she was sure the man would not return, Morgana threw a piece of dry witchwood onto the fire and watched a bleeding eye open in the embers.

"Men are coming to kill me," she said, in the old tongue.

"I count six men, gathering on the edge of the woods." Morgana did not at first recognize Balor's voice. The hearing of it was so natural, she nearly mistook it for her own thoughts. "You could flee."

She shook her head. She would not have Anwen return to find her cottage burned, not when she had trusted Morgana with its protection. "I'm prepared to give you… a finger."

The fire rumbled like a dead man's laughter. "You think a finger worth a life?"

"A hand, then."

The bleeding eye contorted in mirth. "Still only five fingers, and not one of them worth a life. For six lives, I'll be wanting... a heart."

Morgana's hand drifted to her collarbone, felt for the thrum of her heartbeat. It was steadier now than it ought have been, steadier than it had felt for a long time. She glanced at the blood-smeared sword she'd used to bar the door. Perhaps this was what she had been meant for. It certainly suited her better than healing.

"Deal."

* * *

Morgana waited in front of the little cottage as the morning shadows lengthened. Six men, knights she supposed, emerged at the far end of the clearing, their armor glittering in the golden sunrise. They formed a half circle as they advanced. One moved ahead of the rest and took off his helmet. It was the young man she had pulled from the river. This time, his face was lit brightly by the sun, and only his eyes were dark.

Morgana hefted her sword as he approached, cast a final, fleeting glance at the fading refuge of the night. "Flesh and bone," she shouted, raising the sword aloft, "for Balor of the Bleeding Eye!"

When she leveled the weapon once more, its blade crackled with blood-red flame, and its weight did not trouble her at all.

THE WOMAN WITH THE BLEEDING EYE

The young man took a step back.

Before he could take another, Morgana was on him. He raised his shield, but the flaming sword cleaved straight through it, melting armor, sizzling flesh. He fell to the ground in pieces that rattled like pots knocked from the stove. His comrades fared no better.

* * *

Morgana awoke with a shudder and a jolt. She sat up sharply, drew a heaving breath and clawed at her chest. The pulse above her collar bone was frantic but present. She looked around, recognized the wide-eyed face of Tomas Farrel from the village.

"Sorry to shake you, miss." His voice lisped around the rotting tooth Morgana had never quite cured. "Only I came with news and saw…"

She followed his gaze to the chunks of metal-plated gore strewn across the clearing. "News," she said, pressing a palm to her forehead. "What news?"

He swallowed nervously. "It's Anwen. She was just back into town when she… collapsed. Never seen nothing like it, not even when Old Mathers keeled over. It was like her heart just—"

"Vanished." Morgana lay back down and closed her eyes.

* * *

Morgana sat alone for a long time, twisting her sword around in the dirt. When the blood spread to her toes, she looked up. Amidst the viscera, a lone eye rolled over like a loose marble.

"My heart not good enough for you?" she asked.

"Too good." Though the eye had no lids, she sensed Balor's wink. "You'll need it."

Morgana glanced aside. She should have hated the wretched creature, but she didn't. It was in the Fomorian's nature to be wicked. No one could say she hadn't been warned.

She looked to the heaps of melted armor and felt her lip curl. There, she found the hatred when she searched for it. "Why couldn't he just leave us alone?"

"You have power," Balor said. "That threatens him."

"I hadn't even heard of him."

She felt the vile grin as keenly as if it were her own. "And now?"

* * *

"Morgana!" Tomas came running down the dirt road after her. He cast a dubious glance at a sword and a horse that were not hers. "Where are you going?"

"I don't know," she said, gathering the reins into her hand. "Wherever I need to go to find a man named Arthur."

To Cut the Rot
Caroline Fleischauer

I was the only one who saw my father return. The moon was a sliver, thin and curved like the pared clipping of a fingernail. There was a heaviness in the air, despite the oncoming cool that signaled the imminent changing of the seasons. In the great bed behind me, my two sisters slept, their hair fanned on the pillows beneath their heads, chestnut and silvery blonde mingling together. My own, black as the surrounding night, hung around my shoulders, freed from its plait in my tossing and turning. And so I sat on the ledge by my window, looking out at the sea.

My name came from the sea. I was born during a storm, when the white-capped waves crested high and battered the stolid rock walls of Tintagel. I came into the world wailing like the wind, Mother said. But as I settled, so too did the tempest. Morgan, she named me. One who is born by the sea.

The sea was quiet tonight. Only the gentle lapping of the water against the land told me that it remained, had not been magicked up leaving us abandoned on this rock with nothing to surround us. I shivered, thinking of it, of a life unmoored and untethered to the rhythm of the tides.

I had been thinking of my name, longing to hear Father say it in his deep, warm voice. The way it lifted at the end even as he lifted me into the air and onto his shoulders. The last born, I looked the most like him. His dark hair and his strong nose that was too large for my face. His large eyes, deer-dark and bright.

He had been away over a fortnight, battling back the invaders of Dumnonia. We had not received word of him for days, no messengers passing through the safety of our gates. I knew Mother was worried. The nails on her fine fingers were ragged and red, the skin around her eyes purpled with the mark of sleepless nights. Though only eight, I had learned quickly what fear looked like.

But then, as if summoned by my thoughts, there he was. One man alone on a dark horse, just visible in the pale, struggling light of the strip of moon. From my window perch, I saw the rider dismount and step towards the guards at the gate. Heard the creak of the wood giving way, allowing him to pass through, unmolested.

Father.

I bolted for the door, shaking with excitement. I was already imagining being lifted into his arms, feeling them wrap around me and burying my face in his neck, breathing him in, that smell of sweat and horses and the sea that perfumed his skin. Careful not to make a sound, I pulled the door shut, leaving my sleeping sisters to their own dreams.

Sprinting down the passageway, I saw the flutter of a cape rounding the corner. He was heading to Mother's chamber, and I knew that once he opened that door, he would be swallowed up inside. I put my head down and moved my legs with all the speed I could muster.

As I rounded the corner, I hit something hard enough to knock me down and steal my breath. I wheezed, looking up with squinting eyes. Before me was a head with father's dark hair, wearing his mail and crest. And as he turned, I could see the features mirrored in my own face: the large, hawkish nose, the slanting brows. But though his eyes were still the rich brown I knew so well, there was a coldness in them, as if he did not know me.

"Father?" I whispered, suddenly unsure. Morgause had been telling stories of ghosts, illicit ones she had learned from the village girls who worked in the kitchens. In the near-darkness of the passageway, this man seemed a haunting.

The specter of father seemed to come closer to me, though he did not move. Only its eyes narrowed, turning to arrow slits in its pale face. I turned and fled.

When morning broke, a messenger arrived: Gorlois, Duke of Cornwall, was dead.

* * *

We did not see Mother for days, though we heard her wailing grief keening through every hallway. The walls of Tintagel seemed to echo her despair, grieving alongside her at the loss of their master. My sisters and I were not forced into lessons. Indeed, we were not told to do anything. We stayed in the room we shared and waited, until we got restless enough to scurry out. But the castle was like a grave and the wind whistling through its cracks was cold as the dead.

And yet, in our room the candles burned merrily. We were too young to know the implications of death. Besides, had I not seen Father just the other night, in the very passageway outside our door? But I told no one of what I had seen. If I had been the last to see father, alive or spirit, I wanted to keep that memory to myself.

The rains began. Cold and violent they thrashed against the castle walls. Draughts slipping through cracks in the stone made our candles waver, sending shadows dancing in undulating patterns on the wall.

It was on one such afternoon that Morgause pulled out the knife.

"I nicked it from the kitchens," she said. Morgause was my elder by seven years and when she was not complaining, she was in the bowels of the castle, learning the ways of the world from the kitchen maids with wide-eyed wonder.

"Be careful with that. You'll cut yourself." Elaine, at thirteen, was always the careful one. She balanced us, Morgause with her silver-blonde hair and shrewd eyes and me, hair black and a temper to match. She was the sweet one, the compliant one, the one who most resembled Mother, face full and round. Now, it was pink with worry as Morgause played with the knife, spinning it in circles on the floor.

"The blade isn't even that sharp," Morgause said, picking it up and running her thumb down the blade for emphasis. Though her voice had the same sting as the cold metal, her eyes were red-rimmed from crying. She had always fancied herself Father's favorite, accompanying him on outings with horse and hawk until she had begun to turn her back on such frivolities as the time drew closer for her to be presented as the eldest daughter of the Duke of Cornwall. How she had raged the first time he had taken me instead.

"Put it away," Elaine pleaded. Of late, Elaine had foregone eating all meat. She said it was because it was too close to what she

TO CUT THE ROT

imagined war was like, the violence that had taken Father from us awoken in the paring of flesh. Even now, as Morgause pointed the knife at her, she flinched away.

Morgause, defiant, began tossing the knife from one hand to another. Higher and higher it flew, as if she were a minstrel juggling wooden balls. Elaine reached towards her, to take it from her hands. And then Morgause, as she was wont to do, threw the knife too high, too hard, so that it spun around until it was not the handle facing downwards as it fell, but the point. The knife sliced through Elaine's outstretched hand and clattered the stone floor.

All eyes flew to Elaine's hand, now a closed fist. The rivulet of blood that trailed down her wrist.

The room became a flutter of cries, of color. Morgause leapt to her feet, pulling Elaine's cut hand to her skirts, babbling apologies. Elaine's pink face crumpled and her breaths turned to shallow sobs.

"I didn't mean to," Morgause blubbered, now crying too, her tears dripping off of her chin onto the fabric she was using to stanch the bleeding, already dark with Elaine's blood.

"Open your hand, let me see," Morgause sniffled.

Elaine shook her head emphatically, squeezing her eyes shut. Morgause pried her fingers open, revealing a jagged red line through the center of Elaine's palm, the skin ragged and torn as I had seen the flesh of a deer once while out with Father, its flesh pulled from its body by the sharp teeth of other hungry forest-dwellers.

Still as stone up until now, I leaned forward, fascinated. The cut seemed to pulse with its own life, oozing blood. I felt a tingling in my arms, growing warmer the longer I looked.

"Let me see," I said, my voice a child's whisper.

Morgause ignored me, pressing again against the cut. But it did not crust over, blood continuing to spill into the contours of Elaine's palm until the valley of her hand held a number of red rivers.

Unbidden, I reached my small hands toward the wound. I grasped either side of Elaine's hand, my thumbs on the torn skin. Elaine whimpered at my touch.

"Morgan, let go," Morgause admonished through her tears. Elaine tried to pull her hand from me. But still I held on. Even as I stared at it the cut seemed to grow shallower, the blood seeping from it flowing until it stopped. I could feel the fibers of Elaine's skin reaching out across the gap rent in its surface, the split sides moving towards one another. Could feel it knitting itself back together, becoming smooth and whole.

"Morgan!" Elaine's voice was sharper than I had ever heard it.

I opened my eyes to see my sister's mouth open wide in wonder. I had not realized they were closed, and the light of the candles seemed to burn as if I had emerged from the dark into blazing sunlight.

All three of us looked down. The cut on Elaine's palm was gone, invisible save for a thin silver line marking where it had been.

I sat back on my heels, suddenly weary. My eyelids drooped as Elaine pulled me against her side, catching me before I could fall backward onto the flagstones.

"What was that?" Morgause shrieked. Then, again, quieter this time, an angry hiss. "Morgan, what did you do?"

I gave my eldest sister a half shrug. I was tired. I wanted to sleep, right there, in the comforting curve of Elaine's arm.

"It's just gone," Morgause said. Her voice was heavy, with fear or awe I could not tell. I did not much care.

"Magic." Morgause hissed the word, the last sound harsh as chipped rock in her mouth. Elaine squeezed me more tightly against her.

"We won't tell." Elaine's voice was level, without the teary waver that often came after crying.

"Mother has to know." Morgause was stubborn. But Elaine, too, was a child of Ygraine and Gorlois. She pushed her chin into the air.

"No, we won't. We will all swear now that it will be our secret. No one must know. Swear it, Morgause, or I will tell them how you cut me."

I heard their voices as if from underwater, growing thick and fuzzy as a tongue with thirst. Already, sleep was claiming me.

"Morgan," Elaine shook me gently. "Promise with us. We will not speak of this again."

I nodded, but already I was gone from them, the room, and what had occurred between us. It was many moons before I remembered it again.

* * *

The bells tolled on the day Uther Pendragon wed my mother, but it was not a day of mirth. There was no joy in my mother's face as she placed a hand on the arm of her new husband and allowed him to escort her to the rooms she and my father had once shared. From that day on, there was a shadow over the palace.

Uther was a cruel master. He coveted all that was not his and jealously guarded all that was. His women were no exception. He claimed my mother as he might jewels or horses, emblems of victory, objects piled up in the spoils of war. He tore down my father's banners and removed all signs of him from Tintagel, replacing them with his own. But my sisters and I were remembrances that could not be so easily undone.

Though he banished us to another wing of the castle where he would not be forced to look upon our faces, we were always there, shadows of our father. A reminder that kept him hard and sharp as his sword.

Uther could rid us from his side of the castle, but he could not ban us from our mother's chamber. When Uther rode out with his men, I would sneak off to that familiar door, the room behind it bright with memory, and I would sit with her as she spun wool and stories both, sneaking back through the passageways before her husband returned.

Then the morning came when Morgause awoke in the bed we shared, her nightdress and the bedclothes beneath her stained with blood.

"Morgan!" Morgause cried. "Get mother. Quickly!"

I sprang out of our bed and hurled myself through the castle, feeling nothing except the air ripping through my sleep-slow lungs, the fear for my sister spurring me faster.

It was only when I stood outside the door to my mother's chamber that I realized it was too early, too soon after first light, for Uther to have ventured out on his morning ride. But Morgause needed me. I straightened my shoulders and raised my hand to knock.

Behind the thick door, I heard voices. A man's raised in anger. A woman's, thin and pleading. And then a crash, a cry. I had just enough sense to duck behind a heavy brocaded tapestry in the passage before the door flew open, crashing against the stone wall behind, and Uther stormed out, teeth bared like a feral dog mad with bloodlust. I slipped through the door he had left open into the room beyond.

What I found inside did not at first seem real.

My mother lay in a pile on the floor, weeping silently. Beside her, a shattered chamber pot lay in ruin, shards spread out upon the thick bearskin rug. A swelling the size of an apple was already blossoming on her cheek and her lip was split in two, a trickle of blood running down her chin.

When she saw me, she hastily raised a hand to her face, smarting as she wiped at the blood. I could see her face contort as she tried to hide her pain from me.

She tried to stand, but I threw myself on her, already weeping, Morgause forgotten in my own terror.

"Quiet, child," she soothed, stroking my hair. "It's alright." But I could hear the waver in her voice, and it only made me cry harder.

I reached my hand up to her face, letting my fingers drift across her cheekbone, a purplish bruise already beginning to spread across her face like spilled wine. There was pain in her eyes, and fear. I wished, more than anything, I could take it away. To have my mother before me, standing tall. To be able to believe her when she told me everything would be alright.

Warmth flowed beneath my fingers. And when I pulled back, both swelling and cut were gone.

Mother raised a hand to her cheek then shook me off, standing and hurrying to her looking glass. She gasped at her reflection, touched her fingers to her newly healed lip. A crust of blood still covered her chin, the only remnant of what had been only moments before.

"Morgan," Mother began, "how?"

We were so enthralled by her transformation we did not hear Uther come back into the room.

"I told you never to have them in here."

His voice boomed out though it came through bared teeth. Mother pushed me behind her skirt.

Uther stepped towards her and she shrank against me. He grabbed her chin and held it close to his face, his eyes growing wide and dark.

"You will love me, Ygraine."

"She will not!"

I could not help it, this small act of defiance. Seeing Uther's hands on her had made me burn as if thrown onto hot coals.

Uther turned to me, slowly.

"And what do you know of love, bastard child as you are?"

"My father loved us. All of us." I jutted out my chin.

"You are my family now," Uther took a step towards us. "You belong to me."

Mother took a step between us, holding out an arm, keeping him back.

"You are not my father."

The words crackled through my teeth, a whip. Uther went still against my mother's bracing hand.

"There is no longer room in Tintagel for things that are not mine."

"She doesn't know what she's saying," Mother protested. "She is but a child."

Uther leveled his gaze at me. I stared back, until I saw my own venom and hatred mirrored on his face.

"Uther," Mother said, her voice grown soft. Dangerous. "Touch her, and I will never be yours. Touch her, and you will never have an heir."

Uther peeled his eyes from me, looking at her. Without warning, he swung his hand high, prepared to bring it across her face. In all my life, I had never seen my father raise a hand to any of us. And now this man, this beast, sought to crush us all beneath his heel.

But my mother stood tall. She no longer quailed beneath his threats. Her fingers curled into my shoulder, holding tight.

Uther lowered his hand. He spat at her, a glob of sputum landing on the fine fabric of her skirt. But she did not stir, did not move to wipe it away, did not acknowledge it at all, only looked at her husband with an empty, withering pity. Uther turned and stalked out of the room, the only sound the stamping of his boots on the stone floor.

The next day it was announced that the children of Ygraine would no longer be welcome in Tintagel.

* * *

Morgause was married first. Though he was a king nearly twice her age with beard sprinkled with gray, she did not seem to mind. In her cunning way, she had secured herself a place of power, and when Elaine and I went to bid her goodbye, she only acknowledged us when we referred to her as the Queen of Orkney.

Elaine was next. Though she was shy and demure as she approached the altar, there was a peace in her eyes when they landed on the suitor Uther had chosen for her. He was neither as rich nor as imposing as the king chosen for Morgause, but he was younger, with kind eyes that did not leave his bride throughout the whole of the ceremony. When they stepped down together as man and wife, her arm in his, they seemed to fit together as a hand in a glove. I hoped they would find happiness, that Elaine's goodness would not be usurped by this man.

Then it was my turn.

"She is too young," Mother argued, desperate. Two of her daughters had been stripped from her as easily as the mealy part of an apple is cut away from the rest.

But Uther was adamant: he would have no more of Gorlois's seed in Tintagel. And so I was sent to a nunnery.

There was a ceremony for my departing. Uther's show of patriarchal power. Both he and my mother escorted me as I stepped towards the litter that would bear me from the only home I had ever known.

Uther leaned towards me, a show of fatherly affection. I braced myself as he lowered his lips against my ear.

"As you have taken your mother's love from me, so I will take love from you. You will not see her, or your sisters, again.

You will not wed, and you will die behind abbey walls, alone and forgotten."

Hatred ripped through me, leaving me shaking. He pulled away, lips curled in an approximation of a smile.

Then my mother bent to hug me, holding me tight.

"Here," she said, slipping a bundle into my skirt, arranging my hands so that I held it, out of sight from prying eyes. "Use it well, my Morgan. Never forget that you were born of storms."

She kissed me on the forehead, lips lingering against my skin. I watched from the litter as she grew smaller until she was swallowed up in the shadow of Tintagel.

* * *

It was near winter when we reached the nunnery to which Uther had banished me. High on a hill it stood, but there was no salt in the air, no hint of the sea. We were far from any place that was touched by the tides.

Alone the first night, in clothes that were not mine, in a room that was not mine, cold and desolate without the comforting warmth of my sisters, I could have sobbed. I could hear other girls, newly brought, weeping quietly in their own cells. I dug deep in my travelling trunk, searching, drawing out the knife my mother had given to me, mercifully wrapped up in my plainest underclothes. Though the nuns had searched my belongings, doing away with anything deemed too fine, they had not found this.

I unwrapped the knife like a relic. Its blade reflected the moonlight spilling in through my small window, flat and sharp.

The handle was made of silver, engraved with a deer, a many-pronged stag. And in its pommel sat a sapphire, round as the end of my thumb.

I held the knife up to the pale light, studying its contours. Looking for a sign of my father in its length.

Then, I brought it down against my flesh.

I let the blood pool in my palm, spill over the sides and drip down the narrow bones at my wrist. I placed the knife on the cold stone floor and held up my hand. In the moonlight it looked ghostly, my blood black.

I reached down inside, for that desire to heal myself. To cleanse myself of Tintagel, of the scourge of Uther, the darkness he had brought to my home of light and love.

When I opened my eyes, the cut was gone, leaving only a crescent of silver across my palm.

My lips twisted into a smile. It was a promise. Uther would not long taint the halls of Tintagel, leave marks upon my mother's skin. I would heal my family of his foulness the same way I could heal flesh, sew it back together until it was whole. For the first time, I could feel it, that tingling beneath my skin. Magic, Morgause had said. In the quiet of the nunnery, the solitude of my cell, I felt something I had not since Uther had come into our lives with his armor and his bloodlust.

Power.

Gelato

Micah Giddens

I was in my woods communing with the beasts, listening to the secrets they'd gathered from across the realm, when Merlin burst into the glen, huffing and puffing, completely shattering my good mood, as was his habit.

"Morgana!" the wizard said, blue robe sticking to him from sweat. "I've got some bad news and some bad news."

"That's not how the saying goes."

"So the bad news is," he continued, "young Arthur, heir to the throne of Camelot, had an accident. And the other bad news is that, he's in fact dead."

"Come again?"

"Don't look at me with those witchy judgmental eyes," Merlin said. "You know the sword in the stone thing – which, I might add, was your idea – well, the sword was stuck in there real tight, and he wasn't going to get it on his own. I mean, look at the kid, he's like five and weighs less than my beard. So he was getting frustrated, about to give up, but I convinced him to give it one more go, and, to ensure he got it out, I may have turned the stone to water, you know, with magic. He was yanking real hard when it happened, and the momentum carried the sword backwards faster than expected, and, well, he may have cut his face. In half. And subsequently, he succumbed to his wounds."

I glared at him for a long time.

"You do realize—"

"Yes, yes, the prophesy." Merlin waved his hand.

"That if—"

"That if Arthur does not become king, then crops will rot, rivers will turn to pus, cows will combust, etc. I get it."

I wasn't surprised by these developments. Merlin was a classically trained moron. "Anything else, or can I spend my remaining time on earth blissfully alone?"

"I have a contingency plan."

He had that look in his eye. The one where he's just made some stupid magic broom or something, and he's super proud that it sweeps on its own, but then the broom starts having independent thoughts and begins asking for a fair living wage, and eventually Merlin gets annoyed with its whining, and ends up drowning his creation in the river, its sad desperate broom-screams keeping the whole village up all night.

"What you make this time?"

"Time travel, baby!" Merlin did a little jig. "We'll just hop in my Time Contraption, hi-jinx ensue, and that boy's face will be reconstructed in no time!"

I'd heard of Merlin's famed Time Contraption before but never had the misfortune of seeing its pompous glory up close. He kept it in his lair, atop a tower mounted on the back of a chicken-legged tortoise, because he conflated performative eccentricity with intelligence. It took us two hours to find his tortoise lair, by the way, because Merlin forgot to feed the thing, and the damn tortoise wandered into town and was eating some peasant's roof when we found it, but that's besides the point. The Time Contraption was this ridiculous bronze chair with a large orb of ether and a bunch of useless clocks and gears.

"Now, it's made for one, but we're both delicate in frame, so I figure we can squeeze into the seat," Merlin said.

"Isn't this thing busted?"

"I've fixed it," Merlin said.

"But didn't it explode and now you're aging backwards?"

"That was a Phase One bug," Merlin said. "Now please, time is of the essence, pun intended."

I considered leaving him to his own nonsense, but I also considered the consequences of such lack of supervision. When I ran into young Arthur in the market place, I saw his possible future in a flash:

Arthur lying dead; fields aflame, sky blackened; my woods obliterated; bodies spanning the earth.

Merlin often struggled to keep his cloak from snagging in doors, so this task was too important for his hands alone.

"Fine. I'm not sitting on your lap, though."

"Excellent." Merlin clapped. "I'll sit on yours."

We arranged ourselves on the contraption, and Merlin put the orb between us.

"I need your help channeling magical energy into this orb. All you need to do is close your eyes, gather all your magical ether into your bowels, and squeeze with all your might."

"Why do you have to phrase it like that?"

Merlin fiddled with a dial on the chair arm.

Without warning the orb began to glow blue.

"Squeeze now!"

I quickly focused my energy on the orb and the world around us dissipated like paint in a pond. With a violent pop, the swirling cleared, and we were somewhere else:

A busy stone-cobbled street, ornate buildings surrounding us, church bells, merchants calling in another tongue, the smell of garlic and the sea.

"This doesn't look right."

"Blazes!" Merlin was squinting down at the dial. The orb was shattered, green noxious haze sputtering out of it.

"What'd you do?"

"This dial is infuriatingly difficult to read."

"You're the one who designed it!"

"Yeah, well, now I know."

Around us people of diverse origins haggled with merchants, a painter captured the market with remarkable accuracy, women strolled by wearing styles I'd never seen.

"I may have misplaced a few decimal points," Merlin conceded.

"How many?"

"No more than five or six."

Groaning, I stood up.

"Must've over-exerted the orb's capabilities..." Merlin mused.

Tuning him out, I reached out and called a crow to me. Whispering to the bird in its tongue, I got the information I needed.

"We're in Italy."

"Disgusting."

"900 years in the future," I added.

"Well, that's certainly not ideal."

"But you're in luck," I said, still not believing the coincidence of it all. "I happen to have a friend in town."

Using my new crow companion, I learned my friend resided in a grungy loft sandwiched between a cathedral and a bakery. I first met him through a magical mailbox that appeared in my woods. He wrote that he was a craftsman from a distant future and was testing his new invention, trying to commune across time. We began writing as friends, exchanging gossip and knowledge. I told him of my animal companions and their fragile egos. He sent me back the design of a magic box that holds a blizzard within it, and taught me how to use it to create a treat he called 'gelato'. By all accounts he was an impressive man, and I looked forward to meeting him in the flesh.

I sent a note with my crow to alert him to our arrival and navigated the narrow cobbled streets to his residence.

I knocked on his door, and a man with a strong Italian accent called, "Come in, Come in!"

We entered the loft.

"I'm just making some spaghetti," he yelled from the kitchen.

"Typical," Merlin muttered, taking in the decor with an unimpressed sneer.

It was messy, clothes and rubbish strewn about the floor, every surface splattered with paint and charcoal. Artwork plastered the walls: anatomical sketches of many-armed men, splayed animals, plans for an armored carriage spewing fire.

"I don't like the cut of this guy's gib," Merlin said.

"Morgana le Fay." Our host appeared, grabbing my hand and kissing it. "*Bella donna*, it's been too long since our last correspondence."

"Leonardo," I said.

"Of Vinci, yes it is I, ah-ha ha!" he said with a flourish.

"I'm so glad we landed here. We need your help—"

"I'm Merlin!" Merlin butted in, grabbing Leonardo's hand roughly. "I'm a world-class wizard. Women of the Court swoon and enemies of Camelot cower with the reputation of my eldritch powers."

"*Piacere*," Leonardo da Vinci nodded.

"Speak English, you dog!" Merlin spat.

"Anyhoo," I glided between the bristling pair. "Would you mind taking a look at our invention?"

We took Da Vinci to the crashed Time Contraption in the middle of the piazza. For a long time, the inventor strode around it, prodding at various mechanisms, tisk-tisking the superfluous clockwork. Merlin was at his heels, barely restraining himself from assaulting the other man. After half an hour had passed, both men were stroking their long beards in unison, wordlessly competing in who could strike the sagest pose.

"So you think you know how to get it running?" I asked, growing impatient.

"Well," Da Vinci looked at me, coy smile forming. "I'm a bit of a Renaissance Man." He burst out laughing.

Neither Merlin nor I made any show of understanding the reference.

"It's fine. That joke would kill in a couple hundred years. But yes, I can help."

"What can you, a swarthy mortal, teach me about my own Time Contraption?" Merlin asked.

"To start, your power source is too weak."

"Whoa, whoa, whoa," Merlin said. "You don't see me coming into your studio apartment, telling you how to draw genitalia, or whatever it is you do."

"Merlin, shut up," I said. "He's a respected polymath. Listen to his advice."

"A polymath?" Merlin scoffed. "Can a polymath conjure beasts from the Abyss?"

Merlin snapped and a frog appeared in a puff of smoke.

"Fascinating." Da Vinci bent forward to examine the frog. "May I dissect it?"

"You may not." Merlin pulled his frog away. "Pervert."

"Please, boys," I said. "We don't have time for this. Leonardo, do you have a more efficient fuel source for us or don't you?"

Da Vinci smiled and told us where to find the source of our salvation.

* * *

"Kraken tears?" Merlin said, as we hovered over the Atlantic Ocean.

We travelled there in one of Da Vinci's flying machines. Merlin was muttering the whole flight about "shoddy craftsmanship," but despite his misgivings, the machine was miraculous.

"Certainly an unconventional power source, but I trust him," I said as we waited for the kraken to appear. It was a Tuesday, and the clouds were prickly and mean, like an old woman squeezing an overpriced pear at the market, the perfect environment to glimpse the legendary creature, according to Da Vinci.

"How do kraken tears even differ from regular water?" Merlin asked. "The man's pranking us."

"He says it's more viscous."

"Bet he loves that."

Three large ships appeared on the horizon, and the sea began to swell and bristle. Upon closer examination, many tentacles were churning the waves; the beast must've been excited, its lunch slowly approaching.

"Alright, let's get these tears before those poor sailors find themselves in a watery grave," Merlin said, all noble like.

"How do we make a kraken cry?"

"Easy," Merlin said, navigating the machine closer to the mass of writhing tentacles. "Insult its appearance."

Merlin crawled out on the mast of the flying machine and raised his arms.

"Hey, you with the creepy arms!" Merlin yelled at the kraken. The great squid rose out of the sea, turning its black eyes to the wizard. "Why does your head look like a dick?"

In an instant a tentacle whipped out and struck Merlin. He flew into the gathering mist out of sight.

"Idiot," I muttered, and the kraken turned its gaze on me, raising another of its tentacles. Behind me, the three ships drifted closer to their doom.

I could have called on the clouds and smote the beast with lightning, hoping to inflict enough pain to produce tears, but that would surely just anger it.

And there was something about its black eyes. Not angry, but...

I leapt off the flying machine and landed directly on the kraken's long face, clinging to its slippery hide with a desperate hug.

I saw her life in an instant:

An older squid with a kindly face placing fresh anemone in the kraken's beak; a great net pulling her parents beyond her grasp; alone in the reef, growing large, bigger than all her peers, their ridicule, rejection; peaking her head above the surface, dreaming of kinder beings above the waves; small angry creatures hurling spears at her, blasting her back into the depths with their fire...

"You are beautiful," I told the kraken. "You are worthy of love."

The kraken went still and turned her eyes on me.

"You have lovely tentacles, and a striking blue hue in your complexion. You deserve friends who treat you like the miracle you are."

A single, thick tear ran down the kraken's face, and I collected it with the jar Da Vinci gave me.

"Thank you, my friend," I said.

The kraken patted my head and complimented my hair.

"Die, barnacled freak!"

I looked up to see Merlin diving towards us in the flying machine, his staff alight with fire.

"No, Merlin—" It was too late. Merlin shot a fireball at the kraken, hitting her between the eyes.

The kraken twitched away, unharmed but infuriated. I tumbled high into the air, barely holding onto the jar of tears. Using my magic, I caught the wind and landed in the flying machine next to Merlin.

"I have the tears already, you idiot."

"Oh, neat," Merlin said. "Let's get out of here, I may have angered it."

"You think?"

Below us, the kraken retreated into the depths, spinning her tentacles into a terrifying maelstrom.

"Sorry, girl," I whispered.

The three ships were caught in the whirlpool.

"Those poor sailors," Merlin said. "Alas, nothing to be done."

I watched as a ship named *La Santa María* disappeared into the depths, its captain screaming as the waves overtook him.

"Whatever," I said. "Like the world needs more horny sailors."

* * *

We flew back to Florence, and Da Vinci taught us how to use the kraken tears to fuel our machine.

I told Da Vinci I would update him on the experiment using his magic mail box, and Merlin told him he looked like a homeless ferret, and we disappeared back into the void of time.

Surprisingly, we landed exactly where we were meant to: next to the stone, Excalibur protruding from it, the young Arthur reaching for the hilt.

"Wait!" Merlin called out before Arthur could grab the sword. To me he said, "Give the boy this butter I stole from the painter. Have him grease the blade a bit."

I walked over to the kid and handed him the glob of butter,

which, despite the strangeness of the situation, Arthur took without question. He seemed to be a nice, polite kid.

When I brushed the boy's hand, I saw his prophesy again, only this time, more completely:

Arthur wearing a crown; his descendants multiplying; a myriad of boats filled with horny sailors spreading across the globe, smoke and corpses in their wake; terrifying inventions like those on Da Vinci's wall; the woods burning; bearded men like Merlin directing each generation's new king with their dripping red hands.

I knew what I must do.

Before Merlin could defend himself with his staff, I zapped him, transforming him into a squirrel.

"Wow," Arthur said, taking his hand off the sword. "How'd you do that?"

I shrugged and picked up the Merlin-squirrel.

"Can I pet it?"

"Sure," I said. "But be careful. He's very fragile."

Arthur gently pet the Merlin-squirrel (already a cuter, less tedious improvement over the original), a wonderful idea occurred to me.

"Would you like some gelato?"

"What's that?" the little boy asked.

"It's magic," I smiled. "You're going to love it."

The Story that I Want
Lyndsay E. Gilbert

We live underground, in a palace of a hundred thousand mirrors – a mixture of gods and goddesses, heroes and villains, nightmares and dreams. We cannot touch the world above until it calls for us.

I don't know my name. My reflection, unlike others, shows a creature in constant metamorphosis – so many different faces – but which of them is true? Flaming red curls, raven dark braids, cornfield yellow waves. Pointed features, a crooked nose, a smile that holds too many secrets. Eyes wide with innocence and narrowed too, with a truth that no one wants to hear. Gowns through the ages, short skirts, and jeans from the mad, modern Earth.

I am running out of time. I feel the Stagnant Waters lapping at my bare feet – there is an ending waiting for me unless I remember who I am. Which of the reflections is truly me? I roam the halls, hoping to see someone I remember, something that sparks an ancient memory to life. All I see is pity or disgust, eyes drop to take in my soaked feet and dripping gown. 'Poor thing' is the best I can hope for. 'What a waste, what a pathetic sight, what a mess' – these are more common.

I give up on all of it and lie in bed feeling sorry for my ever-shifting body. I contemplate my ending. Will I learn who I am before my head sinks beneath the Depths? A soft knock on my door startles me. It is rare to have visitors. Most are busy begging to be known, to be called upon in stories, songs and dreams. We are desperate to enter the Flowing River that winds like a snake around the palace. If we cannot swim in its living current, the Stagnant Depths are all that is left.

As I walk to the door I realise I am knee deep now. I cannot see the Depths itself but I feel it, and I drip with it. Warm and thick, clinging and slopping like slime instead of water. My current reflection beckons to me from the mirror that covers the door. She tosses her waist-length hair and laughs with manic energy. She winks at me as I grab the doorknob and fling the door open.

My caller is beautiful. She wears her thick golden hair in a long braid down to her hips. Her dress is modest, pale blue with medieval intricacies. But most stunning of all is the crown on her head. This is a queen, or a princess.

"Morgana," she says, and before I can step back she grabs hold of both my hands. I see us in the mirrors of the hallway. My long, wild hair is black as coal, my eyes cat-like and green. Morgana?

My dress becomes like hers, but bold and crimson red. She pulls me into a hug, and in the flowery smell of her being, a name rises to my throat. "Gwynevere?"

I am shaking as I pull myself away from her. She drops the embrace but keeps ahold of my hands. Images tumble through my mind, diving through my whole being. I see regal knights on steeds, swords glinting at their hips or held aloft in their leather-gloved hands. I see Gwynevere in the arms of a king. But I see her too in the arms of others. My arms ache once more to wrap around her. I feel her lips against mine.

Hot tears trickle from my eyes and I manage to pull away from her, to dash the tears away. I don't understand. I want her gone. "Can I help you?" I ask, and curse the fragility of my voice.

"Yes," she says. "But I can help you too, Morgana."

The name reaches into me. It wraps around my hidden faces and draws them out. The images come again. Her lips are no longer on mine. She lies in the dark of deep woods I remember, blood staining the chest of her pale gown. The knife is in my hand. I cast it aside, only to realise it is just a dream, she is with me now, alive and well. Claiming she will help me. A war begins inside me, the pull of a hundred Morganas and the rising fear that every single one of them is me. "How can you help me?"

Gwynevere hums thoughtfully, as though we are merely playing a game of riddles. "I think first you must rest and let the truth bathe your mind a little while."

"But what if I simply forget it all again?"

She smiles. "I will stay with you. And I promise I will help you on your journey after."

"What journey?" I am scared and excited all at once.

Gwynevere points to my soaking gown. "You have to reconnect with yourself. Otherwise this will continue and you will go under. We must find the cause of your forgetfulness and cut it out."

* * *

She falls asleep in mere minutes, her hand in mine. I lie beside her on my bed staring up at the mirrored ceiling, at this reflection of me that does not change. Moving carefully, I slip my hand free of her. Immediately my reflection starts to warp. Weakness floods my limbs and I feel small and useless and broken. I close my eyes and take Gwynevere's hand again. I wonder in what way exactly I can help her in return as I sink into sleep.

* * *

I am in an ancient library, one that grows with each passing minute. A place that holds knowledge of the past and guesses of the future. The books are giant tomes, and each is chained with iron to the dusty stone shelves. Voices whisper in a hundred languages and twist together in a harrowing song. Chains rattle and the deeper I go into the hall, the stronger the voices become. Worse, I hear my own, calling out for help. The prisoners appear, their skinny limbs attached to their books. I start to read as fast as I can, the crying voices have woken the keeper of this place and I hear its footsteps thundering.

* * *

I am Morgana le Fay, with wings that make me one of the Sidhe. A Faery. A member of the Tuatha de Danaan. Morgan and Morgaine. The sorceress, the priestess, the saviour, the villain. Older still, I fly with crow wings, and my body shifts from bird to woman to goddess. I am the Washer at the Ford. An Irish warrior I know well approaches me on the way to his death, thinking I am just an omen he can overcome. Cuchulain. I smile at him as I scrub blood from my clothing at the riverside. Morrigan, goddess of death. A maiden, mother, crone. The trees know this version of me. The land too is old enough to cradle all my tales and tell them with the seasons. But mankind holds them too, and just like Morgana, their stories each are different but have the same thread that links them through thousands of years.

* * *

I gasp, sitting up in bed. I am the thread.

* * *

"We must find this library." Gwynevere speaks with a gentle resolve. "Those chains are keeping you fractured."

I try not to think of the thundering footsteps. I have my own great tome of questions. "How will that stop me from drowning in the Depths?"

She nods toward the hem of my dress. It is dry. I wriggle my toes, discovering my feet are clad in delicate red shoes.

"Our stories get reread, Morgana. Our stories get retold. And when this happens it gives us life and strength. We can even guide those stories, and explore the world as we wish. People are still telling tales of you, but so many parts of you are stuck in that library. Too many parts of you have been starved for generations. You deserve your place in the Flowing River." Now she helps me stand up from the bed. "You deserve to be a part of us."

My cheeks grow hot and I look away from her. "How can I be so many things at once?"

THE STORY THAT I WANT

"Lots of folk here are. That's the point in the river, it is a stream of consciousness."

"How do I know I won't get trapped in it too, slave to everyone else's imagination?"

She puts her hands on her hips. "Like I said, we can guide these stories. Like muses."

I can tell she's a little exasperated, but I have a final question. "So, how is it that I can help you?"

Now it is her turn to flush with red cheeks. She spins away from me, pretending to fix her hair in the mirrors. But I can still see her writhing in her skin.

* * *

We go to the Round Table, and Gwynevere has no need to introduce me. Arthur smiles at me, but he pulls Gwynevere close to him and I hear his harshly whispered words. "I told you she will bring trouble."

How right he is. I did not tell her about the Morrigan. This goddess deep within me. I want to steal the crown from his noble brow and challenge him to fight me for it. Sword and sorcery, hero and villain. But before I can do this, Gwynevere straightens her back and raises her voice. "I take no orders now," she says. "Each of us is free here to flow as the River flows."

I see a handsome, dark-haired man staring at her and know immediately that he is Lancelot. Do these knights forgive each other for their stories? Or do jealousy and vengeance linger here?

"I will be no trouble here. I simply wish to know how I may find a certain library. An ever-growing hall of darkness that holds stories captive."

Lancelot laughs and the other men join him. "That sounds exactly like trouble."

As he speaks, I remember the faces of me that wanted him. Faces that looked his way with longing, while he looked only at Gwynevere. The image of her body rises in me like sickness. Her blood and pale face. I feel the sticky knife in my hand again. No. This is just one story. Soon there will be many more, stories I am free to tell as I wish.

Arthur dismisses us, but Gwynevere doesn't seem worried. A few hours later I understand why. Lancelot seeks us out and offers to escort us to the Library.

* * *

We ride horses around the Depths, and I cannot help but stare at its absolute stillness. It is like a pool of ink. Ink that could only ever scribe a horror tale. The library is a giant building. Statues of goddesses hold up its ceiling. Pleasure and fear raise goosebumps on my skin. Lancelot helps Gwynevere from her white horse. I prepare to climb down from my own beautiful black horse. To my surprise, both Lancelot and Gwynevere come to my side and help me down like a lady.

They stand on either side of me, my hands in theirs. We stare up the steep stairway of the hall. I expect Lancelot to let me go and ask Gwynevere to leave with him, to let me get into as much trouble

THE STORY THAT I WANT

as I want. I feel his gaze on me, but looking up I see a softness in his eyes. "It is dangerous in here. But you know that already." He smirks. For just a moment I am sinking into a memory from another time, the strangest story. His lips on mine, his kiss harder than Gwynevere's, his hands sinking into my hair and holding me in place, flush against his tall body.

I shake free of both of them and run up the stairs. I turn to face them at the top. "There's something in here, something guarding all the books. I don't expect you both to endanger yourselves. I have my sorcery to call upon."

Gwynevere shakes her head. "How can you rely on it so readily, after everything?"

I stand my ground. "Well, it's a lot better than you. At least he has a sword." I glance at Lancelot, not daring to meet his eye.

"You can help me with that." She goes back to her horse and pulls a bow and sling of arrows from the saddlebag. "I can shoot this, and I can swing a sword too. That's where you come in."

I shrug. "How exactly?"

She raises her eyebrows. "You'll see."

I feel like demonstrating my sorcery on her right now. It rises in my blood, pumping fast around my body. Lancelot climbs the rest of the steps and pulls his sword from his sheath. "Lead on."

The giant door is made of stone. I might not be strong enough to push it open, but soon I hear the iron hinges groan. I step inside. The floor is like a desert made of stones and dust. The air is cold and stings with each breath. Looking up, I see giant stone chandeliers that flicker with firelight, but still too dim to encourage reading. I stand still for a moment, expecting the librarian to show up, or at least begin making their ground-shaking way toward us. But there is silence. Perhaps the keeper only existed in my dreams.

I realise just how unlikely that is, since the hall itself exists.

"How do we find the right books?" Lancelot asks. He steps up to the nearest shelf and checks the weight of one of the many chains. "I thought chains in libraries were simply to stop folk from stealing." He looks up at the chandeliers. "Seems strange here. It's not exactly easy or comfortable to read."

Gwynevere coughs on dust. "Do you remember the prisoners?"

I nod, walking deeper into the hall. "Hello?" My voice is just a whisper but it echoes all around. Then the cries begin. Lancelot and Gwynevere move toward each other, and close in behind me. Just as it was in my dream, I hear my own voice, so many all at once. Tears come to my eyes, but I blink them away. The rattling of the chains starts up, and the prisoners appear. The nearest one is just a girl. A version of me still in early maidenhood. The cuff which binds her ankle cuts into her flesh. A symbol has been carved into her forehead, a crescent moon. It looks green and black with pus and infection. She sees me walking toward her. "Please, please help."

I don't know what to say to her. I want to reassure her, but false hope is the last thing she needs. I reach up and slide the book down. It is made of tough leather. One chain ties it to the shelf and a second, longer one ties it to the girl. The young me. I tug on it, hoping the pages will rip, that the leather will tear. Nothing happens.

Lancelot holds out a hand to take it. He tugs too, but it makes no difference.

"Help me," the girl says again. And all around the hall I see that every book has a prisoner, some more than one. How can we possibly find only my stories? How can we ignore the others?

One solution comes to mind. "We have to burn this place."

Gwynevere's eyes are round and wide. "But it's a library."

I take the book back from Lancelot, and he speaks as if reading my mind. "This is no library. It is a prison. There is no learning done here, no actual reading. And as you said, without freeing Morgana, she will be lost to the Depths. These others are the same. A library is supposed to protect knowledge."

I hold out my hand and conjure up a flame. In the back of my mind I hear the voice of Merlin. But he is just one of my teachers. The Morrigan knows the magics of her own folk, and she is always ready to go to war. Wings break through the back of my gown, a set like gauze and smoke, a second set with crow feathers. The flame in my hand grows taller. I hold the book over it and will it to catch fire.

It flares up brilliant and orange, a blue centre that destroys the leather and turns the pages to ash. The chain on the girl clinks to the ground. I expect that she will run for the door, but instead she smiles and steps right into me, disappearing.

Lancelot resheaths his sword and claps his hands together. "Fantastic!" His clapping slows. "Uh… Now we just need you to do that thousands of times."

In answer I hover into the air, my fey wings buzz like bees and the crow wings are slow and heavy, blowing a strong wind over everything. I conjure up more fire, and then I blow it over the top shelf. Every book lights up, crackling like lightning. More chains fall and more prisoners fade away into their freedom. All that are mine float into me, filling me with more memories, more joy, more tragedy. I keep setting each shelf on fire. Below, Gwynevere and Lancelot use burning books to set as many of the ground-floor shelves alight as possible.

I feel powerful, happy, supported.

Then the footsteps start. I keep setting my fires, but the whole hall quakes. Gwynevere loses her balance and sprawls on the floor. A prisoner reaches for her. I scream, not knowing what will happen. But I see it is one of mine, and she rises from the ground as though from a lake, dripping wet and holding out a sword, offering it to Gwynevere. The young queen takes a hold of it and gets to her feet again. Lancelot redraws his own sword. I swoop down and burn the book that binds the Lady of the Lake to it. A lady who is me.

Now we walk through thick smoke, the three of us together. The footsteps stop and we march onward.

A monster appears, taller than the highest shelves. Its body is a mix of flesh and stone, thick long legs coated in layers of dust. It wears a leather belt from which hang instruments of torture – whips and flails, saws and thumbscrews and daggers. Many things I do not recognise, but I see dried blood on everything and know the purpose is pain.

In one hand it carries a giant wine chalice, and standing, staring down at us, it raises the chalice in a toast, then brings it to its pustule-ruptured lips and pours a thick, familiar liquid down its throat.

This creature survives on the liquid of the Depths. Its eyes are gone, carved out of its face, but the more it drinks the darker each pit becomes. Figures writhe inside, trying to climb out. It seems the Depths are not the final resting place of the forgotten. "Pitiful souls," it rumbles. "You should not have come here."

Lancelot moves first, striking his sword against the giant's stone leg. It merely laughs at him, a strangely jolly sound that does not match its evil countenance. Lancelot keeps striking until the stone chips. Then Gwynevere runs to it, swinging toward the small damage already done. The stone cracks, tiny lines spider out. The creature collapses onto one knee.

"Morgana, finish the burning!" Gwynevere calls out to me, dodging the swipe of the keeper's hand. Now it roars in anger.

I take flight, soaring over the shelves to the next row. The fire is already there, but I spur it on and wonder at the many prisoners it frees. I see gods from all around the world, characters from faery tales, ancient and new. I hurry back to the creature, conjuring ice instead of flame. Looking down I see that Lancelot is on the ground, face down, unmoving. Gwynevere shakes him, begging him to wake up. The creature lifts its hand in a fist, ready to slam down on her. I form the ice into a spear, and aim for the thing's heart. As it pierces true, a splash of the Stagnant Waters of the Depths slops across its chest. The spear goes deeper still, just as I will it to.

The creature crashes down, motionless, like Lancelot. I swoop down and land beside Guinevere. The smoke is now unbearable. Lancelot's body is bloodied beyond recognition. He is gone. Must get Guinevere out of here.

She struggles against me. I call on the power of the Morrigan for strength, for fearlessness in the presence of death. I grab her around the waist and fly us both through the acrid smoke and out of the building.

"I shouldn't have enticed him to come," Guinevere says.

Guilt winds itself around me. If not for me none of this would have happened. But instead of allowing myself to give in, I look inside, Morgana the Sorceress, Morrigan the goddess of death. There is more in my future, stories yet untold. "I will bring him back."

We stand side by side, staring into the clouds of smoke streaming from the hall. I keep one hand on Gwynevere's shoulder, scared she will run back into the fire. My eyes sting, and my breath is shallow. Where can I find the strength to do this? My mind plays dozens of memories, dozens of times when my magic healed instead of hurt. I see myself at King Arthur's side, as his sister, determined to keep him from the clutches of death.

Now I close my eyes and force myself to breathe deeply. "By the maiden, mother, crone, by the servant, by the throne. By the wind, the land, the sea. Return this soul I lost to me." I chant over and over, until Gwynevere joints in, her voice strong despite her tears and fear.

I reach out my hand and see a dark blue energy winding out of the smoke. It touches my palm and I grab hold of it, knowing it is Lancelot's soul, the thread that weaves through all his stories.

I wrap it round my hand like a spindle. Eventually, it comes to an end. Guinevere keeps chanting as I stare desperately into the smoke. I give the thread another heave. Lancelot stumbles out of the smoke, attached to me by the wound-up thread.

THE STORY THAT I WANT

Gwynevere and I both run to him, we go to either side of him and hold him up under his arms. "I think we three make a good team," he says, voice weak from the smoke still in his lungs.

* * *

A little stolen sun still shines outside the castle, a small star burrowed in the ceiling of dirt. I am no longer the changing girl I was. As time passes I discover new stories and aspects of me. I accept them all. I get to choose which face I wear, what powers I will call on.

I sit on the edge of the Flowing River, dipping my feet into its cool waters. Gwynevere and Lancelot take it a little further, swimming in the river, splashing each other.

They beckon to me, but I shake my head, too aware of the River's purpose. I fear being dragged into a story full of hate.

Gwynevere knows how I feel. "Morgana, you are strong now, you can choose the story you wish to be written. You are the muse."

I smile. "Even if that's so, I don't think this River is for swimming."

The two of them roll their eyes, but they laugh and swim toward me, pulling themselves up beside me.

I put my arms around them and pull us all close together. I kiss them each without embarrassment. Gwynevere no longer blushes, even when Lancelot kisses her too. In my mind's eye, I see our colourful threads weaving together, a beautiful design.

I know the story that I want.

Under Avalon
Liam Hogan

Never mind where the tunnel begins, it ends at two wooden doors, the solid timbers as black and ancient as the iron that binds them.

You're not expecting two doors. One... maybe?

You dither. Sunken eyes in the top half of a skull, the doors are almost identical, almost mirror images. One has the shape of a crow or raven, carved deep into a roundel at head height. The bird's wings are extended the full span, the talons reaching out, so that it looks like it is coming in to land. To *attack*.

The other door has a more stylised image, that of a dragon. Strictly (you count the limbs), a *wyvern*. Which makes it obvious which door you came here looking for.

Doesn't it?

Still, you hesitate. Thrown by the choice; by the fact there is a choice. Peering through each of the keyholes there's a sense of space, of a chamber, beyond. But no light, no torch, as there is in this antechamber (and who lit that, you wonder?). You try the door on the right, the wyvern. And then the raven. Both of them firmly locked.

Suspended on the wall between these two impassive doors, there's a bell, in the same blackened metal, with a clapper attached to a short length of dangling rope. The triangular start of a nasal cavity. The rest of the imagined skull – the upper and lower jaws, the *teeth* – lies hidden beneath the packed dirt at your feet.

What you must do next is obvious. But you tremble, as you reach out and yank that rope, stiff and coarse. The sudden bright noise of the bell sounds three times, then fades away.

"*Greetings, visitor,*" a resonant voice declares from somewhere unfathomable, making you jump, sending your heart into your stomach. "You have trod a long and difficult journey and you may be justly impatient. But, please listen carefully to this message; it will not be repeated.

"No doubt you are here because your land is in peril. Britain, is in peril. You may have done all that you think you can, marshalled every resource, reached out to every ally, only to find the sum lacking. Now, perhaps in a lull as the enemy gathers for a final assault, you cling in desperate hope to a legend, to a promise made a long time ago, to a supernatural force you only half believe in.

"Believe *fully*, petitioner. Behind these two doors, within each chamber, lies a powerful figure from ancient history, ready to awaken and once more come to Britain's rescue.

"To the right, behind the emblem of his name, lies Arthur Pendragon, scion of Uther Pendragon, King of Britain, defeater of Saxons, keeper of the Grail, one-time apprentice to the fabled magician, Merlinus Ambrosius. *Cough*. That's me, by the way.

"To the sinister left, behind the raven, the darkness to his light, lies Morgana le Fay, also known as Morganda Fatata, scion of Gorlois, queen, enchantress, shape-shifter, healer and deceiver of men, guide, to this place and others, and *also* my apprentice. Though I learned as much from her as she learned from me.

"Hers was a different path from that of her half-brother, Arthur. And you might ask yourself, wasn't Morgana the antagonist in Arthur's story? Mother of Mordred, adversary of Guinevere, luster after Lancelot. Ambiguous, at best. Capricious, vindicative, and powerful. Sometimes malevolent. You might wonder, then, why anyone would call upon Morgana in their hour of need?"

There's a pregnant silence. Hanging on this disembodied voice and intrigued by these questions as you are, you're equally desperate to know if this whole thing is an elaborate and exceedingly bad-taste prank. A voice message? From *Merlin*? Who are they trying to kid? Though is that any less likely than the legend you seek?

"In all of this, you might be right," the sonorous voice continues, as though it had merely stopped to sip from a glass of water. "Just as you would also be right to further contemplate the story of King Arthur, his search for religious significance, the tight shackles of chivalry, the code of honour to which he bound himself and his knights, the destruction that that code wreaked upon them, and, ultimately, on him.

"You might wisely ask yourself: this grave peril that we are facing, does it *need* a hero? Bravery, and courage, and respect for your enemies? A king, with a sword? A figurehead to rally and lead the troops, mostly into senseless slaughter?

"Or do you require native cunning? Machiavellian intelligence, to anticipate their every move? A master of subterfuge? Someone whose moral compass allows them to contemplate the impossible? A cloak-and-dagger architect of counter-plans, with which to thwart the plots set in motion against you?

"*That* is the choice that lies here. When you are ready, closely inspect the clapper of the bell you rang. Detach it. You will find it unlocks either door.

"But it will unlock only *one* of them. Whichever door you choose, the other will be sealed the moment the key begins to turn.

"So pick wisely, petitioner. Choose *well*."

You try to argue yourself out of the decision you've already made. The doubts you had in pursuing this last-ditch measure in the first place. The crazy romance of chivalrous knights in shining armour, arraigned against the most terrible weapons the world has ever seen.

You unhitch the clapper from the bell – here you find the teeth you've half-expected – and insert it into the keyhole. Feel the rumble as you turn it, as the mechanism activates, so that an iron plate slides over the lock on the second door.

You keep turning until there's a surprisingly soft click. When you tentatively push, the counterweighted door moves easily, releasing a breath of cold air.

The light from behind penetrates reluctantly. It takes a moment for your eyes to adjust. The chamber dimly revealed is small, barely wider than the door. There's a stone bed, or altar, around knee height, about the length of a prone adult.

It is bare.

Disbelief freezes you in place. Then you jolt forward, hectic and frustrated, scouring the walls, crouching to make your way around that empty plinth, looking for a crack that might indicate a lid. Looking for something, anything, that would tell you it *isn't* solid rock; that what you're looking for is contained within.

There is no such reassurance, no glimmer of hope.

All this way! For *this*? You feel cheated, feel you should demand a refund. An exchange for the occupant – if there is one! – of the second chamber. A chance to make the other choice.

"*Ah*." The resonant voice rings out once again, chuckling softly. "*Please* don't be disappointed. Morgana le Fay, prophetess and seer, has divined this very moment; both the need for it, and your choice. And so she is *already* at work on your behalf, on Britain's behalf, gathering intelligence, employing counter-measures, spreading rumours. She works in the shadows – did you really expect anything different?

"Return from whence you came, petitioner, and know that even though your foes be mighty, they are no match for Morgana's guile, for her spells and enchantments. Keep strong, and carry the faith. Britain *will* persevere, if all pull together, and those at the top do not shy away from making the hard choices that survival requires. And if, behind the scenes, Morgana le Fay works her clandestine magics.

"Oh – and don't forget to close the door behind you."

* * *

In a chamber deep beneath a hill that crowns a mystical island – which may or may not be the same one that contains a tunnel that ends in a pair of doors and an empty room – two figures lean over the chessboard between them. The tops of the pieces are worn smooth by their fingertips, by all the games that they have played.

They have different strategies, the two of them. The man, plainly attired, tall, eyes as sharp as a hawk, marshals his forces and plays for position, reluctant to sacrifice a piece, any piece, though he will do so, when necessary. The woman, dressed in black, her slender fingers ringed with silver grotesques, sets traps, snipes at her opponent from beneath her cobweb veil, tries to lull him with unexpected moves that appear to give him the advantage. For all that, they are evenly matched, and though there is no tally kept, the overall score would not embarrass either of them.

Many games end in a protracted draw.

At some signal, detected by some other-worldly sense, the man, with a pawn between his fingers, looks up and beyond the chamber's rough-hewn stone walls. He appears to listen, for a moment, as though to the ringing of a bell. When he slowly, deliberately, makes his move, his fingers linger on the piece, not quite ready to relinquish it.

"You're *still* using Merlin's recorded message?" he asks, arching an eyebrow.

The woman shrugs. "Updated, somewhat. For each century, each crisis."

"How many times is that, now?"

"This?" She appears to ponder, to count. "This is the seventh."

"I feel vaguely put out."

"Don't be." She offers him a wry grin. "I believe the choices made says more about the nature of the assumed peril, as was intended. If it is truly as unambiguous a danger as they might claim, then they would select an unambiguous hero. That they don't... that they settle for an empty chamber, and the belief that someone is working on their behalf behind the scenes… well. This is why we slumber on, brother."

Neither of them actually sleeps. To sleep, it feels, is to let eternity catch up with them. The chess game is just one diversion to pass the time. There are many others. There are the laborious rituals that maintain this precarious ageless state, that reset the stage every hundred years or so for the next petitioners. There is reminiscing, and there is discussion, far ranging. Covering, as often as not, the same thorny dilemmas as face petitioners who come to wake them up, just as it faces kings and Lord Protectors and secretive councils through the ages. What are the necessary properties of a successful leader? Of a strong and stable government, even in wartime? Must good men be willing to do bad things, and must bad men – and women – sometimes work for the common good?

It is a puzzle to which they have yet to find a definitive solution.

"You know," Arthur says, "*eventually* someone will pick the dragon over the raven, will need a good man, a man of conscience, a man of honour, to ride forth to save the day. And I will awaken to aid my people, as I promised a long time ago. Champion in some battle of good versus evil, where things are perhaps more clear cut."

"Perhaps." Morgana le Fay slides her queen out onto the chequered board, obliquely threatening Arthur's king. "But when you *do* ride forth, dear brother, I will ride with you. For better or, perhaps more likely, for worse."

Arthur nods as he holds her icicle gaze. "I wouldn't want it any other way," he says, and returns his attention to the chessboard.

An Offense of Memory
Larry Ivkovich

Isle of Gorre, Britain
537 BCE

Morgana rose from her sleeping furs, a disturbing unease settling over her. The hypnotic rhythm of the Tembre river always lulled her to sleep, no matter her mood. Yet, now, a sense of forewarning awakened her.

Something is amiss, she thought, draping a hooded cloak over her nakedness.

A fluttering of wings caught her attention. The light of the Wolf Moon revealed a large raven perched on a window ledge of the old roundhouse Morgana lived in. The bird cawed softly, yet with a definite urgency.

"What is it, my lovely?" Morgana said, approaching the bird. "What brings you here at this late hour?" Her familiar, unlike her suppressed magic, still answered her call. But now, the raven had come to her unbidden.

The bird cocked its head and ruffled its wings. It squawked and croaked, its ebon eyes fixed on Morgana.

"An intruder?" Morgana frowned. "Show me."

She stepped outside through the roundhouse's front entry door. Concealed by the forest above the Tembre's dark rocky shoreline, the conical, thatched dwelling had been Morgana's home, more so a *prison*, for the last three years. Here she'd subsisted since her banishment from the Court of Gorre by her husband King Uriens and Merlin, the High King's Enchanter.

The raven rose into the sky and flew toward the river. Chills ran through Morgana's tall, lean frame as a gust of cold wind kicked up, her long, dark hair whipping behind her. Wrapping the cloak tightly around her and raising its hood over her head, she followed the bird through the surrounding greenwood and looked below.

Her familiar circled high over a tall figure standing like a shimmering ghost on the rocky bank.

Morgana stared. *How has this one gotten here?*

Travelers to Gorre could only reach the isle by two causeways, the Sword Bridge and the Underwater Bridge. Morgana's abode was far from both. The Binding spell placed upon her by the cursed Merlin kept her rooted to this remote spot, unable to leave in any case, most of her magic blunted.

Decreed as punishment for her murderous attempts on the High King's life: the wool cloak of fire, the turning of Arthur's great sword, Excalibur, against him.

She seethed at the memories. Was this being below some foolhardy soul come to gawk at the once-great but now fallen sorceress and Queen of Gorre, Morgana le Fay, half-sister and mortal enemy of Arthur, the High King?

The being raised a hand and sketched a glittering white glyph in the air. The symbol flashed once, twice. After a heartbeat, arcs of blue luminous light sparked at the edge of the river bank. Morgana watched spellbound as a flickering orb coalesced at the river's edge. A blazing blue nimbus shaped and grew wider, higher, and taller than a man, shining like a star fallen to earth.

She gaped, struck dumb by the sight. *A conjuring of dark magic.* Like a giant glowworm, the orb hovered, pulsing to a hidden beat. A shadowy form gradually materialized within the orb's luminous interior. It grew in substance and shape, becoming a second, shorter being, who *stepped* from the orb to the shore.

Morgana clenched her fists, gritting her teeth. Could it be? *A portal through the Veil Between Worlds*, she thought, realization dawning. *From a separate realm of existence.* She'd heard of such spectral gateways, of course, but had always assumed they were the stuff of legends and bards' tales. Yet what else could this be?

In the combined brightness of the moon and the orb's light, the two beings appeared garbed in long robes, faces hidden within thick cowls. The conjurer lowered its hands as its newly arrived companion moved with a feminine, almost feline, grace. It held a bundle of wrapped swaddling in its arms.

Morgana's dark eyes widened. Something within that bundle moved.

For the first time, a shiver of fear coursed through her. She must find out who these two were and what their purpose was! *My lovely,* she sent her thoughts skyward toward her familiar. The raven had moved further away at the appearance of the orb but descended at Morgana's mental call. *Get as close as you safely can and let me see through your eyes.*

The raven did so. Morgana felt the mind of the familiar blend with hers. Her sight became the bird's sight. As the raven beat its great wings to hover, the scene at the riverbank jumped in size and clarity.

The second being bowed its head and offered the swaddling to the conjurer. The conjurer took the bundle and gently held it to its chest. Words were exchanged between the two but Morgana couldn't hear them clearly. Yet, the speech of the second being sounded unusual, voiced in some sibilant, foreign tongue.

As if by some hidden sense, the second being jerked its head upward toward the raven and then pivoted in Morgana's direction. Two pinpoints of bright amber light flashed within the dark oval of its cowl. For a moment, a shaft of moonlight revealed the being's face.

Human, yet... not.

The raven broke its mental tether, radiating waves of fear as it flew upward. Before Morgana could react, the second being moved. It glided swiftly over the ground like a wraith, reaching the forest's edge and looming over Morgana. Morgana had faced many adversaries in her lifetime: Niniane, the Lady of the Lake; Merlin, the King's Enchanter; and King Arthur himself. But none exuded such fearsome menace as this... *creature*. As if bespelled, Morgana couldn't pull her gaze away.

The cowl had fallen back from the creature's head because of its blindingly fast movements. A sharp-featured female face, covered in subtle, blue reptilian scales and topped with long, feathery white hair, pierced Morgana with a heated serpent gaze.

A hissing intake of breath sounded from its lipless mouth. The creature leaned in close and reached out a hand. Four long claws extended from the fingertips. *No!* Morgana thought. *I will not die like this!* She stood tall, defiant in the face of this eldritch threat.

But, instead of attacking, the creature touched Morgana's forehead with a single claw. Then the monstrous being turned and moved sinuously back to join the conjurer, her robe billowing behind her. Morgana released a held breath and placed a tentative finger against the spot where the creature's claw had rested. The skin felt warm; it tingled as if the creature had somehow marked her, had given her a kind of... consent.

Morgana turned her gaze back to the river's edge.

The creature faced the conjurer and, like she had done to Morgana, gently, almost *lovingly*, touched the held bundle with her inhuman hand. She bowed her head again to her taller companion, turned and entered the glowing orb, vanishing within its cocooning depths. Unlike its quiet opening, the orb fell in upon itself loudly, winking out of existence with a sound like a great wind.

Morgana averted her eyes, covering her ears at the sharp whooshing noise. Her heart thudded in her chest, her thoughts whirled. What deviltry had she just beheld? She looked again.

The conjurer had turned in her direction.

Taking a deep breath, Morgana walked toward the river and stopped an arm's length from where the magic-wielder stood. The conjurer pulled its robe's cowl back. Far above, Morgana's familiar shrieked.

A male of middle years faced Morgana. Shoulder-length, graying hair framed a pale yet strong-featured face, which bore the beginnings of a beard. His eyes, strikingly familiar to Morgana, glinted blue-green in the moonlight. This was a man she knew. Yet, was not.

"Merlin?" she asked, not believing. Was this truly the King's Enchanter? Younger and fitter physically but still the same. How could this be?

"It is, Morgana le Fay," he replied in a familiar voice. "But I am not the Merlin who's punished you and caused your exile, binding you to this place. Nor are you the Morgana le Fay I know."

A strange feeling came over Morgana, one of both fear and awe. "Taking in riddles, whoever you may be," she said with a bravado she didn't feel.

"I *am* Merlin, but from a Camelot of another place and time."

Then she knew, with a chill, it was as she suspected. Morgana forced a laugh. "So the great bard Taliesin's fantastic tales are true then? Of different realms able to be traversed within the so-called Veil Between Worlds?"

The Veil had long been described as a numinous barrier, separating realms like Faerie and other spheres of existence from the mortal world. Some of those realms were said to be inhabited by spectral and mysterious beings. Morgana was certain she'd just seen such a being.

"The tales are true," Merlin answered.

"And does *my* Merlin know of your presence here? Of your meddling in the matters of *this* world, for surely meddling is what this is."

"I am bound by certain precepts, as *your* enchanter is."

"Liar!" A sudden rage rose within Morgana. "This is a trick. A trap! Come to finish with me, are you, whoever you are? It's not enough for Merlin to sap my magic, but sends a minion to do his final, foul work!"

AN OFFENSE OF MEMORY

She raised her hands, her bound magic straining for release. Her anger reached deep, grasping a portion of her power. Hands glowing with a red aura of arcing numinous energy, Morgana cried out and cast a Fire spell. A bolt of flame shot from her fingertips at the man standing before her.

With a wave of his hand, Merlin deflected the bolt, turning it into harmless vapor. "Listen well, sorceress!" the conjurer cried, his own anger evident. "You cannot deny me."

Morgana felt spent. The Fire spell had weakened her because of the long disuse of her magic. She lowered her hands. *Gaea damn my enfeebled state!*

He who called himself Merlin knelt and tenderly placed the bundle he held on the ground at his feet. "The child before you must be raised until his destiny takes him elsewhere," he said. "On a different and bloody path. I leave him in your care as has been foretold." He appraised Morgana as if studying her. "The Morgana of my world has a different role to play as you do in your world. You have no choice." Then Merlin turned and walked back the way he had come. Once again he conjured a glowing portal at the river's edge and vanished into it.

By the goddess, what have I witnessed? What did he mean I have a role to play?

A soft, warbling cry from the bundle startled Morgana, breaking through her confusion. With suddenly trembling hands, she knelt and gently parted the swaddling.

It is a child, she thought, beholding tiny eyes and a puckered mouth. *A boy.* Merlin's words came back to her: *I leave him in your care as has been foretold.*

No, I will not! She whirled from the babe and began walking away but stopped as another plaintive cry gripped her heart. Her own son Yvain, like Urien, had turned against her because of her crimes. She never admitted, even to herself, the crushing loneliness she suffered.

Her familiar cawed loudly as it circled closer. Morgana turned, picked up the bundled infant, and strode quickly back to her roundhouse.

* * *

She stayed up the remainder of the night tending to the babe. The child cried, cooed, and slept fitfully, waking hungry and needy. She fed him some pottage and milk from the feral goats she'd caught and kept penned near the roundhouse. She washed the babe's pink, plump body after his soilings, and kept him warm by the stone hearth in the middle of the roundhouse's earthen floor. Her singing lulled him to sleep.

She felt drawn to the child, his presence awakening long-buried emotions. She knew the babe wouldn't understand her, yet she felt compelled to speak to him, to tell him about her exile.

She'd made a life here, lonely and hard, but a life, nonetheless. She tended a vegetable garden, fished, trapped small animals for food, and harvested berries and edible roots from the forest. She'd fallen far but had adapted and survived.

As the babe finally slept and dawn broke over the forest, exhaustion overcame Morgana. She lay down on her sleeping furs beside the infant and fell into her own deep but troubled slumber.

AN OFFENSE OF MEMORY

* * *

She awoke gasping and covered in sweat. A nightmare had shaken her from sleep. Unlike the fading nature of dreams, elements of this... *vision* remained, flitting through her mind.

They revealed the female creature she'd encountered lying with a human, a perverse, blasphemous crime even among the creature's own kind. They were called the Great Old Ones. The Elder Gods. Unfamiliar and terrifying names. Morgana knew them not. And one other...

"Starborn," Morgana murmured, her lips and tongue fumbling with the strangeness of the word. The babe was part Starborn, its mother an inhabitant of a dark realm beyond the Veil Between Worlds. As part of a pact between the rulers of Fairie and the Great Old Ones, the mother became one of the nine guardians of Fairie's fabled treasure, the Cauldron of Inspiration. The babe's father, a knight of Arthur's Court, along with the High King and others, invaded Fairie's Glass Tower in hopes of stealing the cauldron.

There the knight had been bespelled by the guardian creature's Starborn beauty. Helpless to refuse her as she was helpless to resist him. Then, helped by the Merlin of that other Camelot, the mother fled with her spawn to avoid the punishment which would surely be meted out by her masters, the Great Old Ones.

Morgana checked on the babe. He slept soundly, peacefully, but... Did the child look different? She drew back, shaking her head. No, no, a trick of the light, that was all.

A whooshing noise she now recognized came from the direction of the Tembre. An orb, a portal, had opened again on the Isle of Gorre.

Morgana rose and quickly donned a tunic, trousers, and sandals. With a last look at the babe, she walked outside. The forest surrounded her as quiet and undisturbed as always.

Too quiet. No birds sang. No insects flitted. Her goats lay asleep within their fenced enclosure; no breeze stirred. Even her familiar was nowhere to be seen or heard. Despite an unnatural chill enveloping Morgana, she walked toward the river.

No orb was present. The sound she'd heard was the portal closing, not opening. It seemed someone had come through the Veil Between Worlds to pay her a visit.

At that moment, the bushes and ferns on both sides of the dirt path leading to the river parted. Two chainmail and leather-armored men appeared, hands resting upon the pommels of their sheathed swords. As she stared in shock, Morgana discerned the High King's crest upon their leather breastplates. Of an older style and time, it consisted of three crowns backed by a field of blue.

"Who are you?" Morgana demanded. "Why are you here?"

The foremost man, the bigger of the two, stood the more imposing, though dirt stained his garb, his face unshaven and scarred beneath a leather helm. Once, his brown eyes may have been formidable, but now their depths looked glazed and haunted through the helm's eye slits. The knight's words brought her up short.

"We've come for the demon spawn, Mistress. We've searched for more time than can be reckoned, throughout countless realms cordoned off by the cursed Veil. We know the child is here and will

AN OFFENSE OF MEMORY

take it by force if need be. I promised his father before he died. Such a monster shall not exist in *any* world! Now, move aside."

So. These were the surviving companions of the babe's father. The knights who'd raided Fairie in a time long past in another realm.

"No," Morgana said. "You shall not have him. Do you not know who I am?"

"It matters not." The knights drew their swords.

Again, Morgana's magic churned within her. She struck the men with a Changing spell, one she'd employed before, her strength sufficiently returned to withstand it. The knights jerked as if hit by a physical blow. Their movements became sluggish. Their bodies stiffened, their faces frozen into rictuses of terror. In a heartbeat, two stone statues faced Morgana.

It was too easy and perhaps too cruel, but she must protect the child!

The warning caw of her familiar broke the silence. She whirled as a chorus of bloodcurdling screams erupted from the direction of the roundhouse. Ripping, banging, and crunching sounds shattered the morning stillness. Gurgling cries followed, shrieks of agony.

She'd been tricked! Distracted by the two knights while others stole to the roundhouse from the opposite direction.

Fool! Morgana raced back up the path and rushed through the roundhouse's open door. A beam of sunlight lanced through the fire hole at the roof's peak, illuminating the interior. Blood, bones, body parts, remnants of clothing, and entrails lay strewn everywhere on the floor. Morgana's wooden table and chair had been broken; the stone hearth lay smashed, clay pots scattered.

Morgana stood aghast at the carnage and the blinding speed with which it had been carried out. She looked to her sleeping furs. The child was gone but no blood stains were present where he'd lain. Something had brutally killed these other knights, striking with aberrant ferocity. Had such a monster spared the babe and taken him for some other nefarious purpose?

A scrabbling sounded from a corner of the room. Morgana espied a small, shadowy figure crouching there. She moved closer. The beat of her heart drummed in her ears, her breath ragged with anticipation. A clicking noise, like that of an insect, emanated from the figure.

She gasped as the figure's appearance resolved. It was the babe. But…

Upon awakening, Morgana had thought the infant looked different, but dismissed that as wild imaginings. She knew now she had seen truly, and more so at this moment. The face looking up at her from the nightmarish form huddled on the floor was no longer completely human.

Morgana stared, fascinated by the creature. Yes, yes, she was certain this was the infant, but he was bigger, about the size of a small child. How had he grown so quickly? Pale blue scales covered his flesh. He possessed two human-like arms and legs, but the hands and feet were tipped with wicked-looking, bloody claws.

And the eyes… those slit, amber, glistening orbs were the eyes of the female creature Morgana had encountered on the beach. The creature she'd seen in her nightmare. The child's Starborn mother.

Blood covered the beast-child's mouth; a slim, pointed tongue licked the stains eagerly. Merlin's mysterious words from the night before rushed back to Morgana. *His destiny lies elsewhere on another bloody path.*

Bloody path. It had been the child who had slaughtered the knights. His alien gaze locked onto Morgana, enthralling, reassuring her no danger existed here.

She knelt in front of the beast-child, devouring its unworldly aspect, then spotted a round stone, the size of a fist, lying on the floor. *What is this?* The stone must have belonged to one of the knights, perhaps ripped away by the child's attack. Morgana picked up the stone, its surface warm to the touch. Covered in runic symbols, the stone suddenly tingled beneath her fingertips. As if alive.

The runes. She'd seen the likes of them once long ago when she'd been a part of Arthur's court at Camelot. She'd been so young then…

A sudden clarity dawned, rushing through Morgana like a storm. This stone was the power, the *key*, the knights used to travel the Veil Between Worlds. It was a piece of the Siege Perilous, the mystical chair at Arthur's Round Table used in the hunt for the Holy Grail. She'd seen the rune-engraved chair and remembered the tales of its ability to transport whoever sat in it to other realms if they were deemed worthy. Had Arthur given the stone to the surviving knights after their escape from Fairie, directing them to find the child? It must be so!

The beast-child crawled to her, making the clicking sound Morgana had heard. This close, she could see the mix of human and reptile more clearly on his face and body.

Just like his mother, who had touched Morgana in approval, and returned through the portal to whatever fate awaited her, her *role* at an end.

Morgana picked up the child and rocked him as he curled within her arms. His own sweet scent overpowered the stench of blood pervading the roundhouse. His scaled flesh felt surprisingly soft and warm. Morgana smiled, her heart soaring at the child's touch.

"We must leave Gorre," she said softly, her mind awhirl with plans and ideas. "Go somewhere far from here where no one can find us, where we will be safe. We'll entrench ourselves there until you're grown, until you're ready to do what you must. And I know you won't forsake me as Yvain did."

The stone's warmth increased, throbbing in her hand. She rose, and with the child in her arms, walked outside. The binding spell placed upon her was gone. She felt its absence clearly, indicating her Merlin was in league with the younger one. Only her world's enchanter could have released the binding he'd cast.

Well, you've gotten rid of me after all, haven't you, old man? No matter. Morgana accepted this new fate gladly.

She went to the goat enclosure and opened the gate to allow the animals to run free. She took a final look at the roundhouse, turned, and began walking to the river for the last time.

As she passed the stone knights, she continued speaking, "With some of my magic returned to me, the power of the Siege Perilous, and the great goddess Gaea's blessing, I'll open a portal through the Veil. We'll travel to whatever land is revealed. Yes, my beauty? Do you approve?"

A flickering of his eyes as the child drifted off to sleep was the only answer given. Well, it was no wonder. He'd had a trying morning, had he not?

AN OFFENSE OF MEMORY

With the air calm, the river still, the sky cloudless, Morgana stood near the spot where the portals had appeared. Her familiar was already there, waiting on the riverbank. It lifted upward and gently perched on Morgana's shoulder.

"So, my lovely," Morgana addressed the raven, a new confidence and purpose surging through her. "Let us begin this journey, shall we?"

She held the stone out in front of her. The Siege Perilous' power flared into bright light, its sudden heat encompassing her. An orb materialized at the river's edge, whirling, lambent tendrils welcoming her into the Veil. Through its numinous portal, a snow-covered, forested realm became visible. Morgana recognized it from traveler's tales, the songs of Taliesin and her own readings at the remote island convent where she'd studied her magical arts.

The Norse Lands. *Yes,* she thought. *That will do.*

Morgana stepped forward and then hesitated. She realized a great offense on her part, something she'd forgotten. How could she be so remiss? Her memory so befogged? No more time must pass before she set it aright! "You have no name," Morgana said simply, gazing at the sleeping child. "I must give you one. A name of power, one that will be held in high regard."

And there it was, appearing in her mind and forming on her tongue like the comforting taste of honey wine. Yes, it was a good name. A name of great import. A name not likely to be forgotten.

"Grendel," Morgana said dreamily. "I shall call you Grendel."

Satisfied, she stepped into the light.

Mirror, Mirage
Alexis Kaegi

A swift flurry of hooves pounded the damp earth, sending a warning pulse across the roots of the Val sans retour. I followed the snapping twigs and the sudden wingbeats of songbirds, roused from early slumber, to its source. A white mare leapt through dark trees, heedless of root or bramble. I crossed the pond to head her off, lest she break a leg in her panicked frenzy. The sight of my open arms, calm and steady, slowed her gait to a trot, and though her eyes still flashed with fear, we were soon circling a small grove together, speaking in huffs and apples and gentle pleasantries.

Her leather bridle and saddle looked unworn, not yet weathered by travel or battle. The woven padding was of a knightly crimson; her rider, now stranded without steed or travel bags, likely braved the Val on a quest to rescue the two hundred knights lost within.

"Let's have a happy reunion, shall we?" I stroked her neck and led her onward.

We walked a winding path in the quiet night, returning to the entrance of the enchanted wood. Her knight was an easy find: his unnatural steel pauldrons gleamed in the moonlight. He sat at the base of a mother tree, helmet and gauntlets on the ground at his side. His chin rested on balled fists, and he wore a face of total contemplation.

His horse introduced us with a swish of her tail and a swing of her head, newly restless at the sight of him. His eyes lit up, and he clambered to his feet, glad to see her.

"Lost?" I asked, and only then did he notice me: a strange, cloaked figure with hair so dark it bled into shadow. I shaped myself into a fearsome sight, sharp-jawed, pale-skinned, and dark-eyed, but this man was hardly startled – only wary, perhaps, as he squinted to see me.

"You are most kind, dear stranger," he said with the wisdom of one raised by fairy folk, hiding gratitude behind a shield of words. "Estrid is still learning these paths."

"They are not yours – or hers – to learn," I said, stroking Estrid's mane as she nuzzled into her rider's hands. "I advise you return from whence you came, while still you can."

"I cannot heed your warning, though I would know your name. I myself go by Lancelot." He bowed his head, and for a moment his reddish curls hid his eyes.

Lancelot – it was a name I had heard before. A newer knight of Arthur's.

"I am a woman who walks these woods," I offered in return. It is rare the soul who can walk these paths freely; of the nine enchantresses on the Isle of Avalon, only I could be tasked with the keeping of this vale. Indeed, it was my creation.

The knight straightened with a curious tilt of his head. "Then you must be Morgan le Fay. I must admit, I have been warned of your... past pursuits."

I did not gift him with him a response, and when I searched his bright eyes, they gave me nothing in return – no contempt, no fear, no *desire*. I breathed and unclenched my jaw.

Whispers shape a woman, even when they are as vaporous as smoke. Despite rampant rumors of my lustfulness, I had always felt detached from the earthly desire that wracked the spirits of so-called chivalrous knights. Though many had propositioned me, wanted me, or hunted me, only one had ever caught my heart in return. It was no mere courtly love; Guiomar could read the depths of my young soul, and I his. He knew that no noble conquest would move me, and thus he rarely left my side. The one star-crossed night I found him in bed with another, I created this humble habitat for him and his ilk – betrayers of the ones they love most.

Once a silence had bloomed between us, Lancelot nodded. "You know this vale better than anyone, I should think." He bent down to collect his helmet and gauntlets, then stuffed them in his saddlebags. "Any way to avoid those dragons? Would make it heaps easier."

Knights had attempted the noble quest of rescuing their unfaithful fellows before. None had succeeded, of course. A few fell to the dragons, but many more succumbed to the simple task of staying true to one's love – burned in the wall of fire or lost by the cliff-lined pool. I wondered, as I looked into his bright eyes, which would be the demise of Sir Lancelot?

"There's no way 'round, but through," I said. "And no way back, once in."

"For some, perhaps."

The knight took Estrid's reins and climbed into the saddle. She nosed my satchel, and I obliged her with another of my apples. Lancelot bowed his head once more in farewell, giving his horse a humored smirk, before carrying forward, into the dark.

* * *

The dragons appeared no matter which path you took. Wherever the trees thinned, there the lair would be: a cave tucked beneath a stony outcrop, the source of a pristine, slow-moving brook that invited the unwary to drink.

Lancelot dismounted at the tree line, tactically leaving Estrid under the safety of the canopy. He stepped into the glade, fully armored and hand on hilt.

I watched from atop the outcrop as my girls materialized, one red and one blue, crawling on their bellies in the moonlight. Their tongues flicked to taste the intentions of this man; their bodies would respond accordingly. Whenever a knight drew closer, they grew in size – imperceptibly, at first – and their once languid movements turned ever more erratic. A sudden twitch of the tail. Claws kneading the earth. Subtle baring of teeth. At the sight of sharp steel, they swelled into fortresses of fire and fangs.

They became what the knight envisioned them to be: a monster, a challenge, an obstacle, a threat.

Lancelot froze at the sight of them, then slowly dropped into a crouch. His helmet hid his face, shielding his emotions from my view, but my girls would sense the truth of his heart. They wormed around one another on the opposite bank, keeping an eye on their invader, but he remained still, observing the dragons for a long while.

Then, inexplicably, his gaze turned up toward me.

"Do they mean me harm?" he called, and the girls grumbled and grew.

How could he possibly have spotted me, enveloped as I was in the night sky? I clicked my tongue as he stood. The illusion had broken. He even removed his helmet, passing a gloved hand through his hair.

"You carry death in knife and blade," I snapped. "Why would they not?"

That contemplative face again, as he looked between me and the beasts.

Heaps easier. Never did I think one might wield laziness to defeat my dragons. I took my leave with a swish of a cloak, pausing briefly when I caught his response on the wind.

"Good point."

* * *

I sailed ahead on wings of night, arcing toward the ember glow that cut the Val in twain. Ordinarily I flew over these parts, but the ease at which Lancelot had handled my dragons irked me. I wished to ensure the wall of fire would not be so easily avoided.

I descended toward the heat of hungry embers, then flew the length of it. The wall burned bright lines across my vision, visible in every blink. No gaps, no holes, no dips in height. Still fiendishly hot. Rather than fly over the wall, I dropped down in front of it.

My feet touched earth, and sweat pooled at the base of my back. I hadn't attempted this trial since creating it. I wondered what vestiges remained.

For whom does your heart yearn?
Nobody.
What longings do you keep alight?
I walked into the wall.

* * *

The human heart can hold many flames and many cinders and hide it all from view. Scalding as it was, the wall was no match for a love well-kindled – an incense stick to a well-fed bonfire. The task was simple: follow this cherished flame through to the other side, or get lost in a rampant wildfire of your own making, choking on the fumes of your own burning flesh.

Where once I tended a hearth, I now felt a comforting breeze, without any billows of smoke. Eight candles, my sisters of Avalon, guided me through the open sea of my soul. Here, their wax would never cease to burn – a reminder of how far I was from the only place that felt like home. I swiftly reached the other side cool-skinned and bare-faced, my glamour burned away. My cloak had dissipated, as had my wings. I was, truly, nothing more than a woman who walked these woods. I was my crudest self – whole once more.

I had only time for a single deep, steady breath before the knight materialized behind me.

My stomach writhed at his sudden appearance, and I instinctively took a step back. *Quick as a fox*, I thought, searching him for a trickster's tell. But I saw the whites of his eyes in the glowing light. His shining armor had melted away, leaving only linen clothes. He patted himself down, noting the loss of sword and shield and helmet, then slowly met my gaze.

"Hello again," he said, straightening and struggling to find a place to rest his hands.

So he recognized me. I waited for a moment more, prepared for a display of rage or aggression, but I only received a half-smile.

He gestured behind him. "I presume Estrid will *not* be coming through next?"

A laugh – my own – caught me by surprise. "I would not imagine she'd like to, no."

"By foot then. Care to join me, or will you always be flying off?" He offered an arm.

I took it.

Well. Why not? In traversing the wall of fire, he had successfully proven himself faithful to the one he loves most. Few – *very few* knights had successfully reached the other side. And so we walked through the heart of the Val together, arm in arm.

"May I ask who has captured the entirety of your heart?" I began, and he grimaced. With all pretenses lost to the embers, his face betrayed a deep, harrowing pain.

"A miracle of a lady, well beyond my grasp. And yet I cannot think of an obstacle that would keep me from her."

"Not even a wall of fire," I offered.

He nodded, then turned to me. "And who does your heart belong to? Truly."

"You wouldn't believe me."

"Try me."

"No one."

He paused. "Ever?"

"Once," I said. "And then he pierced it with the sharp blade of betrayal."

"Hence all this," Lancelot said, sweeping his other arm across the shadowy trees. "You place a terrifyingly great value in loyalty. I understand, in a way. In a lot of ways."

My insides squirmed, and I could sense my body readying itself to bolt at the slightest hint of dalliance. But his skin was still warm from the fire, and his heart was still with her. He wasn't even looking at me, now; he was focused on the task at hand. His arm, his question, his conversation – it appeared to be nothing more than kinship, freely offered.

We walked at a leisurely pace and talked all the while. We exchanged stories of Nimue, for I knew well the fairy who had raised him, and he confessed his desire to discover his true parentage. We spoke of loyalty to one's friends, and I teased him with a dramatic lecture on the restrictive nature of knighthood. I found myself at ease in his presence, and in the course of our discussions, I found in him a safe haven in the world outside of Avalon.

"If loyalty is as important to you as it is for me," I said, my mind wandering back to his earlier admission, "then why do you continue on this quest?"

"The knights in this wood have loved ones who miss them. Imperfect as they are," he added. "Not everyone can live up to a sorceress's expectations."

"Surely the knights."

"*Especially* the knights," he said with a flash of a grin. "But you know that."

My breath caught unexpectedly, and I slid my arm out of his. "I should leave you here. The next trial..."

He eased me out of my fumbled excuse. "I hope to see you on the other side."

Me too, I wanted to say, but I held my tongue, praying the shadows obscured my flush.

* * *

No man had succeeded in returning from the third and final trial. I darted ahead, barefoot in the underbrush, heart racing. A warm sensation pulsed through my arm, emanating from the crook of my elbow, where our had skin touched. I imagined leaning into his shoulder. *Laughing*. Sharing bites of an apple in between stories of our youth. Rubbing dirt off of his cheek.

It was too much, too much all at once. My head went dizzy. Did I want his friendship, or his circumstance? Was it love? Was it kindness? He saw me as I was, and still he offered warmth. But as quickly as hope rose, it sank into despair; perhaps it was simply *chivalry* – that chauvinistic, meaningless, illusory bastardization of courtesy. Perhaps it was nothing at all.

I approached the still lake, water flecked with lilies and starlight. The full moon hung over the opposite shore, casting a strong, pale light on the glassy surface. Cliffs rose over either side, impossible to scale. The Val ended here, for all knights who had attempted the rescue. They only saw their own reflection in the black, mirrored expanse: heroes of Camelot, champions of virtue, victors of godly warfare.

When caught up in their self-righteous quest, they could not find the narrow walkway, waiting just below the surface – or visages of the trapped knights, who all pointed toward it.

I pushed the closest illusions back, clearing the early depths of mirages, and stepped into the waters myself. It was a steep drop-off – the secret path was knee-deep, and the lake bed fell even further. I submerged myself and laid beside the walkway.

Can you see past your own reflection, into the depths of another?

My body quickly numbed to the icy waters. Gills opened from my neck, and I stopped my shifting there; I did not want to frighten Lancelot with fins or scales. Breathing was enough.

As I waited, I saw the shining pinpricks of Andromeda through a gap in the lily leaves, floating overhead. The damsel hung miserably in the night sky alongside her mother – a woman cursed for the misdeed of loving herself. As the knights tell it, the two are powerless, vain, and idling. Condemnable, yet nobly liberated. But this reading bores me as much as it emboldens them. I imagine instead Cassiopeia leaping to her daughter's side, fending off monsters of beast and man while Andromeda breaks her chains. Together, they flee on the winged stars of Pegasus.

The night sky and her stories are not governed by the Round Table. Camelot has no control over celestial bodies; the moon moves of her own accord. Their starspun tales are not set in stone, but rather etched on the face of a looking glass.

Lancelot strolled out from the tree line as if he were roaming a neighbor's garden. He studied the area, approached the shoreline, and, finally, considered the water.

I did not know why I wanted him to see past the surface, or why I wanted him to accomplish what no knight had thus far. I did not know why I was so willing to put my enchantment at risk for one of *Arthur's knights*.

I watched him look at his own reflection. Paste-like dirt lined his collarbones. Red curls stuck to his forehead. His linen tunic bunched up under his arms, damp from sweat. But he didn't adjust his hair, his face, or his clothes. He only looked, and looked, and looked.

A lily leaf drifted over my view, and I touched it with a slow, outstretched finger.

He was looking at me.

My heart skipped a beat. Lancelot furrowed his brow and crouched down low. He searched my face for a moment, then reached in and grabbed my outstretched hand.

He pulled me from the water with such force that I fell forward, onto my knees. I struggled for air for a few moments, shifting out of gills and into lungs.

"You're a shape shifter," he said.

Once my head had stopped spinning, I rolled into a sitting position. "And?"

"You could be anything. Anyone."

I coughed. "And yet you've seen me at my barest." Especially at present; my clothes, now drenched, clung to my body and chilled me to my bones. But he did not offer warmth now.

He glanced over me and took a step back. "You're just showing me what you think I want to see. It's bewitchery – distraction."

"Distraction? After what you and I—"

"You wish to beguile me." His eyes, once bright, now burned like coals.

"No," I said, my own guard raising. "It is you knights who think yourselves beguiled. But you only trap yourselves in this wood." It has always been thus: if I so much as offer an apple in good faith, they only ever fixate on the noble hand that gifts it.

Lancelot flashed his teeth, then turned toward the water. "And what of this path? Will it trap me, too, after everything?"

"No one has seen it before," I said, my voice now hushed. "It leads to those who are bound by their own vices."

That was all he needed to hear. He leapt in with a splash, then fought his way across the lake. He left me alone – drenched and cold – on the shore.

* * *

I sprouted wings and flew.

The end of the Val was not an unhappy place, if anyone would believe my word over that of the king. I was only here this night to deliver a feast of smoked ham and wine, after which the captive knights wrestled together in play. They were merely lost to the outside world. Previous rescue attempts had only added to their numbers.

I had thought – foolishly, I saw now – that the hero who could surmount the Val would understand why these men must remain here. They were disloyal, faithless, dishonorable, and in the dark night of the Val sans retour, no act of chivalry could mask their truest selves. But outside, in purest daylight, infidelity hid beneath tapestries of bravery and conquest. It was so much harder to see them for who they truly were.

Lancelot had proven faithful. He discerned and respected my dragons, followed the light of his heart through the flames, and saw past his own valor into the pool of my soul. And yet, in the end, he painted me his enemy. Molded my power in the shape of a threat. These knights saw in me what they wanted to see, and never was it a sister, a friend, a confidant.

So they empower me. So they destroy me.

I had thought Lancelot different. *I still thought him different.* Nevertheless, I sharpened my face before my descent into camp. The woman of the wood became the Empress of the Wilderness, and she would carry out the demands of this quest to the final question.

The men were lounging on beds of moss when Lancelot stepped into the glade. I headed him off and opened my wings to shield them from him. The men behind me cooed. One whistled. A few laughed. Lancelot flushed red and avoided looking at me – my eyes, my face, my very presence. So *that* is what our story came to: the knight who escaped the seductress.

"Let them go," he growled.

"Are these really the men you want at your side? Frail-minded, weak-willed? If they betrayed their lover's trust, how can you rely on them to stay loyal to their king?"

Lancelot wrestled with this thought for a few moments. The men behind me fell silent. "Enough of your riddles," he said. "Only the most faithful can free them. Here I am."

"And to whom are you faithful, Sir Lancelot?" The final question.

Lancelot opened his arms and finally returned my gaze. "I am devoted, body and soul, to Lady Guinevere. In her name, I have vanquished your trials. It is finished."

"The queen? Your love is for *the queen?*"

My mind whirled at this revelation, and my astonishment only incensed him further. Fire leapt in his eyes, and his chest rose and fell. *This* – whatever this was – I did not like to see. Yet I knew his love was pure as the mountain spring, and entirely unobtainable. How could Guin not remain faithful to my brother, the king? She was as bound by her duty to Camelot as he was. My heart broke for Lancelot.

But his anger, once directed inward, had found a new target. The blame sloughed off of his shoulders and slithered onto mine: that salacious woman, seducer of men…

I put him to sleep with a swift flick of the wrist, before he could finish the thought.

The earliest rays of sunlight glowed on the horizon. The enchantment had been lifted, and the knights began to congregate around me. I beat my wings and took to the sky, back to Avalon. Soon, Lancelot would wake and lead the men home to Camelot. I did not wish to learn whether he went looking for me on the way out. I knew the answer would cut deeper than a sword ever could.

* * *

Every once in a while, Sir Lancelot encountered an ordinary damsel on the road. Once, she guided him to the secret manor of two villainous knights and helped trick the scoundrels out of their lair. Another time, she entertained the loyal knight at a woodland castle. Then there was the day he fell deathly ill from a snake-poisoned fountain; miraculously, she was there to nourish him back to health with various herbal healing tinctures. *Amable*, she was called.

She thought that surely Estrid would give her away, nuzzling into her satchel like that.

It was after this last recovery that the damsel admitted to falling in love with him, but he explained that he could not return her love, for a lady had already taken his heart.

"What if it was the love of a friend?" she asked, pressing her hand into his. "That is all I ask, that we are forever in each other's lives. Be my confidant, always and everywhere. Thus you may love your lady and love me, without wronging either of us."

He contemplated this for a long moment, watching her carefully, then squeezed her hand.

"To love you as my friend," he said, with that light in his eyes, "would be my honor."

She grinned, teary-eyed, and touched her forehead to his grasp, hiding the aguish she felt at this jagged truth. He could love her… but only in mirage.

A plain girl. Easy to understand. Traveled by foot, rather than wing.

Oh, how close he was to embracing her true form! She had glimpsed it, on the other side of the fire. But her power, like sun-glitter on the sea, blinded men. Even bright-eyed Lancelot, once threatened, had lost sight of her – the woman who walked those woods. A mighty woman did not fit the stories of their stars. She terrified them, and so they remapped her into a more recognizable form: a lascivious enchantress, a masterful healer, an envious woman.

Condemnable, vain, too perfect for this world.

Destiny Forged
Damien Mckeating

Morgana saw a vision of herself stretched across time and possibility. She was recast, reshaped; seductress, villain, lover, goddess, victim of her own jealousy and anger. The possibilities swirled around her as rainbow veins of light carved through a glistening glass structure of time.

It reminded her of something, an idea just on the edge of remembering.

"Morgana!" Arthur's shout from outside her chambers brought her awake.

She stared at the desk, the diagram-covered parchment, the dried leaves, jars of preserved insects, and realised she'd fallen asleep while studying.

Her gaze fell on an oak leaf by her right hand, the pattern of its veins echoing her strange dream. The leaf, for a moment, was a physical reminder of the ephemeral place she had seen. The potentiality of everything, drawn by nature's hand, fallen to the ground, and dried on her desk.

"Morgana!" Arthur hammered at the door.

"I'm here," she called, wiping drool from the corner of her mouth, and gathering together her midnight-crow's nest of hair.

"It's Lancelot," Arthur said as she opened the door.

Morgana moved past him, hurrying down the corridor with Arthur following in her wake. She ran through the cold, stone halls of Camelot until she reached Lancelot's quarters and barged her way inside.

The room was dim and stale, the shutters closed. Lancelot sat on his cot, head in his hands, stripped to the waist, his dark hair falling over his face. He didn't react as Morgana and Arthur arrived.

"Go on," Morgana said, waving Arthur away.

When it was just the two of them, Morgana stepped silently through the shadowed room and knelt at Lancelot's side. His body was tense, muscles clenched, lashes and scars breaking the skin.

"You've hurt yourself," she said. She stroked a finger down the line of a scar, avoiding the fresh wounds. He flinched at her touch but did not resist.

"I think I'm mad," he said, voice broken and pained.

"Nothing that can't be soothed."

He looked up at her, his beauty highlighted by the pain in his tearful eyes, by the lines of worry and anguish that marked his skin. "There are so many voices," he said.

"I can help you." She said it almost as a question and he nodded in return.

Morgana brewed him a drink from her herbs, and set about cleaning the fresh wounds while he drank. Lancelot was troubled in his heart and soul. Passionate and brave, he suffered from dark and dangerous moods when not occupied. Morgana knew his temperaments well, as a sailor knew the tides.

She cleaned the cuts, the wounds that drowned out the voices, and guided his head to the pillow as the herbal brew took hold of him. She sat with him, in his simple and sparse cell, and stroked his hair until he fell asleep.

"Thank you, Guinevere," he mumbled as dreams took him.

Morgana froze and pulled her hand away. It was not the first time he'd called her that while delirious, but each time was a fresh stab in her heart. She choked down her own pain, kissed his forehead, and left him to sleep.

She found Arthur in his study, maps unfurled on a table with troop movements marked by carved stone tokens. Guinevere stood with him, looking anxious as always, her complexion pale, body held like a deer that has caught a scent.

"How is he?" Arthur asked as he saw Morgana.

"Sleeping."

"Will he be okay?" Guinevere asked.

"I know how to take care of him," Morgana replied pointedly.

Guinevere gave a thin smile, excused herself, and drifted from the room like a wan spirit. Morgana watched her leave, satisfied that the queen would not meet her gaze.

"Will he be ready to fight?" Arthur asked when he was alone with Morgana, his attention flitting from her to his maps.

"He'll probably be better when he's fighting. I think the physical action and the clarity of purpose soothe him."

"Good," Arthur nodded. He gestured at the table, the parchments, the tokens. "I never thought talking of peace would bring so much war."

"You talk of uniting the kingdom," Morgana corrected. "People don't like to see themselves swallowed up by something bigger."

"I am king," Arthur replied.

Morgana stayed silent, resisting the temptation to point out the very kingdoms he was battling had their own kings too. She looked at the maps, at the branching of the rivers, and was slammed back into the memory of her vision. What path was Arthur treading? What version of himself would he be? Would his choices affect her, or was she free to choose her own path?

Was she free?

The question felt heavy in her heart.

"We need Merlin's wisdom," Arthur said.

"I have the same power he does," Morgana replied.

"You're still his apprentice," Arthur said with a laugh, his good-hearted intent a barb that lodged in Morgana's chest. "Maybe one day."

She clenched her fist at her side and felt her jaw go tight, her throat constrict. If her life was a branching river then she would carve a course through the soil and stone to reach her own destination.

"I always value your wisdom," Arthur said, reading her mood. "There's no one I'd trust more with healing arts than you."

"I've seen that," Morgana murmured. In her vision, in part of it, Arthur had been on the ground, lying in her arms, blood staining his armour. Together with other women, figures she did not recognise, they had been moving him onto a boat and across the water.

"I wish you had," Arthur said. "Merlin's gift of prophecy would be useful now. To know where and when Mordred will strike." He gave a roguish smile. "No doubt we'll know one way or another soon enough."

Morgana left him to his plans, but his talk of prophecy stayed with her. Was she caught on a pre-ordained path? Were all of her wants and desires for nothing? She struggled to remember more of her vision, but there was nothing beyond a murky aftertaste of emotions, feelings disentangled from knowledge.

Her questions took her to Merlin. She went deep into the forest, following tracks no woodsman would ever guess at. She found the wizard outside of the cave he called home, mixing something in a mortar and pestle. Morgana glanced at it, at the strips of bark on a nearby stone, and guessed it was something to numb pain. More than likely to ease the aches and discomfort the old man must feel.

"Destiny?" Merlin muttered when Morgana raised her question with him. He scratched at his wild, grey hair that bloomed from his wizened head to merge with a wild, grey beard. His robes were old, stained by the land and its animals.

"I saw time like a great crystal, cut through with rivers of colours," Morgana said. "Each one was a different version of me. But each one was done, finished, the course already set."

Merlin chuckled and turned his attention to grinding the pestle. "The gift and curse of prophecy, my lovely apprentice. No man or woman can escape their fate. Not even me."

She caught his tone and seized on it. "You've seen your own."

"Oh, yes."

"And you don't resist it?"

"Morgana, I might as well resist the tide." He laid down his tools and took hold of one of her hands. His crooked, dirty fingers traced the veins in her palm and wrist. "Patterns, just like in the leaves and rivers you saw. They flow through your body too." He slid a finger up her arm and across her chest. "The reflections you would see, if you would only open yourself up." His fingers lingered there, drifting across her body.

Morgana glared at him. She would never recoil, but in her eyes glittered a promise of brutal retribution if he should ever push too far.

"There are things I could show you," Merlin said. "If you were willing. Deeper secrets that can only be accessed by the knowledge of two together."

"I'll find it for myself," Morgana defied him.

"Yes, I can imagine you doing that." He smiled and withdrew his hand. "I have power," he continued as he turned his back to her. "I get the things that I want." He took up the mortar and pestle again.

"Not everything," she said. The thought of the lecherous old man touching her made her chest burn with anger. He was sickening, and nothing compared to her beautiful and tortured Lancelot.

"Some things I have already seen. Some things will always come to pass." His shoulders shook with mirth as he ground the pestle, the gesture and movement of his arm become obscene as Morgana looked from behind him.

She left him without saying another word. It was not the first time they had parted on an argument, or with Morgana spurning his lewd advances. He was never angry, and it made her afraid that he did know something, that he saw a time when she did succumb to him.

That night she lay on her cot, huddled under furs, and let her thoughts run wild. Curse Arthur, and curse Merlin. Kings and wizards and their talk of destiny. They were powerful, with lives of greatness; what desire would they ever have to change the course of time? They were happy to tread destiny's path, for they believed destiny favoured them.

"A curse on destiny," Morgana spit into the night.

Anger propelled her back into the forest as dawn blossomed across the horizon. They said she was half-wild, half-fairy, and it showed when she was surrounded by the trees and wilderness. She moved with a predator's grace, setting a fast pace through the forest with sure feet and unwavering direction.

A break in the trees at a high ridge line showed a distant tower below her, surrounded by a sea of thick fog that hid the forest and gave the illusion of water. Morgana had seen maps where the forest was even drawn as a lake, the tower shown on an island in the middle.

She scoffed at people's stupidity and began her climb down the ridge, heading towards the tower and the Lady who lived there.

The fog would confuse even the most experienced traveller. It was easy to get lost, to be turned around, to lose your footing and tumble down a steep ditch. But Morgana, as always, could see to the heart of things. She had been to the tower before and she felt it pull to her, like a string from her heart to its stone, drawing her in.

She heard the ringing of the forge long before she reached it. The tower loomed up through the fog and Morgana went towards the sound, towards the bright sun-fire glow spilling out of the forge's open door.

There was a woman at the anvil. She held a hammer in one hand, tongs in the other, in turn gripping a red-hot blade. The woman was tall, muscular from her work, shining with sweat, the fire of the forge reflected in her pale arms. Nimue; the Lady of the Lake. The woman who not only gave Excalibur to Arthur, but who forged the blade herself.

"You've come a long way," Nimue said. "What brings you to my door?"

"Destiny," Morgana said.

"And what about it?"

"I want to break it."

Nimue paused a beat and then laughed loud and long. "Then we should talk." She resumed her hammering, the blows ringing out in the fog-shrouded world. When her work was finished to her satisfaction, she led Morgana into the tower.

They came to a room filled with books, trinkets, and oddities. A fire crackled in a stone hearth, and from the window the forest was lost in its shimmering false lake. On a bracket stood an object that caught Morgana's eye. A sword. Long and fine, the blade honed to a sharp edge. It was simple, and in its simplicity radiated a power.

"Excalibur," Morgana said.

"A blade that forged a destiny," Nimue said. She had rinsed the sweat from her arms and face and stood, hands on hips, glowing from the forge and intensity of her work. "Take it, if you want it."

Morgana looked to see if she was joking, but Nimue was serious. Morgana studied the fabled sword and then turned her back on it.

"That's their symbol," she said. "Their destiny. I want my own."

She told Nimue of her vision, of her many selves trapped in their colourful glass pathways. As set and immutable as the leaves, the branches, the rivers, the veins in her body.

Nimue poured them both wine and then sat in a chair, lounging, legs crossed, taking a great swig of the deep red liquid.

"Metal is folded and beaten into shape," Nimue said. "Reality is no different. You want a blade able to cut those folds, to carve for yourself a... What? A kingdom? An empire?"

"A free choice," Morgana said.

They held each other's gaze, each studying the other, until Nimue let a smile play at her lips.

"I've had the same vision," she said. "No doubt Merlin has too, although he never seems to have questioned whether it could be changed. He sees destiny as an immoveable mountain."

"Mountains crumble over time," Morgana shot back. "Merlin's a lecherous old man."

"I agree on both counts. I have plans for that man of the wilds."

"Can you help me?" Morgana asked.

"Yes."

The fire cackled into the silence, a chuckling spectre of consuming incandescence. Morgana sensed the deeper question.

"Will you help me?"

"To see if it could be done?" Nimue drained her cup. "I'll help you."

The work consumed them. Magic and metal folded together, the two women working at the forge and their spells, as days and nights tumbled into each other. The blade was shaped, the weapon bent to their will. It was honed in sunlight and moonlight, it was sharpened on a spider's web.

"It has been made sacred," Nimue said when they were done. She stared at the sword, wrapped up in leather and hidden away. Sacred things, she knew, were removed from reality. The blade existed in their world, but was not part of it.

"It will work?" Morgana asked with just a shadow of doubt.

"That depends on you."

Morgana left the Lady of the Lake and returned to the liminal, shifting waters of the fog-drenched forest. She travelled quickly, filled with an excited energy. The sword rested on her back, and its weight radiated power and potential. Free from the commands of her brother-king, free from the machinations of a lecherous teacher, she would carve her own destiny.

"I wish you'd stayed," Arthur said on her return. "Or told me how long you'd be away."

"I needed supplies from the forest," Morgana replied.

Arthur followed her to her room. "You're a lady of the court, Morgana, you can't just go disappearing into the forest for days on end. You're not Merlin."

Morgana dropped her pack onto her cot and scowled down at it. She kept her back to Arthur, not willing to let him see her anger, not wanting pity or his clumsy attempt at understanding.

"We only need one mad man living in trees and caves," Arthur joked.

"How is Lancelot?" she asked to change the subject.

"Better, thanks to you. I'm sure he misses you."

Hope kindled in her heart and she hated Arthur for sparking it. She knew it was a false hope, a fairy-fire that signalled delusion and not romance. She was thankful when he left her alone. There was work to be done and she needed her thoughts clear and calm. With the sword as a focus, she would work the most powerful magic she had ever attempted.

Despite her best efforts, she saw Lancelot the following day. She carried a sack of the herbs and ingredients she needed for her ritual. He was glowing and gleaming from sword drills in the yard, his body filled with energy and vigour.

"I wanted to thank you," he said, bounding over when he saw her. "You always help me. I don't know what I'd do without you."

Emboldened by the knowledge that she had the power to change the world, Morgana spoke her mind. "Then have me. Always."

Lancelot stared, dumbfounded. "You're the king's sister," he managed to say at last.

"And you would prefer the king's wife," Morgana shot back in a vicious whisper.

"She is our queen," he replied as he paled, his jaw going tense.

Morgana had seen this in her vision. She told Arthur of the affair, and became the woman who broke the knights of Camelot. Never mind that the betrayal belonged to Lancelot and Guinevere, it would rest on her for being the one to bring it all into the light.

She stepped around Lancelot. He reached for her and she glared at him, daring him to touch her.

He let her go.

More certain than ever of her next step, Morgana prepared the ritual.

She burnt herbs to purify her room and laid out a circle of salt for protection. She appealed to the spirits in the cardinal points, to the elements that they commanded, and set her intent: to unravel reality.

The spells she wove did not come quickly or easily. Her body went through the movements and her lips invoked the words until it was a trance, as powerful and unstoppable as her heartbeat.

There was a bend in her vision, like the world curved around her, as if she had become trapped inside a drop of rain. She pushed against it, encouraging it, moving further towards and beyond it.

Cracks appeared, branching lines that increased exponentially, until she saw all of the flow of time, and all of its tributaries and end points.

Morgana held the sword.

She raised it.

It was just a symbol, she knew, a focus for her desire. But both her focus and her desire were pure, and the power they summoned shook the stones of Camelot.

A transcendent rainbow flood of possibilities swept over her. Morgana saw her fates, all of them, every possibility. In none of them did she see what she had achieved now: commander of her own destiny.

She raised the sword and began to cut, the action guiding the magic, the movement becoming the focus that made the spell real. She did not hack or slash. She did not destroy. She moved with careful intent, like she did when she treated a wound. She cut away what wasn't needed; threaded together broken weaves; and made a tapestry of her future.

She wove herself a crown.

She bound to her side a loving consort.

She stitched herself free of the shadows of the brothers, mad men, and lovers that surrounded her.

In the flowing weave of forever, Morgana found herself.

To Catch a Name
Nico Martinez Nocito

I cobble him together, that imagined night-time boy, out of hawthorn boughs and apple blossoms and the gentle, thumping rhythm of my own heartbeat.

Then I hide him in my garden.

The body is nearly invisible among the overgrown tangle of zucchini vines, and, anyway, anyone who sees him will just assume he is one with the weeds and grasses. After all, those are as much part of him as the consciousness I have yet to imbue him with. Until I give him his name, my name, he will be just a pile of scraps, eminently forgettable.

"Merlin," I say, and he appears.

Did I forget to mention that names have power?

He lands beside the bean trellis, almost stepping on the spiky, covert bundle of nightshade with a disgruntled clumsiness that makes it clear he was half-asleep moments earlier. Surely, he now wishes that I didn't know his name, and still thought of him as the old wizard who stole into my garden at night to take plants too illegal for him to grow himself. But names cannot simply be discarded, forgotten. They must be freely given and accepted, or yours will cling to you forever, eating away at your very flesh until you and it are inseparable.

"I am not simply a lapdog to be summoned at will," he says.

"I know," I tell him. "What if I said I was ready to cast the spell?"

Merlin scoffs. "Names are hardly an easy commodity to obtain." He clears a spot for himself among the weeds and plops down before me. I'm already taller than him, but he acts like his extra two hundred years mean he knows everything.

"The last time I made a child, it took me three years to find a suitable name. Three years, do you hear me? I tried a few battlefields – I tracked down the men who would meet their demise that day every morning and asked them to sacrifice their names for a noble cause before getting killed and rendering them unusable. But no, they all refused. I don't blame them entirely – I hear it's a terrible thing to wander the world without a name. Still, couldn't they help an old wizard just trying to make a living?"

I stay silent, because it's in my best interest to learn where Merlin finds his names. After sixteen months beneath his tutelage, I've discovered what's arguably his most helpful trait: he very much enjoys the sound of his own voice.

"I went off to Wales after that, because there's a cliff there where I've heard you can catch a name with your bare hands if you run quickly enough, but all I managed to snag were a few drops of love and a handful of butterflies. At last I found a man half a meter from death who knew it, too, and he agreed to give me his name in exchange for a week longer with his daughter. Three years, I tell you, and—"

"I have a name for him," I say, and that stops him short.

"That's not—" He frowns, restarts. Merlin is knowledgeable, like I said. He doesn't underestimate me. "Show me," he says instead.

I laugh. "If I show it to you, you'll take it, and then I won't have my fair chance to perform the spell."

"You'd risk wasting a perfectly good name on your own stubbornness?"

"It's not stubbornness."

I meet his gaze steadily. He looks away first.

"Thirteen years old and already making life," he mutters.

I roll my eyes. "Don't pretend you weren't doing the same."

He sighs and smooths his ruffled beard. I can't look at the thin hairs growing from his chin without getting lost in a shuddering revulsion of my own body, so I compensate by not looking at him at all.

Shapeshifting. Memory alteration. Merlin has taught me a bevy of useful skills in exchange for easy access to my garden, the only place in all Britain where dangerous, magical plants can be grown and the king looks the other way. It is, I feel, the only good part about the peculiar fascination that Uther Pendragon, King of Britain, has for my mother.

"Lay the body in the moonlight on a blanket of ash leaves," he says. "Then walk around it three times counterclockwise and say *I name you...*"

He looks at me expectantly.

"I won't fall for that trick," I say.

I've learned all I need to about Merlin over the past sixteen months. Maybe he's failed to do the same.

"It's just a name," he says halfheartedly.

I raise my eyebrows, and Merlin sighs.

We both know there's nothing *just* about names. Your name shoulders the essence of your being; it is a powerful, volatile thing that dictates your very existence. To live without one is to be disconnected from that consistent reality.

No wonder so few were willing to part with their names for the sake of a haggling wizard.

He removes the leaves from an ash branch while I check on the body. My spells have held. The woven boughs remain undisturbed, whether by mice or magical decay. Its essential components still hover, suspended, among the apple blossoms at its center: a coil of Uther Pendragon's hair and three drops of my mother's blood, given willingly to Merlin in exchange for the impossible.

I glance at Merlin over my shoulder. He kneels in the dirt as he peels leaf after leaf from their stem, his grubby hands and baggy eyes belying the vast power he can manipulate. My mother knows the truth about him, though, and when she sought him out last month her entreaty was simple: make her a child belonging to herself and Uther Pendragon, so the king would panic and leave her be. He's visited her regularly for years now, and though she cowers nightly beneath his touch, she lacks the authority to refuse him.

"It's ready," Merlin murmurs.

That night, I heard Mother ask Merlin to make her a child. But without any money offered in exchange, he refused.

When I saw Merlin next, I made him my own bargain: I would do the work of creating the body and finding the name, if only he showed me the spells and gave the child to Mother free of charge.

Merlin is brilliant, yes – a genius, even. No other mortal I know can perform his vast catalogue of spells. But he can also be oblivious, and lazy, and I knew he'd leap at any opportunity not to track down a name for the bastard boy himself.

He didn't realize that I already had a name that I needed to be rid of.

Merlin helps me move the cocoon of hawthorn and apple flowers onto the ash leaf nest, and then steps back. He folds his arms and watches as I stand over the body of my half-brother-to-be.

I flex my fingers, letting the familiar rush of power that precedes a spell set my veins on fire. Then I begin to walk.

Each step I take leaves a dazzling sheet of light in my wake, wrapping a translucent wall around myself and the body. The first circle is gold, the second, silver. The third lap shimmers icy blue.

I stop, and hesitate. Emotion coils through me, overwhelming: a bottomless well of joy that comes from knowing that I will finally rid myself of the name that has burdened me since birth, stubbornly labeling me as something I have never been.

"I name you Arthur."

I see the exact moment that what I have just done hits Merlin: his eyes shoot wider, and his voice shatters out of him. "Arthur, what are you—"

The light flairs, coils, funnels into the body. A baby boy lies on the leaves in front of me, with Uther Pendragon's dark hair and my mother's narrow nose.

"What reason could you possibly have—" But Merlin stops, his lips groping for the name that no longer belongs to me and finding only air. His eyes are wide and confused; it's as if I've done the first surprising thing in his two hundred years of life.

And I just smile.

The name Arthur belongs to this baby boy now.

Merlin's face falls, as he seems to realize that I know precisely what I have done, and I'm glad for it.

"My boy, why did you do that?"

"Because I've never been a boy," I say quietly.

To lack a name has always been described as an emptiness, an absence. How, then, do I feel so free? I've rid myself of the one thing binding me to a gender that was never truly mine to begin with.

Understanding dawns then on Merlin's wrinkled face, and he rests one hand on my shoulder. "In that case, I suggest Wales," he says. "A sorceress like you will have no problem finding a name there."

He bundles baby Arthur in his arms and vanishes just like that, leaving me alone in the garden. It occurs to me that he hasn't taught me teleportation yet.

Oh well.

Nothing more ties me to this place. My note to Mother already lies on my bed: *Tell everyone that I have left on religious vocation – I will be back when I have found my name.*

I can envision my mother's confusion, then the odd feeling in her mouth as she tries to speak of me, her lips suddenly missing that mess of syllables that used to belong to me. She will understand, then, at least some small portion of what I've done. She's always known that I'm not really a boy.

TO CATCH A NAME

I become a bird and take to the sky.
It's time to find my own name now.

* * *

The birds accept me easily. The birds don't have names either.

They move as a flock, their decisions made collectively, and when I merge into their cluster of warm bodies hurdling through a wind-swept sky, they do not make note of me or ask what my name is, that question which I no longer possess an answer to. Their wings tilt westward, and I too am headed west, so I fly with them for a while. With every wingbeat I feel that odd gap in my chest, the absence shaped like the apple blossoms I used to craft my half-brother's body.

Arthur's body. That name is his now, and liberation sings on every syllable of this acknowledgement.

When the birds start to turn north, I splinter off from their flock and dive toward the earth. The birds did not greet me. They don't say goodbye, either.

* * *

The cliffs that Merlin spoke of rear tall on the west edge of Britain, glowing softly in the fading light. I find myself in human form again and camp on their edge, but I don't sleep. All night, I watch secrets dart through the air, glassy bubbles of magic that are only there when the moonlight strikes them just right to set them ablaze.

The next morning, I journey out among them.

I spin nettles into thin thread and fashion them into a net, an odd, fluttering affair that leaps as if into wind despite the air holding utterly still. I can hear the things that stir around me, scattered whispers and half-baked dreams. I listen for names.

Guinevere.

I take off after it, my feet leaping easily from the hard and tired earth to pursue this dim whisper of hope. It drums alongside my heartbeat, and I *run*—

I stumble away from the main section of the cliffs and into the wood nearby. The name whispers to me, echoes in my ears, and I taste its beauty on my tongue.

Come...

There is a clearing. A cottage lies at its center.

I open the door.

An old woman lies on a cot, white hair streaming around her head. She does not look surprised to see me. Instead, she points to a pitcher of water on the table beside her bed.

"Bring that to me."

I obey – I know better than to refuse orders from old women – and she accepts the pitcher with shaking hands. She takes two swift sips, then sets it down again.

"What's your name, girl?" she says, and then croaks out a low cackle, eyes dancing with mirth. "Oh, I forgot. You don't have one, do you?"

Guinevere, I realize. This is Guinevere. No wonder the name sang so loudly; it already has a home.

I turn to go.

"I wouldn't leave so quickly," Guinevere says. "Why rush? You won't be able to catch a name now anyway." She nods at the pitcher of water. "The cliffs took a disliking to me long ago. Now that you've helped me, they won't listen to your pleas."

I realize then that I've been tricked. She sits up in her bed, and I see that even if her age is not an illusion, her appearance is; her face is young now, and her eyes glint with malice.

She snaps her fingers, and the walls of the small hut shudder. I move to the door, but it burns beneath my fingertips, and the hinges melt into the wall.

"What are you?" I ask.

Who is a question I'd answered before entering this house.

Guinevere stands and circles me. "I suppose I can always use you for more magic, another nameless wench no one will ever notice is missing. My other sources of power are running a little dry." Her voice turns harder, commanding. "Give me your hand."

I do not give her my hand.

Instead, I summon a fissure of magic and let it *snap* out of me. She reels as if I've slapped her, and I waste no time; I become a bird and bolt for the window, wings slashing at the air.

A wind drives me back, and Guinevere is waiting for me, cat-formed now. Long claws slash through my feathers, and I tumble down to the floor, human again, my shoulder and my arm burning from sudden pain. She moves before I can reconcile my own surprise and latches onto me, vines rising from the floor and coiling about me, holding me, strangling me.

I cannot move.

I feel my magic leaching out into those vines, and I try to thrash but I can't move. I'm thrust back into my old body suddenly, the forced change knocking what little breath I have left in my body out of me, and now I burn with not just internal but external pain.

I never thought I'd be stuck in this form, this boy's body, again.

But there is one place in me she does not know to steal magic out of, one small gap that goes unnoticed beneath her searching gaze. A gap in my chest the size of an apple blossom, holding nothing but raw power.

Guinevere stands over me and laughs.

I say nothing.

* * *

She leaves me there, on the floor, for three days, materializing only to drip soup down my paralyzed gullet. I know she's trying to punish me, but all I want is a little more time: time to nurse that small blossom of magic into something more, time to reimagine my former strength.

When Guinevere comes to retrieve me that night, I form a dagger out of shards of wood using only my gaze and propel it through the air and into her heart.

She staggers, falls. Green swarms out of her, and I think she is casting a spell until I realize she is already dead. This is stolen magic, fleeing her body – taken from other hapless wanderers, tasting of human and fey power – and when that strange, earthy power coils its way through my bones, her vines can no longer hold me.

I stand. I am free. Guinevere is dead, and her name dead with her.

I leave the cottage.

My throat burns with thirst. I find a stream and drink from it, the rich water cascading down my throat, and then walk back to the cliffs.

It is just as Guinevere said. They are silent to me now.

I scream into the night, at the injustice of this place, at the deceptive magic that led me to a name that I could not steal. I scream until every pebble upon these cliffs bears an echo of my nameless self, and even the crumpled remains of the sorceress who tried to cage me vibrate with the sound.

Then I take to the sky on an eagle's sharp-edged wings.

* * *

A year passes.

* * *

I do not make the mistake of trusting someone again.

Magic is sharper now, or perhaps I am. I keenly feel the churning earth around me, and the steady heft of my own power. I do not feel helpless anymore.

I enter villages seeking names borne by the forgotten or the dying. I promise their bearers miracles. All I receive in return is the searching, possessive gaze of the men of the towns, and hands that grope and touch and make this body feel alien to me as the boy's form that I used to bear.

I do not leave them with miracles. I leave them scared.

* * *

Two years pass.

* * *

I underestimated the monotony that is living without a name. It becomes swiftly difficult to nail down variety without that indelible anchor to hold on to. Some days my body frays into raw magic, and when I glance down at my hands, they shimmer into the red, gold, and icy blue of the spell I used to cast away my old name. Other days, I don't see myself at all.

Magic is easier than living: power, movement, light. *Sorceress*, Merlin called me, and the word seems accurate enough.

Merlin was right about another thing, too. People are unwilling to part with their names.

I start to lie, even, telling them that we can share the name, telling them it won't hurt, not even a little. And still, no one says yes.

Three years, Merlin said.

* * *

Three years pass.

* * *

One day, I find my way to Merlin's cabin.

His propensity for teleportation makes it easy to forget that he only lives a few leagues from Camelot, though his home is admittedly so deeply tucked into the woods that one would be hard-pressed to find it on foot. I circle down in bird-form and land outside his door. When I knock, he lets me in immediately.

"I predicted your arrival within one minute of the current time," he says.

He sounds pleased with himself. I step inside.

"You haven't changed," I say.

"You have," he replies.

He's right. Inch by inch, I've discovered a human form that feels right to me: the body of the girl I've always been. But without that ever-present revulsion of my body, the gap of my missing name looms even larger.

Without discussion, I sit at Merlin's table, and he pours tea from the kettle, the water already conveniently boiled. I've never visited his house before, but it feels familiar in the same way that a dream is familiar: it reflects of the lessons that taught me so much about the workings of his mind. This room is all of our shared moments clustered and crammed into a single building. I recognize cuttings of a few of my plants.

"I had to hide Arthur," he tells me. "Your mother feared for his life."

"Interesting," I say.

"I thought you'd be more fascinated by the boy you gave your name to."

"I thought you'd be more curious about why I'm here."

Merlin hands me a mug of tea.

"I've been searching," he says. "I think I've found you a name."

* * *

I shape a boat from reeds and beach sand and push off into the shore of the lake that Merlin pointed me toward. My odd dinghy skims over the water rather than through it. When I reach the lake's center, she is already there.

Her body has the cast of sea foam, all pale fluidity and unpredictable movements, and water lilies stream through her luscious hair. She simply *rises* through the lake, rather than swimming up to meet me.

She does not introduce herself.

"You are the girl Merlin mentioned," she says. "The one in search of a name." She sets one elbow upon the edge of my boat and raises herself slightly out of the water, so we can look eye to eye.

She dances with such power, such fluid self-assurance, that I can't believe that she would help me. "Why would you give up your name?"

She smiles. "I have so many – what is losing one of them to aid a friend of a friend? Merlin is no stranger to me. Neither, one day, will be your half-brother, the one made from apple blossoms and the power of the name that your mother gave you."

"Arthur," I say.

She smiles.

"Soon, little girl" – I can't decide whether to smart at being called *little girl* at seventeen, or surrender to the gentle warmth of being seen as a woman – "you will learn that once you become known, it is far easier to gain a name than it is to lose one."

"Easy?" I have to laugh. Nearly four years now have come and gone. "I have crisscrossed Britain more times than I can count, been caught and mocked and touched and laughed at, turned to wind to catch a name and still felt it slip between my fingers. If gaining names is so easy, then what have I done wrong these past four years?"

"I don't mean the sort of name you choose to accept. I speak of those foisted upon you, which often anchor themselves to you with that same incorrigible strength." She spreads her arms wide, and silver waves dance along her blue-tinged skin. "I am called Ninianne. I too am the Lady of the Lake. And in my youth, when I took interest in roaming beyond the waves, I was known as Morgana le Fay. They will call you sorceress, witch, seductress, monster. You will bear those names with no choice and no relief, and all the spells in the world will not shake them from your back. In time, all the earth will curse you as a villain, and you must bear it or become what they accuse you of. And that choice will, I think, hinge on a girl who also bears the name of Guinevere – a name that already has hurt you."

"Perhaps," I say, but her warnings bury themselves beneath my own sense of urgency, the old itch and emptiness in that apple-blossom gap which craves the name that she can give me.

"What name?" I ask. "What name would you part with?"

"Morgana le Fay." She turns away from me, tasting it against the rhythm of the waves. "An old name, and a powerful one. I've carried it for three hundred years, and I doubt it'll last you a day less."

When the Lady of the Lake faces me again, she's smiling. "Are you ready?"

"Yes," I say.

She does not need to circle my boat, or bother with a bier of ash leaves. She simply faces me, grey eyes open, lips slightly parted. Power stirs in the air between us, and a rush of anticipation flickers up my spine.

"I name you Morgana le Fay."

The name catches me, and I it. It flickers on my tongue. And then it sinks into my bones and fills up that little hollow spot, that apple blossom of regret, and defines me and my body as my own.

The Many-Hued Land
John J. O'Hara

You're not dead, Arthur. You're only dreaming, and in dreams there is no pain, only a vision weightless and unending. So dream of plains of silver grass and orchards of bronze-boughed trees bearing apples like little moons, of hills that curve ghostly and blue, of turrets of crystal and walls of glass that touch a sunless sky as bright and clear as ice, for I will take you there to rest. A place of dreams is Annwn, the Otherworld, a place of death. In life you wondered how the land of our ancestors could encompass both. So long as it remained out of your sight you could bear it. Wheresoever it touched upon the world of men, it became a repugnant irruption, hideous to you in its voluptuousness.

It was all hideous to you, unbearable, an affront to the ordered workings of your mind, of the kingdom you thought yourself fated to build. You must have felt your connection to it in some way. It was part of you, all too seductive to you, and therefore something to be subdued, denied, destroyed. A land of monsters and trickery polluting Prydain. And even now, even as you lay dying in my arms, I am a monster to you. We are all monsters to you, we witches and faeries, dragons and giants, but we were never monsters to ourselves. You never learned that. Perhaps you still might.

What, then, did you learn in this brief blazing life of yours? Foremost you learned war. But have we not heard enough of your battles?

On the day you drew Caliburn from the stone of Logres, I felt the earth shiver. Even at Myrddin's tower in Annwn I felt it. He had left me there, alone, for he had custom in the land of men, or so he had said, and I took the rattle and gasp of the Middle World as an ill omen, knowing that it was somehow his doing.

Before he left I said to him: "It is never for good reasons that you venture into that land. What draws you away from me now?"

"Your task is to study the stars, to learn their paths across the sky, to feel what moves inside you as the vastness of existence moves about you. You will join me when the right moment arrives."

So alone I lay atop that tower as an etheric fire spiraled about me, and I recorded in memory the flowing mercury of my soul as the stars and moon pulled it here and there like an ocean tide. We are all at their mercy, ultimately, and as the stars are impossible to comprehend in their infinity, so too are our own souls. It is a terrifying idea, that we might never know ourselves, is it not? The night sky always felt vaster to me than the blue dome of daylight, for where the sunlit sky ends, the black and inchoate void extends evermore to the beginning and end of time. It is only in death that beginnings and endings fall away and we learn all that could have been.

Though you were born and lived under a sunlit sky, you doubted what the old man told you about the sword. You knew not the name Uthyr Pendragon, but the old man told you he was your father and a very important man, and you could one day live a life of even greater importance. It was all so incomprehensible to you. How many men had tried and failed to wield that sword? Where would a boy such as you find the strength? What would happen to you if you succeeded? That question filled you with a greater terror than the thought of failing. If you failed, you would return to the life you knew, the rhythm of the farm, the weight of the plow, the stern discipline of the man you called "uncle." If you succeeded, who knows what you would become?

The sword needed no coaxing. Your small fingers grasped at the hilt and you pulled with all your strength and the blade soared skyward in your grasp as though under its own power. And even before the sword spilt its first drop of blood something died by its edge: the self-doubt that kept you humble, the shame that checked your pride. All that was childish and naive in you, cut to ribbons by the song of the blade as it rang against stone, by the arc of the rainbow it painted above your head. All that could have saved the boy named Arthur cut away so that only a king remained, for a king has not the luxury of introspection, of doubt.

Blade against stone, the earth cried out, and its echo planted in me a seed of dread that my own dreary soul watered daily. That seed blossomed into a message: you have no choice: take up this burden of dread, for what has happened cannot be reversed; you may not cast it off, for it is already inside you. It was the same dread that rose inside you in that moment as you saw yourself transform from a boy into Arthur, son of Uthyr

Pendragon, King of the Britons – and I from Morgan, apprentice of Myrddin, to Morgan the Faerie. No one ever let me forget my faerie blood. No one ever reminded you of yours.

Our lives forever intertwined. I studied the art. You studied war. Your pack of wolves with gleaming swords swept across this land like a storm and claimed it all for your father, and the Otherworld receded. You took the crown after Uthyr's death and you stalked the Otherworld's margins, stole its treasures, just to taste some morsel of its magic. Something inside you beckoned you to it, and you put it to the sword. You brought death to the dog-heads of Eidyn, raided the palace of the giant Diwrnach, hunted Twrch Trwyth, the untamed boar. You blazed from one end of these islands to the other and left nothing but ash behind you.

And what of me?

* * *

My heart breaks in my chest as your head lies heavy upon it. I am not angry, dear brother. I am merely sad. As sad as I was the day we met. Our boat fast approaches the Isle of Apples, and my words paint images in the mist closing in around you, and I see what you see: the pile of stones Uthyr Pendragon had heaped around his throne and called a castle, his dozen warriors arrayed about him in the dim and drafty great hall. It is the day I arrived at your court, not as a learned magician, pride of Myrddin, but as your humble half-sister, head bowed, face veiled, hands nervously fidgeting as I stood timidly behind my teacher.

You and your queen stood among Uthyr's knights, Caliburn gripped tightly in your right hand as your left held not her hand but Caliburn's empty scabbard.

"Your sister Morgan, daughter of Ygraine." Myrddin's tone suggested that I was a mud-soaked hunting dog dragged back to the kennel from which it had escaped. "She will serve Gwenhwyfar as a lady in waiting."

I raised my head and allowed my eyes to meet Gwenhwyfar's. I had never seen serenity and puzzlement reside so snugly together in one countenance, a mask of naiveté she wore beneath her halo of ruddy hair. It seemed she had mastered the same art I had, the mummer's art, the art of survival.

Inside me swirled a power far vaster than you could imagine, yet I submitted to the whims of your weak and small courtiers who thought themselves grand and powerful. I learned how to navigate the tides of your rages and melancholies. Such fickle creatures men are, puppets of pride, with no love in their hearts save for the love of power. Myrddin, the great warrior Cai, Gwenhwyfar's lover Llenlleog, and even you, though touched by the blood of faerie, you all lived like animals, prisoners of a desire that could never be sated. Yet I lowered my head and answered demurely when spoken to, gave counsel when asked, healed the wounded brought to me, flitted in silence through the cold stone towers of men, all while a fire of rage a million knights could not extinguish burned within me. Is this why Myrddin had taken me in and trained me to carry in my soul the strange power of Annwn?

After I had served Gwenhwyfar for some time, I had gained her trust, and she had gained mine. I looked the other way when she ran off to meet with Llenlleog, and she would pay no mind when I would disappear to Annwn to guard its borderlands and advance my art. And you: we both became ghosts in your life, summoned only when you returned from a raid bearing the spoils of Annwn: a cask of wine that would replenish itself when drunk; a cauldron that would boil meat only for the brave; diadems of gold and bangles of silver forged by the gods in the fires of the sun.

And every time your war band ranged into Annwn, every time you toppled its towers, cleared its forests, killed the creatures you called monsters, and stole its treasures, you severed a link between the two worlds, and a piece of your world died. The expanding frontiers of your kingdom turned to dust, and desert spread like a rash across the mountains and forests that bordered your kingdom.

"You see that none of these treasures brings him happiness," Gwenhwyfar told me one night. "None of them are what he truly seeks: the cauldron that flows perpetually with faerie blood that will restore life to the land." She sighed. "But at least I need not fear for his safety, for so long as the scabbard of Caliburn hangs at his side, no harm may come to him."

I studied the music of her voice and the silent speech of her body but could not discern the motive behind her words. Though we had grown close, I never truly came to understand Gwenhwyfar. It seemed that you always stood between us. Perhaps she reckoned that I knew the location of such an artifact and would help you find it, or that I would use this knowledge of the scabbard to rid her of Llenlleog's rival for her love. Though I carried the learning of a thousand generations within me, I must confess that I knew nothing of this cauldron, but I would not say as much to her. I only knew that you would stop at nothing to find such an artifact, that you would repeat the greatest evil you had visited upon me a thousand times over if it would bring that cauldron to you.

Yes, you had done evil to me before. The day I arrived at Caer Lleon was not our first meeting. Go back in your mind. I am sure you now recognize my power like the scent of a flower carried by summer wind, the one that reminds you of all summers past. Yes – there. Look there, Arthur. I wish to go back there no more than you do. Consider this an indemnity for us both.

You see it now, don't you? The Glowing Castle of the Witches of Ystawingun. You heard of our power and came seeking a boon. The nine witches welcomed you to share in their magic so long as you were within the walls of our castle. You sought instead to kill us all and take that power back to your world. I was among the witches you scattered. And before that...

The great panther Cath Palug who protected the coast of the western sea, which linked this world and the Otherworld. You sent an army to kill her. And then you sent Cai to kill her. He found her prowling amid the heaped and torn dead and still he fought valiantly but returned to you battle-scarred and defeated. So you went yourself, and with the polished shield bestowed upon you by Myrddin Cath Palug fell to the only beast her equal: her own reflection. She too was me. I had animated her with a piece of my soul. And even before that...

The magic of Annwn is mother to great beasts found nowhere on Earth, which you call dragons. Out of the mists of mountain vales they are born, which they come to guard fiercely, for it is the mist that binds together our two worlds. But your ever-expanding kingdom needed land, and so the dragon needed slaying. On the shores of a lake of the valley lived an old druid whose isolated life had made his speech strange. He warned you against slaying the dragon, for its death would anger the powers of the upper world that lies even beyond Annwn. Brandishing Caliburn, you told him that you had an even greater power at your side, and you and your men raced into the mist, possessed by a battle frenzy, to kill a dragon. I thought that if I appeared in my own form, you and your men would do harm to me, that you would at least heed the words of a learned old druid who had become one with the land. But you would obey no one and nothing but your own thirst for glory.

The witch, the cat, the druid, the dragon. They were all me in some form. Even after Myrddin brought me to you, even as I healed the wounded you brought back to Caer Lleon, I sought to stymie your forays into Annwn, for I dreamed of a world where man and faerie could find a balance. But I could not protect Annwn from you, so I sought to deprive you of your kingdom instead.

I delved into the deepest caverns of the Otherworld and carved the likeness of a great warrior into the side of a volcano, and I fed its molten maw with bronze swords to entice Gofannon, the god of smiths, to appear before me. After some time Gofannon answered and granted me the boon I so desired: a warrior of bronze and stone called Accolon, a homunculus animated by the force of my magic.

Meanwhile, you rested at Caer Lleon, recovering your strength after a long journey in Annwn. If only you hadn't so thoroughly rejected your faerie half, you could have withstood the rigors of that realm. Instead, you needed Myrddin to administer a potion that put you into a deep sleep. You placed Caliburn and its scabbard into my care and your kingdom into Myrddin's. I took Caliburn and its scabbard to my quarters and laid them out on a pillow of Otherworldly silk.

I watched over them like a lioness caring for her lionets. These were faerie artifacts, and to steal them would be to profane them. Why could I not act? Why did I suddenly feel this loyalty not only to Caliburn, but to its bearer?

Outside, the Earth rumbled, and the gatekeepers on the parapets blew their horns. Your knights sought out Myrddin with a message: a giant has appeared on the horizon, and he calls for Arthur to give up his crown or die.

The appearance of Accolon stirred me to action. I concluded that you had already profaned these sacred objects. Caliburn belonged in the stone, not in your hands. The scabbard belonged to Annwn, and to Annwn it would return. I took them both up, felt their power surge through my body, and I suddenly thought to slay you myself. I went to you, where you slept, but Gwenhwyfar found me first.

"Myrddin is coming to rouse Arthur."

Your queen had felt some prescient urge to seek me out not to prevent your death, but to prevent me from doing something I would regret.

She placed her hand upon mine, and Caliburn fell from my grip. "I will give this to him. It would be best if you were gone," she said, "before he wakes."

Yet I still held the scabbard. I fled from her, and she fulfilled her obligation as your queen and summoned the guards.

I became a raven and carried the scabbard in my claws. As I soared over the field of battle, I saw you on the ground between the stone pillars of Accolon's legs. I saw his blade strike your thigh, I saw your blood spill upon the bare earth, and I thought your reign had ended.

In truth, I felt nothing in that moment, focused as I was on the task I had set for myself. I cast the scabbard into a lake, and to escape the men who gave chase on horseback, loosing arrows in my path, I landed on the shores of the lake and turned myself to stone.

I remained stone for years, for a stone does not hate, does not regret, does not brood upon failure. If only I could have lived a life in which my flesh could have been so strong.

But soon I felt the grass curl beneath my stony form, and I felt it desiccate, stiffen, and die. I felt the softness of the earth become hard and cracked. I felt the waters of a lake that lapped at my feet recede and turn to sand. I felt the hot air of summer become hotter with the turn of the seasons. But I felt no pain.

The days turned to years, and where the wind once sang the song of Annwn, I heard only silence. Though stone I was, sadness and longing returned, so I became flesh once again.

I wandered the world that you had made in my absence. I walked from Logres in the south to Gorre in the north and found a land that was once lush with thick forests and fens and moors now nothing but desert and brush, like the lands of the distant south. Your lords drove their starved serfs to till the barren land. In the north, emaciated sheep grazed on what threads of grass sprouted from the dead hills, and lambs sucked in vain at the dry teats of their mothers. Everywhere I smelled the rot in the air, and nowhere did I hear the song of Annwn.

I came to feel as though I had abdicated a great obligation that had been thrust upon me, for my years in stone had unbalanced the world. Everywhere the bards sang of Arthur, who tamed the wild forests, who drove mischief from the land. They said you had been cursed by the jealous faerie, who no longer had their run of this world, who no longer stole eggs and chickens and children, who no longer seduced and slew men and women. None of them knew that the kingdom conquered by your sword was now dying by it.

How could you have known the true power of Caliburn? The sword had been sunk into the stone of Logres long before men first set foot upon Prydain's shores. My soul has lived a thousand lives, yet none has memory of the forging of Caliburn. I dare not summon an answer from the world-memory contained within the Isle of Deep Recollection. We of the Otherworld are wise enough to know when something is not ours to know.

Still, it is tempting to journey to that island, where all lives lived and unlived are kept, and observe the unfolding of the life of another Morgan, but those who visit the past often find themselves trapped there. If only our mother's blood had run thicker in your veins, and your fingertips resisted the beckoning thrum of the blade, I would not be left to speculate.

What would I have been had you not taken up the sword? I would have lived out my time in this world studying magic, learning the workings of the universe, the nature of the soul. I would have been a healer, a warrior, a trickster, a bard. I would have taken whatever form I wished and loved whomever I wished, shared joy and pain and life and death with someone. I glimpsed some portion of this life as I wandered the wasteland and helped whom I could. I gave this sheep some milk, that mother of a dead child a song of solace. But soon, magic had drained completely from this world.

In turn, hope drained from my heart. I could feel myself becoming stone again, but it was not fear that changed me this time but grief. I wandered south again to make my grave beside Accolon's. I crossed the marshy remains of the gray river that divided the land, crossed the desert that had become of your kingdom, and came upon the pasture where you had killed Accolon, expecting to find it as barren as the rest of your kingdom. But there amid the ruined field grew a great oak tree.

This was the very spot where Accolon's blade had torn through your mail and pierced your skin – the very spot where the blood of your life had spilt. It had not fallen upon a sapling in that battle; your own blood had been the seed from which emerged this life. You, your body, was the very cauldron that your knights had sought.

Rather than end my life, I journeyed to Myrddin's cave beneath Caer Lleon to seek his counsel. He was not there, only the slightest residue of his existence. He was dead. Much had transpired during my exile.

So I carved the runes into the walls of the cave and I put upon myself the visage of Mabon.

That night you awoke alone. You were not meant to wake until morning, after you had taken the herbs Gwenhwyfar had steeped in your wine so that she could spend the night beside Llenlleog. But you woke at the sound of Mabon's voice – my voice – and the sight of her presence glowing and divine, and I showed you what I had kept from you. Why had I kept it from you? To repay Gwenhwyfar, perhaps, for the slightest kindness she had shown me? To protect you? To protect myself from the rage you would surely feel? Or did I keep it in reserve, to deploy at the decisive moment of the battle? I cannot say what kept my lips sealed for so long. Perhaps it was merely how the stars had arranged my soul. We cannot know the workings of fate. At least, I do not wish to know.

I came to you that night and I painted upon your chamber wall the image that would end your reign: Gwenhwyfar, in love.

You threw your blankets back and my spell finished. I sat there with the weight of Caer Lleon pressing down upon me, and the impression came over me that each of its stones had been a woman once, one who could no longer bear the chaos of the flesh and opted for the surety of stone, and that they all knew what I had done, and that they all felt a deep shame.

So I left Myrddin's cave and his ghost and lumbered, burdened by grief, along the dry riverbed to the mouth of the river, and waited for your rage and jealousy to destroy you, and for your knights to carry your body to me.

* * *

The world had fallen silent by then. There was nothing left of Annwn in this place. Yet hope had returned. Medraut, more Gwenhwyfar's son than yours, had taken up the sword to defend his mother's honor. Blinded by your anger, your pain, you swung Caliburn wildly against him. Medraut disarmed you and ran you through, and where the blood spilled from your wound and ran down Medraut's blade and pooled on the cracked colorless earth of Camlann, there sprouted blades of grass like fingers reaching up to the sun, and great shrubs that blushed with flowers and trees like gods rising from an epochal slumber. And as your men bore your dying body to me, a parade of greenery trailed them.

When I took Caliburn from Bedwyr, I felt its power, the last faerie power left, once again overtake my senses, and I must admit I thought for a moment to turn its blade on him, and on the men who attended him, and to leave you there until the last life leaked from you, and fly all the way back to Caer Lleon and put an end to all our family, and ultimately eradicate humanity as you sought to destroy faerie. But when I saw the light fading from your eyes and the faith drain from Bedwyr's sullen countenance, I knew this struggle had finished. Not that I had won, but that it was finished. All that I had lived for was gone. Our lives in this world were over.

Hate me if you wish, Arthur. In some sense, it would be just. And I believe I would be justified in leaving you to die in the world of your father. Instead, I grant you mercy.

You hear my voice waver. I don't know whether I smile with joy or grimace in pain. I laugh in anticipation of what is to come, and I choke it back with a cry for all I have lost. The Otherworld, Arthur. It is not the end for you yet. The world will heal, and we will return. I only hope that next time, things can be different.

Hound, Hart, Crow, Queen
M.R. Robinson

On the morning of my brother's wedding day, Myrddin flung a candlestick and two fine silver dishes through the window. Once upon a time, I would have cowered while he raged. After nine years as his student, I did not so much as flinch as he swept books and parchment from the shelves.

"All will be well," I said as gently as I could. "My brother—"

He spun to face me, grasping at his beard like he meant to tear it off and hurl that through the window too. "Your *brother!* You have no brother!"

"My half-brother. You know he has no choice in this marriage. Would you have him make an enemy of Leodogran?"

"I would have him listen to my counsel, Leodogran and his sorry sheep-brained daughter be damned! Have I not served Arthur faithfully all his life?"

I inclined my head and did not say *you have planned to kill him all his life*.

Myrddin buried his head in his hands. When he straightened again, he looked impossibly tired, all the anger gone from his face but for a certain sharpness in his eyes. "Will the future I have dreamt come to nothing? This woman will unweave fate. If there is a child – an heir—"

He did not have to finish. I understood: an heir meant that it mattered not whether Arthur lived or died. An heir meant I would never take Caer Lleon from my brother. My half-brother.

"What must we do?"

"We must *act*." He jerked towards me, hand raised as if he meant to strike me. When I did not react, he laughed. "Oh, you are a faithful creature, Morgan, and a brave one. Good. You will need that courage for the task ahead."

I smiled. With my hands behind my back and my chin held high, I picked at the skin around my thumbnail until it bled.

* * *

Caer Lleon had never looked as lovely as it did that night. Gilded petals carpeted the stones; a thousand candles shone like stars. I would have liked to sit at Arthur's table and fill my belly with wine and lamb and pastries in the shapes of wondrous beasts. But it mattered not that I was his sister. His half-sister. I was no lady of the court. No, my place at Arthur's wedding feast was the corner of the great hall, back against the wall.

"What do you see?" Myrddin asked. His fingers on my shoulder were bone-cold; his sharp nails stung even through the linen of my dress.

I hesitated. Arthur looked – perfect. Like a king. When one of his knights whispered in his ear, he threw his head back and howled with laughter. I stared at his throat and tried not to think overlong about slitting it.

His bride sat silently at his side. They suited one another, though Gwenhwyfar looked nearer my age than his. I was as dark as he was fair, as ugly as she was fine. When I looked at him, I saw everything I was not. I saw my mother leaving. I saw the home I had lost, the home his father had stolen, and I saw how carelessly he treated the power I longed to taste.

When I looked at her, I saw—

Well. She was beautiful. Even from afar, I could see how her green eyes outshone the jewels at her throat, the way one lock of copper hair kept escaping her veil, freckles like constellations on her cheeks. When her eyes met mine, her smile widened.

I hated her at once. That much I knew, even if the sweetness of her smile made my stomach cramp. Even if the firelight in her eyes made my mouth dry.

"I see a problem we must solve," I answered. Only then did I remember to tear my eyes from hers, a feat I managed by pinching the skin between my thumb and forefinger. Though Myrddin had taught me much of magic, his first and greatest lesson was the usefulness of pain.

Myrddin laughed. "So we shall, my creature."

His laugh was not bright like my brother's. My half-brother's. And when I looked once more between my teacher and my queen, his smile was as cruel as hers was kind.

* * *

That night I dreamt I stood in Arthur's hall. No candles burned; no petals softened the stones beneath my feet. I was alone –

alone but for the golden-haired child slumped at the head of the table.

"Arthur," I said, soft. He did not stir. I licked my lips and tried again, reaching for the name I called him as a boy, when first I came to Caer Lleon: "*Arth fach*. Little bear."

Again he did not answer. A terrible coldness seized me. Oh, but what did I care? I should rejoice to see him still and broken on the table. I should be relieved.

I did not feel relieved. I felt afraid.

The doors of the hall parted with a creak. I spun, my fingertips crackling with magic. I expected to see a knight. Some warrior come to avenge his boy-king.

A hart, white from his tail to the tip of his antlers, nosed his way into the hall. A black hound followed. They both looked at me as if startled to find another there.

"You cannot help him," I said.

The hound went to Arthur; the poor creature did not understand it had come too late. But the hart moved towards me. I could not run. I could not breathe. Only when he lowered his head and pressed his hot nose to my chest could I fling out my hand and—

"Sister?" the dead boy asked. "Sister?"

* * *

I woke awash in sweat. Stumbling from my bed, I sucked in air and let the cold stones beneath my feet steady me. I had never had a dream so strange. Oh, I knew the taste of shame well enough to understand why I would dream of my brother – my half-brother

– dead. Yet I did not understand the hart, the hound, that sweet soft voice. All I knew was this: though only he could tell me what it meant, I could not speak a word of this to Myrddin.

He had taught me much. Promised me much. It would be wrong to be ungrateful. But I feared it would be wrong, too, to trust him with something as precious as a dream.

I was a girl of fifteen when we met at the convent where Arthur's father had sent me. Myrddin's face was not so lined then, but his beard was white, and he wore a pauper's robes. I remember thinking he looked kind.

"You must choose between two paths," he said. "The first is this: you will marry Urien, son of Cynfarch, and give him sons. The second will take you to Arthur's court at Caer Lleon. I will teach you all I know, and we shall make his throne our own."

"Arthur is my brother," I said, uncertain. My mother's son, but a stranger. Newly orphaned, newly crowned.

"Your half-brother."

"What will you teach me?"

"Making," he said, and raised one fist. When he opened it, he held a raven's feather. When he closed his fingers, dust spilled between his knuckles. "Unmaking."

"Why me?"

I do not know what answer I expected. That he knew I was smart and brave and good, perhaps. That I was worth teaching. That I did not deserve the life I had been given.

He smiled. "He is lonely. He will not think to doubt his own blood."

I remember still how my chest tightened. But the choice he offered was no choice at all. I had no wish to marry Urien. No wish to give him sons. And all my life, I had been powerless. Was it so wrong that my heart jumped at the promise of reward? At *making* and *unmaking*?

Myrddin held out his hand.

I took it, though I shivered at his touch.

* * *

Though it was Arthur's blade that made him brave, it was the scabbard that kept him safe – the scabbard that meant he could not bleed – and thus it was the scabbard Myrddin would have me steal.

One morning, I waited until I heard clanging steel and laughter in the yard. Arthur and his knights. He would not have Caledfwlch with him: he prized the sword too dearly to blunt its edge in play. Simple enough, then, to take the shape of a crow and wing my way to his window.

Arthur made no secret of the fact that he kept the blade by his bedside. If it vanished – well, it would not be the first time he had misplaced something precious. Perhaps he would not even notice its absence before Myrddin's work was done. I returned to my body and knelt by his bed.

I do not know where I went wrong: too focused on my task, I suppose, or too distracted by the unexpected emptiness of the scabbard. But the moment my fingers curled around cold metal, I felt steel at the back of my neck. I froze.

"Arthur—"

The sword left my skin. "Stand."

The voice was not Arthur's. Bewildered, I turned to find my brother's wife in his place, Caledfwlch in her hand. She wore a silver gown that gleamed like mail; bracelets covered her forearms like vambraces. I dropped the scabbard and felt blood well where the sword had been.

"I wonder what you mean to do with my husband's scabbard," Gwenhwyfar said.

"He asked me to fetch it for him," I said, haughtily enough I hoped she would not ask another question. "I wonder what you mean to do with his blade."

She looked at the sword as if surprised to find it in her hand. "I— he said I might look upon it sometimes. I have no brothers. My father trained me like a son. I never wished to be a king's bride gathering dust upon the shelf."

Only then could I hear a tremor in her voice; only then did Caledfwlch waver. I found I did not care for the way her green eyes shone with unshed tears. I pressed my nails into my palms until the strange impulse to touch her arm had passed.

"Arthur would not keep you from the yard if you wished to shake the dust from your shoulders. Indeed, if you asked, he might yield command to you." I smiled despite myself at a memory: Arthur at ten, sulky and clumsy in equal measure, the worst student any swordmaster could hope for. I was the only one who could coax him back to his feet when he fell.

"How should I ask, when he spends his nights hiding from me? How am I to serve him as a wife should when he sends me away from him?"

"It is not a slight. He also had not wished to be wed so soon. Your father insisted."

"I see. Then my father has disappointed us both. Perhaps he and I will prove friends after all." She looked towards the window, the sunlight sharpening her features. "Still, he has his knights, and you, and the wizard. I am alone."

"You need not envy him. Myrddin and I make poor company."

"No?" she asked, and frowned. "He talks of you fondly. And the wizard – why does Arthur seem to fear him so?"

I hesitated, not knowing how to describe Myrddin to one who did not know what it meant to dwell under his shadow. "He is a stern teacher, but he has been a loyal advisor to Arthur."

"An advisor."

"A prophet."

A muscle twitched in her jaw. "I do not believe in prophets. Why should I let some stranger choose my future?"

"He *dreams* the future – he does not choose it—"

"I think he does. I think he is not so different from my father and his lords. Bitter old men who cannot bear the thought of the world leaving them behind. Men who have mistaken what is for what must be. Well, I am tired of these men and their dreaming."

I bit the inside of my cheek to keep from crying out. Even Arthur, whose patience for Myrddin's dreams seemed less with every year, would not have dared to speak so. "You are ridiculous," I said.

"Perhaps." She stared at me, then smiled. "Perhaps I am, but – oh, Morgan, I am not such dreadful company. Would you walk with me in the gardens sometime? I will tell you ridiculous things, and you may tell me they are so."

I opened my mouth to tell her I would not.

"I would like that very much," I said instead.

* * *

One walk turned into another, and soon there was not an afternoon we did not spend together. She told me stories of a girlhood with reins in her hands and the wind in her hair. In return, I answered her questions – stumblingly, then easily, lured into saying too much by her sidelong smile. No one had ever been so interested in me.

How beautiful, she kept repeating. I suppose the gardens must have been so. In truth, I do not remember. I only remember this: her smile, her laugh, her fingers bumping mine when I dared walk too close.

Only this: how her fingers curled around mine before I could retreat.

Only this: how she dragged her gaze from my mouth to my eyes and to my mouth again.

* * *

Arthur was not dead, I did not have his scabbard, and Myrddin's patience grew ever thinner. But what could I do when a pack of knights followed at his heels like yelping dogs? When Gwenhwyfar called me to the gardens every afternoon?

No, no, Arthur was very much alive the morning he knocked on my door. "Would you walk with me?" he asked. "I have missed you, sister."

Without his crown, he looked not like a king but like himself. I opened my mouth, *half-sister* on the tip of my tongue, and found I could not correct him.

"I have not been hiding," I said, though my cheeks felt hot. "Only— busy."

"I feel like we have grown apart, and I do not care for that feeling. I love you, Mo. I miss you, and I need you at my side. I would like to name you to a seat at my table."

My stomach twisted so fiercely I thought I might be sick. "You cannot offer that."

"Why not?"

"What would your knights say to the idea of a woman in their company?"

"Why should I care what they say? I am the king."

"Even a king must have the sense to know that a woman cannot follow any path she wishes. If I will not be a wife, I must be a witch," I said, bitterness thick on my tongue. For all his promises of power, Myrddin would be the first to remind me no queen could rule alone.

"The world need not be so. We could change it, you and I."

"You sound like Gwenhwyfar," I said, thinking of the way her eyes flamed when she spoke to me of *what is* and *what might be*.

"I have found her a better friend than I had imagined – though I hear you know more of her charms than I do." When I lunged for him, he cackled and ducked away before I could pinch his ear. "I hear she enjoys your company very, very much!"

I scowled to keep from laughing. He was such a *boy*. An overgrown child. And for a moment everything felt like when we were young, when my only charge was to be his companion and not his killer.

"I am glad for it," he added, serious again. "It makes me happy. Like the three of us might make a sort of family."

I opened my mouth, not knowing what to say, then stopped: in the distance, I could hear a raven's cry.

"Arthur – you must not speak so. You— you should not—"

"Mo—"

"You should not go anywhere without your scabbard, little bear," I said, and fled before I could say anything more foolish.

* * *

In the nights that followed, whenever I could not slow my racing thoughts, I made myself a crow and circled Caer Lleon. More than once I went to Gwenhwyfar's windowsill. More than once she smiled as if she knew me. But I was not brave enough to enter, and dawn always came too soon, leaving my mind no more rested than my body.

"Pay attention," Myrddin barked during our lessons when my attention wavered for the second time that morning. "What is the matter with you?"

"I am sorry. I did not sleep—"

His expression blackened. "You have turned into a coward. *That* is the matter. You spend your days with the queen, and Arthur walks the halls with Caledfwlch at his side."

I pressed one thumbnail into the raw spot by the other. "What would you have me do?"

"I would have you do as you are told!" Fire bloomed in his palm, then vanished again. "This dalliance with the queen must end before your sins are seen by less keen eyes than mine."

"You are threatening me," I whispered. I did not think to say *I have not sinned*. My thoughts of late were sin enough.

"Not at all. I am threatening her. But the longer Arthur lives, the more it seems to me that she must die. Do you understand? Be a good creature, Morgan. Do not fail me."

"I understand," I said. My throat felt so thick I could hardly swallow. When I did, I tasted salt and copper and something sour. "I will be good."

* * *

That night my wings brought me to her window. When I took my own shape, she laughed. "I knew it was you," she said, and touched the back of my hand. "I could tell by the brown of your eyes. Where have you been? All day I looked for you."

I pulled my hand away. I could not think straight with her fingers brushing mine. "I have been with Myrddin."

"Ah," she said, her smile sharpening. "I suppose he had much to tell you of his dreams."

"Something of that sort."

"I had a dream last night, too." She looked to the window, moonlight silvering her skin. "I dreamed I was a white hart bearing Arthur on my back. What do you think that means?"

For once, I was glad she was not looking at me. "I— I cannot guess—"

"I could not outrun the hunters at our heels. When they cornered us, I felt certain we would die. But a black hound came through the trees, hardly more than a shadow. She chased the rest away. And I woke."

"I do not understand dreams as Myrddin does—"

"Oh, how tired I am of your wizard and his wisdom! Have you snuck into my bedchamber at midnight only to speak his name to me?"

I reached for the edge of her bed to steady myself, but even touching her sheets seemed suddenly a wicked thing. I withdrew as if stung. "Gwenhwyfar," I managed, hoarse.

"My ladies-in-waiting say I should not trust you," she said, her voice lifting. "They say you are *his* creature. Myrddin's creature."

I could not lie. Not with her eyes so aching-dark. Not with her tilting towards me like she thought I might be brave enough to reach for her. But I was not. It took all the courage I had just to speak the truth. "I have been his student for so long. I do not know how to be anything else."

Her eyes blazed so brightly I could barely meet her gaze. "You must find a way. For I do not want you to be his. Sometimes— oh, Morgan, sometimes I do not even want you to be your own. I want you to be *mine*."

Before I could form an answer, she was against me, her hands in my hair, her mouth almost touching mine.

"Please," she said. "If you will have me."

I found I had courage enough for that.

* * *

After, she kissed each of my ragged fingertips, then brought my palm to her lips. "Do not let him tell you who you are," she murmured against my skin. "I know you, Morgan, my Morgan. Let us dream something new together."

"I am afraid," I whispered, more honest than I had ever dared to be.

"I know," she said. She drew me to the crook of her neck. I breathed her in, salt and sweat and garden-green, and understood what I must do.

* * *

I found my master sitting at his desk, nothing in front of him but his steepled hands. As I entered the study, he released a heavy sigh. A fine show of sorrow, too late to be believed.

"So you have come to betray me. What a fool I have been to think so highly of you."

I bit my tongue against the instinct to beg for his praise. "I have come to tell you I will not serve you any longer. I will not help you kill my brother."

"Your *brother*," he began, then caught himself. "And what do you think that means? Do you think you will dwell in your tower, and I in mine, and Arthur will sit upon his throne until the end of his days?"

"I would have it so, if you would."

"I would not!" He leapt from his seat, the chair clattering against the stones. "So be it! You have bought your freedom at a high price. Send me away if you must – I will return, and I will have his head, yes, and yours, and I will see your queen upon the pyre!"

With a snap, he took a raven's shape and made for the window. Before he breached the walls, I was a crow. Though he was larger, I was faster. I dove and felt his flesh split beneath my talons even as his beak went through my belly.

We fell to the ramparts – not crow and raven but student and teacher, my hands red with his blood, his mouth smeared with mine. I pinned him beneath me against the stones. My teacher had forgotten our first lesson: pain was a better trick than any spell. With my right hand, I held the dagger Gwenhwyfar had given me underneath his chin and watched the tip redden. With my left, I pulled threads of magic to my palm.

"I was mistaken," I told him. "I wanted to serve you because I thought you were strong. Because I thought you would make me strong, too."

"Morgan— Morgan – you have been my faithful creature, do not turn against me—"

"I am not your creature any longer. I have found a power greater than yours."

"There is no greater power than mine! Do not refuse it now!"

I thought of Arthur's laughter bouncing off the stones. My blood, my brother, no matter what Myrddin said. I thought of Gwenhwyfar and the freckles on her nose. *I love you* in his voice, the truth of those words shining out of eyes as brown as mine. *Morgan, my Morgan* against my lips, her arms around me like a promise. I thought of what was and what might be.

"You are wrong," I said. At last I knew it to be true. I placed my left hand upon his chest and I showed my teacher all he had taught me of unmaking.

Sea-born
C.J. Subko

We were swimming in the cold sea when the net came around us and snatched us up. Our body flailed in the net, our tail and our flippered hands useless to prize apart the strong knots that held it together, but it was no use. We were not heavy enough to flop our way to freedom, and we were pulled up roughly against the side of a wooden hull onto the deck of a boat.

We looked at the men, human men, standing around us and we hissed, our sharp, pointed teeth bared. We were used to seeing men from a distance, jumping from the rocks and lounging on the beaches. We had never been so close.

One of the men approached. Taller than the others, broad-shouldered, he held out a knife that caught the sunlight and he said, "I will not hurt you if you do not fight."

We could understand his tongue, as we could understand the tongues of all creatures, and we hissed back, "Let us go, or you will repent it."

He sneered at his men and then at us, and stroked his long hair and his short dark beard, so stark against skin as pale as the belly of a clam. "I think it is you who would repent." But he sheathed his knife. Stupidity? Did he mean to curry our favor with his gesture? He bellowed, "I am King Uriens of Gore. Be my wife or I will be your death."

"How can we," we said, "when we are a daughter of the sea?"

Uriens took something out of his pocket then, a glowing turquoise stone as clear as glass. The light of it spiked through the cracks in his fingers. "I have Merlin's magic. I will give you the shape of a woman, and you will be mine."

Before we could budge or scream, Uriens cast the stone at us. It shattered against our gray skin. The pain was immediate, sharp and wrenching, as though someone were actively scissoring the fins away from our fingers, parting our legs and flensing our skin. We were consumed by the blast of agony, and then all was light and gone.

When we woke, it was in the softness and the darkness, and Uriens was standing over us.

"Now to make you mine," he said, his hands fumbling at the ties of his trousers.

We did what we do best – retreated into ourself, until the pain was gone and we were alone.

* * *

He called us Morgen, sea-born, and when we returned to the mainland he married us in a great ceremony where our forearms were tied together and we were crowned with flowers and everyone in the kingdom was invited for the hunt and the feast. We were put on display like a fine vase, clad in a beautifully embroidered gown and a crown of golden thorns, and all the other humans came up to kiss our hands and kneel at our feet and swear us fealty.

We did not want fealty. We wanted the sea, our mother, which we could still hear lilting on the wind, but we nodded at them all.

There was one who was specially introduced to us by our new husband. The man was tall, straight-backed and slender-waisted, with ruddy brown hair and eyes the color of our mother.

"Morgen," said Uriens gruffly, "this is Sir Accolon, one of my finest knights. He will be personally assigned to you as your guard and will accompany you any time you are outside of the castle."

"I am to leave?" we asked. We had learned to call ourselves 'I', as the humans did not understand our triune nature.

Uriens chuffed Accolon on the arm and laughed. "No, my bride, but this place is your home now, and you may go about it as you please."

Our eyes widened. For the first time, we understood that, while we were to be a bird in a cage, it was to be a spacious, glorious cage full of wonders.

"But Accolon?" Uriens added, looking straight at us. "Don't let her near the ocean."

* * *

Our first days in Gore were lonely ones. We longed for the fresh, salty air of the sea, but we dared not leave our chambers, lest we be harmed by any of the humans around us or used by Uriens as he wished. And he did wish, often, so often that by our first autumn in the castle, we became with child. Accolon was the only constant in our life, the only solace, for he never asked anything of us, and always did as we wanted.

"Accolon, bring me a bouquet of flowers," we would say, and he would dutifully return to the door of our chambers with a bouquet of honeysuckle and tea roses.

"Accolon, I'm weary. Tell me a tale." And he would spin us a story of Merlin and his magic or King Arthur and his Knights of the Round Table, tales of glorious, righteous men who seemed impossible to exist given what we were used to.

Yet none of this pleased us as well as the wilds, so at last we were forced to reckon with our fear. "Accolon," we asked one day, "take me out to the grounds. I would like to have a walk."

"Milady?" Accolon asked, surprise evident in the quirk of his sleek dark brows.

Even in the sea, we were prized, worshipped, and not accustomed to be made waiting. We fixed him in our gaze and he blushed and bowed.

"Very well, milady. Please, follow me."

Accolon walked with brisk strides to the tower stairs and we followed apace down the tower stairs to the central hallway. We were not prepared for the glut of people who occupied it. Our throat began to close up as though we were choking, and it became difficult to breathe. "I can't," we whispered. "I can't."

"Make way for the queen!" Accolon announced, and people began to move aside like the parting of waves. "Make way for the queen!"

He hurried us along through the tunnel of humans until we were outside, out in the fresh air, and oh, it was fresh and sweet and it ballooned our withered lungs. We stood with our palms out in prayer, drinking it in.

If we imagined, we could almost taste the salty tang of the sea on the wind.

But no! It was not our imagination. There it was, the cut of salt, the brine of fish. We were close.

"Accolon," we begged, "show it to me. Show me the sea."

Accolon looked aghast. "I cannot, milady, I have been forbidden to take you to the sea."

"Please!" We fell to our knees before him in supplication. "Please, there must be a way. I only want to see."

Accolon looked divided within himself. He looked toward the door, which had not stirred, then at me, and said furtively, "Follow, milady. Do you trust me?"

We had to. We followed.

We followed across the carefully pruned pleasure grounds, all grass and cultivated garden, to the wilds of the forest at the back of the estate – still within the walls, but used mostly for hunting and other such delights.

We sniffed the spicy, woody air. It was different from our muggy, briny home, but it was not unpleasant. We hoped that Accolon knew where he was taking us, and that this was not a trap.

We found ourselves at last on a rise. Accolon stopped, and then... oh, Mother Ocean, there she was in the distance, over the wall and beyond, stretched out in dark gray-blue as far as the eye could see. We found ourselves reaching out towards her, towards the salt we smelled on the wind, but she was so small we could have held her in our hand at this distance. And yet, we felt our connection to her was not lost, whatever magic had been done.

We turned to Accolon, who had been watching us with widened eyes, and now endeavored to look easy. We, too, attempted to look as though we were not so affected. "Sir Accolon," we said, "you will take me to this place every day unless I request otherwise. You have given me a gift, and I will not repent of it. Nor," I added, "will I tell his majesty my husband anything of the sort."

Accolon perceived his danger, no doubt. Making a secret pact with the queen. But perhaps he had already found himself bewitched by my beauty then, or perhaps he was just kind, for he knelt down before me. "I swear it to you, milady, I will not falter."

* * *

Our child was born in winter, a boy we named Yvain, whom the Crone insisted would be a Knight of the Round Table someday. He was a peevish, human thing and we left him often to his wetnurse. Our thoughts and our heart were elsewhere, with the rise of hill where Accolon faithfully brought us every day, even on the snowy days when we must don our beaver fur boots and fur-lined coat for warmth.

We were standing there with Accolon on the rise, looking out over the unchanged ocean, when he asked us with a strange tone to his voice, "Milady, have you ever made a snow angel?"

I looked at him askance, and with a little roll of my eyes. "Sir Accolon, you very well know I have not."

"Come," he said, "we have all this bright, fine, fresh powder, it seems a pity to waste it. Here, I'll show you. You just lay down like this." He lay down in the snow with his limbs out in an X. "And then you move your arms and legs to make the robes and wings like this!"

We furrowed our brow. "What is this winged creature you speak of?"

Accolon sat up, incredulous. "You don't know of God's angels?"

"Ah," we said knowingly, "they are creatures of your god. We do not have such things below the sea."

"You do not worship the Lord?"

We don't know why we said it. We all came to a sort of agreement about it at once and blurted, "I do not worship anyone but my Mother the ocean, for in her realm, I am a goddess."

Accolon staggered to his feet. Now his cheeks were spotty red. "That's blasphemy, milady!"

We waved our hand. "Call the truth whatever name you will, that does not make the sun shine a different color."

We fell silent for a while, and then Accolon said gravely, "You miss the sea, I can see that."

Our eyes welled up with tears. "More than anything."

Then he reached out and with his thumb he pressed away the tears drizzling down my cheek. "I am sorry," he said, with all the sincerity we believed him to possess. "It is a hard life, to be divided from what you want."

We stood dumbfounded. He did not react and, in fact, looked cheery again. "Well, we can make a day of it, at least. Let us look out on the sea as long as you wish, and then we will go get you a nice cup of glug."

* * *

After that day, Accolon was finding more and more excuses to touch us. He would brush past us as we walked, or pluck a fallen leaf from our shoulder, or touch our waist to turn us when we had made a wrong path. It was becoming obvious to our mind, not untutored in the ways of the world – he desired us.

What surprised us, then, was the way our stomach and loins warmed when we thought of desiring him back. In the day, we smiled at memories of our time together. At night, he visited us in our dreams.

Typically, the Maiden was in charge of us, but now the Mother and Crone wanted their say too, all three offering arguments and counterarguments in regards to pursuing Accolon's affections. Mother was deadest against the danger of it, but at last the Crone demanded, "She is young. Let her have her way." And the Maiden was at last given leave to use the body as she saw fit.

We were nervous all the next day in a way we had not felt in a long time. Accolon kept asking us what was wrong, and was becoming increasingly dissatisfied with our noncommittal answers. When we were finally up to the rise, he stopped us.

"Milady, you are not easy! Please, we are…friends, I believe. Tell me what ails you."

We took a step towards him. "Sir Accolon," we said firmly, "I am in grave danger."

Accolon looked around, and one hand went to the hilt of his sword. "Where, milady? What is it?"

"I am in grave danger of the acutest kind from my heart. It belongs by my troth to my lord husband, but it belongs in truth to another."

Accolon's cheeks reddened consciously. Was he thinking of himself? "Milady, you must guard yourself. Your virtue and purity are more precious than gold. I must protect you in all ways."

We stepped still forward. "Would you protect me from yourself? For you are the man who haunts my dreams and waking hours. I can have no peace until you tell me you cannot be with me."

Accolon looked anguished. He looked left, right, as though readying himself to flee, but then back into our eyes, and he took my hands in his and said, "I cannot! I cannot tell you that. For my heart has belonged to you since the moment I saw you look upon the sea."

Like waves, we crashed together, our lips finding each other, parting, breath and tongues mingling, teeth clashing. "Morgen," he whispered into us, and we smiled, for it was as good a name as any; our true name would be unpronounceable in his tongue. And when he spoke it, it was a revelation. A new-naming.

We ended up on the ground, our furred cloaks shed beneath us, our dress rucked up to our thighs and his trousers down, and he thrust into us gently, sweetly, his fingers threaded through our hair and his mouth on ours. Each thrust was like the crash of a wave onto shore, each kiss the spray of the sea. When he juddered into me at last, I held him tightly to me, not ready to let go.

So we lay there in the nest of furs, and I told him the story of myself. Accolon listened without interrupting, until we were done.

"So there are three of you in there?" he said at last.

We laughed and kissed him. "We are one goddess, and we are three spirits," we said.

Accolon shook his head. "I don't pretend to understand, but I will try."

"And that is more than any other man has done," we admitted. And perhaps that is why we had grown to love Accolon. Because he was so different from Uriens, so gentle and so sweet. Because he listened to our desires.

"We must go," he said at last, pressing a hot kiss to our cool forehead. "You'll be wanted."

"We are wanted," we agreed, although we were not sure he quite understood. We allowed him to pull us to our feet and refasten our cloak around us and then, hand in hand, we walked back down towards the castle.

* * *

The coming months were some of the happiest we had ever spent, even though we were on land. Every day, Accolon and I would go to the rise that overlooked the sea and we would make love in the salty air. Sated with a male heir, Uriens no longer came to our chambers quite so often and, when he did, I could pretend the callous rutting was just practice, and dip into pleasanter memories.

As queen, it was still our duty to attend all the fetes and parties our lord Uriens was pleased to throw. In the spring, he ordered a grand feast to celebrate the oncoming gentle weather and the old gods who were called angels now, and it was then that he and we sat in our thrones in the grand hall one night, while a raucous party of acrobats and ramblers performed tricks for the delight of us and our court. The nursemaid kept Yvain by her side; he was ever trying to steal the leather balls the juggler used and to gambol into the fray.

We clapped politely, having only a passing interest in the feats of the human body, but we must clap, because Uriens kept looking to us waiting for our approbation. Satisfied, or not, he clapped his hands and dismissed the acrobats, then said, "We shall hear from the Court Jester, Davance the Fool!"

Our stomach squirmed. We did not like Davance and his quick, penetrating wit, like a knife poked into the stomachs of so many victims, but we clapped all the same as he came out dressed in his motley and did a little jig.

He had sung several vicious songs that made ladies and men blush alike when he announced, "A song for the queen!"

Our eyes found Accolon; he was already looking at us. He must know how horrid we would find this spectacle. And now Davance was grinning at us, his mismatched teeth glinting awfully in the light.

"There was once a queen of the sea,

Or so it was told,

Who married the king even though he was old.

She was passing fair, with thick black hair,

And was beautiful to see.

Says the golden knight, who kissed her there, and on her nether eye!"

A hush fell over the room, and then some clapping and tittering, even a sob from one of the ladies in waiting. People didn't know how to react.

We turned surreptitiously towards Uriens, whose cheeks had gone pale with rage. The implication was clear enough that a clever man like Uriens could not fail to surmise who the man in question was, or what was meant by Davance's song.

We dared not look at Accolon, lest by a look we betray our confidence with him. Instead, we turned to Uriens. "My lord husband, you must not believe such frivolous rumor. The Fool Davance has spoken in jest."

Ignoring us, Uriens demanded Davance draw near. The sycophant slid up on his knees and bowed before his master. "Yes, my king?" His voice dripped syrup and treachery.

"Is this true? Did you witness the lady queen in such indiscretion?"

Did he mean to ask him before the whole court? Although they were not shouting, their voices carried. Yet Uriens did not shush Davance, but encouraged him to continue. Davance said proudly, "I did not witness what I did not see, your majesty, but I have heard the truth spoken from many lips."

"Lies!" we wanted to scream, but that would surely damn us. Our stomach churned like seafoam. Surely Accolon had not made any confidants of his friends in the knighthood. Surely he had not spread our story abroad.

That was all Uriens needed to hear. Drawing his sword and standing to height, he pointed his blade at Accolon. "Villain, I will have your head!"

We thought to lose our lover then and there, but the Priest of God in attendance stood and cautioned Uriens, "We are in company with ladies, your majesty. Shall you not observe the courtly rules of a duel and set a time and place of meeting?"

"Very well!" said Uriens. "Dawn."

We stood, and a shocked hush came over the crowd. "As it is my honor at stake, I should choose the location. The duel will occur at the seaside."

Uriens looked at me. "Fine." But he leant in, our cheeks together; we could smell mullet on his breath. "Try anything and you will die. I own you."

The party broke up then, and we awayed to our rooms. Accolon was still our guard for another day; he hesitated at our door.

"Come in," we commanded him.

He hesitated, blushed. "Your honor."

"Was never a concern for men to fight over. It is ours. Come in. We would hold you, one more night."

"Oh, Uriens be damned!" Accolon cried softly, and closed and locked the door behind him.

For the first time, we did not feel alone in our bed. We made love with Accolon and, when we were done, he held our naked body in his arms and stroked our skin with his callused hands and kissed our neck and we felt free.

"Accolon," we said finally, "if you come to trouble, run into the sea."

"What?"

"Please," we said. We could promise nothing, because we were not sure ourself if it would work, but we said again, "If it be honor or safety, choose safety, and run to the sea."

Accolon nuzzled my neck, and that would have to be answer enough.

* * *

I stood with a small group of ladies-in-waiting by a pile of dry driftwood on the sandy beach. The salt spray was so strong here, my Mother so near, it took everything I had not to go jump in. I had to be here. Had to be here for Accolon.

He and Uriens stood twenty paces apart from each other. His golden hair glinted in the light, before he put on his helmet, and we could not help recall Davance's song and our last night together. We did not blush. We were not ashamed.

One of the knights called the duel and Uriens exploded forward, but Accolon was ready for him and their blades clashed. We had never heard such a sound before, scraping and grating in our stomach. They clashed, back and forth, Uriens trying to slip under Accolon's guard and Accolon parrying back.

At last, Accolon lunged, his sword tip poking into Urien's stomach and coming away bloody.

The knight arbitrating the duel cried, "First blood, Sir Accolon! The duel is over."

"No!" Uriens cried and, while Accolon turned towards his squire, who had a jug of water and a rag, he slashed across Accolon's side. Blood sticky and iron tangy sprayed. One of our ladies-in-waiting swooned. We ignored her, bent only on Accolon, who staggered back and raised his sword to block Uriens' assault.

We felt our whole body vibrating with tension as Uriens sent a flurry of attacks towards Accolon. Accolon was on the defense and backing up towards the cliffs.

With one lunge, Uriens slashed across Accolon's stomach, splitting him open.

Our entire world narrowed to the point of Accolon's eyes. He was looking at us. *Please*, we thought. *Please*.

He glanced towards the sea. But Uriens was coming after him and he had to bring up his sword to stop myself from being fully gutted.

We couldn't watch him die. We ran forward and shrieked, "Uriens!"

Uriens turned his head, paused, just long enough. Accolon dropped his sword and ran, holding his stomach, as fast as he could, into the sea.

"No!" Uriens cried, but it was too late. As soon as Accolon was away, we sprinted full into the sea, until we were ankle deep.

As soon as the water splashed around our skin, we could feel our Mother flowing through us. We could feel Accolon, floating, dying, leaking his fluids into my Mother's water.

Accolon was dying. There was no future for him as a human. But ours was the magic of the sea, and we wrapped it around him, molding him to our will. By the time Uriens reached us and yanked us back out of the sea, a dolphin squeaking breached the surface, a golden-blue dolphin, and then flapped away into the ocean to find his brethren.

"You're mine," Uriens snapped, jerking us back. We did not speak. We allowed tears to spill down our cheeks, mourning our lover, and we followed our lord husband and the stupefied knights and ladies back to the castle. "Le fay," they whispered. The fairy. The witch. Us.

In the seconds after transforming Accolon we had tried to transform ourself too, but Merlin's magic had blocked us.

That was no matter. We now knew one thing: our magic was not gone but only sleeping. We were still a daughter of the sea. Someday, we would break the spell and return. In the meantime, Uriens now knew to fear us.

And oh, Mother, would we make him repent.

She Made a Doll in Winter
Lana Voos

The red blooms spring up overnight. Thousands of them overwhelm Morgana's grove, all five-petaled, four long and one short, like a beckoning hand.

The Fey Duke of Pox and Posies demands a bride.

Her first instinct is to poison the flowers at the root. At half a millennium old, Morgana is in no shape to become a Fey Duchess even if the idea appealed to her. But this Duke is hot-blooded, impetuous, and powerful, judging by his unsubtle proposal. Perhaps he doesn't understand that even legends fade. That after centuries of otherworldly beauty and power, the world of man has finally forgotten Morgana le Fay.

No, she is no one's wife, and she will not become one ever again.

* * *

She must tread carefully, as the Duke can send worse omens than flowers if offended. A pox is the last thing this blighted isle needs.

As Morgana ponders her response, the posies' pollen renders her wistful, nostalgic, and more than a little foolish. The world used to be better, she thinks. Noble. *Decent.* Men have grown impossibly brutal. Kingdoms rise and fall with the seasons, traitors' heads rot on pikes, clever men in gowns whisper Roman tongues into warlords' ears.

She has nothing to do with any of it.

All she does, now, is tend the border between Fey and folk. Some Fey influence is necessary to keep the parsley and pennyroyal in bloom, but too much, and maidens go missing in the night, whole harvests are trampled by the Hunt. So here she stands, a sorceress of legend, spending the long winter of her life as a glorified watchdog.

It's marvelous.

She feels as if she's slipped from iron manacles to run barefoot in the dead of night. She was worried she'd grow lonely, but no, never before has she felt truly free. Moreover, the aches of age, the deep lines on her face, the rising hump in her spine, are their own great comforts. It's thrilling to cheat death, she knows that well, but it's sweeter to cheat life – to feel the magic in her veins fade beneath the slow drip of mortality, like water eating marble. She is grateful for the chance to die as so many of her friends and family have, to follow them into the unknown.

There are so few unknowns, for a Seer.

That's it. She has an answer for the Duke.

* * *

Morgana sends a dove she's magicked to sleep and trussed in a web of the Duke's flowers. Then, she relaxes in her willow rocking chair by the fire, pleased with herself and more than a little addled on Fey pollen, still. Her omen will inform the Duke that she has foreseen the coming of his bride. No force, however powerful, can rush destiny.

Which gives her time to plot and plan and play.

She fashions a doll out of pale soapstone, which, to her relief, she is still able to pull and bend like molten glass. Oh, but she has *missed* this. There's a delicious irony in sending the Duke a false bride, when the Fey constantly ensnare mortals with manifestations of their own desires. She's confident that any young Duke will take a while to realize he's married a doll-woman with no thoughts or will of her own. Time frolics in Faerie, so it may be centuries before it dawns on him that he's been had. Morgana could be dust by then.

Perhaps. It's a gamble.

As the pollen fades from her blood and her mind spirals down, she fusses with the doll. She runs a spelled ruby comb through the flax silk atop its head, turning the stalky strands to auburn waves. The doll blinks, she walks, she even breathes, but she can't speak. That can be spun as a virtue. The true obstacle is that she can't dance. A fatal flaw, for a Fey duchess – she'll be murdered halfway through her wedding feast, and she won't bleed, but rather crumble, giving the game away.

Morgana trudges into the garden to mull that over, weeding the posies with a cloth mask across her face, this time. She has no bride to offer, but the omen is sent. This is why she stopped meddling.

"Ah yes," a strange girl's voice reaches her, distorted, through her outer wards. "Yes indeed, this looks right witchlike to my eye!"

Morgana's perimeter defenses crash in on her. She rushes back to her home and rolls a bell around a bowl of swamp water once, twice, thrice. An illusion makes her grove appear decrepit. Her gilded mirror transmutes to brass, and in the reflection she's an old crone in the traditional image, spindle-thin and dressed in rags. She wonders for a moment if this version isn't closer to the truth.

"Hello?" The mannerless girl barges in wearing tattered, reeking furs. Her body is strong, though, and her red-gold hair is thick and brilliant. "Granddam! I'm looking for a witch in these woods, is that you?" The girl looks around, finally takes in the empty cupboards, the cobwebbed corners. "No, you haven't even a cauldron to your name."

Morgana shakes her head, willing the girl gone. And yet, part of her wonders if she'll stay where she's not welcome. A strong-willed mortal is likely to survive in Faerie.

The girl's gaze rests upon the doll's comb of ruby and gold. It should look like a dead leaf, but there are hundreds of trinkets in the house, and Morgana's magic isn't what it once was.

"Granddam, you part with this bauble and you'll live out your days warm!" The girl looks at Morgana with a new sharpness in her eyes. The illusion strains under this girl's will. Oh, but it's strong. Morgana has no choice; she lets her magic fall.

"I knew it!" the girl shouts as Morgana's true home roars to life with gold and jewels, hanging herb boughs, sparkling spell reagents. "You're the witch of the woods."

Morgana feels the circlet weigh upon her brow, again, the embroidery drip from her arms. Her hair cascades downward, grey, but still with enough true black in it to mark her.

"Blast it all, you're *Morgana le Fay!*" The girl drops to her knees. "From Ol' King Arthur days! Oh, you're the witchiest witch of them all! My name is Edie, just Edie, mi'lady. I'm in need of your hexes, so very badly – iff'n I believed in Fate, I'd say I was meant to find you."

Morgana *did* believe in fate. She'd lived through too many ballads to doubt that someone or something was penning them all. Had Morgana's omen for the Duke drawn the girl here? But no, she'd come seeking something else. "My hexes? What hexes?"

"Why, the wicked spells you call down on men! See, the minor lord of the gatehouse said he meant to wed me, to give me his mum's jewels and a fat pony, but the craven skipped off with his seneschal's third runt daughter instead. Bastard. He knows I've got nothin', no family of my own left."

Morgana blinked. "You know the name *Morgana le Fay* and think I… poison men?" What absurd specificity. She was too stunned to be properly offended. "That's *all*?"

"No–no," Edie stammered. "They say you grant wishes, too."

Morgana once ruled Avalon. The sheer force of her power made the isle a haven for dying kings and magical sisters alike. She soared as a hawk across all of Britain, swam to the court of the Selkies in the body of an eel, staunched mortal wounds while battle raged around her. Men used to whisper her name as warily as any ancient spirit's, any goddess' or god's. She is known, still, but as a petty sorceress casting hexes on men's pricks. Or else granting fool girls' wishes.

Well, so be it.

"I will not hex your man, but I will grant a wish," Morgana said. "If you're willing to leave this world and every soul in it behind, I can remake you into a Fey Duchess. You will rule in a land of excess and fancy on the arm of a handsome young Duke with a weakness for flowers." No need to mention the pox. "Does that appeal to you?"

Morgana hadn't seen a resemblance between herself and Edie until that moment. Then the lust hits her eyes, and oh, they could have been sisters in a bygone age. Morgana remembers how it felt to stand on the cusp of power – tenfold sweeter than actually obtaining it.

"But o'course it appeals to me!" Edie exclaims, and the deal is done.

* * *

If wanting to be a duchess was all it took to make a woman one, Britain would have far fewer fishwives, Morgana figures. She weighs Edie's dreams against her realities. Edie is far from royal, but she can say *no* to things expected of her, which preserves one's humanity in Faerie. She can also dance well enough to avoid being torn asunder by offended courtiers.

She is, Morgana admits, *slightly* more qualified than the doll.

But the girl's mind is crude and clumsy, incapable of reaching any conclusion beyond the obvious. If Morgana sends her to Faerie now, her first Duel of the Sun and Moon – a battle in verse involving subtle variations on a loop – would send the girl's head spinning. Soon after, it would roll. Morgana should have been long past caring, but old age puts more weight on her every decision, as if she can count the remaining forks in her path. With considerable time and effort, Morgana believes she can mold the girl into a Fey-duchess-shaped-thing.

If the Duke agrees to wait.

His patience may already be waning. Morgana checks herself for pox each day and watches for omens by night. On the first full moon after Edie's arrival, while the little wretch snores loudly in the corner, Morgana dreams she's standing in a ring of posies.

Morgana. The Duke's voice is everywhere. He resolves, a slender figure decked in cloud-spun lace and falling-star jewels. His chain of office is part of his skin, the heirloom-birthmark that designates scions of Pox: A ring of softly bleeding sores. They're a thousand times rarer than rubies, in Faerie, as they're permanent.

Fey eyes are deadly snares, but Morgana slips them by seeking her own reflection. In his eyes, she stands unbowed, uncreased, undiminished, exactly as she was centuries ago. It's only an illusion, but still, she feels an echo of her old Feywild power resonate through her blood.

A Seer should not go backwards, she reminds herself. Dousing a fortune teller in her own past is an uncanny trick typical of Faerie. This is the Duke's dream, too – of course he would summon Morgana at the height of her power and beauty, as he would prefer her. She's grown so used to being idealized and scrutinized at once that the Duke's stare feels as common as a shawl across her shoulders.

"*Morgana*," he intones. "Paint us a portrait of our bride."

"A mortal girl possessed of extraordinary strength of will," she begins. "She has outlived her family and seeks to blight with pox any soul who wrongs her." *She is utterly unschooled, unsubtle, and uninteresting,* Morgana thinks, but doesn't say. None of those failings are the girl's fault. Minds need solitude and books like plants need sun and water, and not every girl can be reared in Avalon.

"Is she a beauty?" the Duke asks.

"Of course, Posies' Grace," Morgana says, bowing low. "You insult me by asking."

"Can she weave cloth?"

Morgana frowns, but thankfully the expression is hidden by her pose. When did Fey Dukes care about mortal handiwork?

"The Frost Prince's new mortal bride weaves all through the night, like a spider," the Duke elaborates. "The Frost Prince says that the choicest mortal women are judged by their weaving, as she-Fey are judged by the speed of their reel-step and the venom of their tongues. I must have a finer weaver-mortal-bride-girl than my rival."

There. The pattern comes together.

"Your destined bride is a paragon of weavers," Morgana lies. "So accomplished, in fact, that she will not wed until she has crafted cloth fit for a duchess." Morgana considers his ambitions. "Nay, fit for a *queen.*"

He smiles, but the ring of posies all tremble to see it. "We can clothe her as a queen with a passing thought."

"Good Duke, she's mortal! You can't expect her to wear the first mewl of an infant hellcat to her *coronation.*" Morgana inhales, exhales, shakes off the unease she feels toying with the girl's fate. "She wishes to impress you, your Grace. Let her prove her worth."

The flowers close, contented, and Morgana hides her flash of triumph.

"Great Lady." The Duke inclines his spectral head, sending the pox-marks around his neck spinning happily. "We are glad to have your aid in this."

The dream dissolves, and Morgana wakes to the crash of Edie rolling herself clear off the bed, followed by a string of commoners' curses.

Watchdog, wish-granter, matchmaker... Morgana is nothing if not *helpful*.

* * *

Morgana had a son, once. Barely. The moment he left her arms, he was swept up in a storm of swords and songs and valor. In her darker moods, she suspects she would have been happier if she'd had a daughter. One with magic, of course, or at least a great destiny. Morgana would have even played mentor, like Merlin, or Athena before him, but Gwen never did have children.

Edie is likely the best Morgana is going to get. The girl is more doll than ward, built for a single purpose: to be dressed in pretty clothes and danced into oblivion. Still, Morgana hauls out her loom, a treasure of a machine gathering dust, and teaches Edie to weave. Luckily Morgana still possesses an eternal spindle she once won in a wager, or Edie would have tangled all the wool in Britain.

When Edie's fingers bleed, she reaches for books until Morgana can be bothered to heal her. Edie is hardworking, and reasonably talented, and before long even Morgana can muster affection for the whelp. The first time Edie pauses and thinks before she speaks, Morgana is reminded painfully of her son's first steps.

After a full cycle of the seasons – a blink to Morgana, and an eternity to Edie – the girl announces she's finished. Morgana is skeptical, but upon inspection, she finds no flaws. The girl's broadcloth is even, sturdy, and competently woven.

"It's good," Morgana says, before incinerating it in a wave of Faerie fire.

Edie cries out as if her body has been burned. "Why did you do that?"

"*Good* is not fit for a Fey Queen," Morgana says, without malice. "This is broadcloth. You must invent a pattern no one has ever woven before."

"Then how am I supposed to learn to weave it?"

"Envision something new and teach yourself."

Edie squints. "This isn't just about cloth, is it."

Morgana says nothing, but hope burns behind her sternum. The girl might yet survive Faerie. And if she does, if she *thrives*, she will sate the Fey appetite towards the mortal realm for a while. Morgana the Watchdog may yet earn some rest.

Edie toils at the loom for eight more years, growing out of her awkward, sapling slenderness and into the full expression of her beauty. Her mind keeps pace with her body and her hands, those tiny thoughts unfolding, broadening. On days when Morgana feels particularly sluggish and vague, especially mortal, Edie can argue philosophy with her or entertain her with some light verse.

Morgana keeps her eye on the loom. Edie's expert work becomes inspired. Her inspired work grows sublime. Just when Morgana thinks she's done it, turned the doll into a duchess after all, she's stricken down by visions. Once the Sight stirs awake, not even Morgana's will can stop it. She falls into a fever. For three days, she shakes and dreams and screams and Sees.

A woman born from a severed neck. Heavenly stars dance about her face, framed with red-gold hair like fire, and she wears a woven gown the likes of which Morgana could never have imagined. Morgana watches the child-queen learn and read as hungrily as she once did, until a fever burns all the child's weakness away, leaves scars on her face and hands. As she grows, the scars fade into an otherworldly glow. Moon-pale, snow-pale, lead-pale. The woman's mind is sharp and solemn, her eyes clear and her hand firm. Her words stir hearts and songs spring up in her shadows. She wields the strength of fire and iron, commands the sprites of the sea, oh, she is a queen of queens! Every scene of her is alone, she is unmatched, unalloyed, unwed. Power unbound, like the peace Morgana once knew. The kind she longs for in secret, even now. Even at the end.

* * *

Morgana wakes with a stone lodged in her throat.

"Edie!" She storms over to the loom.

"Lady Morgana." If Edie is startled by Morgana's manner, she hides it well. She curtsies and steps away, opening her work to her mistress's discerning eye. "I was about to look into the proper method to wake a Seer. My masterwork is complete."

Her cloth has the sensibility of Faerie in it, as the vines and posies rise shimmering into the foreground, wrapping and twisting into impossible patterns. Yet in its form, the weave is impressively solid and heavy, packed full of fine thread and even finer skill. Fey will look favorably on Edie for having created something beautiful that lasts beyond three midnights. Even Morgana can't fault it. She would have worn it at her best.

Morgana helps Edie remove the cloth from the loom, and Edie drapes one corner over her shoulder. Morgana takes in her fiery hair, her keen mind. In between blinks, stars dance about her head.

"Wait!" Morgana yells, but already, vines are spilling in through the windows, bursting up through cracks in the floor, dipping like so many snakes through her ceiling. Red petals unfurl, not grasping hands but full, round fists. Posies so rich with petals they shame roses.

Edie clutches her cloth. "He's here."

"I must tell you what I Saw." Morgana bats an encroaching vine away from Edie's waist. She's able to wrangle Edie's hands, which are unscarred by fever, and yes, the vision was far off in the future, well past Edie's natural lifetime, but still. *Still.*

"I saw a queen," Morgana says, "a brilliant, beloved queen who required no duke, no consort. With fiery red hair like yours, and ivory skin like yours, and—"

Morgana is too late. The Duke's spectral hounds snap their teeth, and his fanfare of the sick and dying blares out from Faerie, itself. He's grown in influence since they last spoke, now venturing out bodily beyond his realm.

Edie swoons into his arms, and Morgana grabs her by the hands again.

"Think, damn you! You could have power without burden, without chaining yourself to a Duke, a Court, a dynasty. It's a beautiful thing, to rule alone, to grow old and wise alone. Look at me—" Morgana grabs Edie by the chin, forces her to look. "You don't have to go with him."

"Milady," Edie says, "you promised me a Duke. For nearly ten years, I did *everything* you asked."

"I was wrong to offer you to this... this *beast!* You can be free. You can build your name alone, write your life with your own hand, just as I did."

"Oh, Morgana, no. I can't. You're an uncanny force, and those can exist alone, are *happiest* alone. Don't deny it – I was always a burden to you."

Morgana grimaces, as the accusation strikes with the weight of truth. But she refuses to let go of Edie's chin. "Alone, you get to choose who you are."

"What if I want to be his wife?" She smiles like a Fey, all teeth. "All these years, and you never knew the first thing about me, *Great Lady*. I'm a woman, not a witch."

The Duke laughs as he wrangles Edie away from her. "She is exquisite! Come, love, our wedding feast awaits."

He sweeps out his cloak of rot-blooming moss to cover them both. Pollen bursts from the flowers as they tangle themselves up in Edie's hair, snake and wriggle below her dress, clench her all along her neck and arms. They drown her head-to-toe in posies, and when the blooms wither and die, only empty air remains.

Even the dry petals have been swept up and delivered back to Faerie. For the first time in a decade, Morgana's house falls silent. She is alone. As she always has been. As she is happiest, apparently. Morgana has a hard time arguing that charge. She let go of her husband, her sisters, the wider world. She let go of her own child.

With Faerie mollified, invisible changelings stop leaving their footprints in the wood. Sheep are all born with the usual number of eyes, and flowers take time to open. Morgana finally rests, and her dreams are thick and heavy with the Sight. She sees Fey Queen Edie, her every wish granted and still unsatisfied, sealing off Faerie itself with the strength of her jealousy.

Dying is exactly like her sisters told her it would be. The future unfolds with a clarity she'd never thought possible, before. She sees a virgin girl-Saint across the strait with an iron sword, all her limbs radiant with flame. Then, she's gifted more visions of Britain's fated Queen, ornamented head-to-toe in pearly starlight, every triumph more glorious than the last.

She sees more and more lone women as the years progress, legions of lone women, not uncanny forces but made of flesh and blood. She sees so many of them that even though her cottage is icy and silent as her breaths heave, as her blood slows in her veins, Morgana's heart swells as if a million souls have all gathered to see her off.

Her descendants in spirit, if not in blood.

Her legacy as a woman, whole.

Every Son a Reaver
Holly Lyn Walrath

1.

The battlefield is drenched with the blood of men, redder than a lion's maw. Bodies are stacked one upon the other, limbs splayed intimately across one another or else thrown askew, leg from torso, hand from arm, fingers twisted in the mud.

The last two men stand sword-locked and sweating, the panting of their breath the only sound on the field. It should be epic, this last final battle; there should be the foreswearing of oaths and declarations for God. But in the end, it is abortive, feckless, and lame. The swords clash one last time. The King draws back in an exhausted strike, his sword slowly, agonizingly piercing his enemy's chest. Alas – his enemy strikes him too, a knife in his already battered ribs like a snake striking through grass.

The King falls back, stumbling over his dead comrades. His enemy collapses. There is no great outcry. No one is left to witness the honorable deed. Silence breathes. The King closes his eyes, relieved to finally die.

The sky is the color of a bloated pumpkin. A great black bird rises from the sunset and its scream pulses across the battlefield – sending bodies melting over bodies, deeper into the ooze of the mud. The bird shakes off her cloak of feathers and steps out of the sky as the shadow of a woman. She is dark of hair and light of eyes, bare of foot as she walks through the bloody death-ground.

Kneeling before the King, she lifts him up in her arms like a babe. She cuddles him to her breast and, blinking, her wings unfurl.

The King is born away, over the sea.

2.

The King awakens to the heady smell of rotten apples and even more rotten flesh. He is lying on his side in a dark bower, an orchard made of stones, bones, and yew. The bed beneath him is thick with golden leaves. In the misty distance are the mounds of graves, heavy with moss. A gray statue of a knight lies half-buried in the earth, tilted, its clasped hands long broken off. The statue's expression is sorrowful. The sky is the color of steel, and the King's head churns as he places a hand on his wound. His fingers come away wet like wine.

The Muirgen approaches. She is wearing the guise of a hag. A dark cloak covers her head and body, but beneath is a wreath of bedraggled gray hair, a face so ancient it might be already dead. The face leers at the King, flaunting teeth like gravestones and a darting green tongue. She shuffles to his bedside and holds up a brilliant red apple.

The King holds out his hand, and she places it in his palm, careful not to touch him. As he begins to eat, she stoops over his wound, staring at it for a long time.

She nods, making some small calculation in her mind, and then begins to retch over him. The regurgitated mess is foamy with bile, yellow and green, rich with herbs, and it seals the wound shut. She smiles again, her lips wet with sick, and limps away.

The King blinks, and she flies into the starless sky.

* * *

When she next comes to him, she is a golden-haired child, eight, perhaps nine. She has brought him herbs to chew, blissfully fresh this time.

"You're feeling better, aren't you, Papa?" she sings in a lilting voice.

The King shudders. "Don't call me that."

"You're the father of this land, aren't you?" She giggles and runs in a circle outside the bower. Today, a golden gleam of sunlight falls on each mound. Tomorrow, it will be shadow and shade again. She flounces to his side and collapses beside him, her golden curls like silk across his calves. "I wish you could run and run! Then we could play."

The King puts his hand on his side. The wound is knitted. A gnarled scab like a tree root grows there, but the pain is unbearable, and the memory of the past worse. "Why did you save me?" It is as if he asks God, and not the godless wench at his knee. He groans, burying his face in the leaves to hide the pain.

"I once had nine sisters," she says, her voice unexpectedly serious in its girlish whisper. "And each one knew a special art to bewitch and bewilder men. Mine was healing. I was raised to save you and for that purpose alone."

The King raises his head and searches her face. "Raised by whom?"

"My sisters, of course." Her bright blue eyes meet his, guileless. "And God. I am his virgin bride."

The King laughs at that. "You almost make me believe you, shapeshifter."

The girl shrugs and races off, twirling between the mounds, dancing wickedly over the mossy earth and the buried bones. She kisses the half-buried statue on its lips.

The King shakes his head. "What do they call you?" he calls into the mist.

"Today, Niamh. Tomorrow? Who knows!"

* * *

He crawls out of the bower in the pouring rain and tries to drown himself unsuccessfully in a puddle. His insides are burning. His head is stuffed full of memories – of the woman who was his queen, who he left at home when he went to war, of his comrades in arms who died bloody, needless deaths.

She pulls his head out of the muck by his hair and drags him back inside. She is wearing a beautiful gold-trimmed red robe. Her hair is braided in a coil, and on her brow is a glimmering star of silver. Her lips are redder than roses. Her skin is paler than an eggshell.

She brews a kettle of herb tea over a fire in a hole in the ground.

"I should let you drown," she hisses in his ear. And then, tenderly, she wipes the mud from his face, and neck, and chest, and wound.

* * *

Curiosity gets the better of him when she does not come, and he finds a downed tree limb to use as a cane. He flounders to the mouth of the bower and looks out. There is a scent of seawater on the wind, as well as the white birds of the shore, flecking the pale blue sky. The orchard surrounds the burial mounds with grapes and apples. Sheep wander between the trees, keeping the grass closely clipped. In the distance are rich grain fields, wet from the storm. A river rushes in the distance, its voice thundering.

His side pulls at him as he stumbles to the seashore, where he finds her in the river's ford.

She bends in the water, washing a chariot.

He stops short when he sees the steeds – two horses made of bone. They graze on the river's edge.

"Hello, my sweet," she calls in a dry voice. Today, she is simple, with a ruddy face, her hair tied up in a peasant's rag on her head. And yet, she is beautiful. Achingly, torturously, dangerously beautiful.

"How do I die?" the King asks, the dreaded question out before he can think whether he should ask it. Is it an offense to admit you wish you hadn't been saved – and to say it to the one who saved you?

"You've forgotten how you died already?" she says, but he knows that she knows the true question. She considers him. She puts her hands on her hips. "I didn't ask to be given this task of healing you."

"Nevertheless." The King sits on a rock and puts his head in his hands.

"You defeated your greatest enemy. Are you not happy, man?" Her flinty eyes regard him with exasperation.

"Yes. No. I am happy he is dead, for he was evil. I am not happy I am still alive. I should have died a hero's death. I am a man who has seen too much life—" his voice cracks.

She takes the heavy leather harness up in her hands and throws it into the water, where it lands on the muddy shore. "Men!" She cries. "You all crave death like the reaver. You think I have not lived as much life as you? I have been living *for* you."

He watches as she holds out a hand and speaks a word. The word seems to fill up the whole world. It makes his head buzz, and his teeth clench so hard he thinks they will break.

The river runs red with blood.

* * *

She comes to him where he lounges, not in the bower now but on the grassy knoll of the grave of one of his ancestors. She has crow's lines in her eyes and sagging breasts. There is a babe wrapped and tied across her body. She holds a cup full of honey mead to his lips, and her violet eyes meet his as he drinks. He can smell the musk of her hair. The babe makes an unnatural clacking sound and fidgets in its rags.

"Summer without blossoms, cattle without milk, women without modesty, men without valour." She takes a drink from the cup next, and golden liquid coats her lips.

"Conquests without a king," the King answers in a low, bitter voice. "I know all this! But I served my people. I killed the evil that plagued them. I should rest. I should be resting beneath this ground." He kicks the dirt beneath him.

"I can give you rest. I have been condemned to serve this place until I have gotten a son by a Christian man." She arches a brow. "Will you not lay with me?" Her lips purse in a half-smile.

The King slaps the cup out of her hand.

She takes the babe out of the rags. It is all pinfeathers and talons.

He turns his head as she regurgitates its dinner into its gullet.

* * *

He finds her again on the shore, with a telescope held to her eye in the dark of night as she studies the stars. She is wearing a monk's robe, and on her head is a jaunty cap. A parchment is unrolled at her feet, and she holds a quill in one hand; with the other, she drinks ale from an iron cup.

"I am sorry to say the stars are not aligned. At least, not for you, dear King. The boat is coming to draw you back to your people. Last chance for a tryst."

"You loathsome lady. You wicked, wicked woman." He grabs her up in his arms and shakes her until the cap falls from her hair and her curls spill over his hands.

She caws laughter, her milky throat like a gull. "Don't be so quick to return to the mortal realm, my King. Don't you know only messiahs die twice?"

He drops her, his hands burning.

* * *

At night in the bower, he feels the brush of feathers on his cheek. She slips a ring on his finger. He holds it to the moonlight and the gold glimmers.

"This will keep you safe," she whispers. "I don't know if I can save you again. I don't know if God will let me. I have lost all my sisters. I am the only woman with any knowledge left in this forsaken land."

Her hands are darting and soft, her lips melting over his. He aches. He burns. He dies a thousand little deaths again and again and again.

* * *

The King awakes, having accepted his fate and this place. He feels nearly whole again. Perhaps a rib or two is missing. What does it matter? One cannot help but feel cheerful when pain is gone.

"Where is that woman?" he asks the wind, as he crawls out of the bower and stands, his back popping in a satisfying way.

When he finds her, she stands under a yew tree in conversation with a shadow. She is wearing her black feathers again, her face masked with a bird's beak. A horned man kneels before her. She dismisses him and turns, blanching at the sight of the King, her beady eyes winking with tears. He did not think it possible.

"Who— who was that?"

"Never you mind," she hisses, bouncing like a bird in a storm on her heels. The wind kicks up the feathers about her face and she preens.

"You would consort with the devil?"

"I am the devil, you silly little man," she says in a voice like death.

He rounds on her. He has never been a man to strike a woman, and yet—

She puts a feathered wing over her belly, protective.

Aghast, chastened, he winces. "So fast?"

"Is there any other fate for a woman?"

3.

A golden boat with the head of a dragon and white sails appears on the shores, helmed by ten strong men. They are not men the King knows, and yet he knows them to be his kinfolk. Sons of sons of friends – of men who died by his side.

They make landfall and serve the King dinner. Familiar food and yet foreign now, to him. Where is she? The question repeats itself in his head as the men gather and make ready to sail away. To take him back to the living world.

"My King, do you not wish to join us?" asks their leader, when the King hesitates. It is not a question they expect an honest answer to.

He has one foot in the waves and one foot on the boat. One foot in death and another in life. His eyes sweep the strange, gray land, seeking in the mist. His fist clenches, the ring biting his skin.

A black bird flies overhead and screams but does not land. Go away, that voice seems to say. Go far, far away, and don't come back until you are dead again.

The King steps into the boat and is drawn away by night's hand.

Biographies

K. Blair
His Head in Your Lap, Dear Brother
(First Publication)
K. Blair is a writer based in London. They were part of Apples and Snakes 'The Writing Room' in 2019 and are part of the 24/25 cohort of Barbican Young Film Programmers. Their microchap 'Jesus Loves You, God Hasn't Decided Yet' is available as part of Ghost City Press's Summer Series 22. They can be found on Bluesky @kblair.bsky.social, Instagram: @urban_barbarian, and their website, kblair.co.uk.

Chris A. Bolton
Morgana and the Morrigan
(First Publication)
Chris A. Bolton lives in a house in a cemetery in Portland, Oregon. His short film *Evil F—ing Clowns* won Exceptional Horror Comedy at the 2023 Portland Horror Film Festival. He wrote the all-ages graphic novels *Smash: Trial by Fire* and *Smash: Fearless* from Candlewick Press. His short stories have been published in *Odin: New & Ancient Norse Tales* (also from Flame Tree), *Portland Noir* and *ParABNormal Magazine*. Haunt him online at chrisabolton.com.

Marta Cobb
Foreword
Marta Cobb has loved medieval stories and legends since she was a child. This love brought her to England to study medieval literature, and she has never left! Marta currently teaches medieval subjects in the School of History at the University of Leeds, focusing in particular on female mystics as well as modern representations and appropriations of the medieval. She has recently published an essay about the portrayal of Morgan le Fay in film and television.

Courtney Danielson
No Need for the Green Knight
(First Publication)
Courtney Danielson is an academic librarian at the University of Charleston. She is currently studying to earn her second Master's Degree, an MA in Humanities, at Marshall University. She loves fantasy, science fiction and horror, and she takes inspiration from the natural beauty of her home in Charleston, West Virginia. When not entering into one-too-many writing contests, she can be found playing video games with her partner or trying to walk her Saint Bernard puppy.

Evan Davies
The Woman with the Bleeding Eye
(First Publication)
Evan Davies is a short-story author and aspiring novelist with a passion for pulp fantasy, new-wave sci-fi and noir detective fiction. His work attempts to blend the style and inventiveness of these genres with contemporary themes and moral frameworks. His most recent story, 'Blood Beneath the Sand', was published by Water Dragon Publishing. In his free time, he enjoys reading, visiting national parks and being an enthusiastically below-average mixed martial artist.

Caroline Fleischauer
To Cut the Rot
(First Publication)
Caroline Fleischauer has long held a fascination with Morgan le Fay. Originally from Ithaca, New York, she holds an MA and MFA, both from the University of Wyoming, where her work focused on representations of women and power in Arthurian literature. She currently resides in Bloemfontein, South Africa, where she teaches as an English Language Fellow at the University of the Free State.

Micah Giddens
Gelato
(First Publication)
Micah Giddens grew up in Elk Grove, California, where he combatted boredom by making ridiculous YouTube videos with his friends. He

now lives in Chicago with his wife and two cats. Like a Ninja Turtle, his favourite foods are pizza and candy. When he's not writing, he's hanging out with his writing group Draft Quest, or taking mediocre photos of the city. His fiction has appeared in *Spooky Magazine* and *Red Sheep Magazine*.

Lyndsay E. Gilbert
The Story that I Want
(First Publication)
Lyndsay E. Gilbert is a hopeful author from Northern Ireland. She lives by an ancient castle looking out to sea. Her interests are reading, writing, fantasy, horror, music, playing the fiddle, movies, gaming, fairy tales, cats, dogs, and the ancient art of belly dance. Lyndsay is published in a number of anthologies and is currently in the editing stage of a novel about post-apocalyptic witches. She can be found writing terrible poetry and procrastinating on Instagram @lyndsayegilbert.

Liam Hogan
Under Avalon
(First Publication)
Liam Hogan is an award-winning short-story writer, with stories in *Best of British Science Fiction* and *Best of British Fantasy* (NewCon Press). He volunteers at the creative writing charities Ministry of Stories, and Spark Young Writers. Host of the live literary event Liars' League for twelve years, he has now escaped London, but remains a Liar. More details at happyendingnotguaranteed.blogspot.co.uk.

Larry Ivkovich
An Offense of Memory
(First Publication)
Larry Ivkovich's speculative fiction has been published in twenty-five online and print publications. He's been a finalist in the L. Ron Hubbard's Writers of the Future contest and was the 2010 recipient of the CZP/Rannu Fund award for fiction. His urban fantasy series *The Spirit Winds Quartet* is published by IFWG Publishing. Just released from IFWG is his steampunk-inspired SF novella, *Hope's Song*. Larry is a member of SFWA and lives in Coraopolis, PA, USA.

Alexis Kaegi
Mirror, Mirage
(First Publication)
Alexis Kaegi is a writer of speculative stories and interactive fiction. Her work has been published in *Abyss & Apex*, *Tree and Stone* and *Deep Magic*, and she holds an MFA from Stonecoast (University of Southern Maine). She has a fondness for unexpected adventurers, ace narratives, and mossy trees. Her writing is deeply influenced by the inherent magic of the Pacific Northwest, where she currently resides with her partner and dog.

Pamela Koehne-Drube
Introductory Essay
Pamela Koehne-Drube is an accomplished historian and ghost-writer with a passion for mythology, fantasy and horror. Her portfolio boasts dozens of ghost-writing credits across imprints of Taylor & Francis and Hachette. As a researcher, she has written extensively about the pipeline of history to mythology and popular culture, with a focus on Arthurian legend and vampire lore, fostered by a lifelong love of the subject. Her haunting short stories have appeared in literary horror magazine *The Ghastling*, receiving a notable mention in Ellen Datlow's annual horror anthology, *Best Horror of the Year*. Alongside her own writing, Pamela dedicates herself to mentoring aspiring authors through their writing and publishing journeys. She is based in Wales, the heartland of Arthurian legend.

Damien Mckeating
Destiny Forged
(First Publication)
Damien Mckeating has written for radio, comics, film prose, and the peculiar folk band Hornswaggle. His short stories have found homes in anthologies ranging from modern takes on Irish mythology to SF adventures for young readers. He is currently preparing his first novel for publication: *Tallulah Belle*, a supernatural coming-of-age story set in a fantasy burlesque theatre. Sometimes he remembers to blog at skeletonbutler.wordpress.com but often doesn't, because writing stories is more fun than writing blog posts.

BIOGRAPHIES

Nico Martinez Nocito
To Catch a Name
(First Publication)
Nico Martinez Nocito (they/them) is a queer, trans writer who pens diverse fantasy stories and poetry. They spend their free time running, singing, and acting in local theater productions. Find them in the anthologies *Grimm Retold*, *Holly & Broom* and *Black Cat Tales*, and on Instagram @nicowritesbooks.

John J. O'Hara
The Many-Hued Land
(First Publication)
John J. O'Hara is a writer and former university lecturer in English at the University of North Carolina Wilmington, where he taught courses on weird fiction and liminality in literature. He has presented at the annual conference of the Popular Culture Association and contributed to *Critical Insights: Jane Eyre*, a volume of scholarship on the novel by Charlotte Brontë. Born in Queens, New York, he currently lives in Madison, Wisconsin.

M.R. Robinson
Hound, Hart, Crow, Queen
(First Publication)
M.R. Robinson is a scholar of early modern literature and a writer of speculative fiction. Her short fiction has appeared in publications including *Beneath Ceaseless Skies*, *Haven Spec* and *Flash Fiction Online*, among others. When not writing, Robinson and her wife are very slowly restoring a crumbly old house, which they share with four pets and far too many books. Find her online at m-r-robinson.com or on most social media platforms as @mruthrobinson.

C.J. Subko
Sea-born
(First Publication)
C.J. Subko is a dreamer and a dabbler. She has a Ph.D. in Clinical Psychology from Michigan State University and a B.A. in Psychology and English from the University of Notre Dame, which makes her highly qualified to think too much. Her short fiction publications include *Skin Anthology* (Bag of

Bones press, June 2024), *Cold Signal* (September 2024), *Die Laughing* (October 2024), *Small Wonders* (November 2024), and upcoming issues of *The Deadlands* and *Penumbric Speculative Fiction*. She is a member of the HWA. Her novels are represented by Maria Brannan at Greyhound Literary Agency. She can be found at cjsubko.com.

Lana Voos
She Made a Doll in Winter
(First Publication)
Lana Voos studied playwriting and acting and has always loved strong women in fantasy. Though she spends most of her time writing contemporary novels, magic, dragons and ever-shifting forests will always be her first loves. She has worked as a go-go dancer and perfume describer and now clerks at an eclectic auction house in Nevada, USA, where she enjoys making up stories about possibly-cursed heirlooms.

Holly Lyn Walrath
Every Son a Reaver
(First Publication)
Holly Lyn Walrath's poetry and short fiction has appeared in *Strange Horizons*, *Fireside Fiction*, *Analog* and *Flash Fiction Online*. Her story 'Stardust' appeared in the Flame Tree Publishing anthology *Robots & Artificial Intelligence Short Stories*. She is the author of *Glimmerglass Girl*, *The Smallest of Bones* and *Numinous Stones*. She holds a BA in English from the University of Texas and a Master's in Creative Writing from the University of Denver. Visit her website: hlwalrath.com.

Authors & Core Sources on Morgana le Fay

Of the main early Morgana sources, the most famous contributors were the Welsh cleric Geoffrey of Monmouth (c. 1095–c. 1155) in his *Vita Merlini*, the French poet Chrétien de Troyes (fl. c. 1160–91) with his chivalric romances, and author of *Le Morte d'Arthur* Thomas Malory (c. 1393 or 1425–c. 1470). Their works were instrumental in the development and popularization of Arthurian legends.

Myths, Gods & Immortals

Discover the mythology of humankind through its heroes, characters, gods and immortal figures. **Myths, Gods and Immortals** brings together the new and the ancient, familiar stories with a fresh and imaginative twist. Each book brings back to life a legendary, mythological or folkloric figure, with completely new stories alongside the original tales and a comprehensive introduction which emphasizes ancient and modern connections, tracing history and stories across continents, cultures and peoples.

Flame Tree Fiction

A wide range of new and classic fiction, from myth to modern stories, with tales from the distant past to the far future, including short story anthologies, **Beyond & Within**, **Collector's Editions, Collectable Classics, Gothic Fantasy collections** and **Epic Tales** of mythology and folklore.

Available at all good bookstores, and online at flametreepublishing.com